Rav...
HIS MA...

"[A] great new book . . . enthralling reading."
—*TIME*

"A completely authentic tale, brimming with . . .
detail and richness [and] the impossible wonder
of gilded fantasy."
—*ENTERTAINMENT WEEKLY*
(Editor's Choice, grade of 'A')

"An amazing performance . . . [I] was immediately
hooked by the writing, the research and the sheer
courage of the whole enterprise."
—*CHICAGO TRIBUNE*

"Very addictive . . . It would be exhilarating to see [*His
Majesty's Dragon*] pulled off on the big screen."
—*AIN'TITCOOLNEWS.COM*

"The Temeraire trilogy could well be this year's
Jonathan Strange and Mr. Norrell."
—*BOOKPAGE*

"Excellent, extraordinary . . . a new way to utilize
dragons. . . . Naomi Novik [will] be one to watch."
—*ANNE MCCAFFREY*

"Impressively original, fully developed, and peopled
with characters you care about."
—*DAVID WEBER*, author of the
Honor Harrington series

"Superbly written . . . characters who win one's
heart from the beginning. Bravo!"
—*BOOKLIST* (starred review)

The Temeraire series by Naomi Novik

HIS MAJESTY'S DRAGON
THRONE OF JADE
BLACK POWDER WAR

Throne of Jade

NAOMI NOVIK

BALLANTINE BOOKS • NEW YORK

A Del Rey Mass Market Original

Copyright © 2006 by Naomi Novik
Excerpt from *Black Powder War* by Naomi Novik copyright © 2006 by Naomi Novik

Published in the United States by Del Rey Books, an imprint of The Random House Publishing Group, a division of Random House, Inc., New York.

DEL REY is a registered trademark and the Del Rey colophon is a trademark of Random House, Inc.

This book contains an excerpt from *Black Powder War* by Naomi Novik. This excerpt has been set for this edition only and may not reflect the final content of the book.

ISBN 978-0-345-48129-0

Printed in the United States of America

www.delreybooks.com

OPM 9 8 7 6

In memory of Chawa Nowik,
in hopes that someday I'll be ready to write her book

I

Chapter 1

THE DAY WAS unseasonably warm for November, but in some misguided deference to the Chinese embassy, the fire in the Admiralty boardroom had been heaped excessively high, and Laurence was standing directly before it. He had dressed with especial care, in his best uniform, and all throughout the long and unbearable interview the lining of his thick bottle-green broadcloth coat had been growing steadily more sodden with sweat.

Over the doorway, behind Lord Barham, the official indicator with its compass arrow showed the direction of the wind over the Channel: in the north-northeast today, fair for France; very likely even now some ships of the Channel Fleet were standing in to have a look at Napoleon's harbors. His shoulders held at attention, Laurence fixed his eyes upon the broad metal disk and tried to keep himself distracted with such speculation; he did not trust himself to meet the cold, unfriendly gaze fixed upon him.

Barham stopped speaking and coughed again into his fist; the elaborate phrases he had prepared sat not at all in his sailor's mouth, and at the end of every awkward, halting line, he stopped and darted a look over at the Chinese with a nervous agitation that approached obsequity. It was not a very creditable performance, but under ordinary circumstances, Laurence would have felt a degree of sympathy for Barham's position: some sort of formal message had been anticipated, even perhaps an envoy, but no one had ever imagined that the Emperor of China would send his own brother halfway around the world.

Prince Yongxing could, with a word, set their two nations at war; and there was besides something inherently awful in his presence: the impervious silence with which he met Barham's every remark; the overwhelming splendor of his dark yellow robes, embroidered thickly with dragons; the slow and relentless tapping of his long, jewel-encrusted fingernail against the arm of his chair. He did not even look at Barham: he only stared directly across the table at Laurence, grim and thin-lipped.

His retinue was so large they filled the boardroom to the corners, a dozen guards all sweltering and dazed in their quilted armor and as many servants besides, most with nothing to do, only attendants of one sort or another, all of them standing along the far wall of the room and trying to stir the air with broad-paneled fans. One man, evidently a translator, stood behind the prince, murmuring when Yongxing lifted a hand, generally after one of Barham's more involved periods.

Two other official envoys sat to Yongxing's either side. These men had been presented to Laurence only perfunctorily, and they had neither of them said a word, though the younger, called Sun Kai, had been watching all the proceedings, impassively, and following the translator's words with quiet attention. The elder, a big, round-bellied man with a tufted grey beard, had gradually been overcome by the heat: his head had sunk forward onto his chest, mouth half open for air, and his hand was barely even moving his fan towards his face. They were robed in dark blue silk, almost as elaborately as the prince himself, and together they made an imposing façade: certainly no such embassy had ever been seen in the West.

A far more practiced diplomat than Barham might have been pardoned for succumbing to some degree of servility, but Laurence was scarcely in any mood to be forgiving; though he was nearly more furious with himself, at having hoped for anything better. He had come expecting to plead his case, and privately in his heart he had even imagined a reprieve; instead he had been scolded in terms he would have scrupled to use to a raw lieutenant, and all in front of a foreign prince and his retinue, assembled like a tribunal to hear his crimes. Still he held his tongue as long as he could manage, but when Barham at last came about to saying, with an air of great condescension, "Naturally, Captain, we have it in mind that you shall be put to another hatchling, afterwards," Laurence had reached his limit.

"No, sir," he said, breaking in. "I am sorry, but no: I will not do it, and as for another post, I must beg to be excused."

Sitting beside Barham, Admiral Powys of the Aerial Corps had remained quite silent through the course of the meeting; now he only shook his head, without any appearance of surprise, and folded his hands together over his ample belly. Barham gave him a furious look and said to Laurence, "Perhaps I am not clear, Captain; this is not a request. You have been given your orders, you will carry them out."

"I will be hanged first," Laurence said flatly, past caring that he was speaking in such terms to the First Lord of the Admiralty: the death of his career if he had still been a naval officer, and it could scarcely do him any good even as an aviator. Yet if they meant to send Temeraire away, back to China, his career as an aviator was finished: he would never accept a position with any other dragon. None other would ever compare, to Laurence's mind, and he would not subject a hatchling to being second-best when there were men in the Corps lined up six-deep for the chance.

Yongxing did not say anything, but his lips tightened; his attendants shifted and murmured amongst themselves in their own language. Laurence did not think he was imagining the hint of disdain in their tone, directed less at himself than at Barham; and the First Lord evidently shared the impression, his face growing mottled and choleric with the effort of preserving the appearance of calm. "By God, Laurence; if you imagine you can stand here in the middle of Whitehall and mutiny, you are wrong; I think perhaps you are forgetting that your first duty is to your country and your King, not to this dragon of yours."

"No, sir; it is you who are forgetting. It was for duty I put Temeraire into harness, sacrificing my naval rank, with no knowledge then that he was any breed truly out of the ordinary, much less a Celestial," Laurence said. "And for duty I took him through a difficult training and into a hard and dangerous service; for duty I have taken him into battle, and asked him to hazard his life and happiness. I will not answer such loyal service with lies and deceit."

"Enough noise, there," Barham said. "Anyone would think you were being asked to hand over your firstborn. I am sorry if you have made such a pet of the creature you cannot bear to lose him—"

"Temeraire is neither my pet nor my property, sir," Laurence snapped. "He has served England and the King as much as I have, or you yourself, and now, because he does not choose to go back to China, you stand there and ask me to lie to him. I cannot imagine what claim to honor I should have if I agreed to it. Indeed," he added, unable to restrain himself, "I wonder that you should even have made the proposal; I wonder at it greatly."

"Oh, your soul to the devil, Laurence," Barham said,

losing his last veneer of formality; he had been a serving sea-officer for years before joining the Government, and he was still very little a politician when his temper was up. "He is a Chinese dragon, it stands to reason he will like China better; in any case, he belongs to them, and there is an end to it. The name of thief is a very unpleasant one, and His Majesty's Government does not propose to invite it."

"I know how I am to take that, I suppose." If Laurence had not already been half-broiled, he would have flushed. "And I utterly reject the accusation, sir. These gentlemen do not deny they had given the egg to France; we seized it from a French man-of-war; the ship and the egg were condemned as lawful prize out of hand in the Admiralty courts, as you very well know. By no possible understanding does Temeraire belong to them; if they were so anxious about letting a Celestial out of their hands, they ought not have given him away in the shell."

Yongxing snorted and broke into their shouting-match. "*That* is correct," he said; his English was thickly accented, formal and slow, but the measured cadences only lent all the more effect to his words. "From the first it was folly to let the second-born egg of Lung Tien Qian pass over sea. *That,* no one can now dispute."

It silenced them both, and for a moment no one spoke, save the translator quietly rendering Yongxing's words for the rest of the Chinese. Then Sun Kai unexpectedly said something in their tongue which made Yongxing look around at him sharply. Sun kept his head inclined deferentially, and did not look up, but still it was the first suggestion Laurence had seen that their embassy might perhaps not speak with a single voice. But Yongxing snapped a reply, in a tone which did not allow of any further comment, and Sun did not venture to make one. Satisfied that he had quelled his subordinate, Yongxing turned back to them and added, "Yet regardless of the evil chance that brought him into your hands, Lung Tien Xiang was meant to go to the French Emperor, not to be made beast of burden for a common soldier."

Laurence stiffened; *common soldier* rankled, and for the first time he turned to look directly at the prince, meeting that cold, contemptuous gaze with an equally steady one. "We are at war with France, sir; if you choose to ally yourself with our enemies and send them material assistance, you can hardly complain when we take it in fair fight."

"Nonsense!" Barham broke in, at once and loudly. "China is by no means an ally of France, by no means at all; we certainly do not view China as a French ally. You are not here to speak to His Imperial Highness, Laurence; control yourself," he added, in a savage undertone.

But Yongxing ignored the attempt at interruption. "And now you make piracy your defense?" he said, contemptuous. "We do not concern ourselves with the customs of barbaric nations. How merchants and thieves agree to pillage one another is not of interest to the Celestial Throne, except when they choose to insult the Emperor as you have."

"No, Your Highness, no such thing, not in the least," Barham said hurriedly, even while he looked pure venom at Laurence. "His Majesty and his Government have nothing but the deepest affection for the Emperor; no insult would ever willingly be offered, I assure you. If we had only known of the extraordinary nature of the egg, of your objections, this situation would never have arisen—"

"Now, however, you are well aware," Yongxing said, "and the insult remains: Lung Tien Xiang is still in harness, treated little better than a horse, expected to carry burdens and exposed to all the brutalities of war, and all this, with a mere captain as his companion. Better had his egg sunk to the bottom of the ocean!"

Appalled, Laurence was glad to see this callousness left Barham and Powys as staring and speechless as himself. Even among Yongxing's own retinue, the translator flinched, shifting uneasily, and for once did not translate the prince's words back into Chinese.

"Sir, I assure you, since we learned of your objections, he has not been under harness at all, not a stitch of it," Barham said, recovering. "We have been at the greatest of pains to see to Temeraire's—that is, to Lung Tien Xiang's— comfort, and to make redress for any inadequacy in his treatment. He is no longer assigned to Captain Laurence, that I can assure you: they have not spoken these last two weeks."

The reminder was a bitter one, and Laurence felt what little remained of his temper fraying away. "If either of you had any real concern for his comfort, you would consult his feelings, not your own desires," he said, his voice rising, a voice which had been trained to bellow orders through a gale. "You complain of having him under harness, and in the same breath ask me to trick him into chains, so you might drag him away against his will. I will not do it; I will never do it, and be damned to you all."

Judging by his expression, Barham would have been glad to have Laurence himself dragged away in chains: eyes almost bulging, hands flat on the table, on the verge of rising; for the first time, Admiral Powys spoke, breaking in, and forestalled him. "Enough, Laurence, hold your tongue. Barham, nothing further can be served by keeping him. Out, Laurence; out at once: you are dismissed."

The long habit of obedience held: Laurence flung himself out of the room. The intervention likely saved him from an arrest for insubordination, but he went with no sense of gratitude; a thousand things were pent up in his throat, and even as the door swung heavily shut behind him, he turned back. But the Marines stationed to either side were gazing at him with thoughtlessly rude interest, as if he were a curiosity exhibited for their entertainment. Under their open, inquisitive looks he mastered his temper a little and turned away before he could betray himself more thoroughly.

Barham's words were swallowed by the heavy wood, but the inarticulate rumble of his still-raised voice followed Laurence down the corridor. He felt almost drunk with anger, his breath coming in short abrupt spurts and his vision obscured, not by tears, not at all by tears, except of rage. The antechamber of the Admiralty was full of sea-officers, clerks, political officials, even a green-coated aviator rushing through with dispatches. Laurence shouldered his way roughly to the doors, his shaking hands thrust deep into his coat pockets to conceal them from view.

He struck out into the crashing din of late-afternoon London, Whitehall full of workingmen going home for their suppers, and the bawling of the hackney drivers and chair-men over all, crying, "Make a lane, there," through the crowds. His feelings were as disordered as his surroundings, and he was navigating the street by instinct; he had to be called three times before he recognized his own name.

He turned only reluctantly: he had no desire to be forced to return a civil word or gesture from a former colleague. But with a measure of relief he saw it was Captain Roland, not an ignorant acquaintance. He was surprised to see her; very surprised, for her dragon, Excidium, was a formation-leader at the Dover covert. She could not easily have been spared from her duties, and in any case she could not come to the Admiralty openly, being a female officer, one of those whose existence was made necessary by the insistence of Longwings on female captains. The secret was but barely known outside the ranks of the aviators, and jealously kept against certain public disapproval; Laurence himself had found it difficult to accept the notion, at first, but he had grown so used to the idea that now Roland looked very odd to him out of uniform: she had put on skirts and a heavy cloak by way of concealment, neither of which suited her.

"I have been puffing after you for the last five minutes," she said, taking his arm as she reached him. "I was wandering about that great cavern of a building, waiting for you to come out, and then you went straight past me in such a ferocious hurry I could scarcely catch you. These clothes are a damned nuisance; I hope you appreciate the trouble I am taking for you, Laurence. But never mind," she added, her voice gentling. "I can see from your face that it did not go well: let us go and have some dinner, and you shall tell me everything."

"Thank you, Jane; I am glad to see you," he said, and let her turn him in the direction of her inn, though he did not think he could swallow. "How do you come to be here, though? Surely there is nothing wrong with Excidium?"

"Nothing in the least, unless he has given himself indigestion," she said. "No; but Lily and Captain Harcourt are coming along splendidly, and so Lenton was able to assign them a double patrol and give me a few days of liberty. Excidium took it as excuse to eat three fat cows at once, the wretched greedy thing; he barely cracked an eyelid when I proposed my leaving him with Sanders—that is my new first lieutenant—and coming to bear you company. So I put together a street-going rig and came up with the courier. Oh, Hell: wait a minute, will you?" She stopped and kicked vigorously, shaking her skirts loose: they were too long, and had caught on her heels.

He held her by the elbow so she did not topple over, and afterwards they continued on through the London streets at a slower pace. Roland's mannish stride and scarred face drew enough rude stares that Laurence began to glare at the passersby who looked too long, though she herself paid them no mind; she noticed his behavior, however, and said, "You are ferocious out of temper; do not frighten those poor girls. What did those fellows say to you at the Admiralty?"

"You have heard, I suppose, that an embassy has come from China; they mean to take Temeraire back with them, and Government does not care to object. But evidently he will have none of it: tells them all to go and hang themselves, though they have been at him for weeks now to go," Laurence said. As he spoke, a sharp sensation of pain, like a constriction just under his breastbone, made itself felt. He could picture quite clearly Temeraire kept nearly all alone in the old, worn-down London covert, scarcely used in the last hundred years, with neither Laurence nor his crew to keep him company, no one to read to him, and of his own kind only a few small courier-beasts flying through on dispatch service.

"Of course he will not go," Roland said. "I cannot believe they imagined they could persuade him to leave you. Surely they ought to know better; I have always heard the Chinese cried up as the very pinnacle of dragon-handlers."

"Their prince has made no secret he thinks very little of me; likely they expected Temeraire to share much the same opinion, and to be pleased to go back," Laurence said. "In any case, they grow tired of trying to persuade him; so that villain Barham ordered I should lie to him and say we were assigned to Gibraltar, all to get him aboard a transport and out to sea, too far for him to fly back to land, before he knew what they were about."

"Oh, infamous." Her hand tightened almost painfully on his arm. "Did Powys have nothing to say to it? I cannot believe he let them suggest such a thing to you; one cannot expect a naval officer to understand these things, but Powys should have explained matters to him."

"I dare say he can do nothing; he is only a serving officer, and Barham is appointed by the Ministry," Laurence said. "Powys at least saved me from putting my neck in a noose: I was too angry to control myself, and he sent me away."

They had reached the Strand; the increase in traffic made conversation difficult, and they had to pay attention to avoid being splashed by the questionable grey slush heaped in the gutters, thrown up onto the pavement by the lumbering carts and hackney wheels. His anger ebbing away, Laurence was increasingly low in his spirits.

From the moment of separation, he had consoled himself with the daily expectation that it would soon end: the Chinese would soon see Temeraire did not wish to go, or the Admiralty would give up the attempt to placate them. It had seemed a cruel sentence even so; they had not been parted a full day's time in the months since Temeraire's hatching, and Laurence had scarcely known what to do with himself, or how to fill the hours. But even the two long weeks were nothing to this, the dreadful certainty that he had ruined all his chances. The Chinese would not yield, and the Ministry would find some way of getting Temeraire sent off to China in the end: they plainly had no objection to telling him a pack of lies for the purpose. Likely enough Barham would never consent to his seeing Temeraire now even for a last farewell.

Laurence had not even allowed himself to consider what his own life might be with Temeraire gone. Another dragon was of course an impossibility, and the Navy would not have him back now. He supposed he could take on a ship in the merchant fleet, or a privateer; but he did not think he would have the heart for it, and he had done well enough out of prize-money to live on. He could even marry and set up as a country gentleman; but that prospect, once so idyllic in his imagination, now seemed drab and colorless.

Worse yet, he could hardly look for sympathy: all his former acquaintance would call it a lucky escape, his family would rejoice, and the world would think nothing of his loss. By any measure, there was something ridiculous in his being so adrift: he had become an aviator quite unwillingly, only from the strongest sense of duty, and less than a year had passed since his change in station; yet already he could hardly consider the possibility. Only another aviator, perhaps indeed only another captain, would truly be able to understand his sentiments, and with Temeraire gone, he would be as severed from their company as aviators themselves were from the rest of the world.

The front room at the Crown and Anchor was not quiet, though it was still early for dinner by town standards. The place was not a fashionable establishment, nor even genteel, its custom mostly consisting of countrymen used to a more reasonable hour for their food and drink. It was not the sort of place a respectable woman would have come, nor indeed the kind of place Laurence himself would have ever voluntarily frequented in earlier days. Roland drew some insolent stares, others only curious, but no one attempted any greater liberty: Laurence made an imposing figure beside her with his broad shoulders and his dress-sword slung at his hip.

Roland led Laurence up to her rooms, sat him in an ugly armchair, and gave him a glass of wine. He drank deeply, hiding behind the bowl of the glass from her sympathetic look: he was afraid he might easily be unmanned. "You must be faint with hunger, Laurence," she said. "That is half the trouble." She rang for the maid; shortly a couple of manservants climbed up with a very good sort of plain single-course dinner: a roast fowl, with greens and beef; gravy sauce; some small cheese-cakes made with jam; calf's feet pie; a dish of red cabbage stewed; and a small biscuit pudding for relish. She had them place all the food on the table at once, rather than going through removes, and sent them away.

Laurence did not think he would eat, but once the food was before him he found he was hungry after all. He had been eating very indifferently, thanks to irregular hours and the low table of his cheap boarding-house, chosen for its proximity to the covert where Temeraire was kept; now he ate steadily, Roland carrying the conversation nearly alone and distracting him with service gossip and trivialities.

"I was sorry to lose Lloyd, of course—they mean to put him to the Anglewing egg that is hardening at Kinloch Laggan," she said, speaking of her first lieutenant.

"I think I saw it there," Laurence said, rousing a little and lifting his head from his plate. "Obversaria's egg?"

"Yes, and we have great hopes of the issue," she said. "Lloyd was over the moon, of course, and I am very happy for him; still, it is no easy thing to break in a new premier after five years, with all the crew and Excidium himself murmuring about how Lloyd used to do things. But Sanders is a good-hearted, dependable fellow; they sent him up from Gibraltar, after Granby refused the post."

"What? Refused it?" Laurence cried, in great dismay: Granby was his own first lieutenant. "Not for my sake, I hope."

"Oh, Lord, you did not know?" Roland said, in equal dismay. "Granby spoke to me very pretty; said he was obliged, but he did not choose to shift his position. I was quite sure he had consulted you about the matter; I thought perhaps you had been given some reason to hope."

"No," Laurence said, very low. "He is more likely to end up with no position at all; I am very sorry to hear he should have passed up so good a place." The refusal could have done Granby no good with the Corps; a man who had turned down one offer could not soon expect another, and Laurence would shortly have no power at all to help him along.

"Well, I am damned sorry to have given you any more cause for concern," Roland said, after a moment. "Admiral Lenton has not broken up your crew, you know, for the most part: only gave a few fellows to Berkley out of desperation, he being so short-handed now. We were all so sure that Maximus had reached his final growth; shortly after you were called here, he began to prove us wrong, and so far he has put on fifteen feet in length." She added this last in an attempt to recover the lighter tone of the conversation, but it was impossible: Laurence found that his stomach had closed, and he set down his knife and fork with the plate still half-full.

Roland drew the curtains; it was already growing dark outside. "Do you care for a concert?"

"I am happy to accompany you," he said, mechanically, and she shook her head.

"No, never mind; I see it will not do. Come to bed then, my dear fellow; there is no sense in sitting about and moping."

They put out the candles and lay down together. "I have not the least notion what to do," he said quietly: the cover of dark made the confession a little easier. "I called Barham a villain, and I cannot forgive him asking me to lie; very ungentleman-like. But he is not a scrub; he would not be at such shifts if he had any other choice."

"It makes me quite ill to hear about him bowing and scraping to this foreign prince." Roland propped herself upon her elbow on the pillows. "I was in Canton harbor once, as a mid, on a transport coming back the long way from India; those junks of theirs do not look like they could stand a mild shower, much less a gale. They cannot fly their dragons across the ocean without a pause, even if they cared to go to war with us."

"I thought as much myself, when I first heard," Laurence said. "But they do not need to fly across the ocean to end the China trade, and wreck our shipping to India also, if they liked; besides they share a border with Russia. It would mean the end of the coalition against Bonaparte, if the Tsar was attacked on his eastern borders."

"I do not see the Russians have done us very much good so far, in the war, and money is a low pitiful excuse for behaving like a bounder, in a man or a nation," Roland said. "The State has been short of funds before, and somehow we have scraped by and still blacked Bonaparte's eye for him. In any case, I cannot forgive them for keeping you from Temeraire. Barham still has not let you see him at all, I suppose?"

"No, not for two weeks now. There is a decent fellow at the covert who has taken him messages for me, and lets me know that he is eating, but I cannot ask him to let me in: it would be a court-martial for us both. Though for my own part, I hardly know if I would let it stop me now."

He could scarcely have imagined even saying such a thing a year ago; he did not like to think it now, but honesty put the words into his mouth. Roland did not cry out against it, but then she was an aviator herself. She reached out to stroke his cheek, and drew him down to such comfort as might be found in her arms.

Laurence started up in the dark room, sleep broken: Roland was already out of bed. A yawning housemaid was standing in the doorway, holding up a candle, the yellow light spilling into the room. She handed Roland a sealed dispatch and stayed there, staring with open prurient interest at Laurence; he felt a guilty flush rise in his cheeks, and glanced down to be sure he was quite covered beneath the bedclothes.

Roland had already cracked the seal; now she reached out and took the candlestick straight out of the girl's hand. "There's for you; go along now," she said, giving the maid a shilling; she shut the door in the girl's face without further ceremony. "Laurence, I must go at once," she said, coming to the bed to light the other candles, speaking very low. "This is word from Dover: a French convoy is making a run for Le Havre under dragon guard. The Channel Fleet is going after them, but there is a Flamme-de-Gloire present, and the fleet cannot engage without aerial support."

"How many ships in the French convoy, does it say?" He was already out of the bed and pulling on his breeches: a fire-breather was nearly the worst danger a ship could face, desperately risky even with a good deal of support from the air.

"Thirty or more, packed no doubt to the gills with war matériel," she said, whipping her hair into a tight braid. "Do you see my coat over there?"

Outside the window, the sky was thinning to a paler blue; soon the candles would be unnecessary. Laurence found the coat and helped her into it, some part of his thoughts already occupied in calculating the likely strength of the merchant ships, what proportion of the fleet would be detached to go after them, how many might yet slip through to safe harbor: the guns at Le Havre were nasty. If the wind had not shifted since yesterday, they had favorable conditions for their run. Thirty ships' worth of iron, copper, quicksilver, gunpowder; Bonaparte might no longer be a danger at sea after Trafalgar, but on land he was still master of Europe, and such a haul might easily meet his supply needs for months.

"And just give me that cloak, will you?" Roland asked, breaking into his train of thought. The voluminous folds concealed her male dress, and she pulled the hood up over her head. "There, that will do."

"Hold a moment; I am coming with you," Laurence said, struggling into his own coat. "I hope I can be some use. If Berkley is short-handed on Maximus, I can at least pull on a strap or help shove off boarders. Leave the luggage and ring for the maid: we will have them send the rest of your things over to my boarding-house."

They hurried through the streets, still mostly empty: night-soil men rattling past with their fetid carts, day laborers beginning on their rounds to look for work, maids in their clinking pattens going to market, and the herds of animals with their lowing breath white in the air. A clammy, bitter fog had descended in the night, like a prickling of ice on the skin. At least the absence of crowds meant Roland did not have to pay much mind to her cloak, and they could go at something approaching a run.

The London covert was situated not far from the Admiralty offices, along the western side of the Thames; despite the location, so eminently convenient, the buildings immediately around it were shabby, in disrepair: where those lived who could afford nothing farther away from dragons; some of the houses even abandoned, except for a few skinny children who peered out suspiciously at the sound of strangers passing. A sludge of liquid refuse ran along the gutters of the streets; as Laurence and Roland ran, their boots broke the thin skim of ice on top, letting the stench up to follow them.

Here the streets were truly empty; but even so as they hurried a heavy cart sprang almost as if by malicious intent from the fog: Roland hauled Laurence aside and up onto the pavement just quick enough he was not clipped and dragged under the wheels. The drover never even paused in his careening progress, but vanished around the next corner without apology.

Laurence gazed down at his best dress trousers in dismay: spattered black with filth. "Never mind," Roland said consolingly. "No one will mind in the air, and maybe it will brush off." This was more optimism than he could muster, but there was certainly no time to do anything about them now, and so they resumed their hurried progress.

The covert gates stood out shining against the dingy streets and the equally dingy morning: ironwork freshly painted black, with polished brass locks; unexpectedly, a pair of young Marines in their red uniforms were lounging nearby, muskets leaned against the wall. The gatekeeper on duty touched his hat to Roland as he came to let them in, while the Marines squinted at her in some confusion: her cloak was well back off her shoulders for the moment, revealing both her triple gold bars and her by no means shabby endowment.

Laurence stepped into their line of sight to block their view of her, frowning. "Thank you, Patson; the Dover courier?" he said to the gatekeeper, as soon as they had come through.

"Believe he's waiting for you, sir," Patson said, jerking his thumb over his shoulder as he pulled the gates to again. "Just at the first clearing, if you please. Don't you worry about them none," he added, scowling at the Marines, who looked properly abashed: they were barely more than boys, and Patson was a big man, a former armorer, made only more awful by an eye-patch and the seared red skin about it. "I'll learn them properly, never fret."

"Thank you, Patson; carry on," Roland said, and on they went. "Whatever are those lobsters doing here? Not officers, at least, we may be grateful. I still recall twelve years ago, some Army officer found out Captain St. Germain when she got wounded at Toulon; he made a wretched to-do over the whole thing, and it nearly got into the papers: idiotic affair."

There was only a narrow border of trees and buildings around the perimeter of the covert to shield it from the air and noise of the city; they almost at once reached the first clearing, a small space barely large enough for a middling-sized dragon to spread its wings. The courier was indeed waiting: a young Winchester, her purple wings not yet quite darkened to adult color, but fully harnessed and fidgeting to be off.

"Why, Hollin," Laurence said, shaking the captain's hand gladly: it was a great pleasure to see his former ground-crew master again, now in an officer's coat. "Is this your dragon?"

"Yes, sir, indeed it is; this is Elsie," Hollin said, beaming at him. "Elsie, this is Captain Laurence: which I have told you about him, he helped me to you."

The Winchester turned her head around and looked at Laurence with bright, interested eyes: not yet three months out of the shell, she was still small, even for her breed, but her hide was almost glossy-clean, and she looked very well-tended indeed. "So you are Temeraire's captain? Thank you; I like my Hollin very much," she said, in a light chirping voice, and gave Hollin a nudge with enough affection in it to nearly knock him over.

"I am happy to have been of service, and to make your acquaintance," Laurence said, mustering some enthusiasm, although not without an internal pang at the reminder. Temeraire was here, not five hundred yards distant, and he could not so much as exchange a greeting with him. He did look, but buildings stood in the line of his sight: no glimpse of black hide was to be seen.

Roland asked Hollin, "Is everything ready? We must be off at once."

"Yes, sir, indeed; we are only waiting for the dispatches," Hollin said. "Five minutes, if you should care to stretch your legs before the flight."

The temptation was very strong; Laurence swallowed hard. But discipline held: openly refusing a dishonorable order was one thing, sneaking about to disobey a merely unpleasant one something else; and to do so now might well reflect badly on Hollin, and Roland herself. "I will just step into the barracks here, and speak to Jervis," he said instead, and went to find the man who was overseeing Temeraire's care.

Jervis was an older man, the better part of both his left limbs lost to a wicked raking stroke across the side of the dragon on whom he had served as harness-master; on recovering against all reasonable expectations, he had been assigned to the slow duty of the London covert, so rarely used. He had an odd, lopsided appearance with his wooden leg and metal hook on one side, and he had grown a little lazy and contrary with his idleness, but Laurence had provided him with a willing ear often enough to now find a warm welcome.

"Would you be so kind as to take a word for me?" Laurence asked, after he had refused a cup of tea. "I am going to Dover to see if I can be of use; I should not like Temeraire to fret at my silence."

"That I will, and read it to him; he will need it, poor fellow," Jervis said, stumping over to fetch his inkwell and pen one-handed; Laurence turned over a scrap of paper to write the note. "That fat fellow from the Admiralty came over again not half-an-hour ago with a full passel of Marines and those fancy Chinamen, and there they are still, prating away at the dear. If they don't go soon, I shan't answer for his taking any food today, so I won't. Ugly sea-going bugger; I don't know what he is about, thinking he knows aught about dragons; that is, begging your pardon, sir," Jervis added hastily.

Laurence found his hand shook over the paper, so he

spattered his first few lines and the table. He answered somehow, meaninglessly, and struggled to continue the note; words would not come. He stood there locked in mid-sentence, until suddenly he was nearly thrown off his feet, ink spreading across the floor as the table fell over; outside a terrible shattering noise, like the worst violence of a storm, a full North Sea winter's gale.

The pen was still ludicrously in his hand; he dropped it and flung open the door, Jervis stumbling out behind him. The echoes still hung in the air, and Elsie was sitting up on her hind legs, wings half-opening and closing in anxiety while Hollin and Roland tried to reassure her; the few other dragons at the covert had their heads up as well, peering over the trees and hissing in alarm.

"Laurence," Roland called, but he ignored her: he was already halfway down the path, running, his hand unconsciously gone to the hilt of his sword. He came to the clearing and found his way barred by the collapsed ruins of a barracks building and several fallen trees.

For a thousand years before the Romans first tamed the Western dragon breeds, the Chinese had already been masters of the art. They prized beauty and intelligence more than martial prowess, and looked with a little superior disdain at the fire-breathers and acid-spitters valued so highly in the West; their aerial legions were so numerous they had no need of what they regarded as so much showy flash. But they did not scorn all such unusual gifts; and in the Celestials they had reached the pinnacle of their achievement: the union of all the other graces with the subtle and deadly power which the Chinese called the *divine wind*, the roar with a force greater than cannon-fire.

Laurence had seen the devastation the divine wind wrought only once before, at the battle of Dover, where Temeraire had used it against Napoleon's airborne transports to potent effect. But here the poor trees had suffered the impact at point-blank range: they lay like flung matchsticks, trunks burst into flinders. The whole rough structure of the barracks, too, had smashed to the ground, the coarse mortar crumbled away entirely and the bricks scattered and broken. A hurricane might have caused such wreckage, or an earthquake, and the once-poetic name seemed suddenly far more apt.

The escort of Marines were nearly all of them backed up against the undergrowth surrounding the clearing, faces white and blank with terror; Barham alone of them had stood his ground. The Chinese also had not retreated, but they were one and all prostrated upon the ground in formal genuflection, except for Prince Yong-xing himself, who remained unflinching at their head.

The wreck of one tremendous oak lay penning them all against the edge of the clearing, dirt still clinging to its roots, and Temeraire stood behind it, one foreleg resting on the trunk and his sinuous length towering over them.

"You will not say such things to me," he said, his head lowering towards Barham: his teeth were bared, and the spiked ruff around his head was raised up and trembling with anger. "I do not believe you for an instant, and I will not hear such lies; Laurence would never take another dragon. If you have sent him away, I will go after him, and if you have hurt him—"

He began to gather his breath for another roar, his chest belling out like a sail in high wind, and this time the hapless men lay directly in his path.

"Temeraire," Laurence called, scrambling ungracefully over the wreckage, sliding down the heap into the clearing in disregard of the splinters that caught at his clothing and skin. "Temeraire, I am well, I am here—"

Temeraire's head had whipped around at the first word, and he at once took the two paces needed to bring him across the clearing. Laurence held still, his heart beating very quickly, not at all with fear: the forelegs with their terrible claws landed to either side of him, and the sleek length of Temeraire's body coiled protectively about him, the great scaled sides rising up around him like shining black walls and the angled head coming to rest by him.

He rested his hands on Temeraire's snout and for a moment laid his cheek against the soft muzzle; Temeraire made a low wordless murmur of unhappiness. "Laurence, Laurence, do not leave me again."

Laurence swallowed. "My dear," he said, and stopped; no answer was possible.

They stood with their heads together in silence, the rest of the world shut out: but only for a moment. "Laurence," Roland called from beyond the encircling coils: she sounded out of breath, and her voice was urgent. "Temeraire, do move aside, there is a good fellow." Temeraire lifted up his head and reluctantly uncurled himself a little so they could speak; but all the while he kept himself between Laurence and Barham's party.

Roland ducked under Temeraire's foreleg and joined Laurence. "You had to go to Temeraire, of course, but it will look very bad to someone who does not understand dragons. For pity's sake do not let Barham push you into anything further: answer him as meek as mother-may-I, do anything he tells you." She shook her head. "By God, Laurence; I hate to leave you in such straits, but the dispatches have come, and minutes may make the difference here."

"Of course you cannot stay," he said. "They are likely waiting for you at Dover even now to launch the attack; we will manage, never fear."

"An attack? There is to be a battle?" Temeraire said, overhearing; he flexed his talons and looked away to the east, as if he might see the formations rising into the air even from here.

"Go at once, and pray take care," Laurence said hastily to Roland. "Give my apologies to Hollin."

She nodded. "Try and stay easy in your mind. I will speak with Lenton even before we launch. The Corps will not sit still for this; bad enough to separate you, but now this outrageous pressure, stirring up all the dragons like this: it cannot be allowed to continue, and no one can possibly hold you to blame."

"Do not worry or wait another instant: the attack is more important," he said, very heartily: counterfeit, as much as her assurances; they both knew that the situation was black. Laurence could not for a moment regret having gone to Temeraire's side, but he had openly disobeyed orders. No court-martial could find him innocent; there was Barham himself to lay the charges, and if questioned Laurence could hardly deny the act. He did not think they would hang him: this was not a battlefield offense, and the circumstances offered some excuse, but he would certainly have been dismissed the service if he had still been in the Navy. There was nothing to be done but face the consequences; he forced a smile, Roland gave his arm a quick squeeze, and she was gone.

The Chinese had risen and collected themselves, making a better show of it than the ragged Marines, who looked ready to bolt at any moment's notice. They all together were now picking their way over the fallen oak. The younger official, Sun Kai, more deftly scrambled over, and with one of the attendants offered a hand to the prince to help him down. Yongxing was hampered by his heavy embroidered gown, leaving trailers of bright silk like gaily colored cobwebs upon the broken branches, but if he felt any of the same terror writ large on the faces of the British soldiers, he did not show it: he seemed unshaken.

Temeraire kept a savage, brooding eye upon them all. "I am not going to sit here while everyone else goes and fights, no matter what those people want."

Laurence stroked Temeraire's neck comfortingly. "Do

not let them upset you. Pray stay quite calm, my dear; losing our tempers will not improve matters." Temeraire only snorted, and his eye remained fixed and glittering, the ruff still standing upright with all the points very stiff: in no mood to be soothed.

Himself quite ashen, Barham made no haste to approach any closer to Temeraire, but Yongxing addressed him sharply, repeating demands both urgent and angry, judging by his gestures towards Temeraire; Sun Kai, however, stood apart, and regarded Laurence and Temeraire more thoughtfully. At last Barham came towards them scowling, evidently taking refuge from fear in anger; Laurence had seen it often enough in men on the eve of battle.

"This is the discipline of the Corps, I gather," Barham began: petty and spiteful, since his life had very likely been saved by the disobedience. He himself seemed to perceive as much; he grew even angrier. "Well, it will not stand with me, Laurence, not for an instant; I will see you broken for this. Sergeant, take him under arrest—"

The end of the sentence was inaudible; Barham was sinking, growing small, his shouting red mouth flashing open and shut like a gasping fish, the words becoming indistinct as the ground fell away beneath Laurence's feet. Temeraire's talons were carefully cupped around him and the great black wings were beating in broad sweeps, up up up through the dingy London air, soot dulling Temeraire's hide and speckling Laurence's hands.

Laurence settled himself in the cupped claws and rode in silence; the damage was done, and Laurence knew better than to ask Temeraire to return to the ground at once: there was a sense of true violence in the force behind his wing-strokes, rage barely checked. They were going very fast. He peered downward in some anxiety as they sped over the city walls: Temeraire was flying without harness or signals, and Laurence feared the guns might be turned on them. But the guns stayed silent: Temeraire was distinctive, with his hide and wings of unbroken black, save for the deep blue and pearlescent grey markings along the edges, and he had been recognized.

Or perhaps their passage was simply too swift for a response: they left the city behind them fifteen minutes after leaving the ground, and were soon beyond the range even of the long-barreled pepper-guns. Roads branched away through the countryside beneath them, dusted with snow, the smell of the air already much cleaner. Temeraire paused and hovered for a moment, shook his head free of dust, and sneezed loudly, jouncing Laurence about a little; but afterwards he flew on at a less frantic pace, and after another minute or two he curled his head down to speak. "Are you well, Laurence? You are not uncomfortable?"

He sounded more anxious than the subject deserved. Laurence patted his foreleg where he could reach it. "No, I am very well."

"I am very sorry to have snatched you away so," Temeraire said, some tension gone at the warmth in Laurence's voice. "Pray do not be angry; I could not let that man take you."

"No, I am not angry," Laurence said; indeed, so far as his heart was concerned there was only a great, swelling joy to be once again aloft, to feel the living current of power running through Temeraire's body, even if his more rational part knew this state could not last. "And I do not blame you for going, not in the least, but I am afraid we must turn back now."

"No; I am not taking you back to that man," Temeraire said obstinately, and Laurence understood with a sinking feeling that he had run up against Temeraire's protective instincts. "He lied to me, and kept you away, and then he wanted to arrest you: he may count himself lucky I did not squash him."

"My dear, we cannot just run wild," Laurence said. "We would be truly beyond the pale if we did such a thing; how do you imagine we would eat, except by theft? And we would be abandoning all our friends."

"I am no more use to them in London, sitting in a covert," Temeraire said, with perfect truth, and left Laurence at a loss for how to answer him. "But I do not mean to run wild; although," a little wistfully, "to be sure, it would be pleasant to do as we liked, and I do not think anyone would miss a few sheep here and there. But not while there is a battle to be fought."

"Oh dear," Laurence said, as he squinted towards the sun and realized their course was southeast, directly for their former covert at Dover. "Temeraire, they cannot let us fight; Lenton will have to order me back, and if I disobey he will arrest me just as quick as Barham, I assure you."

"I do not believe Obversaria's admiral will arrest you," Temeraire said. "She is very nice, and has always spoken to me kindly, even though she is so much older, and the flag-dragon. Besides, if he tries, Maximus and Lily are there, and they will help me; and if that man from London tries to come and take you away again, I will kill him," he added, with an alarming degree of bloodthirsty eagerness.

Chapter 2

❦

*T*HEY LANDED IN the Dover covert amid the clamor and bustle of preparation: the harness-masters bellowing orders to the ground crews, the clatter of buckles and the deeper metallic ringing of the bombs being handed up in sacks to the bellmen; riflemen loading their weapons, the sharp high-pitched shriek of whetstones grinding away on sword-edges. A dozen interested dragons had followed their progress, many calling out greetings to Temeraire as he made his descent. He called back, full of excitement, his spirits rising all the while Laurence felt his own sinking.

Temeraire brought them to earth in Obversaria's clearing; it was one of the largest in the covert, as befitted her standing as flag-dragon, though as an Anglewing she was only slightly more than middling in size, and there was easily room for Temeraire to join her. She was rigged out already, her crew boarding; Admiral Lenton himself was standing beside her in full riding gear, only waiting for his officers to be aboard: minutes away from going aloft.

"Well, and what have you done?" Lenton asked, before Laurence had even managed to unfold himself out of Temeraire's claw. "Roland spoke to me, but she said she had told you to stay quiet; there is going to be the devil to pay for this."

"Sir, I am very sorry to put you in so untenable a position," Laurence said awkwardly, trying to think how he could explain Temeraire's refusal to return to London without seeming to make excuses for himself.

"No, it is my fault," Temeraire added, ducking his head and trying to look ashamed, without much success; there was too distinct a gleam of satisfaction in his eye. "I took Laurence away; that man was going to arrest him."

He sounded plainly smug, and Obversaria abruptly leaned over and batted him on the side of the head, hard enough to make him wobble even though he was half again her size. He flinched and stared at her with a surprised and wounded expression; she only snorted at him and said, "You are too old to be flying with your eyes closed. Lenton, we are ready, I think."

"Yes," Lenton said, squinting up against the sun to examine her harness. "I have no time to deal with you now, Laurence; this will have to wait."

"Of course, sir; I beg your pardon," Laurence said quietly. "Pray do not let us delay you; with your permission, we will stay in Temeraire's clearing until you return." Even cowed by Obversaria's reproof, Temeraire made a small noise of protest at this.

"No, no; don't speak like a groundling," Lenton said impatiently. "A young male like that will not stay behind when he sees his formation go, not uninjured. The same bloody mistake this fellow Barham and all the others at the Admiralty make, every time a new one is shuffled in by Government. If we ever manage to get it into their heads that dragons are not brute beasts, they start to imagine that they are just like men, and can be put under regular military discipline."

Laurence opened his mouth to deny that Temeraire would disobey, then shut it again after glancing round; Temeraire was plowing the ground restlessly with his great talons, his wings partly fanned out, and he would not meet Laurence's gaze.

"Yes, just so," Lenton said dryly, when he saw Laurence silenced. He sighed, unbending a little, and brushed his sparse grey hair back off his forehead. "If those Chinamen want him back, it can only make matters worse if he gets himself injured fighting without armor or crew," he said. "Go on and get him ready; we will speak after."

Laurence could scarcely find words to express his gratitude, but they were unnecessary in any case; Lenton was already turning back to Obversaria. There was indeed no time to waste; Laurence waved Temeraire on and ran for their usual clearing on foot, careless of his dignity. A scattered, intensely excited rush of thoughts, all fragmentary: great relief; of course Temeraire would never have stayed behind; how wretched they would have looked, jumping into a battle against orders; in a moment they would be aloft, yet nothing had truly changed in their circumstances: this might be the last time.

Many of his crewmen were sitting outside in the open, polishing equipment and oiling harness unnecessarily, pretending not to be watching the sky; they were silent and downcast; and at first they only stared when Laurence came running into the clearing. "Where is Granby?" he demanded. "Full muster, gentlemen; heavy-combat rig, at once."

By then Temeraire was overhead and descending, and the rest of the crew came spilling out of the barracks, cheering him; a general stampede towards small-arms and gear ensued, that rush which had once looked like chaos to Laurence, used as he was to naval order, but which accomplished the tremendous affair of getting a dragon equipped in a frantic hurry.

Granby came out of the barracks amid the cavalcade: a tall young officer dark-haired and lanky, his fair skin, ordinarily burnt and peeling from daily flying, but for once unmarred thanks to the weeks of being grounded. He was an aviator born and bred, as Laurence was not, and their acquaintance had not been without early friction: like many other aviators, he had resented so prime a dragon as Temeraire being claimed by a naval officer. But that resentment had not survived a shared action, and Laurence had never yet regretted taking him on as first lieutenant, despite the wide divergence in their characters. Granby had made an initial attempt out of respect to imitate the formalities which were to Laurence, raised a gentleman, as natural as breathing; but they had not taken root. Like most aviators, raised from the age of seven far from polite society, he was by nature given to a sort of easy liberty which looked a great deal like license to a censorious eye.

"Laurence, it is damned good to see you," he said now, coming to seize Laurence's hand: quite unconscious of any impropriety in addressing his commanding officer so, and making no salute; indeed he was at the same time trying to hook his sword onto his belt one-handed. "Have they changed their minds, then? I hadn't looked for anything like such good sense, but I will be the first to beg their Lordships' pardon if they have given up this notion of sending him to China."

For his part, Laurence had long since accepted that no disrespect was intended; at present he scarcely even noticed the informality; he was too bitterly sorry to disappoint Granby, especially now knowing that he had refused a prime position out of loyalty. "I am afraid not, John, but there is no time now to explain: we must get Temeraire aloft at once. Half the usual armaments, and leave the bombs; the Navy will not thank us for sinking the ships, and if it becomes really necessary Temeraire can do more damage roaring away at them."

"Right you are," Granby said, and dashed away at once to the other side of the clearing, calling out orders all around. The great leather harness was already being carried out in double-quick time, and Temeraire was doing his best to help matters along, crouching low to the ground to make it easier for the men to adjust the broad weight-bearing straps across his back.

The panels of chainmail for his breast and belly were heaved out almost as quickly. "No ceremony," Laurence said, and so the aerial crew scrambled aboard pell-mell as soon as their positions were clear, disregarding the usual order.

"We are ten short, I am sorry to say," Granby said, coming back to his side. "I sent six men to Maximus's crew at the Admiral's request; the others—" He hesitated.

"Yes," Laurence said, sparing him; the men had naturally been unhappy at having no part of the action, and the missing four had undoubtedly slipped away to seek better or at least more thorough consolation in a bottle or a woman than could be found in busy-work. He was pleased it was so few, and he did not mean to come the tyrant over them afterwards: he felt at present he had no moral ground on which to stand. "We will manage; but if there are any fellows on the ground crew who are handy with pistol or sword, and not prone to height-sickness, let us get them hooked on if they choose to volunteer."

He himself had already shifted his coat for the long heavy one of leather used in combat, and was now strapping his carabiner belt over. A low many-voiced roar began, not very far away; Laurence looked up: the smaller dragons were going aloft, and he recognized Dulcia and the grey-blue Nitidus, the end-wing members of their formation, flying in circles as they waited for the others to rise.

"Laurence, are you not ready? Do hurry, please, the others are going up," Temeraire said, anxiously, craning his head about to look; above them the middle-weight dragons were coming into view also.

Granby swung himself aboard, along with a couple of tall young harness-men, Willoughby and Porter; Laurence waited until he saw them latched onto the rings of the harness and secure, then said, "All is ready; try away."

This was one ritual that could not in safety be set aside: Temeraire rose up onto his hind legs and shook himself, making certain that the harness was secure and all the men properly hooked on. "Harder," Laurence called sharply: Temeraire was not being particularly vigorous, in his anxiety to be away.

Temeraire snorted but obeyed, and still nothing pulled loose or fell off. "All lies well; please come aboard now," he said, thumping to the ground and holding out his foreleg at once; Laurence stepped into the claw and was rather quickly tossed up to his usual place at the base of Temeraire's neck. He did not mind at all: he was pleased, exhilarated by everything: the deeply satisfying sound as his carabiner rings locked into place, the buttery feel of the oiled, double-stitched leather straps of the harness; and beneath him Temeraire's muscles were already gathering for the leap aloft.

Maximus suddenly erupted out of the trees to the north of them, his great red-and-gold body even larger than before, as Roland had reported. He was still the only Regal Copper stationed at the Channel, and he dwarfed every other creature in sight, blotting out an enormous swath of the sun. Temeraire roared joyfully at the sight and leapt up after him, black wings beating a little too quickly with over-excitement.

"Gently," Laurence called; Temeraire bobbed his head in acknowledgment, but they still overshot the slower dragon.

"Maximus, Maximus; look, I am back," Temeraire called out, circling back down to take his position alongside the big dragon, and they began beating up together to the formation's flying height. "I took Laurence away from London," he added triumphantly, in what he likely thought a confidential whisper. "They were trying to arrest him."

"Did he kill someone?" Maximus asked with interest in his deep echoing voice, not at all disapproving. "I am glad you are back; they have been making me fly in the middle while you were gone, and all the maneuvers are different," he added.

"No," said Temeraire, "he only came and talked to me when some fat old man said he should not, which does not seem like any reason to me."

"You had better shut up that Jacobin of a dragon of yours," Berkley shouted across from Maximus's back, while Laurence shook his head in despair, trying to ignore the inquisitive looks from his young ensigns.

"Pray remember we are on business, Temeraire," Laurence called, trying to be severe; but after all there was no sense in trying to keep it a secret; the news would surely be all over in a week. They would be forced to confront the gravity of their situation soon enough; little enough harm in letting Temeraire indulge in high spirits so long as he might.

"Laurence," Granby said at his shoulder, "in the hurry, the ammunition was all laid in its usual place on the left, though we are not carrying the bombs to balance it out; we ought to restow."

"Can you have it done before we engage? Oh, good Lord," Laurence said, realizing. "I do not even know the position of the convoy; do you?" Granby shook his head, embarrassed, and Laurence swallowed his pride and shouted, "Berkley, where are we going?"

A general explosion of mirth ran among the men on Maximus's back. Berkley called back, "Straight to Hell, ha ha!" More laughter, nearly drowning out the coordinates that he bellowed over.

"Fifteen minutes' flight, then." Laurence was mentally running the calculation through in his head. "And we ought to save at least five of those minutes for grace."

Granby nodded. "We can manage it," he said, and clambered down at once to organize the operation, unhooking and rehooking the carabiners with practiced skill from the evenly spaced rings leading down Temeraire's side to the storage nets slung beneath his belly.

The rest of the formation was already in place as Temeraire and Maximus rose to take their defensive positions at the rear. Laurence noticed the formation-leader flag streaming out from Lily's back; that meant that during their absence, Captain Harcourt had at last been given the command. He was glad to see the change: it was hard on the signal-ensign to have to watch a wing dragon as well as keep an eye forward, and the dragons would always instinctively follow the lead regardless of formal precedence.

Still, he could not help feeling how strange that he should find himself taking orders from a twenty-year-old girl: Harcourt was still a very young officer, promoted over-quick due to Lily's unexpectedly early hatching. But command in the Corps had to follow the capabilities of the dragons, and a rare acid-spitter like one of the Longwings was too valuable to place anywhere but the center of a formation, even if they would only accept female handlers.

"Signal from the Admiral: *proceed to meeting*," called the signal-ensign, Turner; a moment later the signal *formation keep together* broke out on Lily's signal-yard, and the dragons were pressing on, shortly reaching their cruising speed of a steady seventeen knots: an easy pace for Temeraire, but all that the Yellow Reapers and the enormous Maximus could manage comfortably for any length of time.

There was time to loosen his sword in the sheath, and load his pistols fresh; below, Granby was shouting orders over the wind: he did not sound frantic, and Laurence had every confidence in his power to get the work completed in time. The dragons of the covert made an impressive spread, even though this was not so large a force in numbers as had been assembled for the Battle of Dover in October, which had fended off Napoleon's invasion attempt.

But in that battle, they had been forced to send up every available dragon, even the little couriers: most of the fighting-dragons had been away south at Trafalgar. Today Excidium and Captain Roland's formation were back in the lead, ten dragons strong, the smallest of them a middle-weight Yellow Reaper, and all of them flying in perfect formation, not a wingbeat out of place: the skill born of many long years in formation together.

Lily's formation was nothing so imposing, as yet: only six dragons flying behind her, with her flank and end-wing positions held by smaller and more maneuverable beasts with older officers, who could more easily compensate for any errors made from inexperience by Lily herself, or by Maximus and Temeraire in the back line. Even as they drew closer, Laurence saw Sutton, the captain of their mid-wing Messoria, stand up on her back and turn to look over at them, making sure all was well with the younger dragons. Laurence raised a hand in acknowledgment, and saw Berkley doing the same.

The sails of the French convoy and the Channel Fleet were visible long before the dragons came into range. There was a stately quality to the scene below: chess-board pieces moving into place, with the British ships advancing in eager haste towards the great crowd of smaller French merchantmen; a glorious spread of white sail to be seen on every ship, and the British colors streaming among them. Granby came clambering back up along the shoulder-strap to Laurence's side. "We'll do nicely now, I think."

"Very good," Laurence said absently, his attention all on what he could see of the British fleet, peering down over Temeraire's shoulder through his glass. Mostly fast-sailing frigates, with a motley collection of smaller sloops, and a handful of sixty-four- and seventy-four-gun ships. The Navy would not risk the largest first- and second-rate ships against the fire-breather; too easy for one lucky attack to send a three-decker packed full of powder up like a light, taking half-a-dozen smaller ships along with her.

"All hands to their stations, Mr. Harley," Laurence said, straightening up, and the young ensign hurried to set the signal-strap embedded in the harness to red. The riflemen stationed along Temeraire's back let themselves partly down his sides, readying their guns, while the rest of the topmen all crouched low, pistols in their hands.

Excidium and the rest of the larger formation dropped low over the British warships, taking up the more important defensive position and leaving the field to them. As Lily increased their speed, Temeraire gave a low growling rumble, the tremor palpable through his hide. Laurence spared a moment to lean over and put his bare hand on the side of Temeraire's neck: no words necessary, and he felt a slight easing of the nervous tension before he straightened and pulled his leather riding glove back on.

"Enemy in sight," came faint but audible in the shrill high voice of Lily's forward lookout, carrying back to them on the wind, echoed a moment later by young Allen, stationed near the joint of Temeraire's wing. A general murmur went around the men, and Laurence snapped out his glass again for a look.

"La Crabe Grande, I think," he said, handing the telescope over to Granby, hoping privately that he had not mangled the pronunciation too badly. He was quite sure that he had identified the formation style correctly, despite his lack of experience in aerial actions; there were few composed of fourteen dragons, and the shape was highly distinct, with the two pincer-like rows of smaller dragons stretched out to either side of the cluster of big ones in the center.

The Flamme-de-Gloire was not easy to spot, with several decoy dragons of similar coloring shifting about: a pair of Papillon Noirs with yellow markings painted over their natural blue and green stripes to make them confusingly alike from a distance. "Hah, I have made her: it is Accendare. There she is, the wicked thing," Granby said, handing back the glass and pointing. "She has a talon missing from her left rear leg, and she is blind in the right eye: we gave her a good dose of pepper back in the battle of the Glorious First."

"I see her. Mr. Harley, pass the word to all the lookouts. Temeraire," he called, bringing up the speaking-trumpet, "do you see the Flamme-de-Gloire? She is the one low and to the right, with the missing talon; she is weak in the right eye."

"I see her," Temeraire said eagerly, turning his head just slightly. "Are we to attack her?"

"Our first duty is to keep her fire away from the Navy's ships; have an eye on her as best you can," Laurence said, and Temeraire bobbed his head once in quick answer, straightening out again.

He tucked away the glass in the small pouch hooked onto the harness: no more need for it, very soon. "You had better get below, John," Laurence said. "I expect they will try a boarding with a few of those light fellows on their edges."

All this while they had been rapidly closing the distance: suddenly there was no more time, and the French were wheeling about in perfect unison, not one dragon falling out of formation, graceful as a flock of birds. A low whistle came behind him; admittedly it was an impressive sight, but Laurence frowned though his own heart was speeding involuntarily. "Belay that noise."

One of the Papillons was directly ahead of them, jaws spreading wide as if to breathe flames it could not produce; Laurence felt an odd, detached amusement to see a dragon play-acting. Temeraire could not roar from his position in the rear, not with Messoria and Lily both in the way, but he did not duck away at all; instead he raised his claws, and as the two formations swept together and intermingled, he and the Papillon pulled up and collided with a force that jarred all of their crews loose.

Laurence grappled for the harness and got his feet back underneath him. "Clap on there, Allen," he said, reaching; the boy was dangling by his carabiner straps with his arms and legs waving about wildly like an overturned tortoise. Allen managed to get himself braced and clung, his face pale and shading to green; like the other lookouts, he was only a new ensign, barely twelve years old, and he had not quite learned to manage himself aboard during the stops and starts of battle.

Temeraire was clawing and biting, his wings beating madly as he tried to keep hold of the Papillon: the French dragon was lighter in weight, and plainly all he now wanted was to get free and back to his formation. "Hold position," Laurence shouted: more important to keep the formation together for the moment. Temeraire reluctantly let the Papillon go and leveled out.

Below, distantly, came the first sound of cannon-fire: bow-chasers on the British ships, hoping to knock away some of the French merchantmen's spars with a lucky shot or two. Not likely, but it would put the men in the right frame of mind. A steady rattle and clang behind him as the riflemen reloaded; all the harness he could see looked still in good order; no sign of dripping blood, and Temeraire was flying well. No time to ask how he was; they were coming about, Lily taking them straight for the enemy formation again.

But this time the French offered no resistance: instead the dragons scattered; wildly, Laurence thought at first, then he perceived how well they had distributed themselves around. Four of the smaller dragons darted upwards; the rest dropped perhaps a hundred feet in height, and Accendare was once again hard to tell from the decoys.

No clear target anymore, and with the dragons above the formation itself was dangerously vulnerable: *engage the enemy more closely* went up the yard on Lily's back, signaling that they might disperse and fight separately. Temeraire could read the flags as well as any signalofficer: he instantly dived for the decoy with bleeding scratches, a little too eager to complete his own handiwork. "No, Temeraire," Laurence called, meaning to direct him after Accendare herself, but too late: two of the smaller dragons, both of the common Pêcheur-Rayé breed, were coming at them from either side.

"Prepare to repel boarders," Lieutenant Ferris, captain of the topmen, shouted from behind him. Two of the sturdiest midwingmen took up stations just behind Laurence's position; he glanced over his shoulder at them, his mouth tightening: it still rankled him to be so shielded, too much like cowardly hiding behind others, but no dragon would fight with a sword laid at its captain's throat, and so he had to bear it.

Temeraire contented himself with one more slash across the fleeing decoy's shoulders and writhed away, almost doubling back on himself. The pursuers overshot and had to turn back: a clear gain of a minute, worth more than gold at present. Laurence cast an eye over the field: the quick light-combat dragons were dashing about to fend off the British dragons, but the larger ones were forming back into a cluster and keeping pace with their convoy.

A powder-flash below caught his eye; an instant later came the thin whistling of a pepper-ball, flying up from the French ships. Another of their formation members, Immortalis, had dived just a hair too low in pursuit of one of the other dragons. Fortunately their aim was off: the ball struck his shoulder instead of his face, and the best part of the pepper scattered down harmlessly into the sea; even the remainder was enough to set the poor fellow sneezing, blowing himself ten lengths back at a time.

"Digby, cast and mark that height," Laurence said; it was the starboard forward lookout's duty to warn when they entered the range of the guns below.

Digby took the small round-shot, bored through and tied to the height-line, and tossed it over Temeraire's shoulder, the thin silk cord paying out with the knotted marks for every fifty yards flying through his fingers. "Six at the mark, seventeen at the water," he said, counting from Immortalis's height, and cut the cord. "Range five hundred fifty yards on the pepper-guns, sir." He was already whipping the cord through another ball, to be ready when the next measure should be called for.

A shorter range than usual; were they holding back, trying to tempt the more dangerous dragons lower, or was the wind checking their shot? "Keep to six hundred yards' elevation, Temeraire," Laurence called; best to be cautious for the moment.

"Sir, lead signal to us, *fall in on left flank Maximus*," Turner said.

No immediate way to get over to him: the two Pêcheurs were back, trying to flank Temeraire and get men aboard, although they were flying somewhat strangely, not in a straight line. "What are they about?" Martin said, and the question answered itself readily in Laurence's mind.

"They fear giving him a target for his roar," Laurence said, making it loud for Temeraire's benefit. Temeraire snorted in disdain, abruptly halted in mid-air, and whipped himself about, hovering to face the pair with his ruff standing high: the smaller dragons, clearly alarmed by the presentation, backwinged out of instinct, giving them room.

"Hah!" Temeraire stopped and hovered, pleased with himself at seeing the others so afraid of his prowess; Laurence had to tug on the harness to draw his attention around to the signal, which he had not yet seen. "Oh, I see!" he said, and dashed forward to take up position to Maximus's left; Lily was already on his right.

Harcourt's intention was clear. "All hands low," Laurence said, and crouched against Temeraire's neck even as he gave the order. Instantly they were in place, Berkley sent Maximus ahead at the big dragon's top speed, right at the clustered French dragons.

Temeraire was swelling with breath, his ruff coming up; they were going so quickly the wind was beating tears from Laurence's eyes, but he could see Lily's head drawing back in similar preparation. Maximus put his head down and drove straight into the French dragons, simply bulling through their ranks with his enormous advantage in weight: the dragons fell off to his either side, only to meet Temeraire roaring and Lily spraying her corrosive acid.

Shrieks of pain in their wake, and the first dead crewmen were being cut loose from harness and sent falling into the ocean, rag-doll limp. The French dragons' forward motion had nearly halted, many of them panicking and scattering, this time with no thought to the pattern. Then Maximus and they were through: the cluster had broken apart and now Accendare was shielded from them only by a Petit Chevalier, slightly larger than Temeraire, and another of Accendare's decoys.

They slowed; Maximus was heaving for breath, fighting to keep elevation. Harcourt waved wildly at Laurence from Lily's back, shouting hoarsely through her speaking-trumpet, "Go after her," even while the formal signal was going up on Lily's back. Laurence touched Temeraire's side and sent him forward; Lily sprayed another burst of acid, and the two defending dragons recoiled, enough for Temeraire to dodge past them and get through.

Granby's voice came from below, yelling: " 'Ware boarders!" So some Frenchmen had made the leap to Temeraire's back. Laurence had no time to look: directly before his face Accendare was twisting around, scarcely ten yards distant. Her right eye was milky, the left wicked and glaring, a pale yellow pupil in black sclera; she had long thin horns curving down from her forehead and to the very edge of her jaws, her opening jaws: a heat-shimmer distorted the air as flames came bursting out upon them. Very like looking into the mouth of Hell, he thought for that one narrow instant, staring into the red maw; then Temeraire snapped his wings shut and fell out of the way like a stone.

Laurence's stomach leapt; behind him he heard clatter and cries of surprise, the boarders and defenders alike losing their footing. It seemed only a moment before Temeraire opened his wings again and began to beat up hard, but they had plummeted some distance, and Accendare was flying rapidly away from them, back to the ships below.

The rearmost merchant ships of the French convoy had come within the accurate range of long guns of the British men-of-war: the steady roar of cannon-fire rose, mingled with sulfur and smoke. The quickest frigates had already moved on ahead, passing by the merchant-men under fire and continuing for the richer prizes at the front. In doing so, however, they had left the shelter of Excidium's formation, and Accendare now stooped towards them, her crew throwing the fist-sized iron in-cendiaries over her sides, which she bathed with flame as they fell towards the vulnerable British ships.

More than half the shells fell into the sea, much more; mindful of Temeraire's pursuit, Accendare had not gone very low, and aim could not be accurate from so high up. But Laurence could see a handful blooming into flame below: the thin metal shells broke as they struck the decks of the ships, and the naphtha within ignited against the hot metal, spreading a pool of fire across the deck.

Temeraire gave a low growl of anger as he saw fire catch the sails of one of the frigates, instantly putting on another burst of speed to go after Accendare; he had been hatched on deck, spent the first three weeks of his life at sea: the affection remained. Laurence urged him on with word and touch, full of the same anger. Intent on the pursuit and watching for other dragons who might be close enough to offer her support, Laurence was star-tled out of his single-minded focus unpleasantly: Croyn, one of the topmen, fell onto him before rolling away and off Temeraire's back, mouth round and open, hands reach-ing; his carabiner straps had been severed.

He missed the harness, his hands slipping over Teme-raire's smooth hide; Laurence snatched at him, uselessly: the boy was falling, arms flailing at the empty air, down a quarter of a mile and gone into the water: only a small splash; he did not resurface. Another man went down just after him, one of the boarders, but already dead even as he tumbled slack-limbed through the air. Laurence loosened his own straps and stood, turning around as he drew his pistols. Seven boarders were still aboard, fight-ing very hard. One with lieutenant's bars on his shoul-

ders was only a few paces away, engaged closely with
Quarle, the second of the midwingmen who had been set
to guard Laurence.

Even as Laurence got to his feet, the lieutenant knocked
aside Quarle's arm with his sword and drove a vicious-
looking long knife into his side left-handed. Quarle
dropped his own sword and put his hands around the
hilt, sinking, coughing blood. Laurence had a wide-open
shot, but just behind the lieutenant, one of the boarders
had driven Martin to his knees: the midwingman's neck
was bare to the man's cutlass.

Laurence leveled his pistol and fired: the boarder fell
backwards with a hole in his chest spurting, and Martin
heaved himself back to his feet. Before Laurence could
take fresh aim and set off the other, the lieutenant took
the risk of slashing his own straps and leapt over Quarle's
body, catching Laurence's arm both for support and to
push the pistol aside. It was an extraordinary maneuver,
whether for bravery or recklessness; "Bravo," Laurence
said, involuntarily. The Frenchman looked at him startled, and then smiled, incongruously boyish in his blood-
streaked face, before he brought his sword up.

Laurence had an unfair advantage, of course; he was
useless dead, for a dragon whose captain had been killed
would turn with utmost savagery on the enemy: uncontrolled but very dangerous nonetheless. The Frenchman
needed him prisoner, not killed, and that made him
overly cautious, while Laurence could freely aim for a
killing blow and strike as best as ever he could.

But that was not very well, currently. It was an odd
battle; they were upon the narrow base of Temeraire's
neck, so closely engaged that Laurence was not at a dis-
advantage from the tall lieutenant's greater reach, but
that same condition let the Frenchman keep his grip on
Laurence, without which he would certainly have slipped
off. They were more pushing at one another than truly

sword-fighting; their blades hardly ever parted more than an inch or two before coming together again, and Laurence began to think the contest would only be ended if one or the other of them fell.

Laurence risked a step; it let him turn them both slightly, so he could see the rest of the struggle over the lieutenant's shoulder. Martin and Ferris were both still standing, and several of the riflemen, but they were outnumbered, and if even a couple more of the boarders managed to get past, it would be very awkward for Laurence indeed. Several of the bellmen were trying to come up from below, but the boarders had detached a couple of men to fend them off: as Laurence watched, Johnson was stabbed through and fell.

"*Vive l'Empereur,*" the lieutenant shouted to his men encouragingly, looking also; he took heart from the favorable position and struck again, aiming for Laurence's leg. Laurence deflected the blow: his sword rang oddly with the impact, though, and he realized with an unpleasant shock that he was fighting with his dress-sword, worn to the Admiralty the day before: he had never had a chance to exchange it.

He began to fight more narrowly, trying not to meet the Frenchman's sword anywhere below the midpoint of his sword: he did not want to lose his entire blade if it were going to snap. Another sharp blow, at his right arm: he blocked it as well, but this time five inches of steel did indeed snap off, scoring a thin line across his jaw before it tumbled away, red-gold in the reflected firelight.

The Frenchman had seen the weakness of the blade now, and was trying to batter it into pieces. Another crack and more of the blade went: Laurence was fighting with only six inches of steel now, with the paste brilliants on the silver-plated hilt sparkling at him mockingly, ridiculous. He clenched his jaw; he was not going to surrender and see Temeraire ordered to France: he would be damned first. If he jumped over the side, calling, there was some hope Temeraire might catch him; if not, then at least he would not be responsible for delivering Temeraire into Napoleon's hands after all.

Then a shout: Granby came swarming up the rear tail-strap without benefit of carabiners, locked himself back on and lunged for the man guarding the left side of the belly-strap. The man fell dead, and six bellmen almost at once burst into the tops: the remaining boarders drew into a tight knot, but in a moment they would have to surrender or be killed. Martin had turned and was already clambering over Quarle's body, freed by the relief from below, and his sword was ready.

"*Ah, voici un joli gâchis,*" the lieutenant said in tones of despair, looking also, and he made a last gallant attempt, binding Laurence's hilt with his own blade, and using the length as a lever: he managed to pry it out of Laurence's hand with a great heave, but just as he did he staggered, surprised, and blood came out of his nose. He fell forward into Laurence's arms, senseless: young Digby was standing rather wobblingly behind him, holding the round-shot on the measuring cord; he had crept along from his lookout's post on Temeraire's shoulder, and struck the Frenchman on the head.

"Well done," Laurence said, after he had worked out what had happened; the boy flushed up proudly. "Mr. Martin, heave this fellow below to the infirmary, will you?" Laurence handed the Frenchman's limp form over. "He fought quite like a lion."

"Very good, sir." Martin's mouth kept moving, he was saying something more, but a roar from above was drowning out his voice: it was the last thing Laurence heard.

The low and dangerous rumble of Temeraire's growl, just above him, penetrated the smothering unconsciousness. Laurence tried to move, to look around him, but the light stabbed painfully at his eyes, and his leg did not want to answer at all; groping blindly down along his thigh, he found it entangled with the leather straps of his harness, and felt a wet trickle of blood where one of the buckles had torn through his breeches and into his skin.

He thought for a moment perhaps they had been captured; but the voices he heard were English, and then he recognized Barham, shouting, and Granby saying fiercely, "No, sir, no farther, not one damned step. Temeraire, if those men make ready, you may knock them down."

Laurence struggled to sit up, and then suddenly there were anxious hands supporting him. "Steady, sir, are you all right?" It was young Digby, pressing a dripping waterbag into his hands. Laurence wetted his lips, but he did not dare to swallow; his stomach was roiling. "Help me stand," he said, hoarsely, trying to squint his eyes open a little.

"No, sir, you mustn't," Digby whispered urgently. "You have had a nasty knock on the head, and those fellows, they have come to arrest you. Granby said we had to keep you out of sight and wait for the Admiral."

He was lying behind the protective curl of Temeraire's foreleg, with the hard-packed dirt of the clearing underneath him; Digby and Allen, the forward lookouts, were crouched down on either side of him. Small rivulets of dark blood were running down Temeraire's leg to stain the ground black, not far away. "He is wounded," Laurence said sharply, trying to get up again.

"Mr. Keynes is gone for bandages, sir; a Pêcheur hit us across the shoulders, but it is only a few scratches," Digby said, holding him back; which attempt was successful, because Laurence could not make his wrenched leg even bend, much less carry any weight. "You are not to get up, sir, Baylesworth is getting a stretcher."

"Enough of this, help me rise," Laurence said, sharply;

Lenton could not possibly come quickly, so soon after a battle, and he did not mean to lie about letting matters get worse. He made Digby and Allen help him rise and limp out from the concealment, the two ensigns struggling under his weight.

Barham was there with a dozen Marines, these not the inexperienced boys of his escort in London but hard-bitten soldiers, older men, and they had brought with them a pepper-gun: only a small, short-barreled one, but at this range they hardly needed better. Barham was almost purple in the face, quarreling with Granby at the side of the clearing; when he caught sight of Laurence his eyes went narrow. "There you are; did you think you could hide here, like a coward? Stand down that animal, at once; Sergeant, go there and take him."

"You are not to come anywhere near Laurence, at all," Temeraire snarled at the soldiers, before Laurence could make any reply, and raised one deadly clawed foreleg, ready to strike. The blood streaking his shoulders and neck made him look truly savage, and his great ruff was standing up stiffly around his head.

The men flinched a little, but the sergeant said, stolidly, "Run out that gun, Corporal," and gestured to the rest of them to raise up their muskets.

In alarm, Laurence called out to him hoarsely, "Temeraire, stop; for God's sake settle," but it was useless; Temeraire was in a red-eyed rage, and did not take any notice. Even if the musketry did not cause him serious injury, the pepper-gun would surely blind and madden him even further, and he could easily be driven into a truly uncontrolled frenzy, terrible both to himself and to others.

The trees to the west of them shook suddenly, and abruptly Maximus's enormous head and shoulders came rising up out of the growth; he flung his head back yawning tremendously, exposing rows of serrated teeth, and shook himself all over. "Is the battle not over? What is all the noise?"

"You there!" Barham shouted at the big Regal Copper, pointing at Temeraire. "Hold down that dragon!"

Like all Regal Coppers, Maximus was badly farsighted; to see into the clearing, he was forced to rear up onto his haunches to gain enough distance. He was twice Temeraire's size by weight and twenty feet more in length now; his wings, half-outspread for balance, threw a long shadow ahead of him, and with the sun behind him they glowed redly, veins standing out in the translucent skin.

Looming over them all, he drew his head back on his neck and peered into the clearing. "Why do you need to be held down?" he asked Temeraire, interestedly.

"I do not need to be held down!" Temeraire said, almost spitting in his anger, ruff quivering; the blood was running more freely down his shoulders. "Those men want to take Laurence from me, and put him in prison, and execute him, and I will not let them, ever, and I do not *care* if Laurence tells me not to squash you," he added, fiercely, to Lord Barham.

"Good God," Laurence said, low and appalled; it had not occurred to him the real nature of Temeraire's fear. But the only time Temeraire had ever seen an arrest, the man taken had been a traitor, executed shortly thereafter before the eyes of the man's own dragon. The experience had left Temeraire and all the young dragons of the covert crushed with sympathetic misery for days; it was no wonder if he was panicked now.

Granby took advantage of the unwitting distraction Maximus had provided and made a quick, impulsive gesture to the other officers of Temeraire's crew: Ferris and Evans jumped to follow him, Riggs and his riflemen scrambling after, and in a moment they were all ranged defensively in front of Temeraire, raising pistols and rifles. It was all bravado, their guns spent from the battle, but that did not in any way reduce the significance. Laurence shut his eyes in dismay. Granby and all his men had just flung themselves into the stew-pot with him, by such direct disobedience; indeed there was increasingly every justification to call this a mutiny.

The muskets facing them did not waver, though; the Marines were still hurrying to finish loading the gun, tamping down one of the big round pepper-balls with a small wad. "Make ready!" the corporal said. Laurence could not think what to do; if he ordered Temeraire to knock down the gun, they would be attacking fellow-soldiers, men only doing their duty: unforgivable, even to his own mind, and only a little less unthinkable than standing by while they injured Temeraire, or his own men.

"What the devil do you all mean here?" Keynes, the dragon-surgeon assigned to Temeraire's care, had just come back into the clearing, two staggering assistants behind him laden down with fresh white bandages and thin silk thread for stitching. He shoved his way through the startled Marines, his well-salted hair and blood-spattered coat giving him a badge of authority they did not choose to defy, and snatched the slow-match out of the hands of the man standing by the pepper-gun.

He flung it to the ground and stamped it out, and glared all around, sparing neither Barham and the Marines nor Granby and his men, impartially furious. "He is fresh from the field; have you all taken leave of your senses? You cannot be stirring up dragons like this after a battle; in half a minute we will have the rest of the covert looking in, and not just that great busybody there," he added, pointing at Maximus.

Indeed more dragons had already lifted their heads up above the tree cover, trying to crane their heads over to see what was going on, making a great noise of cracking branches; the ground even trembled underfoot when the abashed Maximus dropped lower, back down to his

haunches, in an attempt to make his curiosity less obvious. Barham uneasily looked around at the many inquisitive spectators: dragons ordinarily ate directly after a
battle, and many of them had gore dripping from their
jaws, bones cracking audibly as they chewed.

Keynes did not give him time to recover. "Out, out at
once, the lot of you; I cannot be operating in the middle
of this circus, and as for you," he snapped at Laurence,
"lie down again at once; I gave orders you were to be
taken straight to the surgeons. Christ only knows what
you are doing to that leg, hopping about on it. Where is
Baylesworth with that stretcher?"

Barham, wavering, was caught by this. "Laurence is
damned well under arrest, and I have a mind to clap the
rest of you mutinous dogs into irons also," he began,
only to have Keynes wheel on him in turn.

"You can arrest him in the morning, after that leg has
been seen to, and his dragon. Of all the blackguardly,
unchristian notions, storming in on wounded men and
beasts—" Keynes was literally shaking his fist in Barham's
face; an alarming prospect, thanks to the wickedly hooked
ten-inch tenaculum clenched in his fingers, and the moral
force of his argument was very great: Barham stepped
back, involuntarily. The Marines gratefully took it as a
signal, beginning to drag the gun back out of the clearing
with them, and Barham, baffled and deserted, was forced
to give way.

The delay thus won lasted only a short while. The surgeons scratched their heads over Laurence's leg; the bone
was not broken, despite the breathtaking pain when they
roughly palpated the limb, and there was no visible wound,
save the great mottled bruises covering nearly every
scrap of skin. His head ached fiercely also, but there was
little they could do but offer him laudanum, which he refused, and order him to keep his weight off the leg: ad-

vice as practical as it was unnecessary, since he could not stand for any length of time without suffering a collapse.

Meanwhile, Temeraire's own wounds, thankfully minor, were sewed up, and with much coaxing Laurence persuaded him to eat a little, despite his agitation. By morning, it was plain Temeraire was healing well, with no sign of wound-fever, and there was no excuse for further delay; a formal summons had come from Admiral Lenton, ordering Laurence to report to the covert headquarters. He had to be carried in an elbow-chair, leaving behind him an uneasy and restive Temeraire. "If you do not come back by tomorrow morning, I will come and find you," he vowed, and would not be dissuaded.

Laurence could do little in honesty to reassure him: there was every likelihood he was to be arrested, if Lenton had not managed some miracle of persuasion, and after these multiple offenses a court-martial might very well impose a death-sentence. Ordinarily an aviator would not be hanged for anything less than outright treason. But Barham would surely have him up before a board of Navy officers, who would be far more severe, and consideration for preserving the dragon's service would not enter into their deliberations: Temeraire was already lost to England, as a fighting-dragon, by the demands of the Chinese.

It was by no means an easy or a comfortable situation, and still worse was the knowledge that he had imperiled his men; Granby would have to answer for his defiance, and the other lieutenants also, Evans and Ferris and Riggs; any or all of them might be dismissed the service: a terrible fate for an aviator, raised in the ranks from early childhood. Even those midwingmen who never passed for lieutenant were not usually sent away; some work would be found for them, in the breeding grounds or in the coverts, that they might remain in the society of their fellows.

Though his leg had improved some little way overnight, Laurence was still pale and sweating even from the short walk he risked taking up the front stairs of the building. The pain was increasing sharply, dizzying, and he was forced to stop and catch his breath before he went into the small office.

"Good Heaven; I thought you had been let go by the surgeons. Sit down, Laurence, before you fall down; take this," Lenton said, ignoring Barham's scowl of impatience, and put a glass of brandy into Laurence's hand.

"Thank you, sir; you are not mistaken, I have been released," Laurence said, and only sipped once for politeness's sake; his head was already clouded badly enough.

"That is enough; he is not here to be coddled," Barham said. "Never in my life have I seen such outrageous behavior, and from an officer— By God, Laurence, I have never taken pleasure in a hanging, but on this occasion I would call it good riddance. But Lenton swears to me your beast will become unmanageable; though how we should tell the difference I can hardly say."

Lenton's lips tightened at this disdainful tone; Laurence could only imagine the humiliating lengths to which he had been forced in order to impress this understanding on Barham. Though Lenton was an admiral, and fresh from another great victory, even that meant very little in any larger sphere; Barham could offend him with impunity, where any admiral in the Navy would have had political influence and friends enough to require more respectful handling.

"You are to be dismissed the service, that is beyond question," Barham continued. "But off to China the animal must go, and for that, I am sorry to say, we require your cooperation. Find some way to persuade him, and we will leave the matter there; any more of this recalcitrance, and I am damned if I will *not* hang you after all;

yes, and have the animal shot, and be damned to those Chinamen also."

This last very nearly brought Laurence out of his chair, despite his injury; only Lenton's hand on his shoulder, pressing down firmly, held him in place. "Sir, you go too far," Lenton said. "We have never shot dragons in England for anything less than man-eating, and we are not going to start now; I would have a real mutiny on my hands."

Barham scowled, and muttered something not quite intelligible under his breath about lack of discipline; which was a fine thing coming from a man whom Laurence well knew had served during the great naval mutinies of '97, when half the fleet had risen up. "Well, let us hope it does not come to any such thing. There is a transport in ordinary in harbor at Spithead, the *Allegiance*; she can be made ready for sea in a week. How then are we to get the animal aboard, since he is choosing to be balky?"

Laurence could not bring himself to answer; a week was a horribly short time, and for a moment he even wildly allowed himself to consider the prospect of flight. Temeraire could easily reach the Continent from Dover, and there were places in the forests of the German states where even now feral dragons lived; though only small breeds.

"It will require some consideration," Lenton said. "I will not scruple to say, sir, that the whole affair has been mismanaged from the beginning. The dragon has been badly stirred-up, now, and it is no joke to coax a dragon to do something he does not like to begin with."

"Enough excuses, Lenton; quite enough," Barham began, and then a tapping came on the door; they all looked in surprise as a rather pale-looking midwingman opened the door and said, "Sir, sir—" only to hastily clear out of the way: the Chinese soldiers looked as though they would have trampled straight over him, clearing a path for Prince Yongxing into the room.

They were all of them so startled they forgot at first to rise, and Laurence was still struggling to get up to his feet when Yongxing had already come into the room. The attendants hurried to pull a chair—Lord Barham's chair—over for the prince; but Yongxing waved it aside, forcing the rest of them to keep on their feet. Lenton unobtrusively put a hand under Laurence's arm, giving him a little support, but the room still tilted and spun around him, the blaze of Yongxing's bright-colored robes stabbing at his eyes.

"I see this is the way in which you show your respect for the Son of Heaven," Yongxing said, addressing Barham. "Once again you have thrown Lung Tien Xiang into battle; now you hold secret councils, and plot how you may yet keep the fruits of your thievery."

Though Barham had been damning the Chinese five minutes before, now he went pale and stammered, "Sir, Your Highness, not in the least—" but Yongxing was not slowed even a little.

"I have gone through this *covert,* as you call these animal pens," he said. "It is not surprising, when one considers your barbaric methods, that Lung Tien Xiang should have formed this misguided attachment. Naturally he does not wish to be separated from the companion who is responsible for what little comfort he has been given." He turned to Laurence, and looked him up and down disdainfully. "You have taken advantage of his youth and inexperience; but this will not be tolerated. We will hear no further excuses for these delays. Once he has been restored to his home and his proper place, he will soon learn better than to value company so far beneath him."

"Your Highness, you are mistaken; we have every intention to cooperate with you," Lenton said bluntly, while

Barham was still struggling for more polished phrases. "But Temeraire will not leave Laurence, and I am sure you know well that a dragon cannot be sent, but only led."

Yongxing said icily, "Then plainly Captain Laurence must come also; or will you now attempt to convince us that *he* cannot be sent?"

They all stared, in blank confusion; Laurence hardly dared believe he understood properly, and then Barham blurted, "Good God, if you want Laurence, you may damned well have him, and welcome."

The rest of the meeting passed in a haze for Laurence, the tangle of confusion and immense relief leaving him badly distracted. His head still spun, and he answered to remarks somewhat randomly until Lenton finally intervened once more, sending him up to bed. He kept himself awake only long enough to send a quick note to Temeraire by way of the maid, and fell straightaway into a thick, unrefreshing sleep.

He clawed his way out of it the next morning, having slept fourteen hours. Captain Roland was drowsing by his bedside, head tipped against the chair back, mouth open; as he stirred, she woke and rubbed her face, yawning. "Well, Laurence, are you awake? You have been giving us all a fright and no mistake. Emily came to me because poor Temeraire was fretting himself to pieces: whyever did you send him such a note?"

Laurence tried desperately to remember what he had written: impossible; it was wholly gone, and he could remember very little of the previous day at all, though the central, the essential point was quite fixed in his mind. "Roland, I have not the faintest idea what I said. Does Temeraire know that I am going with him?"

"Well, now he does, since Lenton told me after I came

looking for you, but he certainly did not find it in here," she said, and gave him a piece of paper.

It was in his own hand, and with his signature, but wholly unfamiliar, and nonsensical:

> Temeraire—
> Never fear; I am going; the Son of Heaven will not tolerate delays, and Barham gives me leave. Allegiance will carry us! Pray eat something.
>
> —L.

Laurence stared at it in some distress, wondering how he had come to write so. "I do not remember a word of it; but wait, no; *Allegiance* is the name of the transport, and Prince Yongxing referred to the Emperor as the Son of Heaven, though why I should have repeated such a blasphemous thing I have no idea." He handed her the note. "My wits must have been wandering. Pray throw it in the fire; go and tell Temeraire that I am quite well now, and will be with him again soon. Can you ring for someone to valet me? I need to dress."

"You look as though you ought to stay just where you are," Roland said. "No: lie quiet awhile. There is no great hurry at present, as far as I understand, and I know this fellow Barham wants to speak with you; also Lenton. I will go and tell Temeraire you have not died or grown a second head, and have Emily jog back and forth between you if you have messages."

Laurence yielded to her persuasions; indeed he did not truly feel up to rising, and if Barham wanted to speak with him again, he thought he would need to conserve what strength he had. However, in the event, he was spared: Lenton came alone instead.

"Well, Laurence, you are in for a hellishly long trip, I am afraid, and I hope you do not have a bad time of it," he said, drawing up a chair. "My transport ran into a three-days' gale going to India, back in the nineties; rain freezing as it fell, so the dragons could not fly above it for some relief. Poor Obversaria was ill the entire time. Nothing less pleasant than a sea-sick dragon, for them or you."

Laurence had never commanded a dragon transport, but the image was a vivid one. "I am glad to say, sir, that Temeraire has never had the slightest difficulty, and indeed he enjoys sea-travel greatly."

"We will see how he likes it if you meet a hurricane," Lenton said, shaking his head. "Not that I expect either of you have any objections, under the circumstances."

"No, not in the least," Laurence said, heartfelt. He supposed it was merely a jump from frying-pan to fire, but he was grateful enough even for the slower roasting: the journey would last for many months, and there was room for hope: any number of things might happen before they reached China.

Lenton nodded. "Well, you are looking moderately ghastly, so let me be brief. I have managed to persuade Barham that the best thing to do is pack you off bag and baggage, in this case your crew; some of your officers would be in for a good bit of unpleasantness, otherwise, and we had best get you on your way before he thinks better of it."

Yet another relief, scarcely looked for. "Sir," Laurence said, "I must tell you how deeply indebted I am—"

"No, nonsense; do not thank me." Lenton brushed his sparse grey hair back from his forehead, and abruptly said, "I am damned sorry about all this, Laurence. I would have run mad a good deal sooner, in your place; brutally done, all of it."

Laurence hardly knew what to say; he had not expected anything like sympathy, and he did not feel he deserved it. After a moment, Lenton went on, more briskly. "I am sorry not to give you a longer time to recover, but then you will not have much to do aboard ship but rest. Barham has promised them the *Allegiance* will sail in a week's time; though from what I gather, he will be hard put to find a captain for her by then."

"I thought Cartwright was to have her?" Laurence asked, some vague memory stirring; he still read the *Naval Chronicle,* and followed the assignments of ships; Cartwright's name stuck in his head: they had served together in the *Goliath,* many years before.

"Yes, when the *Allegiance* was meant to go to Halifax; there is apparently some other ship being built for him there. But they cannot wait for him to finish a two-years' journey to China and back," Lenton said. "Be that as it may, someone will be found; you must be ready."

"You may be sure of it, sir," Laurence said. "I will be quite well again by then."

His optimism was perhaps ill-founded; after Lenton had gone, Laurence tried to write a letter and found he could not quite manage it, his head ached too wretchedly. Fortunately, Granby came by an hour later to see him, full of excitement at the prospect of the journey, and contemptuous of the risks he had taken with his own career.

"As though I could give a cracked egg for such a thing, when that scoundrel was trying to have you hauled away, and pointing guns at Temeraire," he said. "Pray don't think of it, and tell me what you would like me to write."

Laurence gave up trying to counsel him to caution; Granby's loyalty was as obstinate as his initial dislike had been, if more gratifying. "Only a few lines, if you please—to Captain Thomas Riley; tell him we are bound for China in a week's time, and if he does not mind a transport, he can likely get the *Allegiance,* if only he goes straightaway to the Admiralty: Barham has no one for the ship; but be sure and tell him not to mention my name."

"Very good," Granby said, scratching away; he did not write a very elegant hand, the letters sprawling wastefully, but it was serviceable enough to read. "Do you know him well? We will have to put up with whoever they give us for a long while."

"Yes, very well indeed," Laurence said. "He was my third lieutenant in *Belize*, and my second in *Reliant*; he was at Temeraire's hatching: a fine officer and seaman. We could not hope for better."

"I will run it down to the courier myself, and tell him to be sure it arrives," Granby promised. "What a relief it would be, not to have one of these wretched stiff-necked fellows—" and there he stopped, embarrassed; it was not so very long ago he had counted Laurence himself a "stiff-necked fellow," after all.

"Thank you, John," Laurence said hastily, sparing him. "Although we ought not get our hopes up yet; the Ministry may prefer a more senior man in the role," he added, though privately he thought the chances were excellent. Barham would not have an easy time of it, finding someone willing to accept the post.

Impressive though they might be, to the landsman's eye, a dragon transport was an awkward sort of vessel to command: often enough they sat in port endlessly, awaiting dragon passengers, while the crew dissipated itself in drinking and whoring. Or they might spend months in the middle of the ocean, trying to maintain a single position to serve as a resting point for dragons crossing long distances; like blockade-duty, only worse for lack of society. Little chance of battle or glory, less of prize-money; they were not desirable to any man who could do better.

But the *Reliant*, so badly dished in the gale after Trafalgar, would be in dry-dock for a long while. Riley, left on shore with no influence to help him to a new ship, and virtually no seniority, would be as glad of the opportunity as Laurence would be to have him, and there was every chance Barham would seize on the first fellow who offered.

Laurence spent the next day laboring, with slightly more success, over other necessary letters. His affairs were not prepared for a long journey, much of it far past the limits of the courier circuit. Then, too, over the last dreadful weeks he had entirely neglected his personal correspondence, and by now he owed several replies, particularly to his family. After the battle of Dover, his father had grown more tolerant of his new profession; although they still did not write one another directly, at least Laurence was no longer obliged to conceal his correspondence with his mother, and he had for some time now addressed his letters to her openly. His father might very well choose to suspend that privilege again, after this affair, but Laurence hoped he might not hear the particulars of it: fortunately, Barham had nothing to gain from embarrassing Lord Allendale; particularly not now when Wilberforce, their mutual political ally, meant to make another push for abolition in the next session of Parliament.

Laurence dashed off another dozen hasty notes, in a hand not very much like his usual, to other correspondents; most of them were naval men, who would well understand the exigencies of a hasty departure. Despite much abbreviation, the effort took its toll, and by the time Jane Roland came to see him once again, he had nearly prostrated himself once more, and was lying back against the pillows with eyes shut.

"Yes, I will post them for you, but you are behaving absurdly, Laurence," she said, collecting up the letters. "A knock on the head can be very nasty, even if you have not cracked your skull. When I had the yellow fever I did not prance about claiming I was well; I lay in bed and took my gruel and possets, and I was back on my feet quicker than any of the other fellows in the West Indies who took it."

"Thank you, Jane," he said, and did not argue with her; indeed he felt very ill, and he was grateful when she drew the curtains and cast the room into a comfortable dimness.

He briefly came out of sleep some hours later, hearing some commotion outside the door of his room: Roland saying, "You are damned well going to leave now, or I will kick you down the hall. What do you mean, sneaking in here to pester him the instant I have gone out?"

"But I must speak with Captain Laurence; the situation is of the most urgent—" The protesting voice was unfamiliar, and rather bewildered. "I have ridden straight from London—"

"If it is so urgent, you may go and speak to Admiral Lenton," Roland said. "No; I do not care if you are from the Ministry; you look young enough to be one of my mids, and I do not for an instant believe you have anything to say that cannot wait until morning."

With this she pulled the door shut behind her, and the rest of the argument was muffled; Laurence drifted again away. But the next morning there was no one to defend him, and scarcely had the maid brought in his breakfast—the threatened gruel and hot-milk posset, and quite unappetizing—than a fresh attempt at invasion was made, this time with more success.

"I beg your pardon, sir, for forcing myself upon you in this irregular fashion," the stranger said, talking rapidly while he dragged up a chair to Laurence's bedside, uninvited. "Pray allow me to explain; I realize the appearance is quite extraordinary—" He set down the heavy chair and sat down, or rather perched, at the very edge of the seat. "My name is Hammond, Arthur Hammond; I have been deputized by the Ministry to accompany you to the court of China."

Hammond was a surprisingly young man, perhaps twenty years of age, with untidy dark hair and a great intensity of expression that lent his thin, sallow face an illuminated quality. He spoke at first in half-sentences, torn between the forms of apology and his plain eagerness to come to his subject. "The absence of an introduction, I beg you will forgive, we have been taken completely, completely by surprise, and Lord Barham has already committed us to the twenty-third as a sailing date. If you would prefer, we may of course press him for some extension—"

This of all things Laurence was eager to avoid, though he was indeed a little astonished by Hammond's forwardness; hastily he said, "No, sir, I am entirely at your service; we cannot delay sailing to exchange formalities, particularly when Prince Yongxing has already been promised that date."

"Ah! I am of a similar mind," Hammond said, with a great deal of relief; Laurence suspected, looking at his face and measuring his years, that he had received the appointment only due to the lack of time. But Hammond quickly refuted the notion that a willingness to go to China on a moment's notice was his only qualification. Having settled himself, he drew out a thick sheaf of papers, which had been distending the front of his coat, and began to discourse in great detail and speed upon the prospects of their mission.

Laurence was almost from the first unable to follow him. Hammond unconsciously slipped into stretches of the Chinese language from time to time, when looking down at those of his papers written in that script, and while speaking in English dwelt largely on the subject of the Macartney embassy to China, which had taken place fourteen years prior. Laurence, who had been newly made lieutenant at the time and wholly occupied with naval matters and his own career, had hardly remembered the existence of the mission at all, much less any details.

He did not immediately stop Hammond, however: there was no convenient pause in the flow of his conversation, for one, and for another there was a reassuring quality to the monologue. Hammond spoke with authority beyond his years, an obvious command of his subject, and, still more importantly, without the least hint of the incivility which Laurence had come to expect from Barham and the Ministry. Laurence was grateful enough for any prospect of an ally to willingly listen, even if all he knew of the expedition himself was that Macartney's ship, the *Lion*, had been the first Western vessel to chart the Bay of Zhitao.

"Oh," Hammond said, rather disappointed, when at last he realized how thoroughly he had mistaken his audience. "Well, I suppose it does not much signify; to put it plainly, the embassy was a dismal failure. Lord Macartney refused to perform their ritual of obeisance before the Emperor, the kowtow, and they took offense. They would not even consider granting us a permanent mission, and he ended by being escorted out of the China Sea by a dozen dragons."

"That I do remember," Laurence said; indeed he had a vague recollection of discussing the matter among his friends in the gunroom, with some heat at the insult to Britain's envoy. "But surely the kowtow was quite offensive; did they not wish him to grovel on the floor?"

"We cannot be turning up our noses at foreign customs when we are coming to their country, hat in hand," Hammond said, earnestly, leaning forward. "You can see yourself, sir, the evil consequences: I am sure that the bad blood from this incident continues to poison our present relationship."

Laurence frowned; this argument was indeed persuasive, and made some better explanation why Yongxing had come to England so very ready to be offended. "Do you think this same quarrel their reason for having offered Bonaparte a Celestial? After so long a time?"

"I will be quite honest with you, Captain, we have not the least idea," Hammond said. "Our only comfort, these last fourteen years—a very cornerstone of foreign policy—has been our certainty, our complete certainty, that the Chinese were no more interested in the affairs of Europe than we are in the affairs of the penguins. Now all our foundations have been shaken."

Chapter 3

THE *ALLEGIANCE* WAS a wallowing behemoth of a ship: just over four hundred feet in length and oddly narrow in proportion, except for the outsize dragondeck that flared out at the front of the ship, stretching from the foremast forward to the bow. Seen from above, she looked very strange, almost fan-shaped. But below the wide lip of the dragondeck, her hull narrowed quickly; the keel was fashioned out of steel rather than elm, and thickly covered with white paint against rust: the long white stripe running down her middle gave her an almost rakish appearance.

To give her the stability which she required to meet storms, she had a draft of more than twenty feet and was too large to come into the harbor proper, but had to be moored to enormous pillars sunk far out in the deep water, her supplies ferried to and fro by smaller vessels: a great lady surrounded by scurrying attendants. This was not the first transport which Laurence and Temeraire had traveled on, but she would be the first true ocean-going one; a poky three-dragon ship running from Gibraltar to Plymouth with barely a few planks in increased width could offer no comparison.

"It is very nice; I am more comfortable even than in my clearing." Temeraire approved: from his place of solitary glory, he could see all the ship's activity without being in the way, and the ship's galley with its ovens was placed directly beneath the dragondeck, which kept the surface warm. "You are not cold at all, Laurence?" he asked, for perhaps the third time, craning his head down to peer closely at him.

"No, not in the least," Laurence said shortly; he was a little annoyed by the continuing oversolicitude. Though the dizziness and headache had subsided together with the lump upon his head, his bruised leg remained stubborn, prone to giving out at odd moments and throbbing with an almost constant ache. He had been hoisted aboard in a bosun's chair, very offensive to his sense of his own capabilities, then put directly into an elbow-chair and carried up to the dragondeck, swathed in blankets like an invalid, and now had Temeraire very carefully coiling himself about to serve as a windbreak.

There were two sets of stairs rising to the dragondeck, one on either side of the foremast, and the area of the forecastle stretching from the foot of these and halfway to the mainmast was by custom allocated to the aviators, while the foremast jacks ruled the remainder of the space up to the mainmast. Already Temeraire's crew had taken possession of their rightful domain, pointedly pushing several piles of coiled cables across the invisible dividing line; bundles of leather harness and baskets full of rings and buckles had been laid down in their place, all to put the Navy men on notice that the aviators were not to be taken advantage of. Those men not occupied in putting away their gear were ranged along the line in various attitudes of relaxation and affected labor; young Roland and the other two cadet runners, Morgan and Dyer, had been set to playing there by the ensigns, who had conveyed their duty to defend the rights of the Corps. Being so small, they could walk the ship's rail with ease and were dashing back and forth with a fine show of recklessness.

Laurence watched them, broodingly; he was still uneasy about bringing Roland. "Why would you leave her?
Has she been misbehaving?" was all Jane had asked, when
he had consulted her on the matter; impossibly awkward
to explain his concerns, facing her. And of course, there
was some sense in taking the girl along, young as she
was: she would have to face every demand made of a
male officer, when she came to be Excidium's captain on
her mother's retirement; it would be no kindness to leave
her unprepared by being too soft on her now.

Even so, now that he was aboard he was sorry. This
was not a covert, and he had already seen that as with
any naval crew there were some ugly, some very ugly fellows among the lot: drunkards, brawlers, gaol-birds. He
felt too heavily the responsibility of watching over a young
girl among such men; not to mention that he would be
best pleased if the secret that women served in the Corps
did not come out here and make a noise.

He did not mean to instruct Roland to lie, by no
means, and of course he could not give her different duties than otherwise; but he privately and intensely hoped
the truth might remain concealed. Roland was only eleven, and no cursory glance would take her for a girl in
her trousers and short jacket; he had once mistaken her
for a boy himself. But he also desired to see the aviators
and the sailors friendly, or at least not hostile, and a close
acquaintance could hardly fail to notice Roland's real
gender for long.

At present his hopes looked more likely to be answered in her case than the general. The foremast hands,
engaged in the business of loading the ship, were talking
none too quietly about fellows who had nothing better
to do but sit about and be passengers; a couple of men
made loud comments about how the shifted cables had
been cast all ahoo, and set to re-coiling them, unnecessarily. Laurence shook his head and kept his silence; his

own men had been within their rights, and he could not reprove Riley's men, nor would it do any good.

However, Temeraire had noticed also; he snorted, his ruff coming up a little. "That cable looks perfectly well to me," he said. "My crew were very careful moving it."

"It is all right, my dear; can never hurt to re-coil a cable," Laurence said hurriedly. It was not very surprising that Temeraire had begun to extend his protective and possessive instincts over the crew as well; they had been with him now for several months. But the timing was wretchedly inconvenient: the sailors would likely be nervous to begin with at the presence of a dragon, and if Temeraire involved himself in any dispute, taking the part of his crew, that could only increase the tensions on board.

"Pray take no offense," Laurence added, stroking Temeraire's flank to draw his attention. "The beginning of a journey is so very important; we wish to be good shipmates, and not encourage any sort of rivalry among the men."

"Hm, I suppose," Temeraire said, subsiding. "But we have done nothing wrong; it is disagreeable of them to complain so."

"We will be under way soon," Laurence said, by way of distraction. "The tide has turned, and I think that is the last of the embassy's luggage coming aboard now."

Allegiance could carry as many as ten mid-weight dragons, in a pinch; Temeraire alone scarcely weighed her down, and there was a truly astonishing amount of storage space aboard. Yet the sheer quantity of the baggage the embassy carried began to look as though it would strain even her great capacity: shocking to Laurence, used to traveling with little more than a single sea-chest, and seeming quite out of proportion to the size of the entourage, which was itself enormous.

There were some fifteen soldiers, and no less than

three physicians: one for the prince himself, one for the other two envoys, and one for the remainder of the embassy, each with assistants. After these and the translator, there were besides a pair of cooks with assistants, perhaps a dozen body servants, and an equal number of other men who seemed to have no clear function at all, including one gentleman who had been introduced as a poet, although Laurence could not believe this had been an accurate translation: more likely the man was a clerk of some sort.

The prince's wardrobe alone required some twenty chests, each one elaborately carved and with golden locks and hinges: the bosun's whip flew loud and cracking more than once, as the more enterprising sailors tried to pry them off. The innumerable bags of food had also to be slung aboard, and having already come once from China, they were beginning to show wear. One enormous eighty-pound sack of rice split wide open as it was handed across the deck, to the universal joy and delectation of the hovering seagulls, and afterwards the sailors were forced to wave the frenzied clouds of birds away every few minutes as they tried to keep on with their work.

There had already been a great fuss about boarding, earlier. Yongxing's attendants had demanded, at first, a walkway leading *down* to the ship—wholly impossible, even if the *Allegiance* could have been brought close enough to the dock to make a walkway of any sort practical, because of the height of her decks. Poor Hammond had spent the better part of an hour trying to persuade them that there was no dishonor or danger in being lifted up to the deck, and pointing at frustrated intervals at the ship herself, a mute argument.

Hammond had eventually said to him, quite desperately, "Captain, is this a dangerously high sea?" An absurd question, with a swell less than five feet, though in the brisk wind the waiting barge had occasionally bucked against the ropes holding her to the dock, but even Laurence's surprised negative had not satisfied the attendants. It had seemed they might never get aboard, but at last Yongxing himself had grown tired of waiting and ended the argument by emerging from his heavily draped sedan-chair, and climbing down into the boat, ignoring both the flurry of his anxious attendants and the hastily offered hands of the barge's crew.

The Chinese passengers who had waited for the second barge were still coming aboard now, on the starboard side, to the stiff and polished welcome of a dozen Marines and the most respectable-looking of the sailors, interleaved in a row along the inner edge of the gangway, decorative in their bright red coats and the white trousers and short blue jackets of the sailors.

Sun Kai, the younger envoy, leapt easily down from the bosun's chair and stood a moment looking around the busy deck thoughtfully. Laurence wondered if perhaps he did not approve the clamor and disarray of the deck, but no, it seemed he was only trying to get his feet underneath him: he took a few tentative steps back and forth, then stretched his sea-legs a little further and walked the length of the gangway and back more surely, with his hands clasped behind his back, and gazed with frowning concentration up at the rigging, trying evidently to trace the maze of ropes from their source to their conclusion.

This was much to the satisfaction of the men on display, who could at last stare their own fill in return. Prince Yongxing had disappointed them all by vanishing almost at once to the private quarters which had been arranged for him at the stern; Sun Kai, tall and properly impassive with his long black queue and shaved forehead, in splendid blue robes picked out with red and orange embroidery, was very nearly as good, and he showed no inclination to seek out his own quarters.

A moment later they had a still better piece of entertainment; shouts and cries rose from below, and Sun Kai sprang to the side to look over. Laurence sat up, and saw Hammond running to the edge, pale with horror: there had been a noisy splashing. But a few moments later, the older envoy finally appeared over the side, dripping water from the sodden lower half of his robes. Despite his misadventure, the grey-bearded man climbed down with a roar of good-humored laughter at his own expense, waving off what looked like Hammond's urgent apologies; he slapped his ample belly with a rueful expression, and then went away in company with Sun Kai.

"He had a narrow escape," Laurence observed, sinking back into his chair. "Those robes would have dragged him down in a moment, if he had properly fallen in."

"I am sorry they did not all fall in," Temeraire muttered, quietly for a twenty-ton dragon; which was to say, not very. There were sniggers on the deck, and Hammond glanced around anxiously.

The rest of the retinue were heaved aboard without further incident, and stowed away almost as quickly as their baggage. Hammond looked much relieved when the operation was at last completed, blotting his sweating forehead on the back of his hand, though the wind was knife-cold and bitter, and sat down quite limply on a locker along the gangway, much to the annoyance of the crew. They could not get the barge back aboard with him in the way, and yet he was a passenger and an envoy himself, too important to be bluntly told to move.

Taking pity on them all, Laurence looked for his runners: Roland, Morgan, and Dyer had been told to stay quiet on the dragondeck and out of the way, and so were sitting in a row at the very edge, dangling their heels into space. "Morgan," Laurence said, and the dark-haired boy scrambled up and towards him, "go and invite Mr. Hammond to come and sit with me, if he would like."

Hammond brightened at the invitation and came up to the dragondeck at once; he did not even notice as behind him the men immediately began rigging the tackles to hoist aboard the barge. "Thank you, sir—thank you, it is very good of you," he said, taking a seat on a locker which Morgan and Roland together pushed over for him, and accepting with still more gratitude the offer of a glass of brandy. "How I should have managed, if Liu Bao had drowned, I have not the least notion."

"Is that the gentleman's name?" Laurence said; all he remembered of the older envoy from the Admiralty meeting was his rather whistling snore. "It would have been an inauspicious start to the journey, but Yongxing could scarcely have blamed you for his taking a mis-step."

"No, there you are quite wrong," Hammond said. "He is a prince; he can blame anyone he likes."

Laurence was disposed to take this as a joke, but Hammond seemed rather glumly serious about it; and after drinking the best part of his glass of brandy in what already seemed to Laurence, despite their brief acquaintance, an uncharacteristic silence, Hammond added abruptly, "And pray forgive me—I must mention, how very prejudicial such remarks may be—the consequences of a moment's thoughtless offense—"

It took Laurence a moment to puzzle out that Hammond referred to Temeraire's earlier resentful mutterings; Temeraire was quicker and answered for himself. "I do not care if they do not like me," he said. "Maybe then they will let me alone, and I will not have to stay in China." This thought visibly struck him, and his head came up with sudden enthusiasm. "If I were very offensive, do you suppose they would go away now?" he asked. "Laurence, what would be particularly insulting?"

Hammond looked like Pandora, the box open and horrors loosed upon the world; Laurence was inclined to laugh, but he stifled it out of sympathy. Hammond was young for his work, and surely, however brilliant his talents, felt his own lack of experience; it could not help but make him over-cautious.

"No, my dear, it will not do," Laurence said. "Likely they would only blame us for teaching you ill-manners, and resolve all the more on keeping you."

"Oh." Temeraire disconsolately let his head sink back down onto his forelegs. "Well, I suppose I do not mind so much going, except that everyone else will be fighting without me," he said in resignation. "But the journey will be very interesting, and I suppose I would like to see China; only they *will* try to take Laurence away from me again, I am sure of it, and I am not going to have any of it."

Hammond prudently did not engage him on this subject, but hurried instead to say, "How long this business of loading has all taken—surely it is not typical? I made sure we would be halfway down the Channel by noon; here we have not even yet made sail."

"I think they are nearly done," Laurence said; the last immense chest was being swung aboard into the hands of the waiting sailors with the help of a block and line. The men looked all tired and surly, as well they might, having spent time enough for loading ten dragons on loading instead one man and his accoutrements; and their dinner was a good half-an-hour overdue already.

As the chest vanished below, Captain Riley climbed the stairs from the quarterdeck to join them, taking his hat off long enough to wipe sweat away from his brow. "I have no notion how they got themselves and the lot to England. I suppose they did not come by transport?"

"No, or else we would surely be returning by their ship," Laurence said. He had not considered the question before and realized only now that he had no idea how the Chinese embassy had made their voyage. "Perhaps they came overland." Hammond was silent and frowning, evidently wondering himself.

"That must be a very interesting journey, with so many different places to visit," Temeraire observed. "Not that I am sorry to be going by sea: not at all," he added, hastily, peering down anxiously at Riley to be sure he had not offended. "Will it be much faster, going by sea?"

"No, not in the least," Laurence said. "I have heard of a courier going from London to Bombay in two months, and we will be lucky to reach Canton in seven. But there is no secure route by land: France is in the way, unfortunately, and there is a great deal of banditry, not to mention the mountains and the Taklamakan desert to cross."

"I would not wager on less than eight months, myself," Riley said. "If we make six knots with the wind anywhere but dead astern, it will be more than I look for, judging by her log." Below and above now there was a great scurry of activity, all hands preparing to unmoor and make sail; the ebbing tide was lapping softly against the windward side. "Well, we must get about it. Laurence, tonight I must be on deck, I need to take the measure of her; but I hope you will dine with me tomorrow? And you also, of course, Mr. Hammond."

"Captain," Hammond said, "I am not familiar with the ordinary course of a ship's life—I beg your indulgence. Would it be suitable to invite the members of the embassy?"

"Why—" Riley said, astonished, and Laurence could not blame him; it was a bit much to be inviting people to another man's table. But Riley caught himself, and then said, more politely, "Surely, sir, it is for Prince Yongxing to issue such an invitation first."

"We will be in Canton before that happens, in the present state of relations," Hammond said. "No; we must make shifts to engage them, somehow."

Riley offered a little more resistance; but Hammond had taken the bit between his teeth and managed, by a skillful combination of coaxing and deafness to hints, to carry his point. Riley might have struggled longer, but the men were all waiting impatiently for the word to weigh anchor, the tide was going every minute, and at last Hammond ended by saying, "Thank you, sir, for your indulgence; and now I will beg you gentlemen to excuse me. I am a fair enough hand at their script on land, but I imagine it will take me some more time to draft an acceptable invitation aboard ship." With this, he rose and escaped before Riley could retract the surrender he had not quite made.

"Well," Riley said, gloomily, "before he manages it, I am going to go and get us as far out to sea as I can; if they are mad as fire at my cheek, at least with this wind I can say in perfect honesty that I cannot get back into port for them to kick me ashore. By the time we reach Madeira they may get over it."

He jumped down to the forecastle and gave the word; in a moment the men at the great quadruple-height capstans were straining, their grunting and bellowing carrying up from the lower decks as the cable came dragging over the iron catheads: the *Allegiance*'s smallest kedge anchor as large as the best bower of another ship, its flukes spread wider than the height of a man.

Much to the relief of the men, Riley did not order them to warp her out; a handful of men pushed off from the pilings with iron poles, and even that was scarcely necessary: the wind was from the northwest, full on her starboard beam, and that with the tide carried her now easily away from the harbor. She was only under topsails, but as soon as they had cleared moorings Riley called for topgallants and courses, and despite his pessimistic words they were soon going through the water at a respectable clip: she did not make much leeway, with that long deep keel, but went straight down the Channel in a stately manner.

Temeraire had turned his head forward to enjoy the wind of their progress: he looked rather like the figure-head of some old Viking ship. Laurence smiled at the notion. Temeraire saw his expression and nudged at him affectionately. "Will you read to me?" he asked hopefully. "We will have only another couple of hours of light."

"With pleasure," said Laurence, and sat up to look for one of his runners. "Morgan," he called, "will you be so good as to go below and fetch me the book in the top of my sea-chest, by Gibbon; we are in the second volume."

The great admiral's cabin at the stern had been hastily converted into something of a state apartment for Prince Yongxing, and the captain's cabin beneath the poop deck divided for the other two senior envoys, the smaller quarters nearby given over to the crowd of guards and attendants, displacing not only Riley himself but also the ship's first lieutenant, Lord Purbeck, the surgeon, the master, and several other of his officers. Fortunately, the quarters at the fore of the ship, ordinarily reserved for the senior aviators, were all but empty with Temeraire the only dragon aboard: even shared out among them all, there was no shortage of room; and for the occasion, the ship's carpenters had knocked down the bulkheads of their individual cabins and made a grand dining space.

Too grand, at first: Hammond had objected. "We cannot seem to have more room than the prince," he explained, and so had the bulkheads shifted a good six feet forward: the collected tables were suddenly cramped.

Riley had benefited from the enormous prize-money awarded for the capture of Temeraire's egg almost as much as Laurence himself had; fortunately he could afford to keep a good table and a large one. The occasion indeed called for every stick of furniture which could be found on board: the instant he had recovered from the appalling shock of having his invitation even partly accepted, Riley had invited all the senior members of the gunroom, Laurence's own lieutenants, and any other man who might reasonably be expected to make civilized conversation.

"But Prince Yongxing is not coming," Hammond said, "and the rest of them have less than a dozen words of English between them. Except for the translator, and he is only one man."

"Then at least we can make enough noise amongst ourselves we will not all be sitting in grim silence," Riley said.

But this hope was not answered: the moment the guests arrived, a paralyzed silence descended, bidding fair to continue throughout the meal. Though the translator had accompanied them, none of the Chinese spoke at first. The older envoy, Liu Bao, had stayed away also, leaving Sun Kai as the senior representative; but even he made only a spare, formal greeting on their arrival, and afterwards maintained a calm and silent dignity, though he stared intently at the barrel-thick column of the foremast, painted in yellow stripes, which came down through the ceiling and passed directly through the middle of the table, and went so far as to look beneath the table-cloth, to see it continuing down through the deck below.

Riley had left the right side of the table entirely for the Chinese guests, and had them shown to places there, but they did not move to sit when he and the officers did, which left the British in confusion, some men already half-seated and trying to keep themselves suspended in mid-air. Bewildered, Riley pressed them to take their seats; but he had to urge them several times before at last they would sit. It was an inauspicious beginning, and did not encourage conversation.

The officers began by taking refuge in their dinners, but even that semblance of good manners did not last very long. The Chinese did not eat with knife and fork, but with lacquered sticks they had brought with them. These they somehow maneuvered one-handed to bring food to their lips, and shortly the British half of the company were staring in helplessly rude fascination, every new dish presenting a fresh opportunity to observe the technique. The guests were briefly puzzled by the platter of roast mutton, large slices carved from the leg, but after a moment one of the younger attendants carefully proceeded to roll up a slice, still only using the sticks, and picked it up entire to eat in three bites, leading the way for the rest.

By now Tripp, Riley's youngest midshipman, a plump and unlovely twelve-year-old aboard by virtue of his family's three votes in Parliament, and invited for his own education rather than his company, was surreptitiously trying to imitate the style, using his fork and knife turned upside-down in place of the sticks, his efforts meeting without notable success, except in doing damage to his formerly clean breeches. He was too far down the table to be quelled by hard looks, and the men around him were too busy gawking themselves to notice.

Sun Kai had the seat of honor nearest Riley, and, desperate to keep his attention from the boy's antics, Riley tentatively raised a glass to him, watching Hammond out of the corner of his eye for direction, and said, "To your health, sir." Hammond murmured a hasty translation across the table, and Sun Kai nodded, raised his own glass, and sipped politely, though not very much: it was a heady Madeira well-fortified with brandy, chosen to survive rough seas. For a moment it seemed this might rescue the occasion: the rest of the officers were belatedly recalled to their duty as gentlemen, and began to salute the rest of the guests; the pantomime of raised glasses was perfectly comprehensible without any translation, and led naturally to a thawing of relations. Smiles and nods began to traverse the table, and Laurence heard Hammond, beside him, heave out an almost inaudible sigh through open lips, and finally take some little food.

Laurence knew he was not doing his own part; but his knee was lodged up against a trestle of the table, preventing him from stretching out his now-aching leg, and though he had drunk as sparingly as was polite, his head felt thick and clouded. By this point he only hoped he might avoid embarrassment, and resigned himself to making apologies to Riley after the meal for his dullness.

Riley's third lieutenant, a fellow named Franks, had spent the first three toasts in rude silence, sitting woodenly and raising his glass only with a mute smile, but sufficient flow of wine loosened his tongue at last. He had served on an East Indiaman as a boy, during the peace, and evidently had acquired a few stumbling words of Chinese; now he tried the less-obscene of them on the gentleman sitting across from him: a young, clean-shaven man named Ye Bing, gangly beneath the camouflage of his fine robes, who brightened and proceeded to respond with his own handful of English.

"A very—a fine—" he said, and stuck, unable to find the rest of the compliment he wished to make, shaking his head as Franks offered, alternatively, the options which seemed to him most natural: *wind, night,* and *dinner;* at last Ye Bing beckoned over the translator, who said on his behalf, "Many compliments to your ship: it is most cleverly devised."

Such praise was an easy way to a sailor's heart; Riley, overhearing, broke off from his disjointed bilingual conversation with Hammond and Sun Kai, on their likely southward course, and called down to the translator,

"Pray thank the gentleman for his kind words, sir; and tell him that I hope you will all find yourselves quite comfortable."

Ye Bing bowed his head and said, through the translator, "Thank you, sir, we are already much more so than on our journey here. Four ships were required to carry us here, and one proved unhappily slow."

"Captain Riley, I understand you have gone round the Cape of Good Hope before?" Hammond interrupted: rudely, and Laurence glanced at him in surprise.

Riley also looked startled, but politely turned back to answer him, but Franks, who had spent nearly all of the last two days below in the stinking hold, directing the stowage of all the baggage, said in slightly drunken irreverence, "Four ships only? I am surprised it did not take six; you must have been packed like sardines."

Ye Bing nodded and said, "The vessels were small for so long a journey, but in the service of the Emperor all discomfort is a joy, and in any case, they were the largest of your ships in Canton at the time."

"Oh; so you hired East Indiamen for the passage?" Macready asked; he was the Marine lieutenant, a rail-thin, wiry stump of a man who wore spectacles incongruous on his much-scarred face. There was no malice but undeniably a slight edge of superiority in the question, and in the smiles exchanged by the naval men. That the French could build ships but not sail them, that the Dons were excitable and undisciplined, that the Chinese had no fleet at all to speak of, these were the oft-repeated bywords of the service, and to have them so confirmed was always pleasant, always heartening.

"Four ships in Canton harbor, and you filled their holds with baggage instead of silk and porcelain; they must have charged you the earth," Franks added.

"How very strange that you should say so," Ye Bing said. "Although we were traveling under the Emperor's seal, it is true, one captain did try to demand payment, and then even tried to sail away without permission. Some evil spirit must have seized hold of him and made him act in such a crazy manner. But I believe your Company officials were able to find a doctor to treat him, and he was allowed to apologize."

Franks stared, as well he might. "But then why did they take you, if you did not pay them?"

Ye Bing stared back, equally surprised to have been asked. "The ships were confiscated by Imperial edict. What else could they have done?" He shrugged, as if to dismiss the subject, and turned his attention back to the dishes; he seemed to think the piece of intelligence less significant than the small jam tartlets Riley's cook had provided with the latest course.

Laurence abruptly put down knife and fork; his appetite had been weak to begin with, and now was wholly gone. That they could speak so casually of the seizure of British ships and property—the forced servitude of British seamen to a foreign throne— For a moment almost he convinced himself he had misunderstood: every newspaper in the country would have been shrieking of such an incident; Government would surely have made a formal protest. Then he looked at Hammond: the diplomat's face was pale and alarmed, but unsurprised; and all remaining doubt vanished as Laurence recalled all of Barham's sorry behavior, so nearly groveling, and Hammond's attempts to change the course of the conversation.

Comprehension was only a little slower in coming to the rest of the British, running up and down the table on the backs of low whispers, as the officers murmured back and forth to one another. Riley's reply to Hammond, which had been going forward all this time, slowed and stopped: though Hammond prompted Riley again, urgently, asking, "Did you have a rough crossing of it? I hope we do not need to fear bad weather along the way," this came too late; a complete silence fell, except for young Tripp chewing noisily.

Garnett, the master, elbowed the boy sharply, and even this sound failed. Sun Kai put down his wineglass and looked frowning up and down along the table; he had noticed the change of atmosphere: the feel of a brewing storm. There had already been a great deal of hard drinking, though they were scarcely halfway through the meal, and many of the officers were young, and flushing now with mortification and anger. Many a Navy man, cast on shore during an intermittent peace or by a lack of influence, had served aboard the ships of the East India Company; the ties between Britain's Navy and her merchant marine were strong, and the insult all the more keenly felt.

The translator was standing back from the chairs with an anxious expression, but most of the other Chinese attendants had not yet perceived. One laughed aloud at some remark of his neighbor's: it made a queer solitary noise in the cabin.

"By God," Franks said, suddenly, out loud, "I have a mind to—"

His seat-mates caught him by the arms, hurriedly, and kept him in his chair, hushing him with many anxious looks up towards the senior officers, but other whispers grew louder. One man was saying, "—sitting at our table!" to snatches of violent agreement; an explosion might come at any moment, certainly disastrous. Hammond was trying to speak, but no one was attending to him.

"Captain Riley," Laurence said, harshly and overloud, quelling the furious whispers, "will you be so good as to lay out our course for the journey? I believe Mr. Granby was curious as to the route we would follow."

Granby, sitting a few chairs down, his face pale under his sunburn, started; then after a moment he said, "Yes, indeed; I would take it as a great favor, sir," nodding to Riley.

"Of course," Riley said, if a little woodenly; he leaned over to the locker behind him, where his maps lay: bringing one onto the table, he traced the course, speaking somewhat more loudly than normal. "Once out of the Channel, we must swing a ways out to skirt France and Spain; then we will come in a little closer and keep to the coastline of Africa as best we can. We will put in at the Cape until the summer monsoon begins, perhaps a week or three depending on our speed, and then ride the wind all the way to the South China Sea."

The worst of the grim silence was broken, and slowly a thin obligatory conversation began again. But no one now said a word to the Chinese guests, except occasionally Hammond speaking to Sun Kai, and under the weight of disapproving stares even he faltered and was silent. Riley resorted to calling for the pudding, and the dinner wandered to a disastrous close, far earlier than usual.

There were Marines and seamen standing behind every sea-officer's chair to act as servants, already muttering to each other; by the time Laurence regained the deck, pulling himself up the ladder-way more by the strength of his arms than by properly climbing, they had gone out, and the news had gone from one end of the deck to another, the aviators even speaking across the line with the sailors.

Hammond came out onto the deck and stared at the taut, muttering groups of men, biting his lips to bloodlessness; the anxiety made his face look queerly old and drawn. Laurence felt no pity for him, only indignation: there was no question that Hammond had deliberately tried to conceal the shameful matter.

Riley was beside him, not drinking the cup of coffee in his hand: boiled if not burnt, by the smell of it. "Mr. Hammond," he said, very quiet but with authority, more authority than Laurence, who for most of their acquaintance had known him as a subordinate, had ever heard him use; an authority which quite cleared away all traces of his ordinary easy-going humor, "pray convey to the Chinamen that it is essential they stay below; I do not give a damn what excuse you like to give them, but I would not wager tuppence for their lives if they came on this deck now. Captain," he added, turning to Laurence, "I beg you send your men to sleep at once; I don't like the mood."

"Yes," Laurence said, in full understanding: men so stirred could become violent, and from there it was a short step to mutiny; the original cause of their rage would not even necessarily matter by then. He beckoned Granby over. "John, send the fellows below, and have a word with the officers to keep them quiet; we want no disturbance."

Granby nodded. "By God, though—" he said, hard-eyed with his own anger, but he stopped when Laurence shook his head, and went. The aviators broke up and went below quietly; the example might have been of some good, for the sailors did not grow quarrelsome when ordered to do the same. Then, also, they knew very well that their officers were in this case not their enemies: anger was a living thing in every breast, shared sentiment bound them all together, and little more than mutters followed when Lord Purbeck, the first lieutenant, walked out upon the deck among them and ordered them below in his drawling, affected accent, "Go along now, Jenkins; go along, Harvey."

Temeraire was waiting on the dragondeck with head raised high and eyes bright; he had overheard enough to be on fire with curiosity. Having had the rest of the story, he snorted and said, "If their own ships could not have carried them, they had much better have stayed home." This was less indignation at the offense than simple dislike, however, and he was not inclined to great resentment; like most dragons, he had a very casual view of property, saving, of course, jewels and gold belonging to himself: even as he spoke he was busy polishing the great sapphire pendant which Laurence had given him, and which he never removed save for that purpose.

"It is an insult to the Crown," Laurence said, rubbing his hand over his leg with short, pummeling strokes, resentful of the injury; he wanted badly to pace. Hammond was standing at the quarterdeck rail smoking a cigar, the dim red light of the burning embers flaring with his inhalations, illuminating his pale and sweat-washed face. Laurence glared at him along the length of the near-empty deck, bitterly. "I wonder at him; at him and at Barham, to have swallowed such an outrage, with so little noise: it is scarcely to be borne."

Temeraire blinked at him. "But I thought we must at all costs avoid war with China," he said, very reasonably, as he had been lectured on the subject without end for weeks, and even by Laurence himself.

"I should rather settle with Bonaparte, if the lesser evil had to be chosen," Laurence said, for the moment too angry to consider the question rationally. "At least he had the decency to declare war before seizing our citizens, instead of this cavalier offhand flinging of insults in our face, as if we did not dare to answer them. Not that Government have given them any reason to think otherwise: like a pack of damned curs, rolling over to show their bellies. And to think," he added, smoldering, "that scoundrel was trying to persuade me to kowtow, knowing it should be coming after *this*—"

Temeraire gave a snort of surprise at his vehemence, and nudged him gently with his nose. "Pray do not be so angry; it cannot be good for you."

Laurence shook his head, not in disagreement, and fell silent, leaning against Temeraire. It could do no good to vent his fury so, where some of the men left on deck might yet overhear and take it as encouragement to some rash act, and he did not want to distress Temeraire. But much was suddenly made plain to him: after swallowing such an insult, of course Government would hardly strain at handing over a single dragon; the entire Ministry would likely be glad to rid themselves of so unpleasant a reminder, and to see the whole business hushed up all the more thoroughly.

He stroked Temeraire's side for comfort. "Will you stay above-decks with me a while?" Temeraire asked him, coaxing. "You had much better sit down and rest, and not fret yourself so."

Indeed Laurence did not want to leave him; it was curious how he could feel his lost calm restore itself under the influence of that steady heartbeat beneath his fingers. The wind was not too high, at the moment, and not all of the night watch could be sent below; an extra officer on the deck would not be amiss. "Yes, I will stay; in any case I do not like to leave Riley alone with such a mood over the ship," he answered, and went limping for his wraps.

Chapter 4

THE WIND WAS freshening from the northeast, very cold; Laurence stirred out of his half-sleep and looked up at the stars: only a few hours had passed. He huddled deeper into his blankets by Temeraire's side and tried to ignore the steady ache in his leg. The deck was strangely quiet; under Riley's grim and watchful eye there was scarcely any conversation at all among the remaining crew, though occasionally Laurence could hear indistinct murmurs from the rigging above, men whispering to each other. There was no moon, only a handful of lanterns on deck.

"You are cold," Temeraire said unexpectedly, and Laurence turned to see the great deep blue eyes studying him. "Go inside, Laurence; you must get well, and I will not let anyone hurt Riley. Or the Chinese, I suppose, if you would not like it," he added, though without much enthusiasm.

Laurence nodded, tiredly, and heaved himself up again; the threat of danger was over, he thought, at least for the moment, and there was no real sense in his staying above. "You are comfortable enough?"

"Yes, with the heat from below I am perfectly warm," Temeraire said; indeed Laurence could feel the warmth of the dragondeck even through the soles of his boots.

It was a great deal more pleasant in out of the wind;

his leg stabbed unpleasantly twice as he climbed down to the upper berth deck, but his arms were up to his weight and held him until the spasm passed; he managed to reach his cabin without falling.

Laurence had several pleasant small round windows, not drafty, and near the ship's galley as he was, the cabin was still warm despite the wind; one of the runners had lit the hanging lantern, and Gibbon's book was lying still open on the lockers. He slept almost at once, despite the pain; the easy sway of his hanging cot was more familiar than any bed, and the low susurration of the water along the sides of the ship a wordless and constant reassurance.

He came awake all at once, breath jolted out of his body before his eyes even quite opened: noise more felt than heard. The deck abruptly slanted, and he flung out a hand to keep from striking the ceiling; a rat went sliding across the floor and fetched up against the fore lockers before scuttling into the dark again, indignant.

The ship righted almost at once: there was no unusual wind, no heavy swell; at once he understood that Temeraire had taken flight. Laurence flung on his boat-cloak and rushed out in nightshirt and bare feet; the drummer was beating to quarters, the crisp flying staccato echoing off the wooden walls, and even as Laurence staggered out of his room the carpenter and his mates were rushing past him to clear away the bulkheads. Another crash came: bombs, he now recognized, and then Granby was suddenly at his side, a little less disordered since he had been sleeping in breeches. Laurence accepted his arm without hesitation and with his help managed to push through the crowd and get back up to the dragondeck through the confusion. Sailors were running with frantic haste to the pumps, flinging buckets out over the sides for water to slop onto the decks and wet down the sails. A bloom of orange-yellow was trying to grow on the edge of the furled mizzen topsail; one of the midshipmen, a spotty boy of thirteen Laurence had seen skylarking that morning, flung himself gallantly out onto the yard with his shirt in his hand, dripping, and smothered it out.

There was no other light, nothing to show what might be going on aloft, and too much shouting and noise to hear anything of the battle above at all: Temeraire might have been roaring at full voice for all they would have known of it. "We must get a flare up, at once," Laurence said, taking his boots from Roland; she had come running with them, and Morgan with his breeches.

"Calloway, go and fetch a box of flares, and the flash-powder," Granby called. "It must be a Fleur-de-Nuit; no other breed could see without at least moonlight. If only they would stop that noise," he added, squinting uselessly up.

The loud crack warned them; Laurence fell as Granby tried to pull him down to safety, but only a handful of splinters came flying; screams rose from below: the bomb had gone through a weak place in the wood and down into the galley. Hot steam came up through the vent, and the smell of salt pork, steeping already for the next day's dinner: tomorrow was Thursday, Laurence remembered, ship's routine so deeply ingrained that the one thought followed instantly on the other in his mind.

"We must get you below," Granby said, taking his arm again, calling, "Martin!"

Laurence gave him an astonished, appalled look; Granby did not even notice, and Martin, taking his left arm, seemed to think nothing more natural. "I am not leaving the deck," Laurence said sharply.

The gunner Calloway came panting with the box; in a moment, the whistle of the first rising flare cut through the low voices, and the yellow-white flash lit the sky. A dragon bellowed: not Temeraire's voice, too low, and in the too-short moment while the light lingered, Laurence caught sight of Temeraire hovering protectively over the ship. The Fleur-de-Nuit had evaded him in the dark and was a little way off, twisting its head away from the light.

Temeraire roared at once and darted for the French dragon, but the flare died out and fell, leaving all again black as pitch. "Another, another; damn you," Laurence shouted to Calloway, who was still staring aloft just as they all were. "He must have light; keep them going aloft."

More of the crewmen rushed to help him, too many: three more flares went up at once, and Granby sprang to keep them from any further waste. Shortly they had the time marked: one flare followed after another in steady progression, a fresh burst of light just as the previous one failed. Smoke curled around Temeraire, trailed from his wings in the thin yellow light as he closed with the Fleur-de-Nuit, roaring; the French dragon dived to avoid him, and bombs scattered into the water harmlessly, the sound of the splashes traveling over the water.

"How many flares have we left?" Laurence asked Granby, low.

"Four dozen or so, no more," Granby said, grimly: they were going very fast. "And that is already with what the *Allegiance* was carrying besides our own; their gunner brought us all they had."

Calloway slowed the rate of firing to stretch the dwindling supply longer, so that the dark returned full-force between bursts of light. Their eyes were all stinging with smoke and the strain of trying to see in the thin, always-fading light of the flares; Laurence could only imagine how Temeraire was managing, alone, half-blind, against an opponent fully manned and prepared for battle.

"Sir, Captain," Roland cried, waving at him from the starboard rail; Martin helped Laurence over, but before they had reached her, one of the last handful of flares went off, and for a moment the ocean behind the *Allegiance* was illuminated clearly: two French heavy frigates coming on behind them, with the wind in their favor, and a dozen boats in the water crammed with men sweeping towards their either side.

The lookout above had seen also; "Sail ho; boarders," he bellowed out, and all was suddenly confusion once more: sailors running across the deck to stretch the boarding-netting, and Riley at the great double-wheel with his coxswain and two of the strongest seamen; they were putting the *Allegiance* about with desperate haste, trying to bring her broadside to bear. There was no sense in trying to outrun the French ships; in this wind the frigates could make a good ten knots at least, and the *Allegiance* would never escape them.

Ringing along the galley chimney, words and the pounding of many feet echoed up hollowly from the gundecks: Riley's midshipmen and lieutenants were already hurrying men into place at the guns, their voices high and anxious as they repeated instructions, over and over, trying to drum what ought to have occupied the practice of months into the heads of men half-asleep and confused.

"Calloway, save the flares," Laurence said, hating to give the order: the darkness would leave Temeraire vulnerable to the Fleur-de-Nuit. But with so few left, they had to be conserved, until there was some better hope of being able to do real damage to the French dragon.

"Stand by to repel boarders," the bosun bellowed; the *Allegiance* was finally coming up through the wind, and there was a moment of silence: out in the darkness, the oars kept splashing, a steady count in French drifting faintly towards them over the water, and then Riley called, "Fire as she bears."

The guns below roared, red fire and smoke spitting: impossible to tell what damage had been done, except by the mingled sounds of screaming and splintering wood to let them know at least some of the shot had gone home. On went the guns, a rolling broadside as the *Alle-*

giance made her ponderous turn; but after they had spoken once, the inexperience of the crew began to tell.

At last the first gun spoke again, four minutes at least between shots; the second gun did not fire at all, nor the third; the fourth and fifth went together, with some more audible damage, but the sixth ball could be heard splashing into clear water; also the seventh, and then Purbeck called, " 'Vast firing." The *Allegiance* had carried too far; now she could not fire again until she made her turn once more; and all the while the boarding party would be approaching, the rowers only encouraged to greater speed.

The guns died away; the clouds of thick grey smoke drifted over the water. The ship was again in darkness, but for the small, swaying pools of light cast off by the lanterns on deck. "We must get you aboard Temeraire," Granby said. "We are not too far from shore yet for him to make the flight, and in any case there may be ships closer by: the transport from Halifax may be in these waters by now."

"I am not going to run away and hand a hundred-gun transport over to the French," Laurence said, very savagely.

"I am sure we can hold out, and in any case there is every likelihood of recapturing her before they can bring her into port, if you can warn the fleet," Granby argued; no naval officer would have persisted so against his commander, but aviator discipline was far more loose, and he would not be denied; it was indeed his duty as first lieutenant to see to the captain's safety.

"They could easily take her to the West Indies or a port in Spain, far from the blockades, and man her from there; we cannot lose her," Laurence said.

"It would still be best to have you aboard, where they cannot lay hands on you unless we are forced to surrender," Granby said. "We must find some way to get Temeraire clear."

"Sir, begging your pardon," Calloway said, looking up from the box of flares, "if you was to get me one of those pepper-guns, we might pack up a ball with flash-powder, and maybe give himself a bit of breathing room." He jerked his chin up towards the sky.

"I'll speak to Macready," Ferris said at once, and dashed away to find the ship's Marine lieutenant.

The pepper-gun was brought from below, two of the Marines carrying the halves of the long rifled barrel up while Calloway cautiously pried open one of the pepper-balls. The gunner shook out perhaps half the pepper and opened the locked box of flash-powder, taking out a single paper twist and sealing the box again. He held the twist far out over the side, two of his mates holding his waist to keep him steady while he unwound the twist and carefully spilled the yellow powder into the case, watching with only one eye, the other squinted up and his face half-turned away; his cheek was spotted with black scars, reminders of previous work with the powder: it needed no fuse and would go off on any careless impact, burning far hotter than gunpowder, if spent more quickly.

He sealed up the ball and plunged the rest of the twist into a bucket of water. His mates threw it overboard while he smeared the seal of the ball with a little tar and covered it all over with grease before loading the gun; then the second half of the barrel was screwed on. "There; I don't say it will go off, but I allow as it may," Calloway said, wiping his hands clean with no little relief.

"Very good," Laurence said. "Stand ready and save the last three flares to give us light for the shot; Macready, have you a man for the gun? Your best, mind you; he must strike the head to do any good."

"Harris, you take her," Macready said, pointing one

of his men to the gun, a gangly, rawboned fellow of perhaps eighteen, and added to Laurence, "Young eyes for a long shot, sir; never fear she'll go astray."

A low angry rumble of voices drew their attention below, to the quarterdeck: the envoy Sun Kai had come on deck with two of the servants trailing behind, carrying one of the enormous trunks out of their luggage. The sailors and most of Temeraire's crew were clustered along the rails to fend off the boarders, cutlasses and pistols in every hand; but even with the French ships gaining, one fellow with a pike went so far as to take a step towards the envoy, before the bosun started him with the knotted end of his rope, bawling, "Keep the line, lads; keep the line."

Laurence had all but forgotten the disastrous dinner in the confusion: it seemed already weeks ago, but Sun Kai was still wearing the same embroidered gown, his hands folded calmly into the sleeves, and the angry, alarmed men were primed for just such a provocation. "Oh, his soul to the devil. We must get him away. Below, sir; below at once," he shouted, pointing at the gangway, but Sun Kai only beckoned his men on, and came climbing up to the dragondeck while they heaved the great trunk up more slowly behind him.

"Where is that damned translator?" Laurence said. "Dyer, go and see—" But by then the servants had hauled up the trunk; they unlocked it and flung back the lid, and there was no need for translation: the rockets that lay in the padding of straw were wildly elaborate, red and blue and green like something out of a child's nursery, painted with swirls of color, gold and silver, and unmistakable.

Calloway snatched one at once, blue with white and yellow stripes, one of the servants anxiously miming for him how the match should be set to the fuse. "Yes, yes," he said, impatiently, bringing over the slow-match; the rocket caught at once and hissed upwards, vanishing from sight far above where the flares had gone.

The white flash came first, then a great thunderclap of sound, echoing back from the water, and a more faintly glimmering circle of yellow stars spread out and hung lingering in the air. The Fleur-de-Nuit squawked audibly, undignified, as the fireworks went off: it was revealed plainly, not a hundred yards above, and Temeraire immediately flung himself upwards, teeth bared, hissing furiously.

Startled, the Fleur-de-Nuit dived, slipping under Temeraire's outstretched claws but coming into their range. "Harris, a shot, a shot!" Macready yelled, and the young Marine squinted through the sight. The pepper-ball flew straight and true, if a little high; but the Fleur-de-Nuit had narrow curving horns flaring out from its forehead, just above the eyes; the ball broke open against them and the flash-powder burst white-hot and flaring. The dragon squalled again, this time in real pain, and flew wildly and fast away from the ships, deep into the dark; it swept past the ship so low that the sails shuddered noisily in the wind of its wings.

Harris stood up from the gun and turned, grinning wide and gap-toothed, then fell with a look of surprise, his arm and shoulder gone. Macready was knocked down by his falling body; Laurence jerked a knife-long splinter out of his own arm and wiped spattered blood from his face. The pepper-gun was a blasted wreck: the crew of the Fleur-de-Nuit had flung down another bomb even as their dragon fled, and hit the gun dead-on.

A couple of the sailors dragged Harris's body to the side and flung him overboard; no one else had been killed. The world was queerly muffled; Calloway had sent up another pair of fireworks, a great starburst of orange streaks spreading almost over half the sky, but Laurence could hear the explosion only in his left ear.

With the Fleur-de-Nuit thus distracted, Temeraire dropped back down onto the deck, rocking the ship only a little. "Hurry, hurry," he said, ducking his head down beneath the straps as the harness-men scrambled to get him rigged out. "She is very quick, and I do not think the light hurts her as much as it did the other one, the one we fought last fall; there is something different about her eyes." He was heaving for breath, and his wings trembled a little: he had been hovering a great deal, and it was not a maneuver he was accustomed to perform for any length of time.

Sun Kai, who had remained upon deck, observing, did not protest the harnessing; perhaps, Laurence thought bitterly, they did not mind it when it was their own necks at risk. Then he noticed that drops of deep, red-black blood were dripping onto the deck. "Where are you hurt?"

"It is not bad; she only caught me twice," Temeraire said, twisting his head around and licking at his right flank; there was a shallow cut there, and another gouged claw-mark further up on his back.

Twice was a good deal more than Laurence cared for; he snapped at Keynes, who had been sent along with them, as the man was boosted up and began to pack the wound with bandages. "Ought you not sew them up?"

"Nonsense," Keynes said. "He'll do as he is; barely worth calling them flesh wounds. Stop fretting." Macready had regained his feet, wiping his forehead with the back of his hand; he gave the surgeon a dubious look at this reply and glanced at Laurence sidelong, the more so as Keynes continued his work muttering audibly about over-anxious captains and mother hens.

Laurence himself was too grateful to object, full of re-lief. "Are you ready, gentlemen?" he asked, checking his pistols and his sword: this time it was his good heavy cutlass, proper Spanish steel and a plain hilt; he was glad to feel its solid weight under his hand.

"Ready for you, sir," Fellowes said, pulling the final strap tight; Temeraire reached out and lifted Laurence up to his shoulder. "Give her a pull up there; does she hold?" he called, once Laurence was settled and locked on again.

"Well enough," Laurence called back down, having thrown his weight against the stripped-down harness. "Thank you, Fellowes; well done. Granby, send the riflemen to the tops with the Marines, and the rest to repel boarders."

"Very good; and Laurence—" Granby said, clearly meaning to once again encourage him to take Temeraire away from the battle. Laurence cut him short by the expedient of giving Temeraire a quick nudge with his knee. The *Allegiance* heaved again beneath the weight of his leap, and they were airborne together at last.

The air above the *Allegiance* was thick with the harsh, sulfurous smoke of the fireworks, like the smell of flintlocks, cloying on his tongue and skin despite the cold wind. "There she is," Temeraire said, beating back aloft; Laurence followed his gaze and saw the Fleur-de-Nuit approaching again from high above: she had indeed recovered very quickly from the blinding light, judging by his previous experience with the breed, and he wondered if perhaps she was some sort of new cross. "Shall we go after her?"

Laurence hesitated; for the sake of keeping Temeraire out of their hands, disabling the Fleur-de-Nuit was of the most urgent necessity, for if the *Allegiance* was forced to surrender and Temeraire had to attempt a return to shore, she could harry them in the darkness all the way back home. And yet the French frigates could do far more damage to the ship: a raking fire would mean a very slaughter of the men. If the *Allegiance* were taken, it would be a terrible blow to the Navy and the Corps both: they had no large transports to spare.

"No," he said finally. "Our first duty must be to preserve the *Allegiance*—we must do something about those frigates." He spoke more to convince himself than Temeraire; he felt the decision was in the right, but a terrible doubt lingered; what was courage in an ordinary man might often be called recklessness in an aviator, with the responsibility for a rare and precious dragon in his hands. It was Granby's duty to be over-cautious, but it did not follow that he was in the wrong. Laurence had not been raised in the Corps, and he knew his nature balked at many of the restraints placed upon a dragon captain; he could not help but wonder if he were consulting his own pride too far.

Temeraire was always enthusiastic for battle; he made no argument, but only looked down at the frigates. "Those ships look much smaller than the *Allegiance*," Temeraire said doubtfully. "Is she truly in danger?"

"Very great danger; they mean to rake her." Even as Laurence spoke, another of the fireworks went off. The explosion came startlingly near, now that he was aloft on Temeraire's back; he was forced to shield his dazzled eyes with a hand. When the spots at last faded from his eyes, he saw in alarm that the leeward frigate had suddenly club-hauled to come about: a risky maneuver and not one he would himself have undertaken simply for an advantage of position, though in justice he could not deny it had been brilliantly performed. Now the *Allegiance* had her vulnerable stern wholly exposed to the French ship's larboard guns. "Good God; there!" he said urgently, pointing even though Temeraire could not see the gesture.

"I see her," Temeraire said: already diving. His sides were swelling out with the gathering breath required for the divine wind, the gleaming black hide going drumhidetaut as his deep chest expanded. Laurence could feel a palpable low rumbling echo already building beneath Temeraire's skin, a herald of the destructive power to come.

The Fleur-de-Nuit had made out his intentions: she was coming on behind them. He could hear her wings beating, but Temeraire was the faster, his greater weight not hampering him in the dive. Gunpowder cracked noisily as her riflemen took shots, but their attempts were only guesswork in the dark; Laurence laid himself close to Temeraire's neck and silently willed him to greater speed.

Below them, the frigate's cannon erupted in a great cloud of smoke and fury; flames licked out from the ports and flung an appalling scarlet glow up against Temeraire's breast. A fresh cracking of rifle-fire came from the frigate's decks, and he jerked, sharply, as if struck: Laurence called out his name in anxiety, but Temeraire had not paused in his drive towards the ship: he leveled out to blast her, and the sound of Laurence's voice was lost in the terrible thundering noise of the divine wind.

Temeraire had never before used the divine wind to attack a ship; but in the battle of Dover, Laurence had seen the deadly resonance work against Napoleon's troop-carriers, shattering their light wood. He had expected something similar here: the deck splintering, damage to the yards, perhaps even breaking the masts. But the French frigate was solidly built, with oak planking as much as two feet thick, and her masts and yards were well-secured for battle with iron chains to reinforce the rigging.

Instead the sails caught and held the force of Temeraire's roar: they shivered for a moment, then bulged out full and straining. A score of braces snapped like violin strings, the masts all leaning away; yet still they held, wood and sailcloth groaning, and for a moment Laurence's heart sank: no great damage, it seemed, would be done.

But if part would not yield, then all must perforce bend: even as Temeraire stopped his roaring and went flashing by, the whole ship turned away, driven broadside to the wind, and slowly toppled over onto her side. The tremendous force left her all but on her beam-ends, men hanging loose from the rigging and the rails, their feet kicking in mid-air, some falling into the ocean.

Laurence twisted about to look back towards her as they swept on, Temeraire skimming past, low to the water. VALÉRIE was emblazoned in lovingly bright gold letters upon her stern, illuminated by lanterns hung in the cabin windows: now swinging crazily, half overturned. Her captain knew his work: Laurence could hear shouts carrying across the water, and already the men were crawling up onto the side with every sort of sea-anchor in their hands, hawsers run out, ready to try to right her.

But they had no time. In Temeraire's wake, churned up by the force of the divine wind upon the water, a tremendous wave was climbing out of the swell. Slow and high it mounted, as if with some deliberate intent. For a moment all hung still, the ship suspended in blackness, the great shining wall of water blotting out even the night; then, falling, the wave heeled her over like a child's toy, and the ocean quenched all the fire of her guns.

She did not come up again. A pale froth lingered, and a scattered few smaller waves chased the great one and broke upon the curve of the hull, which remained above the surface. A moment only: then it slipped down beneath the waters, and a hail of golden fireworks lit the sky. The Fleur-de-Nuit circled low over the churning waters, belling out in her deep lonely voice, as though unable to understand the sudden absence of the ship.

There was no sound of cheering from the *Allegiance*, though they must have seen. Laurence himself was silent, dismayed: three hundred men, perhaps more, the ocean smooth and glassy, unbroken. A ship might founder in a gale, in high winds and forty-foot waves; a ship might occasionally be sunk in an action, burnt or exploded after a long battle, run aground on rocks. But she had been untouched, in open ocean with no more than a ten-foot swell and winds of fourteen knots; and now obliterated whole.

Temeraire coughed, wetly, and made a sound of pain; Laurence hoarsely called, "Back to the ship, at once," but already the Fleur-de-Nuit was beating furiously towards them: against the next brilliant flare he could see the silhouettes of the boarders waiting, ready to leap aboard, knives and swords and pistols glittering white along their edges. Temeraire was flying so very awkwardly, labored; as the Fleur-de-Nuit came close, he put on a desperate effort and lunged away, but he was no longer quicker in the air, and he could not get around the other dragon to reach the safety of the *Allegiance*.

Laurence might almost have let them come aboard, to treat the wound; he could feel the quivering labor of Temeraire's wings, and his mind was full of that scarlet moment, the terrible muffled impact of the ball: every moment aloft now might worsen the injury. But he could hear the shouting voices of the French dragon's crew, full of a grief and horror that required no translation; and he did not think they would accept a surrender.

"I hear wings," Temeraire gasped, voice gone high and thin with pain; meaning another dragon, and Laurence vainly searched the impenetrable night: British or French? The Fleur-de-Nuit abruptly darted at them again; Temeraire gathered himself for another convulsive burst of speed, and then, hissing and spitting, Nitidus was there, beating about the head of the French dragon in a flurry of silver-grey wings: Captain Warren on his back standing in harness and waving his hat wildly at Laurence, yelling, "Go, go!"

Dulcia had come about them on the other side, nipping at the Fleur-de-Nuit's flanks, forcing the French dragon to double back and snap at her; the two light dragons were the quickest of their formation-mates, and though not up to the weight of the big Fleur-de-Nuit, they might harry her a little while. Temeraire was already turning in a slow arc, his wings working in shuddering sweeps. As they closed with the ship, Laurence could see the crew scrambling to clear the dragondeck for him to land: it was littered with splinters and ends of rope, twisted metal; the *Allegiance* had suffered badly from the raking, and the second frigate was keeping up a steady fire on her lower decks.

Temeraire did not properly land, but half-fell clumsily onto the deck and set the whole ship to rocking; Laurence was casting off his straps before they were even properly down. He slid down behind the withers without a hand on the harness; his leg gave way beneath him as he came down heavily upon the deck, but he only dragged himself up again and staggered half-falling to Temeraire's head.

Keynes was already at work, elbow-deep in black blood; to better give him access, Temeraire was leaning slowly over onto his side under the guidance of many hands, the harness-men holding up the light for the surgeon. Laurence went to his knees by Temeraire's head and pressed his cheek to the soft muzzle; blood soaked warm through his trousers, and his eyes were stinging, blurred. He did not quite know what he was saying, nor whether it made any sense, but Temeraire blew out warm air against him in answer, though he did not speak.

"There, I have it; now the tongs. Allen, stop that foolishness or put your head over the side," Keynes said, somewhere behind his back. "Good. Is the iron hot? Now then; Laurence, he must keep steady."

"Hold fast, dear heart," Laurence said, stroking Temeraire's nose. "Hold as still as ever you may; hold still." Temeraire gave a hiss only, and his breath wheezed in loudly through his red, flaring nostrils; one heartbeat, two, then the breath burst out of him, and the spiked ball rang as Keynes dropped it into the waiting tray. Temeraire gave another small hissing cry as the hot iron was clapped to the wound; Laurence nearly heaved at the scorched, roasting smell of meat.

"There; it is over; a clean wound. The ball had fetched up against the breastbone," Keynes said; the wind blew the smoke clear, and suddenly Laurence could hear the crash and echo of the long guns again, and all the noise of the ship; the world once again had meaning and shape.

Laurence dragged himself up to his feet, swaying. "Roland," he said, "you and Morgan run and see what odds and ends of sailcloth and wadding they may have to spare; we must try and put some padding around him."

"Morgan is dead, sir," Roland said, and in the lantern-light he saw abruptly that her face was tracked with tears, not sweat; pale streaks through grime. "Dyer and I will go."

The two of them did not wait for him to nod, but darted away at once, shockingly small in and among the burly forms of the sailors; he followed after them with his eyes for a moment, and turned back, his face hardening.

The quarterdeck was so thickly slimed with blood that portions shone glossy black as though freshly painted. By the slaughter and lack of destruction in the rigging, Laurence thought the French must have been using canister shot, and indeed he could see some parts of the broken casings lying about on the deck. The French had crammed every man who could be spared into the boats, and there were a great many of those: two hundred desperate men were struggling to come aboard, enraged with the loss of their ship. They were four- and five-deep along the grappling-lines in places, or clinging to the rails, and the British sailors trying to hold them back had all the broad and empty deck behind them. Pistol-shot rang clear, and the clash of swords; sailors with long pikes were jabbing into the mass of boarders as they heaved and pushed.

Laurence had never seen a boarding fight from such a strange, in-between distance, at once near and yet removed; he felt very queer and unsettled, and drew his pistols out for comfort. He could not see many of his crew: Granby missing, and Evans, his second lieutenant, too; down on the forecastle below, Martin's yellow hair shone bright in the lanterns for a moment as he leapt to cut a man off; then he disappeared under a blow from a big French sailor carrying a club.

"Laurence." He heard his name, or at least something like it, strangely drawn out into three syllables more like *Lao-ren-tse,* and turned to look; Sun Kai was pointing northward, along the line of the wind, but the last burst of fireworks was already fading, and Laurence could not see what he meant to point out.

Above, the Fleur-de-Nuit suddenly gave a roar; she banked sharply away from Nitidus and Dulcia, who were still darting at her flanks, and set off due eastward, flying fast, vanishing very quickly into the darkness. Almost on her heels came the deep belly-roar of a Regal Copper, and the higher shrieks of Yellow Reapers: the wind of their passage set all the shrouds snapping back and forth as they swept overhead, firing flares off in every direction.

The remaining French frigate doused her lights all at once, hoping to escape into the night, but Lily led the formation past her, low enough to rattle her masts; two passes, and in a fading crimson starburst Laurence saw the French colors slowly come drooping down, while all across the deck the boarders flung down their weapons and sank to the deck in surrender.

Chapter 5

. . . and the Conduct of your son was in all ways both heroic and gentlemanly. His Loss must grieve all those who shared in the Privilege of his Acquaintance, and none more so than those honoured to serve alongside him, and to see in him already formed the noble Character of a wise and courageous Officer and a loyal Servant of his Country and King. I pray that you may find some Comfort in the sure Knowledge that he died as he would have lived, valiant, fearing nothing but Almighty God, and certain to find a Place of Honour among those who have sacrificed All for their Nation.

Yours, etc.,

William Laurence

HE LAID THE pen down and folded over the letter; it was miserably awkward, inadequate, and yet he could do no better. He had lost friends near his own age enough as a mid and a young lieutenant, and one thirteen-year-old boy under his own first command; even so he had never before had to write a letter for a ten-year-old, who by rights ought still to have been in his schoolroom playing with tin soldiers.

It was the last of the obligatory letters, and the thinnest: there had not been very much to say of earlier acts of valor. Laurence set it aside and wrote a few lines of a more personal nature, these to his mother: news of the engagement would certainly be published in the *Gazette*, and he knew she would be anxious. It was difficult to write easily, after the earlier task; he confined himself to assuring her of his health and Temeraire's, dismissing their collective injuries as inconsequential. He had written a long and grinding description of the battle in his report for the Admiralty; he did not have the heart to paint a lighter picture of it for her eyes.

Having done at last, he shut up his small writing-desk and collected the letters, each one sealed and wrapped in oilcloth against rain or sea-water. He did not get up right away, but sat looking out the windows at the empty ocean, in silence.

Making his way back up to the dragondeck was a slow affair of easy stages. Having gained the forecastle, he limped for a moment to the larboard rail to rest, pretending it was to look over at their prize, the *Chanteuse*. Her sails were all hung out loose and billowing; men were clambering over her masts, getting her rigging back into order, looking much like busy ants at this distance.

The scene upon the dragondeck was very different now, with nearly all the formation crammed aboard. Temeraire had been allotted the entire starboard section, the better to ease his wound, but the rest of the dragons lay in a complicated many-colored heap of entangled limbs, stirring rarely. Maximus alone took up virtually all the space remaining, and lay on the bottom; even Lily, who ordinarily considered it beneath her dignity to curl up with other dragons, was forced to let her tail and wing drape over him, while Messoria and Immortalis, older dragons and smaller, made not even such pretensions, and simply sprawled upon his great back, a limb dangling loose here and there.

They were all drowsing and looked perfectly happy with their circumstances; Nitidus only was too fidgety to like lying still very long, and he was presently aloft, circling the frigate curiously: a little too low for the comfort of the sailors, judging by the nervous way heads on the *Chanteuse* often turned skyward. Dulcia was nowhere in sight, perhaps already gone to carry news of the engagement back to England.

Crossing the deck had become something of an adventure, particularly with his uncooperative and dragging leg; Laurence only narrowly managed to avoid falling over Messoria's hanging tail when she twitched in her sleep. Temeraire was soundly asleep as well; when Laurence came to look at him, one eye slid halfway open, gleamed at him deep blue, and slid at once closed again. Laurence did not try to rouse him, very glad to see him comfortable; Temeraire had eaten well that morning, two cows and a large tunny, and Keynes had pronounced himself satisfied with the present progress of the wound.

"A nasty sort of weapon," he had said, taking a ghoulish pleasure in showing Laurence the extracted ball; staring unhappily at its many squat spikes, Laurence could only be grateful it had been cleaned before he had been obliged to look at it. "I have not seen its like before, though I hear the Russians use something of the sort; I should not have enjoyed working it out if it had gone any deeper, I can tell you."

But by good fortune, the ball had come up against the breastbone, and lodged scarcely half a foot beneath the skin; even so, the ball itself and the extraction had torn the muscles of the breast cruelly, and Keynes said Temeraire ought not fly at all for as long as two weeks, perhaps even a month. Laurence rested a hand upon the broad, warm shoulder; he was glad to have only so much of a price to pay.

The other captains were sitting at a small folding-table wedged up against the galley chimney, very nearly the only open space available on the deck, playing cards; Laurence joined them and gave Harcourt the bundle of letters. "Thank you for taking them," he said, sitting down heavily to catch his breath.

They all paused in the game to look at the large packet. "I am so very sorry, Laurence." Harcourt put the whole into her satchel. "You have been wretchedly mauled about."

"Damned cowardly business." Berkley shook his head. "More like spying than proper combat, this skulking about at night."

Laurence was silent; he was grateful for their sympathy, but at present he was too much oppressed to manage conversation. The funerals had been ordeal enough, keeping his feet for an hour against his leg's complaints, while one after another the bodies were slipped over the side, sewn into their hammocks with round-shot at their feet for the sailors, iron shells for the aviators, as Riley read slowly through the service.

He had spent the remainder of the morning closeted with Lieutenant Ferris, now his acting second, telling over the butcher's bill; a sadly long list. Granby had taken a musket-ball in his chest; thankfully it had cracked against a rib and gone straight out again in back, but he had lost a great deal of blood, and was already feverish. Evans, his second lieutenant, had a badly broken leg and was to be sent back to England; Martin at least would recover, but his jaw was presently so swollen he could not speak except in mumbles, and he could not yet see out of his left eye.

Two more of the topmen wounded, less severely; one of the riflemen, Dunne, wounded, and another, Donnell, killed; Miggsy of the bellmen killed; and worst-hit, the harness-men: four of them had been killed by a single cannon-ball, which had caught them belowdecks while they had been carrying away the extra harness. Morgan had been with them, carrying the box of spare buckles: a wretched waste.

Perhaps seeing something of the tally in his face, Berkley said, "At least I can leave you Portis and Macdonaugh," referring to two of Laurence's topmen, who had been transferred to Maximus during the confusion after the envoys' arrival.

"Are you not short-handed yourself?" Laurence asked.

"I cannot rob Maximus; you will be on active duty."

"The transport coming from Halifax, the *William of Orange,* has a dozen likely fellows for Maximus," Berkley said. "No reason you cannot have your own back again."

"I ought not argue with you; Heaven knows I am desperately short," Laurence said. "But the transport may not arrive for a month, if her crossing has been slow."

"Oh; you were below earlier, so you did not hear us tell Captain Riley," Warren said. "*William* was sighted only a few days ago, not far from here. So we have sent Chenery and Dulcia off to fetch her, and she will take us and the wounded home. Also, I believe Riley was saying that this boat needs something; it could not have been stars, Berkley?"

"Spars," Laurence said, looking up at the rigging; in the daylight he could see that the yards which supported the sails did indeed look very ugly, much splintered and pockmarked with bullets. "It will certainly be a relief if she can spare us some supplies. But you must know, Warren, this is a ship, not a boat."

"Is there a difference?" Warren was unconcerned, scandalizing Laurence. "I thought they were simply two words for the same thing; or is it a matter of size? This is certainly a behemoth, although Maximus is like to fall off her deck at any moment."

"I am not," Maximus said, but he opened his eyes and peered over at his hindquarters, only settling back to sleep when he had satisfied himself that he was not in present danger of tipping into the water.

Laurence opened his mouth and closed it again without venturing on an explanation; he felt the battle was already lost. "You will be with us for a few days, then?"

"Until tomorrow only," Harcourt said. "If it looks to be longer than that, I think we must take the flight; I do not like to strain the dragons without need, but I like leaving Lenton short at Dover still less, and he will be wondering where on earth we have got to: we were only meant to be doing night maneuvers with the fleet off Brest, before we saw you all firing off like Guy Fawkes Day."

Riley had asked them all to dinner, of course; and the captured French officers as well. Harcourt was obliged to plead sea-sickness as an excuse for avoiding the close quarters where her gender might too easily be revealed, and Berkley was a taciturn fellow, disinclined to speak in sentences of more than five words at a time. But Warren was both free and easy in his speech, the more so after a glass or two of strong wine, and Sutton had a fine store of anecdotes, having been in service nearly thirty years; together they carried the conversation along in an energetic if somewhat ramshackle way.

But the Frenchmen were silent and shocked, and the British sailors only a little less so; their oppression only grew more apparent over the course of the meal. Lord Purbeck was stiff and formal, Macready grim; even Riley was quiet, inclined to uncharacteristic and long periods of silence, and plainly uncomfortable.

On the dragondeck afterwards, over coffee, Warren said, "Laurence, I do not mean to insult your old service or your shipmates, but Lord! They make it heavy going. Tonight I should have thought we had offended them mortally, not saved them a good long fight and whoever knows how many bucketsful of blood."

"I expect they feel we came rather late to save them very much." Sutton leaned against his dragon Messoria companionably and lit a cigar. "So instead we have robbed them of the full glory, not to mention that we have a share in the prize, you know, having arrived before the French ship struck. Would you care for a draft, my dear?" he asked, holding the cigar where Messoria could breathe the smoke.

"No, you have mistaken them entirely, I assure you," Laurence said. "We should never have taken the frigate if you had not come; she was not so badly mauled she could not have shown us her heels whenever she chose; every man aboard was wholly glad to see you come." He did not very much wish to explain, but he did not like to leave them with so ill an impression, so he added briefly, "It is the other frigate, the *Valérie*, which we sank before you came; the loss of men was very great."

They perceived his own disquiet and pressed him no further; when Warren made as if to ask, Sutton nudged him into silence and called his runner for a deck of cards. They settled to a casual game of speculation, Harcourt having joined them now that they had parted from the naval officers. Laurence finished his cup and slipped quietly away.

Temeraire was himself sitting and looking out across the empty sea; he had slept all the day, and roused just lately for another large meal. He shifted himself to make a place for Laurence upon his foreleg, and curled about him with a small sigh.

"Do not take it to heart." Laurence was aware he was giving advice he could not himself follow; but he feared that Temeraire might brood on the sinking too long, and drive himself into a melancholy. "With the second frigate on our larboard, we should likely have been brought by the lee, and had they doused all the lights and stopped our fireworks, Lily and the others could hardly have found us in the night. You saved many lives, and the *Allegiance* herself."

"I do not feel guilty," Temeraire said. "I did not intend to sink her, but I am not sorry for that; they meant to kill a great many of my crew, and of course I would not let them. It is the sailors: they look at me so queerly now, and they do not like to come near at all."

Laurence could neither deny the truth of this observation, nor offer any false comfort. Sailors preferred to see a dragon as a fighting machine, very much like a ship which happened to breathe and fly: a mere instrument of man's will. They could accept without great difficulty his strength and brute force, natural as a reflection of his size; if they feared him for it, so might a large, dangerous man be feared. The divine wind however bore an unearthly tinge, and the wreck of the *Valérie* was too implacable to be human: it woke every wild old legend of fire and destruction from the sky.

Already the battle seemed very like a nightmare in his own memory: the endless gaudy stream of the fireworks and the red light of the cannon firing, the ash-white eyes of the Fleur-de-Nuit in the dark, bitter smoke on his tongue, and above all the slow descent of the wave, like a curtain lowering upon a play. He stroked Temeraire's arm in silence, and together they watched the wake of the ship slipping gently by.

The cry of "Sail!" came at the first dim light: the *William of Orange* clear on the horizon, two points off the starboard bow. Riley squinted through his glass. "We will pipe the hands to breakfast early; she will be in hailing distance well before nine."

The *Chanteuse* lay between the two larger ships and was already hailing the oncoming transport: she herself would be going back to England to be condemned as a prize, carrying the prisoners. The day was clear and very cold, the sky that peculiarly rich shade of blue reserved for winter, and the *Chanteuse* looked cheerful with her white topgallants and royals set. It being rare for a transport to take a prize, the mood ought to have been celebratory; a handsome forty-four-gun ship and a trim sailer, she would certainly be bought into the service, and there would be head-money for the prisoners besides. But the unsettled mood had not quite cleared overnight, and the men were mostly quiet as they worked. Laurence himself had not slept very well, and now he stood on the forecastle watching the *William of Orange* draw near, wistfully; soon they would once again be quite alone.

"Good morning, Captain," Hammond said, joining him at the rail. The intrusion was unwelcome, and Laurence did not make much attempt to hide it, but this made no immediate impression: Hammond was too busy gazing upon the *Chanteuse*, an indecent satisfaction showing on his face. "We could not have asked for a better start to the journey."

Several of the crew were at work nearby repairing the shattered deck, the carpenter and his mates; one of them, a cheerful, slant-shouldered fellow named Leddowes, brought aboard at Spithead and already established as the ship's jester, sat up on his heels at this remark and stared at Hammond in open disapproval, until the carpenter Eklof, a big silent Swede, thumped him on the shoulder with his big fist, drawing him back down to the work.

"I am surprised you think so," Laurence said. "Would you not have preferred a first-rate?"

"No, no," Hammond said, oblivious to sarcasm. "It is just as one could wish; do you know one of the balls passed quite through the prince's cabin? One of his guards was killed, and another, badly wounded, passed away during the night; I understand he is in a towering rage. The French navy has done us more good in one night than months of diplomacy. Do you suppose the captain of the captured ship might be presented to him? Of course I have told them our attackers were French, but it would be as well to give them incontrovertible proof."

"We are not going to march a defeated officer about like a prize in some Roman triumph," Laurence said levelly; he had been made prisoner once himself, and though he had been scarcely a boy at the time, a young midshipman, he still remembered the perfect courtesy of the French captain, asking him quite seriously for his parole.

"Of course, I do see—It would not look very well, I suppose," Hammond said, but only as a regretful concession, and he added, "Although it would be a pity if—"

"Is that all?" Laurence interrupted him, unwilling to hear any more.

"Oh—I beg your pardon; forgive my having intruded," Hammond said uncertainly, finally looking at Laurence. "I meant only to inform you: the prince has expressed a desire of seeing you."

"Thank you, sir," Laurence said, with finality. Hammond looked as though he would have liked to say something more, perhaps to urge Laurence to go at once, or give him some advice for the meeting; but in the end he did not dare, and with a short bow went abruptly away.

Laurence had no desire to speak with Yongxing, still less to be trifled with, and his mood was not much improved by the physical unpleasantness of making his halting way to the prince's quarters, all the way to the stern of the ship. When the attendants tried to make him wait in the antechamber, he said shortly, "He may send word when he is ready," and turned at once to go. There was a hasty and huddled conference, one man going so far as to stand in the doorway to bar the way out, and after a moment Laurence was ushered directly into the great cabin.

The two gaping holes in the walls, opposite one another, had been stuffed with wads of blue silk to keep out the wind; but still the long banners of inscribed parchment hanging upon the walls blew and rattled now and again in the draught. Yongxing sat straight-backed upon an armchair draped in red cloth, at a small writing-table of lacquered wood; despite the motion of the ship, his brush moved steadily from ink-pot to paper, never dripping, the shining-wet characters formed up in neat lines and rows.

"You wished to see me, sir," Laurence said.

Yongxing completed a final line and set aside his brush without immediately answering; he took a stone seal, resting in a small pool of red ink, and pressed it at the bottom of the page; then folded up the page and laid it to one side, atop another similar sheet, and folded these both into a piece of waxed cloth. "Feng Li," he called.

Laurence started; he had not even noticed the attendant standing in the corner, nondescript in plain robes of dark blue cotton, who now came forward. Feng was a tall fellow but so permanently stooped that all Laurence could see of him was the perfect line running across his head, ahead of which his dark hair was shaven to the skin. He gave Laurence one quick darting glance, mutely curious, then lifted the whole table up and carried it away to the side of the room, not spilling a drop of the ink.

He hurried back quickly with a footrest for Yongxing, then drew back into the corner of the room: plainly Yongxing did not mean to send him away for the interview. The prince sat up erect with his arms resting upon the chair, and did not offer Laurence a seat, though two more chairs stood against the far wall. This set the tone straightaway; Laurence felt his shoulders stiffening even before Yongxing had begun.

"Though you have only been brought along for necessity's sake," Yongxing said coldly, "you imagine that you remain companion to Lung Tien Xiang and may continue to treat him as your property. And now the worst has been realized: through your vicious and reckless behavior, he has come to grave injury."

Laurence pressed his lips together; he did not trust himself to make anything resembling a civilized remark in response. He had questioned his own judgment, both before taking Temeraire into the battle and all through the long following night, remembering the sound of the dreadful impact, and Temeraire's labored and painful breath; but to have Yongxing question it was another matter.

"Is that all?" he said.

Yongxing had perhaps expected him to grovel, or beg forgiveness; certainly this short answer made the prince more voluble with anger. "Are you so lacking in all right principles?" he said. "You have no remorse; you would have taken Lung Tien Xiang to his death as easily as ridden a horse to foundering. You are not to go aloft with him again, and you will keep these low servants of yours away. I will set my own guards around him—"

"Sir," Laurence said, bluntly, "you may go to the devil." Yongxing broke off, looking more taken aback than offended at finding himself interrupted, and Laurence added, "And as for your guards, if any one of them sets foot upon my dragondeck, I will have Temeraire pitch him overboard. Good day."

He made a short bow and did not stay to hear a response, if Yongxing even made one, but turned and went directly from the room. The attendants stared as he went past them and did not this time attempt to block his way; he was forcing his leg to obey his wishes, moving swiftly. He paid for the bravado: by the time he reached his own cabin, at the very other end of the ship's interminable length, his leg had begun to twitch and shudder with every step as if palsied; he was glad to reach the safety of his chair, and to soothe his ruffled temper with a private glass of wine. Perhaps he had spoken intemperately, but he did not regret it in the least; Yongxing should at least know that not all British officers and gentlemen were prepared to bow and scrape to his every tyrannous whim.

As satisfying a resolution as this was, however, Laurence could not help but acknowledge to himself that his defiance was a good deal strengthened by the conviction that Yongxing would never willingly bend on the central, the essential, point of his separation from Temeraire. The Ministry, in Hammond's person, might have something to gain in exchange for all their crawling; for his own part Laurence had nothing of great importance left to lose. This was a lowering thought, and he put down his glass and sat in silent gloom awhile instead, rubbing his aching leg, propped upon a locker. Six bells rang on deck, and faintly he heard the pipe shrilling away, the scrape and clatter of the hands going to their breakfast on the berth deck below, and the smell of strong tea came drifting over from the galley.

Having finished his glass and eased his leg a little, Laurence at last got himself back onto his feet, and he crossed to Riley's cabin and tapped on the door. He meant to ask Riley to station several of the Marines to keep the threatened guards off the deck, and he was startled and not at all pleased to find Hammond already there, sitting before Riley's writing-desk, with a shadow of conscious guilt and anxiety upon his face.

"Laurence," Riley said, after offering him a chair, "I have been speaking with Mr. Hammond, about the passengers," and Laurence noticed that Riley himself was looking tired and anxious. "He has brought to my attention that they have all been keeping belowdecks, since this news about the Indiamen came out. It cannot go on like this for seven months: we must let them come on deck and take the air somehow. I am sure you will not object—I think we must let them walk about the dragon-deck, we do not dare put them near the hands."

No suggestion could have possibly been more un-welcome, nor come at a worse moment; Laurence eyed Hammond in mingled irritation and something very near despair; the man already seemed to be possessed of an evil genius for disaster, at least from Laurence's view, and the prospect of a long journey spent suffering one after another of his diplomatic machinations was increasingly grim.

"I am sorry for the inconvenience," Riley said, when Laurence did not immediately reply. "Only I do not see what else is to be done. There surely is no shortage of room?"

This, too, was indisputable; with so few aviators aboard, and the ship's complement so nearly full, it was unfair to ask the sailors to give up any portion of their space, and could only aggravate the tensions, already high. As a practical matter, Riley was perfectly correct, and it was his right as the ship's captain to decide where the passengers might be at liberty; but Yongxing's threat had made the matter a question of principle. Laurence would have liked to unburden himself plainly to Riley, and if Hammond had not been there, he would have done so; as it was—

"Perhaps," Hammond put in, hurriedly, "Captain Lau-rence is concerned that they might irritate the dragon. May I suggest that we set aside one portion for them, and that plainly demarcated? A cord, perhaps, might be strung; or else paint would do."

"That would do nicely, if you would be so kind as to explain the boundaries to them, Mr. Hammond," Riley said.

Laurence could make no open protest without expla-nation, and he did not choose to be laying out his actions in front of Hammond, inviting him to comment upon

them; not when there was likely nothing to gain. Riley
would sympathize—or at least Laurence hoped he would,
though abruptly he was less certain; but sympathy or no,
the difficulty would remain, and Laurence did not know
what else could be done.

He was not resigned; he was not resigned in the least,
but he did not mean to complain and make Riley's situation more difficult. "You will also make plain, Mr. Hammond," Laurence said, "that they are none of them to
bring small-arms onto the deck, neither muskets nor
swords, and in any action they are to go belowdecks at
once: I will brook no interference with my crew, or with
Temeraire."

"But sir, there are soldiers among them," Hammond
protested. "I am sure they would wish to drill, from time
to time—"

"They may wait until they reach China," Laurence
said.

Hammond followed him out of the cabin and caught
him at the door to his own quarters; inside, two ground
crewmen had just brought in more chairs, and Roland
and Dyer were busily laying plates out upon the cloth:
the other dragons' captains were joining Laurence for
breakfast before they took their leave. "Sir," Hammond
said, "pray allow me a moment. I must beg your pardon
for having sent you to Prince Yongxing in such a way,
knowing him to be in an intemperate mood, and I assure
you I blame only myself for the consequences, and your
quarrel; still, I must beg you to be forbearing—"

Laurence listened to this much, frowning, and now
with mounting incredulity said, "Are you saying that you
were already aware—? That you made this proposal to
Captain Riley, knowing I had forbidden them the deck?"

His voice was rising as he spoke, and Hammond
darted his eyes desperately towards the open door of the
cabin: Roland and Dyer were staring wide-eyed and in-

terested at them both, not attending to the great silver platters they were holding. "You must understand, we *cannot* put them in such a position. Prince Yongxing has issued a command; if we defy it openly, we humiliate him before his own—"

"Then he had best learn not to issue commands to me, sir," Laurence said angrily, "and you would do better to tell him so, instead of carrying them out for him, in this underhanded—"

"For Heaven's sake! Do you imagine I have any desire to see you barred from Temeraire? All we have to bargain with is the dragon's refusal to be separated from you," Hammond said, growing heated himself. "But that alone will not get us very far without good-will, and if Prince Yongxing cannot enforce his commands so long as we are at sea, our positions will be wholly reversed in China. Would you have us sacrifice an alliance to your pride? To say nothing," Hammond added, with a contemptible attempt at wheedling, "of any hope of keeping Temeraire."

"I am no diplomat," Laurence said, "but I will tell you, sir, if you imagine you are likely to get so much as a thimbleful of good-will from this prince, no matter how you truckle to him, then you are a damned fool; and I will thank you not to imagine that I may be bought by castles in the air."

Laurence had meant to send Harcourt and the others off in a creditable manner, but his table was left to bear the social burden alone, without any assistance from his conversation. Thankfully he had laid in good stores, and there was some advantage in being so close to the galley: bacon, ham, eggs, and coffee came to the table steaming hot, even as they sat down, along with a portion of a great tunny, rolled in pounded ship's biscuit and fried, the rest of which had gone to Temeraire; also a large dish of cherry preserves, and an even larger of marmalade. He ate only a little, and seized gladly on the distraction when Warren asked him to sketch the course of the battle for them. He pushed aside his mostly untouched plate to demonstrate the maneuvers of the ships and the Fleur-de-Nuit with bits of crumbled bread, the salt-cellar standing for the *Allegiance*.

The dragons were just completing their own somewhat less-civilized breakfast as Laurence and the other captains came back above to the dragondeck. Laurence was deeply gratified to find Temeraire wide awake and alert, looking much more easy with his bandages showing clean white, and engaged in persuading Maximus to try a piece of the tunny.

"It is a particularly nice one, and fresh-caught this very morning," he said. Maximus eyed the fish with deep suspicion: Temeraire had already eaten perhaps half, but its head had not been removed, and it lay gap-mouthed and staring glassily on the deck. A good fifteen hundred pounds when first taken, Laurence guessed; even half was still impressive.

Less so, however, when Maximus finally bent his head down and took it: the whole bulk made a single bite for him, and it was amusing to see him chewing with a skeptical expression. Temeraire waited expectantly; Maximus swallowed and licked his chops, and said, "It would not be so very bad, I suppose, if there were nothing else handy, but it is too slippery."

Temeraire's ruff flattened with disappointment. "Perhaps one must develop a taste for it. I dare say they can catch you another."

Maximus snorted. "No; I will leave the fish to you. Is there any more mutton, at all?" he asked, peering over at the herdsmaster with interest.

"How many have you et up already?" Berkley demanded, heaving himself up the stairs towards him. "Four? That is enough; if you grow any more, you will never get yourself off the ground."

Maximus ignored this and cleaned the last haunch of sheep out of the slaughtering-tub; the others had finished also, and the herdmaster's mates began pumping water over the dragondeck to sluice away the blood: shortly there was a veritable frenzy of sharks in the waters before the ship.

The *William of Orange* was nearly abreast of them, and Riley had gone across to discuss the supplies with her captain; now he reappeared on her deck and was rowed back over, while her men began laying out fresh supplies of wooden spars and sailcloth. "Lord Purbeck," Riley said, climbing back up the side, "we will send the launch to fetch over the supplies, if you please."

"Shall we bring them for you instead?" Harcourt asked, calling down from the dragondeck. "We will have to clear Maximus and Lily off the deck in any case; we can just as easily ferry supplies as fly circles."

"Thank you, sir; you would oblige me greatly," Riley said, looking up and bowing, with no evident suspicion: Harcourt's hair was pulled back tightly, the long braid concealed beneath her flying-hood, while her dress coat hid her figure well enough.

Maximus and Lily went aloft, without their crews, clearing room on the deck for the others to make ready; the crews rolled out the harnesses and armor, and began rigging the smaller dragons out, while the two larger flew over to the *William of Orange* for the supplies. The moment of departure was drawing close, and Laurence limped over to Temeraire's side; he was conscious suddenly of a sharp, unanticipated regret.

"I do not know that dragon," Temeraire said to Laurence, looking across the water at the other transport; there was a large beast sprawled sullenly upon their dragondeck, a stripey brown-and-green, with red streaks on his wings and neck rather like paint: Laurence had never seen the breed before.

"He is an Indian breed, from one of those tribes in Canada," Sutton said, when Laurence pointed out the strange dragon. "I think Dakota, if I am pronouncing the name correctly; I understand he and his rider—they do not use crews over there, you know, only one man to a dragon, no matter the size—were captured raiding a settlement on the frontier. It is a great coup: a vastly different breed, and I understand they are very fierce fighters. They meant to use him at the breeding grounds in Halifax, but I believe it was agreed that once Praecursoris was sent to them, they should send that fellow here in exchange; and a proper bloody-minded creature he looks."

"It seems hard to send him so very far from home, and to stay," Temeraire said, rather low, looking at the other dragon. "He does not look at all happy."

"He would only be sitting in the breeding grounds at Halifax instead of here, and that does not make much difference," Messoria said, stretching her wings out for the convenience of her harness-crewmen, who were climbing over her to get her rigged out. "They are all much alike, and not very interesting, except for the breeding part," she added, with somewhat alarming frankness; she was a much older dragon than Temeraire, being over thirty years of age.

"That does not sound very interesting, either," Temeraire said, and glumly laid himself back down. "Do you suppose they will put me in a breeding ground in China?"

"I am sure not," Laurence said; privately, he was quite determined he would not leave Temeraire to any such fate, no matter what the Emperor of China or anyone else had to say about it. "They would hardly be making such a fuss, if that were all they wanted."

Messoria snorted indulgently. "You may not think it so terrible, anyway, after you have tried it."

"Stop corrupting the morals of the young." Captain Sutton slapped her side good-humoredly, and gave the harness a final reassuring tug. "There, I think we are ready. Good-bye a second time, Laurence," he said, as they clasped hands. "I expect you have had enough excitement to stand you for the whole voyage; may the rest be less eventful."

The three smaller dragons leapt one after another off the deck, Nitidus scarcely even making the *Allegiance* dip in the water, and flew over to the *William of Orange*; then Maximus and Lily came back in turns to be rigged-out themselves, and for Berkley and Harcourt to make Laurence their farewells. At last the whole formation was transferred to the other transport, leaving Temeraire alone on the *Allegiance* once more.

Riley gave the order to make sail directly; the wind coming from east-southeast and not over-strong, even the studdingsails were set, a fine and blooming display of white. *William of Orange* fired a gun to leeward as they passed, answered in a moment by Riley's order, and a cheer came to them across the water as the two transports drew finally away from one another, slow and majestic.

Maximus and Lily had gone aloft for a frolic, with the energy of young dragons lately fed; they could be seen for a long while chasing one another through the clouds above the ship, and Temeraire kept his gaze on them until distance reduced them to the size of birds. He sighed a little then, and drew his head back down, curling in upon himself. "It will be a long time before we see them again, I suppose," he said.

Laurence put his hand on the sleek neck, silently. This parting felt somehow more final: no great bustle and noise, no sense of new adventure unfolding, only the crew going about their work still subdued, with nothing to be seen but the long blue miles of empty ocean, an uncertain road to a more uncertain destination. "The time will pass more quickly than you expect," he said. "Come, let us have the book again."

II

Chapter 6

THE WEATHER HELD clear for the first brief stage of their journey, with that peculiar winter cleanliness: the water very dark, the sky cloudless, and the air gradually warming as they continued the journey southward. A brisk, busy time, replacing the damaged yards and hanging the sails fresh, so that their pace daily increased as they restored the ship to her old self. They saw only a couple of small merchantmen in the distance, who gave them a wide berth, and once high overhead a courier-dragon going on its rounds with dispatches: certainly a Greyling, one of the long-distance fliers, but too far away for even Temeraire to recognize if it was anyone they knew.

The Chinese guards had appeared promptly at dawn, the first day after the arrangement, a broad stripe of paint having marked off a section of the larboard dragondeck; despite the absence of any visible weapons they did indeed stand watch, as formal as Marines on parade, in shifts of three. The crew were by now well aware of the quarrel, which had taken place near enough the stern windows to be overheard on deck, and were naturally inclined to be resentful of the guards' presence, and still more so of the senior members of the Chinese party, who were one and all eyed darkly, without distinction.

Laurence however was beginning to discern some individual traces among them, at least those who chose to come on deck. A few of the younger men showed some real enthusiasm for the sea, standing near the larboard end of the deck to best enjoy the spray as the *Allegiance* plowed onwards. One young fellow, Li Honglin, was particularly adventurous, going so far as to imitate the habits of some of the midshipmen and hang off the yards despite his unsuitable clothes: the skirts of his half-robe looked likely to entangle with the ropes, and his short black boots had soles too thick to have much purchase on the edge of the deck, unlike the bare feet or thin slippers of the sailors. His compatriots were much alarmed each time he tried it, and urged him back onto the deck loudly and with urgent gestures.

The rest took the air more sedately, and stayed well back from the edges; they often brought up low stools to sit upon, and spoke freely among themselves in the strange rise-and-fall of their language, which Laurence could not so much as break into sentences; it seemed wholly impenetrable to him. But despite the impossibility of direct conversation, he quickly came to feel that most of the attendants had no strong hostility of their own towards the British: uniformly civil, at least in expression and gesture, and usually making polite bows as they came and went.

They omitted such courtesies only on those occasions when they were in Yongxing's company: at such times, they followed his practice, and neither nodded nor made any gesture at all towards the British aviators, but came and went as if there were no other people at all aboard. But the prince came on deck infrequently; his cabin with its wide windows was spacious enough he did not need to do so for exercise. His main purpose seemed to be to frown and to look over Temeraire, who did not benefit from these inspections, as he was almost always asleep: still recovering from his wound, he was as yet napping nearly all the day, and lay oblivious, now and again send-

ing a small rumble through the deck with a wide and
drowsy yawn, while the life of the ship went on unheeded about him.

Liu Bao did not even make brief visits such as these,
but remained closeted in his apartments: permanently, as
far as any of them could tell; no one had seen so much of
him as the tip of his nose since his first coming aboard,
though he was quartered in the cabin under the poop
deck, and had only to open his front door and step outside. He did not even leave to go down below to take
meals or consult with Yongxing, and only a few servants
trotted back and forth between his quarters and the
galley, once or twice a day.

Sun Kai, by contrast, scarcely spent a moment of daylight indoors; he took the air after every meal and remained on deck for long stretches at a time. On those
occasions when Yongxing came above, Sun Kai always
bowed formally to the prince, and then kept himself quietly to one side, set apart from the retinue of servants,
and the two of them did not much converse. Sun Kai's
own interest was centered upon the life of the ship, and
her construction; and he was particularly fascinated by
the great-gun exercises.

These, Riley was forced to curtail more than he would
have liked, Hammond having argued that they could not
be disturbing the prince regularly; so on most days the
men only ran out the guns in dumb-show, without firing,
and only occasionally engaged in the thunder and crash
of a live exercise. In either case, Sun Kai always appeared
promptly the moment the drum began to beat, if he were
not already on deck at the time, and watched the proceedings intently from start to finish, not flinching even
at the enormous eruption and recoil. He was careful to
place himself so that he was not in the way, even as the
men came racing up to the dragondeck to man its hand-

ful of guns, and by the second or third occasion the gun-crews ceased to pay him any notice.

When there was no exercise in train, he studied the nearby guns at close range. Those upon the dragondeck were the short-barreled carronades, great forty-two-pound smashers, less accurate than the long guns but with far less recoil, so they did not require much room; and Sun Kai was fascinated by the fixed mounting in particular, which allowed the heavy iron barrel to slide back and forth along its path of recoil. He did not seem to think it rude to stare, either, as the men went about their work, aviators and sailors alike, though he could not have understood a word of what they were saying; and he studied the *Allegiance* herself with as much interest: the arrangement of her masts and sails, and with particular attention to the design of her hull. Laurence saw him often peering down over the edge of the dragondeck at the white line of the keel, and making sketches upon the deck in an attempt to outline her construction.

Yet for all his evident curiosity, he had a quality of deep reserve which went beyond the exterior, the severity of his foreign looks; his study was somehow more intense than eager, less a scholar's passion than a matter of industry and diligence, and there was nothing inviting in his manner. Hammond, undaunted, had already made a few overtures, which were received with courtesy but no warmth, and to Laurence it seemed almost painfully obvious that Sun Kai was not welcoming: not the least change of emotion showed on his face at Hammond's approach or departure, no smiles, no frowns, only a controlled, polite attention.

Even if conversation had been possible, Laurence did not think he could bring himself to intrude, after Hammond's example; though Sun Kai's study of the ship would certainly have benefited from some guidance, and thus offered an ideal subject of conversation. But tact forbade it as much as the barrier of language, so for the moment, Laurence contented himself with observation.

At Madeira, they watered and repaired their supplies of livestock from the damage which the formation's visit had done them, but did not linger in port. "All this shifting of the sails has been to some purpose—I am beginning to have a better notion of what suits her," Riley said to Laurence. "Would you mind Christmas at sea? I would be just as happy to put her to the test, and see if I can bring her up as far as seven knots."

They sailed out of Funchal roads majestically, with a broad spread of sail, and Riley's jubilant air announced his hopes for greater speed had been answered even before he said, "Eight knots, or nearly; what do you say to that?"

"I congratulate you indeed," Laurence said. "I would not have thought it possible, myself; she is going beyond anything." He felt a curious kind of regret at their speed, wholly unfamiliar. As a captain he had never much indulged in real cracking on, feeling it inappropriate to be reckless with the King's property, but like any seaman he liked his ship to go as well as she could. He would ordinarily have shared truly in Riley's pleasure, and never looked back at the smudge of the island receding behind them.

Riley had invited Laurence and several of the ship's officers to dine, in a celebratory mood over the ship's newfound speed. As if for punishment, a brief squall blew up from nowhere during the meal, while only the hapless young Lieutenant Beckett was standing watch: he could have sailed around the world six times without a pause if only ships were to be controlled directly by mathematical formulae, and yet invariably managed to give quite the wrong order in any real weather. There was a mad rush from the dinner table as soon as the *Allegiance* first pitched beneath them, putting her head down and protesting, and they heard Temeraire make a startled small roar; even so, the wind nearly carried away the mizzentopgallant sail before Riley and Purbeck could get back on deck and put things to rights.

The storm blew away as quickly as it had come, the hurrying dark clouds leaving the sky washed shell-pink and blue behind them; the swell died to a comfortable height, a few feet, which the *Allegiance* scarcely noticed; and while there was yet enough light to read by on the dragondeck, a party of the Chinese came up on deck: several servants first maneuvering Liu Bao out through his door, trundling him across the quarterdeck and forecastle, and then at last up to the dragondeck. The older envoy was greatly altered from his last appearance, having shed perhaps a stone in weight and gone a distinctly greenish shade under his beard and pouched cheeks, so visibly uncomfortable that Laurence could not help but be sorry for him. The servants had brought a chair for him; he was eased into it and his face turned into the cool wet wind, but he did not look at all as though he were improving, and when another of the attendants tried to offer him a plate of food, he only waved it away.

"Do you suppose he is going to starve to death?" Temeraire inquired, more in a spirit of curiosity than concern, and Laurence answered absently, "I hope not; though he is old to be taking to sea for the first time," even as he sat up and beckoned. "Dyer, go down to Mr. Pollitt and ask if he would be so good as to step up for a moment."

Shortly Dyer came back with the ship's surgeon puffing along behind him in his awkward way; Pollitt had been Laurence's own surgeon in two commands, and did not stand on ceremony, but heaved himself into a chair and said, "Well, now, sir; is it the leg?"

"No, thank you, Mr. Pollitt; I am improving nicely; but I am concerned for the Chinese gentleman's health." Laurence pointed out Liu Bao, and Pollitt, shaking his head, opined that if he went on losing weight at such a pace, he should scarcely reach the equator. "I do not suppose they know any remedies for sea-sickness of this virulent sort, not being accustomed to long voyages," Laurence said. "Would you not make up some physic for him?"

"Well, he is not my patient, and I would not like to be accused of interference; I do not suppose their medical men take any kinder view of it than do we," Pollitt said apologetically. "But in any case, I think I should rather prescribe a course of ship's biscuit. There is very little offense any stomach can take at biscuit, I find, and who knows what sort of foreign cookery he has been teasing himself with. A little biscuit and perhaps a light wine will set him up properly again, I am sure."

Of course the foreign cookery was native to Liu Bao, but Laurence saw nothing to argue with in this course of action, and later that evening sent over a large packet of biscuit, picked-over by a reluctant Roland and Dyer to remove the weevils, and the real sacrifice, three bottles of a particular sprightly Riesling: very light, indeed almost airy, and purchased at a cost of 6s., 3d. apiece from a Portsmouth wine-merchant.

Laurence felt a little odd in making the gesture; he hoped he would have done as much in any case, but there was more calculation in it than he had ever been used to make, and there was just a shade of dishonesty, a shade of flattery to it, which he could not entirely like, or approve of in himself. And indeed he felt some general qualms about any overture at all, given the insult of the confiscation of the East India Company ships, which he had no more forgotten than any of the sailors who still watched the Chinese with sullen dislike.

But he excused himself to Temeraire privately that night, having seen his offering delivered into Liu Bao's cabin. "After all, it is not their fault personally, any more than it would be mine if the King were to do the same to them. If Government makes not a sound over the matter, they can hardly be blamed for treating it so lightly: *they* at least have not made the slightest attempt at concealing the incident, nor been dishonest in the least."

Even as he said it, he was still not quite satisfied. But there was no other choice; he did not mean to be sitting about doing nothing, nor could he rely upon Hammond: skill and wit the diplomat might possess, but Laurence was by now convinced that there was no intention, on his part, of expending much effort to keep Temeraire; to Hammond the dragon was only a bargaining-chip. There was certainly no hope of persuading Yongxing, but so far as the other members of the embassy might be won over, in good faith, he meant to try, and if the effort should tax him in his pride, that was small sacrifice.

It proved worthwhile: Liu Bao crept from his cabin again the next day, looking less wretched, and by the subsequent morning was well enough to send for the translator, and ask Laurence to come over to their side of the deck and join him: some color back in his face, and much relief. He had also brought along one of the cooks: the biscuits, he reported, had worked wonders, taken on his own physician's recommendation with a little fresh ginger, and he was urgent to know how they might be made.

"Well, they are mostly flour and a bit of water, but I cannot tell you anything more, I am afraid," Laurence said. "We do not bake them aboard, you see; but I assure you we have enough in the bread-room to last you twice around the world, sir."

"Once has been more than enough for me," Liu Bao said. "An old man like me has no business going so far away from home and being tossed around on the waves.

Since we came on this ship, I have not been able to eat anything, not even a few pancakes, until those biscuits! But this morning I was able to have some congee and fish, and I was not sick at all. I am very grateful to you."

"I am happy to have been of service, sir; indeed you look much improved," Laurence said.

"That is very polite, even if it is not very truthful," Liu Bao said. He held out his arm ruefully and shook it, the robe hanging rather loose. "I will take some fattening up to look like myself again."

"If you feel equal to it, sir, may I invite you to join us for dinner tomorrow evening?" Laurence asked, thinking this overture, though barely, enough encouragement to justify the invitation. "It is our holiday, and I am giving a dinner for my officers; you would be very welcome, and any of your compatriots who might wish to join you."

This dinner proved far more successful than the last. Granby was still laid up in the sick-berth, forbidden rich food, but Lieutenant Ferris was bent on making the most of his opportunity to impress and in any direction which offered. He was a young officer and energetic, very lately promoted to Temeraire's captain of topmen on account of a fine boarding engagement he had led at Trafalgar. In ordinary course it would have been at least another year and more likely two or three before he could hope to become a second lieutenant in his own right, but with poor Evans sent home, he had stepped into his place as acting-second, and plainly hoped to keep the position.

In the morning, Laurence with some amusement overheard him sternly lecturing the midwingmen on the need to behave in a civilized manner at table, and not sit around like lumps. Laurence suspected that he even primed the junior officers with a handful of anecdotes, as occasionally during the meal he glared significantly at one or the other of the boys, and the target would hastily gulp his wine and start in on a story rather improbable for an officer of such tender years.

Sun Kai accompanied Liu Bao, but as before had the air of an observer rather than a guest. But Liu Bao displayed no similar restraint and had plainly come ready to be pleased, though indeed it would have been a hard man who could have resisted the suckling pig, spit-roasted since that morning and glowing under its glaze of butter and cream. They neither of them disdained a second helping, and Liu Bao was also loud in his approval of the crackling-brown goose, a handsome specimen acquired specially for the occasion at Madeira and still smug and fat at the time of its demise, unlike the usual poultry to be had at sea.

The civil exertions of the officers had an effect also, as stumbling and awkward as some of the younger fellows were about it; Liu Bao had a generous laugh easily provoked, and he shared many amusing stories of his own, mostly about hunting misadventures. Only the poor translator was unhappy, as he had a great deal of work scurrying back and forth around the table, alternately putting English into Chinese and then the reverse; almost from the beginning, the atmosphere was wholly different, and wholly amiable.

Sun Kai remained quiet, listening more than speaking, and Laurence could not be sure he was enjoying himself; he ate still in an abstemious fashion and drank very little, though Liu Bao, himself not at all lacking in capacity, would good-naturedly scold him from time to time, and fill his glass again to the brim. But after the great Christmas pudding was ceremoniously borne out, flickering blue with brandied flames, to shared applause, to be dismantled, served, and enjoyed, Liu Bao turned and said to him, "You are being very dull tonight. Here, sing 'The Hard Road' for us, that is the proper poem for this journey!"

For all his reserve, Sun Kai seemed quite willing to oblige; he cleared his throat and recited:

"Pure wine costs, for the golden bowl, ten thousand
  coppers a flagon,
And a jade platter of dainty food calls for a million
  coins.
I fling aside my bowl and meat, I cannot eat or
  drink . . .
I raise my talons to the sky, I peer four ways in vain.
I would cross the Yellow River, but ice takes hold of
  my limbs;
I would fly above the Tai-hang Mountains, but the
  sky is blind with snow.
I would sit and watch the golden carp, lazy by a
  brook—
But I suddenly dream of crossing the waves, sailing
  for the sun . . .
Journeying is hard,
Journeying is hard.
There are many turnings—
Which am I to follow?
I will mount a long wind some day and break the
  heavy bank of clouds,
And set my wings straight to bridge the wide, wide
  sea."

If there was any rhyme or meter to the piece, it vanished in the translation, but the content the aviators uniformly approved and applauded. "Is it your own work, sir?" Laurence asked with interest. "I do not believe I have ever heard a poem from the view of a dragon."

"No, no," Sun Kai said. "It is one of the works of the honored Lung Li Po, of the Tang Dynasty. I am only a poor scholar, and my verses are not worthy of being shared in company." He was perfectly happy, however, to give them several other selections from classical poets, all recited from memory, in what seemed to Laurence a prodigious feat of recall.

All the guests rolled away at last on the most harmonious of terms, having carefully avoided any discussion of British and Chinese sovereignty regarding either ships or dragons. "I will be so bold as to say it was a success," Laurence said afterwards, sipping coffee upon the dragon-deck while Temeraire ate his sheep. "They are not so very stiff-necked in company, after all, and I can call myself really satisfied with Liu Bao; I have been in many a ship where I should have been grateful to dine with as good company."

"Well, I am glad you had a pleasant evening," Temeraire said, grinding thoughtfully upon the leg bones. "Can you say that poem over again?"

Laurence had to canvass his officers to attempt to reconstruct the poem; they were still at it the next morning, when Yongxing came up to take the air, and listened to them mangling the translation; after they had made a few attempts, he frowned and then turned to Temeraire, and himself recited the poem.

Yongxing spoke in Chinese, without translation; but nevertheless, after a single hearing, Temeraire was able to repeat the verses back to him in the same language, with not the least evidence of difficulty. It was not the first time that Laurence had been surprised by Temeraire's skill with language: like all dragons, Temeraire had learned speech during the long maturity in the shell, but unlike most, he had been exposed to three different tongues, and evidently remembered even what must have been his earliest.

"Laurence," Temeraire said, turning his head towards him with excitement, after exchanging a few more words in Chinese with Yongxing, "he says that it was written by a dragon, not a man at all."

Laurence, still taken aback to find that Temeraire could speak the language, blinked yet again at this intelligence. "Poetry seems an odd sort of occupation for a dragon, but I suppose if other Chinese dragons like books as well as you do, it is not so surprising one of them should have tried his hand at verse."

"I wonder how he wrote it," Temeraire said thoughtfully. "I might like to try, but I do not see how I would ever put it down; I do not think I could hold a pen." He raised his own foreleg and examined the five-fingered claw dubiously.

"I would be happy to take your dictation," Laurence said, amused by the notion. "I expect that is how he managed."

He thought nothing more of it until two days later, when he came back on deck grim and worried after sitting a long while again in the sick-berth: the stubborn fever had recurred, and Granby lay pale and half-present, his blue eyes wide and fixed sightlessly upon the distant recesses of the ceiling, his lips parted and cracked; he took only a little water, and when he spoke his words were confused and wandering. Pollitt would give no opinion, and only shook his head a little.

Ferris was standing anxiously at the bottom of the dragondeck stairs, waiting for him; and at his expression Laurence quickened his still-limping pace. "Sir," Ferris said, "I did not know what to do; he has been talking to Temeraire all morning, and we cannot tell what he is saying."

Laurence hastened up the steps and found Yongxing seated in an armchair on the deck and conversing with Temeraire in Chinese, the prince speaking rather slowly and loudly, enunciating his words, and correcting Temeraire's own speech in return; he had also brought up several sheets of paper, and had painted a handful of their odd-looking characters upon them in large size. Temeraire indeed looked fascinated; his attention was wholly engaged, and the tip of his tail was flicking back and forth in mid-air, as when he was particularly excited.

"Laurence, look, that is 'dragon' in their writing," Temeraire said, catching sight of him and calling him forward: Laurence obediently stared at the picture, rather blankly; to him it looked like nothing more than the patterns sometimes left marked on a sandy shore after a tide, even when Temeraire had pointed out the portion of the symbol which represented the dragon's wings, and then the body.

"Do they only have a single letter for the entire word?" Laurence said, dubiously. "How is it pronounced?"

"It is said *lung*," Temeraire said, "like in my Chinese name, Lung Tien Xiang, and *tien* is for Celestials," he added, proudly, pointing to another symbol.

Yongxing was watching them both, with no very marked outward expression, but Laurence thought perhaps a suggestion of triumph in his eyes. "I am very glad you have been so pleasantly occupied," Laurence said to Temeraire, and, turning to Yongxing, made a deliberate bow, addressing him without invitation. "You are very kind, sir, to take such pains."

Yongxing answered him stiffly, "I consider it a duty. The study of the classics is the path to understanding."

His manner was hardly welcoming, but if he chose to ignore the boundary and speak with Temeraire, Laurence considered it the equivalent of a formal call, and himself justified in initiating conversation. Whether or not Yongxing privately agreed, Laurence's forwardness did not deter him from future visits: every morning now began to find him upon the deck, giving Temeraire daily lessons in the language and offering him further samples of Chinese literature to whet his appetite.

Laurence at first suffered only irritation at these transparent attempts at enticement; Temeraire looked much brighter than he had since parting from Maximus and Lily, and though he might dislike the source, Laurence could not begrudge Temeraire the opportunity for so much new mental occupation, when he was as yet confined to the deck by his wound. As for the notion that Temeraire's loyalty would be swayed by any number of Oriental blandishments, Yongxing might entertain such a belief if he liked; Laurence had no doubts.

But he could not help but feel a rather sinking sensation as the days went on and Temeraire did not tire of the subject; their own books were now often neglected in favor of recitation of one or another piece of Chinese literature, which Temeraire liked to get by rote, as he could not write them down or read them. Laurence was well aware he was nothing like a scholar; his own notion of pleasant occupation was to spend an afternoon in conversation, perhaps writing letters or reading a newspaper when one not excessively out of date could be had. Although under Temeraire's influence he had gradually come to enjoy books far more than he had ever imagined he could, it was a good deal harder to share Temeraire's excitement over works in a language he could not make head or tail of himself.

He did not mean to give Yongxing the satisfaction of seeing him at all discomfited, but it did feel like a victory for the prince at his own expense, particularly on those occasions when Temeraire mastered a new piece and visibly glowed under Yongxing's rare and hard-won praise. Laurence worried, also, that Yongxing seemed almost surprised by Temeraire's progress, and often especially pleased; Laurence naturally thought Temeraire remarkable among dragons, but this was not an opinion he desired Yongxing to share: the prince scarcely needed any additional motive to try and take Temeraire away.

As some consolation, Temeraire was constantly shifting into English, that he might draw Laurence in; and Yongxing had perforce to make polite conversation with him or risk losing what advantage he had gained. But while this might be satisfying in a petty sort of way, Laurence could not be said to *enjoy* these conversations much. Any natural kinship of spirit must have been inadequate in the face of so violent a practical opposition, and they would scarcely have been inclined towards one another in any case.

One morning Yongxing came on deck early, with Temeraire still sleeping; and while his attendants brought out his chair and draped it, and arranged for him the scrolls which he meant to read to Temeraire that day, the prince came to the edge of the deck to gaze out at the ocean. They were in the midst of a lovely stretch of blue-water sailing, no shore in sight and the wind coming fresh and cool off the sea, and Laurence was himself standing in the bows to enjoy the vista: dark water stretching endless to the horizon, occasional little waves overlapping one another in a white froth, and the ship all alone beneath the curving bowl of the sky.

"Only in the desert can one find so desolate and uninteresting a view," Yongxing said abruptly; as Laurence had been on the point of offering a polite remark about the beauty of the scene, he was left dumb and baffled, and still more so when Yongxing added, "You British are forever sailing off to some new place; are you so discontented with your own country?" He did not wait for an answer, but shook his head and turned away, leaving Laurence again confirmed in his belief that he could hardly have found a man less in sympathy with himself on any point.

Temeraire's shipboard diet would ordinarily have been mostly fish, caught by himself; Laurence and Granby had planned on it in their calculations of supply, cattle and sheep intended for variety's sake, and in case of bad weather which might keep Temeraire confined to the ship. But barred from flying because of his wound, Temeraire could not hunt, and so he was consuming their stores at a far more rapid pace than they had originally counted upon.

"We will have to keep close to the Saharan coastline in any case, or risk being blown straight across to Rio by the trade winds," Riley said. "We can certainly stop at Cape Coast to take on supplies." This was meant to console him; Laurence only nodded and went away.

Riley's father had plantations in the West Indies, and several hundred slaves to work them, while Laurence's own father was a firm supporter of Wilberforce and Clarkson, and had made several very cutting speeches in the Lords against the trade, on one occasion even mentioning Riley's father by name in a list of slave-holding gentlemen who, as he had mildly put it, "disgrace the name of Christian, and blight the character and reputation of their country."

The incident had made a coolness between them at the time: Riley was deeply attached to his father, a man of far greater personal warmth than Lord Allendale, and naturally resented the public insult. Laurence, while lacking a particularly strong degree of affection for his own father and angry to be put in so unhappy a position, was yet not at all willing to offer any sort of apology. He had grown up with the pamphlets and books put out by Clarkson's committee all about the house, and at the age of nine had been taken on a tour of a former slave-ship, about to be broken up; the nightmares had lingered afterwards for several months, and made upon his young mind a profound impression. They had never made peace on the subject but only settled into a truce; they neither of them mentioned the subject again, and studiously avoided discussing either parent. Laurence could not now speak frankly to Riley about how very reluctant he was to put in at a slave port, though he was not at all easy in his mind at the prospect.

Instead he privately asked Keynes whether Temeraire was not healing well, and might be permitted short flights again, for hunting. "Best not," the surgeon said, reluctantly; Laurence looked at him sharply, and at last drew from Keynes the admission that he had some concern: the wound was not healing as he would like. "The muscles are still warm to the touch, and I believe I feel some drawn flesh beneath the hide," Keynes said. "It is far too soon to have any real concern; however, I do not intend to take any risks: no flying, for at least another two weeks."

So by this conversation Laurence merely gained one additional source of private care. There were sufficient others already, besides the shortage of food and the now-unavoidable stop at Cape Coast. With Temeraire's injury as well as Yongxing's steadfast opposition precluding any work aloft, the aviators had been left almost entirely idle, while at the same time the sailors had been particularly busy with repairing the damage to the ship and making her stores, and a host of not unpredictable evils had followed.

Thinking to offer Roland and Dyer some distraction, Laurence had called the two of them up to the dragon-deck shortly before the arrival in Madeira, to examine them in their schoolwork. They had stared at him with such guilty expressions that he was not surprised to find they had neglected their studies entirely since having become his runners: very little notion of arithmetic, none at all of the more advanced mathematics, no French whatsoever, and when he handed them Gibbon's book, which he had brought to the deck meaning to read to Temeraire later, Roland stuttered so over the words that Temeraire put back his ruff and began to correct her from memory. Dyer was a little better off: when quizzed, he at least had his multiplication tables mostly by heart, and some sense of grammar; Roland stumbled over anything higher than eight and professed herself surprised to learn that speech even had parts. Laurence no longer wondered how he would fill their time; he only reproached himself for having been so lax about their schooling, and set about his newly self-appointed task as their schoolmaster with a will.

The runners had always been rather pets of the entire crew; since Morgan's death, Roland and Dyer had been cosseted still more. Their daily struggles with participles and division were now looked on by the other aviators with great amusement, but only until the *Allegiance*'s midshipmen made some jeering noises. Then the ensigns took it on themselves to repay the insult, and a few scuffles ensued in dark corners of the ship.

At first, Laurence and Riley entertained themselves by a comparison of the wooden excuses which were offered them for the collection of black eyes and bleeding lips. But the petty squabbling began to take a more ominous shape when older men started to present similar excuses: a deeper resentment on the sailors' part, founded in no small part in the uneven balance of labor and their fear of Temeraire, was finding expression in the near-daily exchange of insults, no longer even touching upon Roland and Dyer's studies. In their turn, the aviators had taken a reciprocal offense at the complete lack of gratitude that seemed to them due to Temeraire's valor.

The first true explosion occurred just as they began to make the turn eastward, past Cape Palmas, and headed towards Cape Coast. Laurence was drowsing on the dragondeck, sheltered by the shadow of Temeraire's body from the direct force of the sun; he did not see himself what had happened, but he was roused by a heavy thump, sudden shouts and cries, and climbing hurriedly to his feet saw the men in a ring. Martin was gripping Blythe, the armorer's mate, by the arm; one of Riley's officers, an older midshipman, was stretched out on the deck, and Lord Purbeck was shouting from the poop deck, "Set that man in irons, Cornell, straightaway."

Temeraire's head came straight up, and he roared: not raising the divine wind, thankfully, but he made a great and thundering noise nonetheless, and the men all scattered back from it, many with pale faces. "No one is putting any of my crew in prison," Temeraire said angrily, his tail lashing the air; he raised himself and spread wide his wings, and the whole ship shivered: the wind was blowing out from the Saharan coast, abaft the beam, the sails close-hauled to keep them on their southeast course, and Temeraire's wings were acting as an independent and contrary sail.

"Temeraire! Stop that at once; at once, do you hear me?" Laurence said sharply; he had never spoken so, not since the first weeks of Temeraire's existence, and Temeraire dropped down in surprise, his wings furling in tight on instinct. "Purbeck, you will leave my men to me, if you please; stand down, master-at-arms," Laurence said, snapping orders quickly: he did not mean to allow the scene to progress further, nor turn into some open struggle between the aviators and seamen. "Mr. Ferris," he said, "take Blythe below and confine him."

"Yes, sir," Ferris said, already shoving through the crowd, and pushing the aviators back around him, breaking up the knots of angry men even before he reached Blythe.

Watching the progress with hard eyes, Laurence added, loudly, "Mr. Martin, to my cabin at once. Back to your work, all of you; Mr. Keynes, come here."

He stayed another moment, but he was satisfied: the pressing danger had been averted. He turned from the rail, trusting to ordinary discipline to break up the rest of the crowd. But Temeraire was huddled down very nearly flat, looking at him with a startled, unhappy expression; Laurence reached out to him and flinched as Temeraire twitched away: not out of reach, but the impulse plainly visible.

"Forgive me," Laurence said, dropping his hand, a tightness in his throat. "Temeraire," he said, and stopped; he did not know what to say, for Temeraire could not be allowed to act so: he might have caused real damage to the ship, and aside from that if he carried on in such a fashion the crew would shortly grow too terrified of him to do their work. "You have not hurt yourself?" he asked, instead, as Keynes hurried over.

"No," Temeraire said, very quietly. "I am perfectly well." He submitted to being examined, in silence, and Keynes pronounced him unharmed by the exertion.

"I must go and speak with Martin," Laurence said, still at a loss; Temeraire did not answer, but curled himself up and swept his wings forward, around his head, and after a long moment, Laurence left the deck and went below.

The cabin was close and hot, even with all the windows standing open, and not calculated to improve Laurence's temper. Martin was pacing the length of the cabin in agitation; he was untidy in a suit of warm-weather slops, his face two days unshaven and presently flushed, his hair too long and flopping over his eyes. He did not recognize the degree of Laurence's real anger, but burst out talking the moment Laurence came in.

"I am so very sorry; it was all my fault. I oughtn't have spoken at all," he said, even while Laurence limped to his chair and sat down heavily. "You cannot punish Blythe, Laurence."

Laurence had grown used to the lack of formality among aviators, and ordinarily did not balk at this liberty in passing, but for Martin to make use of it under the circumstances was so egregious that Laurence sat back and stared at him, outrage plainly written on his face. Martin went pale under his freckled skin, swallowed, and hurriedly said, "I mean, Captain, sir."

"I will do whatever I must to keep order among this crew, Mr. Martin, which appears to be more than I thought necessary," Laurence said, and moderated his volume only with a great effort; he felt truly savage. "You will tell me at once what happened."

"I didn't mean to," Martin said, much subdued. "That fellow Reynolds has been making remarks all week, and Ferris told us to pay him no mind, but I was walking by, and he said—"

"I am not interested in hearing you bear tales," Laurence said. "What did you do?"

"Oh—" Martin said, flushing. "I only said—well, I said something back, which I should rather not repeat; and then he—" Martin stopped, and looked somewhat confused as to how to finish the story without seeming to accuse Reynolds again, and finished lamely, "At any rate, sir, he was on the point of offering me a challenge, and that was when Blythe knocked him down; he only did it because he knew I could not fight, and did not want to see me have to refuse in front of the sailors; truly, sir, it is my fault, and not his."

"I cannot disagree with you in the least," Laurence said, brutally, and was glad in his anger to see Martin's shoulders hunch forward, as if struck. "And when I have to have Blythe flogged on Sunday for striking an officer, I hope you will keep in mind that he is paying for your lack of self-restraint. You are dismissed; you are to keep belowdecks and to your quarters for the week, save when defaulters are called."

Martin's lips worked a moment; his "Yes, sir," emerged only faintly, and he was almost stumbling as he left the room. Laurence sat still breathing harshly, almost panting in the thick air; the anger slowly deserted him in spite of every effort, and gave way to a heavier, bitter oppression. Blythe had saved not only Martin's reputation but that of the aviators as a whole; if Martin had openly refused a challenge made in front of the entire crew, it would have blackened all their characters; no matter that it was forced on them by the regulations of the Corps, which forbade dueling.

And yet there was no room for leniency in the matter whatsoever. Blythe had openly struck an officer before witnesses, and Laurence would have to sentence him to sufficient punishment to give the sailors satisfaction, and all of the men pause against any future capers of the sort. And the punishment would be carried out by the bosun's mate: a sailor, like as not to relish the chance to be severe on an aviator, particularly for such an offense.

He would have to go and speak with Blythe; but a tapping at the door broke in upon him before he could rise, and Riley came in: unsmiling, in his coat and with his hat under his arm, neckcloth freshly tied.

Chapter 7

❦

$\mathcal{T}$HEY DREW NEAR Cape Coast a week later with the atmosphere of ill-will a settled and living thing among them, as palpable as the heat. Blythe had taken ill from his brutal flogging; he still lay nearly senseless in the sick-bay, the other ground-crew hands taking it in turn to sit by him and fan the bloody weals, and to coax him to take some water. They had taken the measure of Laurence's temper, and so their bitterness against the sailors was not expressed in word or direct action, but in sullen, black looks and murmurs, and abrupt silences whenever a sailor came in earshot.

Laurence had not dined in the great cabin since the incident: Riley had been offended at having Purbeck corrected on the deck; Laurence had grown short in turn when Riley refused to unbend and made it plain he was not satisfied by the dozen lashes which were all Laurence would sentence. In the heat of discussion, Laurence had let slip some suggestion of his distaste for going to the slave port, Riley had resented the implication, and they had ended not in shouting but in cold formality.

But worse by far than this, Temeraire's spirits were very low. He had forgiven Laurence the moment of harshness, and been persuaded to understand that some punishment was necessary for the offense. But he had not been at all reconciled to the actual event, and during the flogging he had growled savagely when Blythe had screamed towards the end. Some good had come of that: the bosun's mate Hingley, who had been wielding the cat with more than usual energy, had been alarmed, and the last couple of strokes had been mild; but the damage had already been done.

Temeraire had since remained unhappy and quiet, answering only briefly, and he was not eating well. The sailors, for their part, were as dissatisfied with the light sentence as the aviators were with the brutality; poor Martin, set to tanning hides with the harness-master for punishment, was more wretched with guilt than from his punishment, and spent every spare moment at Blythe's bedside; and the only person at all satisfied with the situation was Yongxing, who seized the opportunity to hold several more long conversations with Temeraire in Chinese: privately, as Temeraire made no effort to include Laurence.

Yongxing looked less pleased, however, at the conclusion of the last of these, when Temeraire hissed, put back his ruff, and then proceeded to all but knock Laurence off his feet in coiling possessively around him. "What has he been saying to you?" Laurence demanded, trying futilely to peer above the great black sides rising around him; he had already reached a state of high irritation at Yongxing's continued interference and was very nearly at the end of his patience.

"He has been telling me about China, and how things are managed there for dragons," Temeraire said, evasively, by which Laurence suspected that Temeraire had liked these described arrangements. "But then he told me I should have a more worthy companion there, and you would be sent away."

By the time he could be persuaded to uncoil himself again, Yongxing had gone, "looking mad as fire," Ferris reported, with glee unbecoming a senior lieutenant.

This scarcely contented Laurence. "I am not going to have Temeraire distressed in this manner," he said to Hammond angrily, trying without success to persuade the diplomat to carry a highly undiplomatic message to the prince.

"You are taking a very short-sighted view of the matter," Hammond said, maddeningly. "If Prince Yongxing can be convinced over the course of this journey that Temeraire will not agree to be parted from you, all the better for us: they will be far more ready to negotiate when finally we arrive in China." He paused and asked, with still more infuriating anxiousness, "You are quite certain, that he will not agree?"

On hearing the account that evening, Granby said, "I say we heave Hammond and Yongxing over the side together some dark night, and good riddance," expressing Laurence's private sentiments more frankly than Laurence himself felt he could. Granby was speaking, with no regard for manners, between bites of a light meal of soup, toasted cheese, potatoes fried in pork fat with onions, an entire roast chicken, and a mince pie: he had finally been released from his sickbed, pallid and much reduced in weight, and Laurence had invited him to supper. "What else was that prince saying to him?"

"I have not the least idea; he has not said three words together in English the last week," Laurence said. "And I do not mean to press Temeraire to tell me; it would be the most officious, prying sort of behavior."

"That none of his friends should ever be flogged there, I expect," Granby said, darkly. "And that he should have a dozen books to read every day, and heaps of jewels. I have heard stories about this sort of thing, but if a fellow ever really tried it, they would drum him out of the Corps quick as lightning; if the dragon did not carve him into joints, first."

Laurence was silent a moment, twisting his wineglass

in his fingers. "Temeraire is only listening to it at all because he is unhappy."

"Oh, Hell." Granby sat back heavily. "I am damned sorry I have been sick so long; Ferris is a right'un, but he hasn't been on a transport before, he couldn't know how the sailors get, and how to properly teach the fellows to take no notice," he said glumly. "And I can't give you any advice for cheering him up; I served with Laetificat longest, and she is easy-going even for a Regal Copper: no temper to speak of, and no mood I ever saw could dampen her appetite. Maybe it is not being allowed to fly."

They came into the harbor the next morning: a broad semicircle with a golden beach, dotted with attractive palms under the squat white walls of the overlooking castle. A multitude of rough canoes, many with branches still attached to the trunks from which they had been hollowed, were plying the waters of the harbor, and besides these there could be seen an assortment of brigs and schooners, and at the western end a snow of middling size, with her boats swarming back and forth, crowded with blacks who were being herded along from a tunnel mouth that came out onto the beach itself.

The *Allegiance* was too large to come into the harbor proper, but she had anchored close enough; the day was calm, and the cracking of the whips perfectly audible over the water, mingled with cries and the steady sound of weeping. Laurence came frowning onto the deck and ordered Roland and Dyer away from their wide-eyed staring, sending them below to tidy his cabin. Temeraire could not be protected in the same manner, and was observing the proceedings with some confusion, the slitted pupils of his eyes widening and narrowing as he stared.

"Laurence, those men are all in chains; what can so many of them have done?" he demanded, roused from his apathy. "They cannot all have committed crimes; look, that one over there is a small child, and there is another."

"No," Laurence said. "That is a slaver; pray do not watch." Fearing this moment, he had made a vague attempt at explaining the idea of slavery to Temeraire, with his lack of success due as much to his own distaste as to Temeraire's difficulty with the notion of property. Temeraire did not listen now, but kept watching, his tail switching rapidly in anxiety. The loading of the vessel continued throughout the morning, and the hot wind blowing from the shore carried the sour smell of unwashed bodies, sweating and ill with misery.

At length the boarding was finished, and the snow with her unhappy cargo came out of the harbor and spread her sails to the wind, throwing up a fine furrow as she went past them, already moving at a steady pace, sailors scrambling in the rigging; but full half her crew were only armed landsmen, sitting idly about on deck with their muskets and pistols and mugs of grog. They stared openly at Temeraire, curious, their faces unsmiling, sweating and grimy from the work; one of them even picked up his gun and sighted along it at Temeraire, as if for sport. "Present arms!" Lieutenant Riggs snapped, before Laurence could even react, and the three riflemen on deck had their guns ready in an instant; across the water, the fellow lowered his musket and grinned, showing strong yellowed teeth, and turned back to his shipmates laughing.

Temeraire's ruff was flattened, not out of any fear, as a musket-ball fired at such a range would have done him less injury than a mosquito to a man, but with great distaste. He gave a low rumbling growl and almost drew a deep preparatory breath; Laurence laid a hand on his side, quietly said, "No; it can do no good," and stayed with him until at last the snow shrank away over the horizon, and passed out of their sight.

Even after she had gone, Temeraire's tail continued to flick unhappily back and forth. "No, I am not hungry," he said, when Laurence suggested some food, and stayed very quiet again, occasionally scraping at the deck with his claws, unconsciously, making a dreadful grating noise.

Riley was at the far end of the ship, walking the poop deck, but there were many sailors in earshot, getting the launch and the officers' barge over the side, preparing to begin the process of supply, and Lord Purbeck was overseeing; in any case one could not say anything on deck in full voice and not expect it to have traveled to the other end and back in less time than it would take to walk the distance. Laurence was conscious of the plain rudeness of seeming to criticize Riley on the deck of his own ship, even without the quarrel already lingering between them, but at last he could not forbear.

"Pray do not be so distressed," he said, trying to console Temeraire, without going so far as to speak too bluntly against the practice. "There is reason to hope that the trade will soon be stopped; the question will come before Parliament again this very session."

Temeraire brightened perceptibly at the news, but he was unsatisfied with so bare an explanation and proceeded to inquire with great energy into the prospects of abolition; Laurence perforce had to explain Parliament and the distinction between the Commons and the Lords and the various factions engaged in the debate, relying for his particulars on his father's activities, but aware all the while that he was overheard and trying as best he could to be politic.

Even Sun Kai, who had been on deck the whole morning, and seen the progress of the snow and its effects on Temeraire's mood, gazed upon him thoughtfully, evidently guessing at some of the conversation; he had come as near as he could without crossing the painted border, and during a break, he asked Temeraire to translate for him. Temeraire explained a little; Sun Kai nodded, and then inquired of Laurence, "Your father is an official then, and feels this practice dishonorable?"

Such a question, put baldly, could not be evaded however much it might offend; silence would be very nearly dishonest. "Yes, sir, he does," Laurence said, and before Sun Kai could prolong the conversation with further inquiries, Keynes came up to the deck; Laurence hailed him to ask him for permission to take Temeraire on a short flight to shore, and so was able to cut short the discussion. Even so abbreviated, however, it did no good for relations aboard ship; the sailors, mostly without strong opinions on the subject, naturally took their own captain's part, and felt Riley ill-used by the open expression of such sentiments on his ship when his own family connections to the trade were known.

The post was rowed back shortly before the hands' dinner-time, and Lord Purbeck chose to send the young midshipman Reynolds, who had set off the recent quarrel, to bring over the letters for the aviators: nearly a piece of deliberate provocation. The boy himself, his eye still blacked from Blythe's powerful blow, smirked so insolently that Laurence instantly resolved on ending Martin's punishment duty, nearly a week before he had otherwise intended, and said quite deliberately, "Temeraire, look; we have a letter from Captain Roland; it will have news of Dover, I am sure." Temeraire obligingly put his head down to inspect the letter; the ominous shadow of the ruff and the serrated teeth gleaming so nearby made a profound impression on Reynolds: the smirk vanished, and almost as quickly so did he himself, hastily retreating from the dragondeck.

Laurence stayed on deck to read the letters with Temeraire. Jane Roland's letter, scarcely a page long, had been sent only a few days after their departure and had very little news, only a cheerful account of the life of the covert; heartening to read, even if it left Temeraire sighing a little for home, and Laurence with much the same sentiments. He was a little puzzled, however, at receiving no other letters from his colleagues; since a courier had come through, he had expected to have something from Harcourt, at least, whom he knew to be a good correspondent, and perhaps one of the other captains.

He did have one more letter, from his mother, which had been forwarded on from Dover. Aviators received their mail quicker than anyone else, post-dragons making their rounds from covert to covert, whence the mail went out by horse and rider, and she had evidently written and sent it before receiving Laurence's own letter informing her of their departure.

He opened it and read most of it aloud for Temeraire's entertainment: she wrote mainly of his oldest brother, George, who had just added a daughter to his three sons, and his father's political work, as being one of the few subjects on which Laurence and Lord Allendale were in sympathy, and which now was of fresh interest to Temeraire as well. Midway, however, Laurence abruptly stopped, as he read to himself a few lines which she had made in passing, which explained the unexpected silence of his fellow-officers:

Naturally we were all very much shocked by the dreadful news of the Disaster in Austria, and they say that Mr. Pitt has taken ill, which of course much grieves your Father, as the Prime Minister has always been a Friend to the Cause. I am afraid I hear much talk in town of how Providence is favoring Bonaparte. It does seem strange that one man should make so great a difference in the course of War, when on both sides numbers are equal. But it is shameful in the extreme, how quickly Lord Nelson's great victory at Trafalgar is Forgot, and your own noble defense of our shores, and men of less resolution begin to speak of peace with the Tyrant.

She had of course written expecting him to be still at Dover, where news from the Continent came first, and where he would have long since heard all there was to know; instead it came as a highly unpleasant shock, particularly as she gave no further particulars. He had heard reports in Madeira of several battles fought in Austria, but nothing so decisive. At once he begged Temeraire to forgive him and hastened below to Riley's cabin, hoping there might be more news, and indeed found Riley numbly reading an express dispatch which Hammond had just given him, received from the Ministry.

"He has smashed them all to pieces, outside Austerlitz," Hammond said, and they searched out the place on Riley's maps: a small town deep in Austria, northeast of Vienna. "I have not been told a great deal, Government is reserving the particulars, but he has taken at least thirty thousand men dead, wounded, or prisoner; the Russians are fleeing, and the Austrians have signed an armistice already."

These spare facts were grim enough without elaboration, and they all fell silent together, looking over the few lines of the message, which disobligingly refused to offer more information regardless of the number of times they were re-read. "Well," Hammond said finally, "we will just have to starve him out. Thank God for Nelson and Trafalgar! And he cannot mean to invade by air again, not with three Longwings stationed in the Channel now."

"Ought we not return?" Laurence ventured, awkwardly; it seemed so self-serving a proposal he felt guilty in making it, and yet he could not imagine they were not badly needed, back in Britain. Excidium, Mortiferus, and Lily with their formations were indeed a deadly force to be reckoned with, but three dragons could not be everywhere, and Napoleon had before this found means of drawing one or the other away.

"I have received no orders to turn back," Riley said, "though I will say it does feel damned peculiar to be sailing on to China devil-may-care after news like this, with a hundred-and-fifty-gun ship and a heavy-combat dragon."

"Gentlemen, you are in error," Hammond said sharply. "This disaster only renders our mission all the more urgent. If Napoleon is to be beaten, if our nation is to preserve a place as anything more besides an inconsequential island off the coast of a French Europe, only trade will do it. The Austrians may have been beaten for the moment, and the Russians; but so long as we can supply our Continental allies with funds and with resources, you may be sure they will resist Bonaparte's tyranny. We *must* continue on; we must secure at least neutrality from China, if not some advantage, and protect our Eastern trade; no military goal could be of greater significance."

He spoke with great authority, and Riley nodded in quick agreement. Laurence was silent as they began to discuss how they might speed the journey, and shortly he excused himself to return to the dragondeck; he could not argue, he was not impartial by any means, and Hammond's arguments had a great deal of weight; but he was not satisfied, and he felt an uneasy distress at the lack of sympathy between their thinking and his own.

"I cannot understand how they let Napoleon beat them," Temeraire said, ruff bristling, when Laurence had broken the unhappy news to him and his senior officers. "He had more ships and dragons than we did, at Trafalgar and at Dover, and we still won; and this time the Austrians and the Russians outnumbered him."

"Trafalgar was a sea-battle," Laurence said. "Bonaparte has never really understood the navy; he is an artillery-man himself by training. And the battle of Dover we won only thanks to you; otherwise I dare say Bonaparte would be having himself crowned in Westminster directly. Do not forget how he managed to trick us into sending the better part of the Channel forces south and concealed the movements of his own dragons, before the invasion; if he had not been taken by surprise by the divine wind, the outcome could have been quite different."

"It still does not seem to me that the battle was cleverly managed," Temeraire said, dissatisfied. "I am sure if we had been there, with our friends, we should not have lost, and I do not see why we are going to China when other people are fighting."

"I call that a damned good question," Granby said. "A great pack of nonsense to begin with, giving away one of our very best dragons in the middle of a war when we are so desperate hard-up to begin with; Laurence, oughtn't we go home?"

Laurence only shook his head; he was too much in agreement, and too powerless to make any alteration. Temeraire and the divine wind *had* changed the course of the war, at Dover. As little as the Ministry might like to admit it, or give credit for a victory to so narrow a cause, Laurence too well remembered the hopeless uneven struggle of that day before Temeraire had turned the tide. To be meekly surrendering Temeraire and his extraordinary abilities seemed to Laurence a willful blindness, and he did not believe the Chinese would yield to any of Hammond's requests at all.

But "We have our orders" was all he said; even if Riley and Hammond had been of like mind with him, Laurence knew very well this would scarcely be accepted by the Ministry as even a thin excuse for violating their standing orders. "I am sorry," he added, seeing that Temeraire was inclined to be unhappy, "but come; here is Mr. Keynes, to see if you can be allowed to take some exercise on shore; let us clear away and let him make his examination."

"Truly it does not pain me at all," Temeraire said anxiously, peering down at himself as Keynes at last stepped back from his chest. "I am sure I am ready to fly again, and I will only go a short way."

Keynes shook his head. "Another week perhaps. No; do not set up a howl at me," he said sternly, as Temeraire sat up to protest. "It is not a question of the length of the flight; launching is the difficulty," he added, to Laurence, by way of grudging explanation. "The strain of getting aloft will be the most dangerous moment, and I am not confident the muscles are yet prepared to bear it."

"But I am so very tired of only lying on deck," Temeraire said disconsolately, almost a wail. "I cannot even turn around properly."

"It will only be another week, and perhaps less," Laurence said, trying to comfort him; he was already regretting that he had ever made the proposal and raised Temeraire's hopes only to see them dashed. "I am very sorry; but Mr. Keynes's opinion is worth more than either of ours on the subject, and we had better listen to him."

Temeraire was not so easily appeased. "I do not see why his opinion should be worth more than mine. It is my muscle, after all."

Keynes folded his arms and said coolly, "I am not going to argue with a patient. If you want to do yourself an injury and spend another two months lying about instead, by all means go jumping about as much as you like."

Temeraire snorted back at this reply, and Laurence, annoyed, hurried to dismiss Keynes before the surgeon could be any more provoking: he had every confidence in the man's skill, but his tact could have stood much improvement, and though Temeraire was by no means contrary by nature, this was a hard disappointment to bear.

"I have a little better news, at least," he told Temeraire, trying to rally his spirits. "Mr. Pollitt was kind enough to bring me several new books from his visit ashore; shall I not fetch one now?"

Temeraire made only a grumble for answer, head unhappily drooping over the edge of the ship and gazing towards the denied shore. Laurence went down for the book, hoping that the interest of the material would rouse him, but while he was still in his cabin, the ship abruptly rocked, and an enormous splash outside sent water flying in through the opened round windows and onto the floor; Laurence ran to look through the nearest porthole, hastily rescuing his dampened letters, and saw Temeraire, with an expression at once guilty and self-satisfied, bobbing up and down in the water.

He dashed back up to the deck; Granby and Ferris were peering over the side in alarm, and the small boats that had been crowding around the sides of the ship, full of whores and enterprising fishermen, were already making frantic haste away and back to the security of the harbor, with much shrieking and splashing of oars. Temeraire rather abashedly looked after them in dismay. "I did not mean to frighten them," he said. "There is no need to run away," he called, but the boats did not pause for an instant. The sailors, deprived of their entertainments, glared disapprovingly; Laurence was more concerned for Temeraire's health.

"Well, I have never seen anything so ridiculous in my life, but it is not likely to hurt him. The air-sacs will keep him afloat, and salt water never hurt a wound," Keynes said, having been summoned back to the deck. "But how we will ever get him back aboard, I have not the least idea."

Temeraire plunged for a moment under the surface

and came almost shooting up again, propelled by his buoyancy. "It is very pleasant," he called out. "The water is not cold at all, Laurence; will you not come in?"

Laurence was by no means a strong swimmer, and uneasy at the notion of leaping into the open ocean: they were a good mile out from the shore. But he took one of the ship's small boats and rowed himself out, to keep Temeraire company and to be sure the dragon did not overtire himself after so much enforced idleness on deck. The skiff was tossed about a little by the waves resulting from Temeraire's frolics, and occasionally swamped, but Laurence had prudently worn only an old pair of breeches and his most threadbare shirt.

His own spirits were very low; the defeat at Austerlitz was not merely a single battle lost, but the overthrow of Prime Minister Pitt's whole careful design, and the destruction of the coalition assembled to stop Napoleon: Britain alone could not field an army half so large as Napoleon's Grande Armée, nor easily land it on the Continent, and with the Austrians and Russians now driven from the field, their situation was plainly grim. Even with such cares, however, he could not help but smile to see Temeraire so full of energy and uncomplicated joy, and after a little while he even yielded to Temeraire's coaxing and let himself over the side. Laurence did not swim very long but soon climbed up onto Temeraire's back, while Temeraire paddled himself about enthusiastically, and nosed the skiff about as a sort of toy.

He might shut his eyes and imagine them back in Dover, or at Loch Laggan, with only the ordinary cares of war to burden them, and work to be done which he understood, with all the confidence of friendship and a nation united behind them; even the present disaster hardly insurmountable, in such a situation: the *Allegiance* only another ship in the harbor, their familiar clearing a short flight away, and no politicians and princes to trouble with. He lay back and spread his hand open against the warm side, the black scales warmed by the sun, and for a little while indulged the fancy enough to drowse.

"Do you suppose you will be able to climb back aboard the *Allegiance*?" Laurence said presently; he had been worrying the problem in his head.

Temeraire craned his head around to look at him. "Could we not wait here on shore until I am well again, and rejoin the ship after?" he suggested. "Or," and his ruff quivered with sudden excitement, "we might fly across the continent, and meet them on the opposite side: there are no people in the middle of Africa, I remember from your maps, so there cannot be any French to shoot us down."

"No, but by report there are a great many feral dragons, not to mention any number of other dangerous creatures, and the perils of disease," Laurence said. "We cannot go flying over the uncharted interior, Temeraire; the risk cannot be justified, particularly not now."

Temeraire sighed a little at giving up this ambitious project, but agreed to make the attempt to climb up onto the deck; after a little more play he swam back over to the ship, and rather bemused the waiting sailors by handing the skiff up to them, so they did not have to haul her back aboard. Laurence, having climbed up the side from Temeraire's shoulder, held a huddled conference with Riley. "Perhaps if we let the starboard sheet anchor down as a counterweight?" he suggested. "That with the best bower ought to keep her steady, and she is already loaded heavy towards the stern."

"Laurence, what the Admiralty will say to me if I get a transport sunk on a clear blue day in harbor, I should not like to think," Riley said, unhappy at the notion. "I dare say I should be hanged, and deserve it, too."

"If there is any danger of capsizing, he can always let go in an instant," Laurence said. "Otherwise we must sit in port a week at least, until Keynes is willing to grant him leave to fly again."

"I am not going to sink the ship," Temeraire said indignantly, poking his head up over the quarterdeck rail and entering into the conversation, much to Riley's startlement. "I will be very careful."

Though Riley was still dubious, he finally gave leave. Temeraire managed to rear up out of the water and get a grip with his foreclaws on the ship's side; the *Allegiance* listed towards him, but not too badly, held by the two anchors, and having raised his wings out of the water, Temeraire beat them a couple of times, and half-leapt, half-scrambled up the side of the ship.

He fell heavily onto the deck without much grace, hind legs scrabbling for an undignified moment, but he indeed got aboard, and the *Allegiance* did not do more than bounce a little beneath him. He hastily settled his legs underneath him again and busied himself shaking water off his ruff and long tendrils, pretending he had not been clumsy. "It was not very difficult to climb back on at all," he said to Laurence, pleased. "Now I can swim every day until I can fly again."

Laurence wondered how Riley and the sailors would receive this news, but was unable to feel much dismay; he would have suffered far more than black looks to see Temeraire's spirits so restored; and when he presently suggested something to eat, Temeraire gladly assented, and devoured two cows and a sheep down to the hooves.

When Yongxing once again ventured to the deck the following morning, he thus found Temeraire in good humor: fresh from another swim, well-fed, and highly pleased with himself. He had clambered aboard much more gracefully this second time, though Lord Purbeck at least found something to complain of, in the scratches to the ship's paint, and the sailors were still unhappy at having the bumboats frightened off. Yongxing himself benefited, as Temeraire was in a forgiving mood and disinclined to hold even what Laurence considered a well-deserved grudge, but the prince did not look at all satisfied; he spent the morning visit watching silently and brooding as Laurence read to Temeraire out of the new books procured by Mr. Pollitt on his visit ashore.

Yongxing soon left again; and shortly thereafter, his servant Feng Li came up to the deck to ask Laurence below, making clear his meaning through gestures and pantomime, Temeraire having settled down to nap through the heat of the day. Unwilling and wary, Laurence insisted on first going to his quarters to dress: he was again in shabby clothes, having accompanied Temeraire on his swim, and did not feel prepared to face Yongxing in his austere and elegant apartment without the armor of his dress coat and best trousers, and a fresh-pressed neckcloth.

There was no theater about his arrival, this time; he was ushered in at once, and Yongxing sent even Feng Li away, that they might be private, but he did not speak at once and only stood in silence, hands clasped behind his back, gazing frowningly out the stern windows: then, as Laurence was on the point of speaking, he abruptly turned and said, "You have sincere affection for Lung Tien Xiang, and he for you; this I have come to see. Yet in your country, he is treated like an animal, exposed to all the dangers of war. Can you desire this fate for him?"

Laurence was much astonished at meeting so direct an appeal, and supposed Hammond proven right: there could be no explanation for this change but a growing conviction in Yongxing's mind of the futility of luring Temeraire away. But as pleased as he would otherwise have been to see Yongxing give up his attempts to divide them from one another, Laurence grew only more uneasy: there was plainly no common ground to be had between them, and he did not feel he understood Yongxing's motives for seeking to find any.

"Sir," he said, after a moment, "your accusations of ill-treatment I must dispute; and the dangers of war are the common hazard of those who take service for their country. Your Highness can scarcely expect me to find such a choice, willingly made, objectionable; I myself have so chosen, and such risks I hold it an honor to endure."

"Yet you are a man of ordinary birth, and a soldier of no great rank; there may be ten thousand men such as you in England," Yongxing said. "You cannot compare yourself to a Celestial. Consider his happiness, and listen to my request. Help us restore him to his rightful place, and then part from him cheerfully: let him think you are not sorry to go, that he may forget you more easily, and find happiness with a companion appropriate to his station. Surely it is your duty not to hold him down to your own level, but to see him brought up to all the advantages which are his right."

Yongxing made these remarks not in an insulting tone, but as stating plain fact, almost earnestly. "I do not believe in that species of kindness, sir, which consists in lying to a loved one, and deceiving him for his own good," Laurence said, as yet unsure whether he ought to be offended, or to view this as some attempt to appeal to his better nature.

But his confusion was sharply dispelled in another moment, as Yongxing persisted: "I know that what I ask is a great sacrifice. Perhaps the hopes of your family will be disappointed; and you were given a great reward for bringing him to your country, which may now be confiscated. We do not expect you to face ruin: do as I ask, and you will receive ten thousand taels of silver, and the gratitude of the Emperor."

Laurence stared first, then flushed to an ugly shade of

mortification, and said, when he had mastered himself well enough to speak, with bitter resentment, "A noble sum indeed; but there is not silver enough in China, sir, to buy me."

He would have turned to go at once; but Yongxing said in real exasperation, this refusal at last driving him past the careful façade of patience which he had so far maintained throughout the interview, "You are foolish; you *cannot* be permitted to remain companion to Lung Tien Xiang, and in the end you will be sent home. Why not accept my offer?"

"That you may separate us by force, in your own country, I have no doubt," Laurence said. "But that will be *your* doing, and none of mine; and he shall know me faithful as he is himself, to the last." He meant to leave; he could not challenge Yongxing, nor strike him, and only such a gesture could have begun to satisfy his deep and violent sense of injury; but so excellent an invitation to quarrel at least gave his anger some vent, and he added with all the scorn which he could give the words, "Save yourself the trouble of any further cajolery; all your bribes and machinations you may be sure will meet with equal failure, and I have too much faith in Temeraire to imagine that he will ever be persuaded to prefer a nation where discourse such as this is the *civilized* mode."

"You speak in ignorant disdain of the foremost nation of the world," Yongxing said, growing angry himself, "like all your country-men, who show no respect for that which is superior, and insult our customs."

"For which I might consider myself as owing you some apology, sir, if you yourself had not so often insulted myself and my own country, or shown respect for any customs other than your own," Laurence said.

"We do not desire anything that is yours, or to come

and force our ways upon you," Yongxing said. "From your small island you come to our country, and out of kindness you are allowed to buy our tea and silk and porcelain, which you so passionately desire. But still you are not content; you forever demand more and more, while your missionaries try to spread your foreign religion and your merchants smuggle opium in defiance of the law. *We* do not need your trinkets, your clockworks and lamps and guns; our land is sufficient unto itself. In so unequal a position, you should show threefold gratitude and submission to the Emperor, and instead you offer one insult heaped on another. Too long already has this disrespect been tolerated."

These arrayed grievances, so far beyond the matter at hand, were spoken passionately and with great energy; more sincere than anything Laurence had formerly heard from the prince and more unguarded, and the surprise he could not help but display evidently recalled Yongxing to his circumstances, and checked his flow of speech. For a moment they stood in silence, Laurence still resentful, and as unable to form a reply as if Yongxing had spoken in his native tongue, baffled entirely by a description of the relations between their countries which should lump Christian missionaries together in with smugglers and so absurdly refuse to acknowledge the benefits of free and open trade to both parties.

"I am no politician, sir, to dispute with you upon matters of foreign policy," Laurence said at last, "but the honor and dignities of my nation and my country-men I will defend to my last breath; and you will not move me with any argument to act dishonorably, least of all to Temeraire."

Yongxing had recovered his composure, yet looked still intensely dissatisfied; now he shook his head, frowning. "If you will not be persuaded by consideration for

Lung Tien Xiang or for yourself, will you at least serve your country's interests?" With deep and evident reluctance he added, "That we should open ports to you, besides Canton, cannot be considered; but we will permit your ambassador to remain in Peking, as you so greatly desire, and we will agree not to go to war against you or your allies, so long as you maintain a respectful obedience to the Emperor: this much can be allowed, if you will ease Lung Tien Xiang's return."

He ended expectantly; Laurence stood motionless, breathtaken, white; and then he said, "No," almost inaudibly, and without staying to hear another word turned and left the room, thrusting the drapery from his way.

He went blindly to the deck and found Temeraire sleeping, peaceful, tail curled around himself; Laurence did not touch him but sat down on one of the lockers by the edge of the deck and bowed his head down, that he should not meet anyone's eyes; his hands clasped, that they should not be seen to shake.

"You refused, I hope?" Hammond said, wholly unexpectedly; Laurence, who had steeled himself to face a furious reproach, was left staring. "Thank Heaven; it had not occurred to me that he might attempt a direct approach, and so soon. I must beg you, Captain, to be sure and not commit us to any proposal whatsoever, without private consultation with me, no matter how appealing it may seem. Either here or after we have reached China," he added, as an afterthought. "Now pray tell me again: he offered a promise of neutrality, and a permanent envoy in Peking, outright?"

There was a quick predatory gleam in his expression, and Laurence was put to dredging the details of the conversation from his memory in answer to his many questions. "But I am sure that I do not misremember; he was quite firm that no other ports should ever be opened," Laurence protested, when Hammond had begun dragging over his maps of China and speculating aloud which might be the most advantageous, inquiring of Laurence which harbors he thought best for shipping.

"Yes, yes," Hammond said, waving this aside. "But if *he* may be brought so far as to admit the possibility of a permanent envoy, how much more progress may we not hope to make? You must be aware that his own opinions are fixed quite immovably against all intercourse with the West."

"I am," Laurence said; he was more surprised to find Hammond so aware, given the diplomat's continuing efforts to establish good relations.

"Our chances of winning Prince Yongxing himself over are small, though I hope we do make some progress," Hammond said, "but I find it most encouraging indeed that he should be so anxious to obtain your cooperation at such a stage. Plainly he wishes to arrive in China *fait accompli,* which should only be the case if he imagines the Emperor may be persuaded to grant us terms less pleasing to himself.

"He is not the heir to the throne, you know," Hammond added, seeing Laurence look doubtful. "The Emperor has three sons, and the eldest, Prince Mianning, is grown already and the presumptive crown prince. Not that Prince Yongxing lacks in influence, certainly, or he would never have been given so much autonomy as to be sent to England, but this very attempt on his part gives me hope there may yet be more opportunity than we heretofore have realized. If only—"

Here he grew abruptly dismal, and sat down again with the charts neglected. "If only the French have not already established themselves with the more liberal minds of the court," he finished, low. "But that would explain a great deal, I am afraid, and in particular why they were ever given the egg. I could tear my hair over it; here they have managed to thoroughly insinuate themselves, I suppose, while we have been sitting about congratulating ourselves on our precious dignity ever since Lord Macartney was sent packing, and making no real attempt to restore relations."

Laurence left feeling very little less guilt and unhappiness than before; his refusal, he was well aware, had not been motivated by any such rational and admirable arguments, but a wholly reflexive denial. He would certainly never agree to lie to Temeraire, as Yongxing had proposed, nor abandon him to any unpleasant or barbaric situation, but Hammond might make other demands, less easy to refuse. If they were ordered to separate to ensure a truly advantageous treaty, it would be his own duty not only to go, but to convince Temeraire to obey, however unwillingly. Before now, he had consoled himself in the belief that the Chinese would offer no satisfactory terms; this illusory comfort was now stripped away, and all the misery of separation loomed closer with every sea-mile.

Two days later saw them leaving Cape Coast, gladly for Laurence's part. The morning of their departure, a party of slaves had been brought in overland and were being driven into the waiting dungeons within sight of the ship. An even more dreadful scene ensued, for the slaves had not yet been worn down by long confinement nor become resigned to their fate, and as the cellar doors were opened to receive them, very much like the mouth of a waiting grave, several of the younger men staged a revolt.

They had evidently found some means of getting loose along their journey. Two of the guards went down at once, bludgeoned with the very chains that had bound the slaves, and the others began to stumble back and away, firing indiscriminately in their panic. A troop of guards came running down from their posts, adding to the general melee.

It was a hopeless attempt, if gallant, and most of the loosed men saw the inevitable and dashed for their personal freedom; some scrambled down the beach, others fled into the city. The guards managed to cow the remaining bound slaves again, and started shooting at the escaping ones. Most were killed before they were out of sight, and search parties organized immediately to find the remainder, marked as they were by their nakedness and the galls from their former chains. The dirt road leading to the dungeons was muddy with blood, the small and huddled corpses lying terribly still among the living; many women and children had been killed in the action. The slavers were already forcing the remaining men and women down into the cellar, and setting some of the others to drag the bodies away. Not fifteen minutes had gone by.

There was no singing or shouting as the anchor was hauled up, and the operation went more slowly than usual; but even so the bosun, ordinarily vigorous at any sign of malingering, did not start anyone with his cane. The day was again stickily humid, and so hot that the tar grew liquid and fell in great black splotches from the rigging, some even landing upon Temeraire's hide, much to his disgust. Laurence set the runners and the ensigns on watch with buckets and rags, to clean him off as the drops fell, and by the end of the day they were all drooping and filthy themselves.

The next day only more of the same, and the three after that; the shore tangled and impenetrable to larboard, broken only by cliffs and jumbled rockfalls, and a constant attention necessary to keep the ship at a safe distance in deep water, with the winds freakish and variable so close to land. The men went about their work silent and unsmiling in the heat of the day; the evil news of Austerlitz had spread among them.

Chapter 8

❧

$\mathscr{B}$LYTHE AT LAST emerged from the sick-berth, much reduced, mostly to sit and doze in a chair on the deck: Martin was especially solicitous for his comfort, and apt to speak sharply to anyone who so much as jostled the makeshift awning they had rigged over him. Blythe could scarcely cough but a glass of grog was put in his hand; he could not speak slightingly of the weather but he would be offered, as appropriate, a rug, an oil-skin, a cool cloth.

"I'm sorry he's taken it so to heart, sir," Blythe told Laurence helplessly. "I don't suppose any high-spirited fellow could have stood it kindly, the way them tars were going on, and no fault of his, I'm sure. I wish he wouldn't take on so."

The sailors were not pleased to see the offender so cosseted, and by way of answer made much of their fellow Reynolds, already inclined to put on a martyr's airs. In ordinary course he was only an indifferent seaman, and the new degree of respect he was receiving from his company went to his head. He strutted about the deck like cock-robin, giving unnecessary orders for the pleasure of seeing them followed with such excess of bows, and nods, and forelock-pulling; even Purbeck and Riley did not much check him.

Laurence had hoped that at least the shared disaster of

Austerlitz might mute the hostility between the sailors and the aviators; but this display kept tempers on both sides at an elevated pitch. The *Allegiance* was now drawing close to the equatorial line, and Laurence thought it necessary to make special arrangements for managing the usual crossing ceremony. Less than half of the aviators had ever crossed the line before, and if the sailors were given license to dunk and shave the lot of them under the present mood, Laurence did not think order could possibly be maintained. He consulted with Riley, and the agreement was reached that he would offer a general tithe on behalf of his men, namely three casks of rum which he had taken the precaution of acquiring in Cape Coast; the aviators would therefore be universally excused.

All the sailors were disgruntled by the alteration in their tradition, several going so far as to speak of bad luck to the ship as a consequence; undoubtedly many of them had privately been looking forward to the opportunity to humiliate their shipboard rivals. As a result, when at last they crossed the equator and the usual pageant came aboard, it was rather quiet and unenthusiastic. Temeraire at least was entertained, though Laurence had to shush him hastily when he said, very audibly, "But Laurence, that is not Neptune at all; that is Griggs, and Amphitrite is Boyne," recognizing the seamen through their shabby costumes, which they had not taken much trouble to make effective.

This produced a good deal of imperfectly suppressed hilarity among the crew, and Badger-Bag—the carpenter's mate Leddowes, less recognizable under a scruffy mop-head for a judicial wig—had a fit of inspiration and declared that this time, all those who allowed laughter to escape should be Neptune's victims. Laurence gave Riley a quick nod, and Leddowes was given a free hand among both sailors and aviators. Fair numbers of each were seized, all the rest applauding, and to cap the occasion Riley sang out, "An extra ration of grog for all, thanks to the toll paid by Captain Laurence's crew," producing an enthusiastic cheer.

Some of the hands got up a set of music, and another of dancing; the rum worked its effect and soon even the aviators were clapping along, and humming the music to the shanties, though they did not know the words. It was perhaps not as wholeheartedly cheerful as some crossings, but much better than Laurence had feared.

The Chinese had come on deck for the event, though naturally not subjected to the ritual, and watched with much discussion amongst themselves. It was of course a rather vulgar kind of entertainment, and Laurence felt some embarrassment at having Yongxing witness it, but Liu Bao thumped his thigh in applause along with the entire crew, and let out a tremendous, booming laugh for each of Badger-Bag's victims. He at length turned to Temeraire, across the boundary, and asked him a question: "Laurence, he would like to know what the purpose of the ceremony is, and which spirits are being honored," Temeraire said. "But I do not know myself; what are we celebrating, and why?"

"Oh," Laurence said, wondering how to explain the rather ridiculous ceremony. "We have just crossed the equator, and it is an old tradition that those who have never crossed the line before must pay respects to Neptune— that is the Roman god of the sea; though of course he is not actually worshiped anymore."

"Aah!" Liu Bao said, approvingly, when this had been translated for him. "I like that. It is good to show respect to old gods, even if they are not yours. It must be very good luck for the ship. And it is only nineteen days until the New Year: we will have to have a feast on board, and that will be good luck, too. The spirits of our ancestors will guide the ship back to China."

Laurence was dubious, but the sailors listening in to the translation with much interest found much to approve in this speech: both the feast, and the promised good luck, which appealed to their superstitious habit of thought. Although the mention of spirits was cause for a great deal of serious belowdecks debate, being a little too close to ghosts for comfort, in the end it was generally agreed that as ancestor spirits, these would have to be benevolently inclined towards the descendants being carried by the ship, and therefore not to be feared.

"They have asked me for a cow and four sheep, and all eight of the remaining chickens, also; we will have to put in at St. Helena after all. We will make the turn westward tomorrow; at least it will be easier sailing than all this beating into the trades we have been doing," Riley said, watching dubiously a few days later: several of the Chinese servants were busy fishing for sharks. "I only hope the liquor is not too strong. I must give it to the hands in addition to their grog ration, not in its place, or it would be no celebration at all."

"I am sorry to give you any cause for alarm, but Liu Bao alone can drink two of me under the table; I have seen him put away three bottles of wine in a sitting," Laurence said ruefully, speaking from much painful experience: the envoy had dined with him convivially several more times since Christmas, and if he were suffering any lingering ill-effects whatsoever from the sea-sickness, it could not be told from his appetite. "For that matter, though Sun Kai does not drink a great deal, brandy and wine are all the same to him, as far as I can tell."

"Oh, to the devil with them," Riley said, sighing. "Well, perhaps a few dozen able seamen will get themselves into enough trouble that I can take away their grog for the night. What do you suppose they are going to do with those sharks? They have thrown back two porpoises already, and those are much better eating."

Laurence was ill-prepared to venture upon a guess, but he did not have to: at that moment the lookout called, "Wing three points off the larboard bow," and they hurried at once to the side, to pull out their telescopes and peer into the sky, while sailors stampeded to their posts in case it should be an attack.

Temeraire had lifted his head from his nap at the noise. "Laurence, it is Volly," he called down from the dragon-deck. "He has seen us, he is coming this way." Following this announcement, he roared out a greeting that made nearly every man jump and rattled the masts; several of the sailors looked darkly towards him, though none ventured a complaint.

Temeraire shifted himself about to make room, and some fifteen minutes later the little Greyling courier dropped down onto the deck, furling his broad grey-and-white-streaked wings. "Temrer!" he said, and butted Temeraire happily with his head. "Cow?"

"No, Volly, but we can fetch you a sheep," Temeraire said indulgently. "Has he been hurt?" he asked James; the little dragon sounded queerly nasal.

Volly's captain, Langford James, slid down. "Hello, Laurence, there you are. We have been looking for you up and down the coast," he said, reaching out to take Laurence's hand. "No need to fret, Temeraire; he has only caught this blasted cold going about Dover. Half the dragons are moaning and sniffling about: they are the greatest children imaginable. But he will be right as rain in a week or two."

More rather than less alarmed by these reassurances, Temeraire edged a little distance away from Volly; he did not look particularly eager to experience his first illness. Laurence nodded; the letter he had had from Jane Roland had mentioned the sickness in passing. "I hope you have not strained him on our account, coming so far. Shall I send for my surgeon?" he offered.

"No, thank you; he has been doctored enough. It'll be another week before he forgets the medicine he swallowed and forgives me for slipping it into his dinner," James said, waving away the request. "Any road, we have not come so very far; we have been down here flying the southern route the last two weeks, and it is a damned sight warmer here than in jolly old England, you know. Volly's hardly shy about letting me know if he don't care to fly, either, so as long as he doesn't speak up, I'll keep him in the air." He petted the little dragon, who bumped his nose against James's hand, and then lowered his head directly to sleep.

"What news is there?" Laurence asked, shuffling through the post that James had handed over: his responsibility rather than Riley's, as it had been brought by dragon-courier. "Has there been any change on the Continent? We heard news of Austerlitz at Cape Coast. Are we recalled? Ferris, see these to Lord Purbeck, and the rest among our crew," he added, handing the other letters off: for himself he had a dispatch, and a couple of letters, though he politely tucked them into his jacket rather than looking at them at once.

"No to both, more's the pity, but at least we can make the trip a little easier for you; we have taken the Dutch colony at Capetown," James said. "Seized it last month, so you can break your journey there."

The news leapt from one end of the deck to the other with speed fueled by the enthusiasm of men who had been long brooding over the grim news of Napoleon's latest success, and the *Allegiance* was instantly afire with patriotic cheers; no further conversation was possible until some measure of calm had been restored. The post did some work to this effect, Purbeck and Ferris handing it out among the respective crews, and gradually the noise collected into smaller pockets, many of the other men deep into their letters.

Laurence sent for a table and chairs to be brought up to the dragondeck, inviting Riley and Hammond to join them and hear the news. James was happy to give them a more detailed account of the capture than was contained in the brief dispatch: he had been a courier from the age of fourteen, and had a turn for the dramatic; though in this case he had little material to work from. "I'm sorry it doesn't make a better story; it was not really a fight, you know," he said apologetically. "We had the Highlanders there, and the Dutch only some mercenaries; they ran away before we even reached the town. The governor had to surrender; the people are still a little uneasy, but General Baird is leaving local affairs to them, and they have not kicked up much of a fuss."

"Well, it will certainly make resupply easier," Riley said. "We need not stop in St. Helena, either; and that will be a savings of as much as two weeks. It is very welcome news indeed."

"Will you stay for dinner?" Laurence asked James. "Or must you be going straightaway?"

Volly abruptly sneezed behind him, a loud and startling noise. "Ick," the little dragon said, waking himself up out of his sleep, and rubbed his nose against his foreleg in distaste, trying to scrape the mucus from his snout.

"Oh, stop that, filthy wretch," James said, getting up; he took a large white linen square from his harness bags and wiped Volly clean with the weary air of long practice. "I suppose we will stay the night," he said after, contemplating Volly. "No need to press him, now that I have found you in time, and you can write any letters you like me to take on: we are homeward bound after we leave you."

. . . so my poor Lily, like Excidium and Mortiferus, has been banished from her comfortable clearing to the Sand Pits, for when she sneezes, she cannot help but spit some of the acid, the muscles involved in this reflex (so the surgeons tell me) being the very same. They all three are very disgusted with their situation, as the sand cannot be got rid of from day to day, and they scratch themselves like Dogs trying to cast off fleas no matter how they bathe.

Maximus is in deep disgrace, for he began sneezing first, and all the other dragons like to have someone to blame for their Misery; however he bears it well, or as Berkley tells me to write, "Does not give a Tinker's Dam for the lot of them and whines all the day, except when busy stuffing his gullet; has not hurt his appetite in the least."

We all do very well otherwise, and all send their love; the dragons also, and bid you convey their greetings and affection to Temeraire. They indeed miss him badly, though I am sorry to have to tell you that we have lately discovered one ignoble cause for their pining, which is plain Greed. Evidently he had taught them how to pry open the Feeding Pen, and close it again after, so they were able to help themselves whenever they liked without anyone the wiser—their Guilty Secret discovered only after note was taken that the Herds were oddly diminished, and the dragons of our formation overfed, whereupon being questioned they confessed the Whole.

I must stop, for we have Patrol, and Volatilus goes south in the morning. All our prayers for your safe Journey and quick return.

Etc.,
Catherine Harcourt

"What is this I hear from Harcourt of your teaching the dragons to steal from the pen?" Laurence demanded, looking up from his letter; he was taking the hour before dinner to read his mail, and compose replies.

Temeraire started up with so very revealing an expression that his guilt could be in no doubt. "That is not true, I did not teach anyone to steal," he said. "The herdsmen at Dover are very lazy, and do not always come in the morning, so we have to wait and wait at the pen, and the herds are meant for us, anyway; it cannot be called stealing."

"I suppose I ought to have suspected something when you stopped complaining of them being always late," Laurence said. "But how on earth did you manage it?"

"The gate is perfectly simple," Temeraire said. "There is only a bar across the fence, which one can lift very easily, and then it swings open; Nitidus could do it best, for his forehands are the smallest. Though it is difficult to keep the animals inside the pen, and the first time I learned how to open it, they all ran away," he added. "Maximus and I had to chase after them for hours and hours—it was not funny, *at all*," he said, ruffled, sitting back on his haunches and contemplating Laurence with great indignation.

"I beg your pardon," Laurence said, after he had regained his breath. "I truly beg your pardon, it was only the notion of you, and Maximus, and the sheep—oh dear," Laurence said, and dissolved again, try as he might to contain himself: astonished stares from his crew, and Temeraire haughtily offended.

"Is there any other news in the letter?" Temeraire asked, coolly, when Laurence had finally done.

"Not news, but all the dragons have sent you greetings and their love," Laurence said, now conciliatory. "You may console yourself that they are all sick, and if you were there you certainly would be also," he added, seeing Temeraire inclined to droop when reminded of his friends.

"I would not care if I were sick, if I were home. Anyway, I am sure to catch it from Volly," Temeraire said gloomily, glancing over: the little Greyling was snuffling thickly in his sleep, bubbles of mucus swelling and shrinking over his nostrils as he breathed, and a small puddle of saliva had collected beneath his half-open mouth.

Laurence could not in honesty hold out much hope to the contrary, so he shifted the subject. "Have you any messages? I will go below now and write my replies, so James can carry them back: the last chance of sending a word by courier we will have for a long time, I am afraid, for ours do not go to the Far East except for some truly urgent matter."

"Only to send my love," Temeraire said, "and to tell Captain Harcourt and also Admiral Lenton it was not stealing in the least. Oh, and also, tell Maximus and Lily about the poem written by the dragon, for that was very interesting, and perhaps they will like to hear of it. And also about my learning to climb aboard the ship, and that we have crossed the equator, and about Neptune and Badger-Bag."

"Enough, enough; you will have me writing a novel," Laurence said, rising easily: thankfully his leg had at last put itself right, and he was no longer forced to limp about the deck like an old man. He stroked Temeraire's side. "Shall we come and sit with you while we have our port?"

Temeraire snorted and nudged him affectionately with his nose. "Thank you, Laurence; that would be pleasant, and I would like to hear any news James has of the others, besides what is in your letters."

The replies finished at the stroke of three, Laurence and his guests dined in unusual comfort: ordinarily, Laurence kept to his habit of formal decorum, and Granby and his own officers followed his lead, while Riley and his subordinates did so of their own accord and naval custom; they one and all sweltered through every meal under thick broadcloth and their snugly tied neckcloths.

But James had a born aviator's disregard for propriety coupled with the assurance of a man who had been a captain, even if only of a single-man courier, since the age of fourteen. With hardly a pause, he discarded his outer garments on coming below, saying, "Good God, it is close in here; you must stifle, Laurence."

Laurence was not sorry to follow his example, which he would have done regardless out of a desire not to make him feel out of place. Granby immediately followed suit, and after a brief surprise, Riley and Hammond matched them, though Lord Purbeck kept his coat and his expression fixed, clearly disapproving. The dinner went cheerfully enough, though at Laurence's request, James reserved his own news until they were comfortably ensconced on the dragondeck with their cigars and port, where Temeraire could hear, and with his body provide a bulwark against the rest of the crew's eavesdropping. Laurence dismissed the aviators down to the forecastle, this leaving only Sun Kai, as usual taking the air in the reserved corner of the dragondeck, close enough to overhear what should be quite meaningless to him.

James had much to tell them of formation movements: nearly all the dragons of the Mediterranean division had been reassigned to the Channel, Laetificat and Excursius and their respective formations to provide a thoroughly impenetrable opposition should Bonaparte once again attempt invasion through the air, emboldened by his success on the Continent.

"Not much left to stop them from trying for Gibraltar, though, with all this shifting about," Riley said. "And we must keep watch over Toulon: we may have taken twenty prizes at Trafalgar, but now Bonaparte has every forest in Europe at his disposal, he can build more ships. I hope the Ministry have a care for it."

"Oh, Hell," James said, sitting up with a thump; his chair had been tilted rather precariously backwards as he reclined with his feet on the rail. "I am being a dunce; I suppose you haven't heard about Mr. Pitt."

"He is not still ill?" Hammond said anxiously.

"Not ill in the least," James said. "Dead, this last fortnight and more. The news killed him, they say; he took his bed after we heard of the armistice, and never got out of it again."

"God rest his soul," Riley said.

"Amen," Laurence said, deeply shocked. Pitt had not been an old man; younger than his father, certainly.

"Who is Mr. Pitt?" Temeraire inquired, and Laurence paused to explain to him the post of Prime Minister.

"James, have you any word on who will form the new government?" he asked, already wondering what this might mean for himself and Temeraire, if the new Minister felt China ought to be dealt with differently, in either more conciliatory or more belligerent manner.

"No, I was off before more than the bare word had reached us," James said. "I promise if anything has changed when I get back, I will do my best and bring you the news at Capetown. But," he added, "they send us down here less than once in a sixmonth, ordinarily, so I shouldn't hope for it. The landing sites are too uncertain, and we have lost couriers without a trace here before, trying to go overland or even just spend a night on shore."

James set off again the next morning, waving at them from Volly's back until the little grey-white dragon disappeared entirely into the thready, low-hanging clouds. Laurence had managed to pen a brief reply to Harcourt as well as appending to his already-begun letters for his mother and Jane, and the courier had carried them all away: the last word they would receive from him for months, almost certainly.

There was little time for melancholy: he was at once called below, to consult with Liu Bao on the appropriate substitute for some sort of monkey organ which was ordinarily used in a dish. Having suggested lamb kidneys, Laurence was instantly solicited for assistance with another task, and the rest of the week passed in increasingly frantic preparations, the galley going day and night at full steam, until the dragondeck grew so warm that even Temeraire began to feel it a little excessive. The Chinese servants also set to clearing the ship of vermin; a hopeless task, but one in which they persevered. They came up to the deck sometimes five or six times in a day to fling the bodies of rats overboard into the sea, while the midshipmen looked on in outrage, these ordinarily serving, late in a voyage, as part of their own meals.

Laurence had not the least idea what to expect from the occasion, but was careful to dress with especial formality, borrowing Riley's steward Jethson to valet him: his best shirt, starched and ironed; silk stockings and knee-breeches instead of trousers with his polished Hessian boots; his dress coat, bottle-green, with gold bars on the shoulders, and his decorations: the gold medal of the Nile, where he had been a naval lieutenant, on its broad blue ribbon, and the silver pin voted recently to the captains of the Dover battle.

He was very glad to have taken so many pains when he entered the Chinese quarters: passing through the door, he had to duck beneath a sweep of heavy red cloth and found the room so richly draped with hangings it might have been taken for a grand pavilion on land, except for the steady motion of the ship beneath their feet. The table was laid with delicate porcelain, each piece of different color, many edged with gold and silver; and the lacquered eating sticks which Laurence had been dreading all week were at every place.

Yongxing was already seated at the head of the table, in imposing state and wearing his most formal robes, in the deep golden silk embroidered with dragons in blue and black thread. Laurence was seated close enough to see that there were small chips of gemstones for the dragons' eyes and talons, and in the very center of the front, covering the chest, was a single dragon-figure larger than the rest, embroidered in pure white silk, with chips of rubies for its eyes and five outstretched talons on each foot.

Somehow they were all crammed in, down to little Roland and Dyer, the younger officers fairly squashed together at their separate table and their faces already shining and pink in the heat. The servants began pouring the wine directly everyone was seated, others coming in from the galley to lay down great platters along the length of the tables: cold sliced meats, interspersed with an assortment of dark yellow nuts, preserved cherries, and prawns with their heads and dangling forelegs intact.

Yongxing took up his cup for the first toast and all hurried to drink with him; the rice wine was served warm, and went down with dangerous ease. This was evidently the signal for a general beginning; the Chinese started in on the platters, and the younger men at least had little hesitation in following suit. Laurence was embarrassed to see, when he glanced over, that Roland and Dyer were having not the least difficulty with their chopsticks and were already round-cheeked from stuffing food into their mouths.

He himself had only just managed to get a piece of the beef to his mouth by dint of puncturing it with one of his sticks; the meat had a smoky, not unpleasant quality. No sooner had he swallowed than Yongxing raised the cup for another toast, and he had to drink again; this succession repeated itself several times more, until he was uncomfortably warm, his head nearly swimming.

Growing slowly braver with the sticks, he risked a prawn, though the other officers about him were avoiding them; the sauce made them slippery and awkward to manage. It wobbled precariously, the beady black eyes bobbing at him; he followed the Chinese example and bit it off just behind the attached head. At once he groped for the cup again, breathing deeply through his nose: the sauce was shockingly hot, and broke a fresh sweat out upon his forehead, the drops trickling down the side of his jaw into his collar. Liu Bao laughed uproariously at his expression and poured him more wine, leaning across the table and thumping him approvingly on the shoulder.

The platters were shortly taken off the tables and replaced with an array of wooden dishes, full of dumplings, some with thin crêpe-paper skins and others of thick, yeasty white dough. These were at least easier to get hold of with the sticks, and could be chewed and swallowed whole. The cooks had evidently exercised some ingenuity, lacking essential ingredients; Laurence found a piece of seaweed in one, and the lamb kidneys made their appearance also. Three further courses of small dishes ensued, then a strange dish of uncooked fish, pale pink and fleshy, with cold noodles and pickled greens gone dull brown with long storage. A strange crunchy substance in the mixture was identified after inquiry by Hammond as dried jellyfish, which intelligence caused several men to surreptitiously pick the bits out and drop them onto the floor.

Liu Bao with motions and his own example encouraged Laurence to literally fling the ingredients into the air to mix them together, and Hammond informed them by translation that this was intended to ensure good luck: the higher the better. The British were not unwilling to make the attempt; their coordination was less equal to the task, however, and shortly both uniforms and the table were graced by bits of fish and pickled greens. Dignity was thus dealt a fatal blow: after nearly a jug of rice wine to every man, even Yongxing's presence was not enough to dampen the hilarity ensuing from watching their fellow-officers fling bits of fish all over themselves.

"It is a dashed sight better than we had in the *Normandy*'s cutter," Riley said to Laurence, over-loud, meaning the raw fish; to the more general audience, interest having been expressed by Hammond and Liu Bao both, he expanded on the story: "We were wrecked in the *Normandy* when Captain Yarrow ran her onto a reef, all of us thrown on a desert island seven hundred miles from Rio. We were sent off in the cutter for rescue—though Laurence was only second lieutenant at the time, the captain and premier knew less about the sea than trained apes, which is how they came to run us aground. They wouldn't go themselves for love or money, or give us much in the way of supply, either," he added, still smarting at the memory.

"Twelve men with nothing but hard tack and a bag of cocoanuts; we were glad enough for fish to eat it raw, with our fingers, the moment we caught it," Laurence said. "But I cannot complain; I am tolerably sure Foley tapped me for his first lieutenant in the *Goliath* because of it, and I would have eaten a good deal more raw fish for the chance. But this is much nicer, by far," he added, hastily, thinking this conversation implied that raw fish was fit only for consumption in desperate circumstances, which opinion he privately held true, but not to be shared at present.

This story launched several more anecdotes from various of the naval officers, tongues loosened and backs unstiffened by so much gluttony. The translator was kept busy rendering these for the benefit of the highly interested Chinese audience; even Yongxing followed the stories; he had still not deigned to break his silence, save for the formal toasts, but there was something of a mellowing about his eyes.

Liu Bao was less circumspect about his curiosity. "You have been to a great many places, I see, and had unusual adventures," he observed to Laurence. "Admiral Zheng sailed all the way to Africa, but he died on his seventh voyage, and his tomb is empty. You have gone around the world more than once. Have you never been worried that you would die at sea, and no one would perform the rites at your grave?"

"I have never thought very much about it," Laurence said, with a little dishonesty: in truth he had never given the matter any consideration whatsoever. "But after all, Drake and Cook, and so many other great men, have been buried at sea; I really could not complain about sharing their tomb, sir, and with your own navigator as well."

"Well, I hope you have many sons at home," Liu Bao said, shaking his head.

The casual air with which he made so personal a remark took Laurence quite aback. "No, sir; none," he said, too startled to think of anything to do but answer. "I have never married," he added, seeing Liu Bao about to assume an expression of great sympathy, which on this answer being translated became a look of open astonishment; Yongxing and even Sun Kai turned their heads to stare. Beleaguered, Laurence tried to explain. "There is no urgency; I am a third son, and my eldest brother has three boys already himself."

"Pardon me, Captain, if I may," Hammond broke in, rescuing him, and said to them, "Gentlemen, among us, the eldest son alone inherits the family estates, and the younger are expected to make their own way; I know it is not the same with you."

"I suppose your father is a soldier, like you?" Yongxing said abruptly. "Does he have a very small estate, that he cannot provide for all his sons?"

"No, sir; my father is Lord Allendale," Laurence said, rather nettled by the suggestion. "Our family seat is in Nottinghamshire; I do not think anyone would call it small."

Yongxing looked startled and somewhat displeased by this answer, but perhaps he was only frowning at the soup which was at that moment being laid out before them: a very clear broth, pale gold and queer to the taste, smoky and thin, with pitchers of bright red vinegar as accompaniment and to add sharp flavor, and masses of short dried noodles in each bowl, strangely crunchy.

All the while the servants were bringing it in, the translator had been murmuring quietly in answer to some question from Sun Kai, and now on his behalf leaned across the table and asked, "Captain, is your father a relation of the King?"

Though surprised by the question, Laurence was grateful enough for any excuse to put down his spoon; he would have found the soup difficult eating even had he not already gone through six courses. "No, sir; I would hardly be so bold as to call His Majesty a relation. My father's family are of Plantagenet descent; we are only very distantly connected to the present house."

Sun Kai listened to this translated, then persisted a little further. "But are you more closely related to the King than the Lord Macartney?"

As the translator pronounced the name a little awkwardly, Laurence had some difficulty in recognizing the name as that of the earlier ambassador, until Hammond, whispering hastily in his ear, made it clear to whom Sun Kai was referring. "Oh, certainly," Laurence said. "He was raised to the peerage for service to the Crown, himself; not that that is held any less honorable with us, I assure you, but my father is eleventh Earl of Allendale, and his creation dates from 1529."

Even as he spoke, he was amused at finding himself so absurdly jealous of his ancestry, halfway around the world, in the company of men to whom it could be of no consequence whatsoever, when he had never trumpeted it among his acquaintance at home. Indeed, he had often rebelled against his father's lectures upon the subject, of which there had been many, particularly after his first abortive attempt to run away to sea. But four weeks of being daily called into his father's office to endure another repetition had evidently had some effect he had not previously suspected, if he could be provoked to so stuffy a response by being compared with a great diplomat of very respectable lineage.

But quite contrary to his expectations, Sun Kai and his countrymen showed a deep fascination with this intelligence, betraying an enthusiasm for genealogy Laurence had heretofore only encountered in a few of his more stiff-necked relations, and he shortly found himself pressed for details of the family history which he could only vaguely dredge out of his memory. "I beg your pardon," he said at last, growing rather desperate. "I cannot keep it straight in my head without writing it down; you must forgive me."

It was an unfortunate choice of gambit: Liu Bao, who had also been listening with interest, promptly said, "Oh, that is easy enough," and called for brush and ink; the servants were clearing away the soup, and there was room on the table for the moment. At once all those nearby leaned forward to look on, the Chinese in curiosity, the British in self-defense: there was another course waiting in the wings, and no one but the cooks was in a hurry for it to arrive.

Feeling that he was being excessively punished for his moment of vanity, Laurence was forced to write out a chart on a long roll of rice paper under all their eyes. The difficulty of forming the Latin alphabet with a paint-brush was added to that of trying to remember the various begats; he had to leave several given names blank, marking them with interrogatives, before finally reaching Edward III after several contortions and one leap through the Salic line. The result said nothing complimentary about his penmanship, but the Chinese passed it around more than once, discussing it amongst themselves with energy, though the writing could hardly have made any more sense to them than theirs to him. Yongxing himself stared at it a long time, though his face remained devoid of emotion, and Sun Kai, receiving it last, rolled it away with an expression of intense satisfaction, apparently for safe-keeping.

Thankfully, that was an end to it; but now there was no more delaying the next dish, and the sacrificed poultry was brought out, all eight at once, on great platters and steaming with a pungent, liquored sauce. They were laid on the table and hacked expertly into small pieces by the servants using a broad-bladed cleaver, and again Laurence rather despairingly allowed his plate to be filled. The meat was delicious, tender and rich with juices, but almost a punishment to eat; nor was this the conclusion: when the chicken was taken away, nowhere close to finished, whole fish were brought out, fried in the rich slush from the hands' salt pork. No one could do more than pick at this dish, or the course of sweets that followed: seedcake, and sticky-sweet dumplings in syrup, filled with a thick red paste. The servants were especially anxious to press them onto the youngest officers, and poor Roland could be heard saying plaintively, "Can I not eat it tomorrow?"

When finally they were allowed to escape, almost a dozen men had to be bodily lifted up by their seat-mates and helped from the cabin. Those who could still walk unaided escaped to the deck, there to lean on the rail in various attitudes of pretended fascination, which were mostly a cover for waiting their turn in the seats of ease below. Laurence unashamedly took advantage of his private facility, and then heaved himself back up to sit with Temeraire, his head protesting almost as much as his belly.

Laurence was taken aback to find Temeraire himself being feasted in turn by a delegation of the Chinese servants, who had prepared for him delicacies favored by dragons in their own land: the entrails of the cow, stuffed with its own liver and lungs chopped fine and mixed with spices, looking very much like large sausages; also a haunch, very lightly seared and touched with what looked very like the same fiery sauce which had been served to the human guests. The deep maroon flesh of an enormous tunny, sliced into thick steaks and layered with whole delicate sheets of yellow noodles, was his fish course, and after this, with great ceremony, the servants brought out an entire sheep, its meat cooked rather like mince and dressed back up in its skin, which had been dyed a deep crimson, with pieces of driftwood for legs.

Temeraire tasted this dish and said, in surprise, "Why, it is sweet," and asked the servants something in their native Chinese; they bowed many times, replying, and Temeraire nodded; then he daintily ate the contents, leaving the skin and wooden legs aside. "They are only for decoration," he told Laurence, settling down with a sigh of deep contentment; the only guest so comfortable. From the quarterdeck below, the faint sound of retching could be heard, as one of the older midshipmen suffered the consequences of overindulgence. "They tell me that in China, dragons do not eat the skins, any more than people do."

"Well, I only hope you will not find it indigestible, from so much spice," Laurence said, and was sorry at once, recognizing in himself a species of jealousy that did not like to see Temeraire enjoying any Chinese customs. He was unhappily conscious that it had never occurred to him to offer Temeraire prepared dishes, or any greater variety than the difference between fish and mutton, even for a special occasion.

But Temeraire only said, "No, I like it very well," unconcerned and yawning; he stretched himself very long and flexed his claws. "Do let us go for a long flight tomorrow?" he said, curling up again more compactly. "I have not been tired at all, this whole last week, coming back; I am sure I can manage a longer journey."

"By all means," Laurence said, glad to hear that he was feeling stronger. Keynes had at last put a period to Temeraire's convalescence, shortly after their departure from Cape Coast. Yongxing's original prohibition against Laurence's taking Temeraire aloft again had never been withdrawn, but Laurence had no intention of abiding by this restriction, or begging him to lift it. However Hammond, with some ingenuity and quiet discussion, arranged matters diplomatically: Yongxing came on deck after Keynes's final pronouncement, and granted the permission audibly, "for the sake of ensuring Lung Tien Xiang's welfare through healthy exercise," as he put it. So they were free to take to the air again without any threat of quarreling, but Temeraire had been complaining of soreness, and growing weary with unusual speed.

The feast had lasted so long that Temeraire had begun eating only at twilight; now full darkness spread, and Laurence lay back against Temeraire's side and looked over the less-familiar stars of the Southern Hemisphere; it was a perfectly clear night, and the master ought to be able to fix a good longitude, he hoped, through the constellations. The hands had been turned up for the evening to celebrate, and the rice wine had flowed freely at their mess tables also; they were singing a boisterous and highly explicit song, and Laurence made sure with a look that Roland and Dyer were not on deck to be interested in it: no sign of either, so they had probably sought their beds after dinner.

One by one the men slowly began to drift away from the festivities and seek their hammocks. Riley came climbing up from the quarterdeck, taking the steps one at a time with both feet, very weary and scarlet in the face; Laurence invited him to sit, and out of consideration did not offer a glass of wine. "You cannot call it anything but a rousing success; any political hostess would consider it a triumph to put on such a dinner," Laurence said. "But I confess I would have been happier with half so many dishes, and the servants might have been much less solicitous without leaving me hungry."

"Oh—yes, indeed," Riley said; distracted, and now that Laurence looked at him more closely, plainly unhappy, discomfited.

"What has occurred? Is something amiss?" Laurence looked at once at the rigging, the masts; but all looked well, and in any case every sense and intuition together told him that the ship was running well: or as well as she ever did, being in the end a great lumbering hulk.

"Laurence, I very much dislike being a tale-bearer, but I cannot conceal this," Riley said. "That ensign, or I suppose cadet, of yours; Roland. He—that is, Roland was asleep in the Chinese cabin, and as I was leaving, the servants asked me, with their translator, where he slept, so they might carry him there." Laurence was already dreading the conclusion, and not very surprised when Riley added, "But the fellow said 'she,' instead; I was on the point of correcting him when I looked—well, not to drag it out; Roland is a girl. I have not the least notion how she has concealed it so long."

"Oh bloody Hell," Laurence said, too tired and irritable from the excess of food and drink to mind his language. "You have not said anything about this, have you, Tom? To anyone else?" Riley nodded, warily, and Laurence said, "I must beg you to keep it quiet; the plain fact of the matter is, Longwings will not go into harness under a male captain. And some other breeds also, but those are of less material significance; Longwings are the kind we cannot do without, and so some girls must be trained up for them."

Riley said, uncertainly, half-smiling, "Are you—? But this is absurd; was not the leader of your formation here on this very ship, with his Longwing?" he protested, seeing that Laurence was not speaking in jest.

"Do you mean Lily?" Temeraire asked, cocking his head. "Her captain is Catherine Harcourt; she is not a man."

"It is quite true; I assure you," Laurence said, while Riley stared at him and Temeraire in turn.

"But Laurence, the very notion," Riley said, grown now appalled as he began to believe them. "Every feeling must cry out against such an abuse. Why, if we are to send women to war, should we not take them to sea, also? We could double our numbers, and what matter if the deck of every ship become a brothel, and children left motherless and crying on shore?"

"Come, the one does not follow on the other in the slightest," Laurence said, impatient with this exaggeration; he did not like the necessity himself, but he was not at all willing to be given such romantical arguments against it. "I do not at all say it could or ought to answer in the general case; but where the willing sacrifice of a few may mean the safety and happiness of the rest, I cannot think it so bad. Those women officers whom I have met are not impressed into service, nor forced to the work even by the ordinary necessities that require men to seek employment, and I assure you no one in the service would dream of offering any insult."

This explanation did not reconcile Riley at all, but he abandoned his general protest for the specific. "And so you truly mean to keep this girl in service?" he said, in tones increasingly plaintive rather than shocked. "And have her going about in male dress in this fashion; can it be allowed?"

"There is formal dispensation from the sumptuary laws for female officers of the Corps while engaged upon their duties, authorized by the Crown," Laurence said. "I am sorry that you should be put to any distress over the matter, Tom; I had hoped to avoid the issue entirely, but I suppose it was too much to ask for, seven months aboard ship. I promise you," he added, "I was as shocked as you might wish when I first learned of the practice; but since I have served with several, and they are indeed not at all like ordinary females. They are raised to the life, you know, and under such circumstances habit may trump even birth."

For his part, Temeraire had been following this exchange with cocked head and increasing confusion; now he said, "I do not understand in the least, why ought it make any difference at all? Lily is female, and she can fight just as well as I can, or almost," he amended, with a touch of superiority.

Riley, still dissatisfied even after Laurence's reassurance, looked after this remark very much as though he had been asked to justify the tide, or the phase of the moon; Laurence was by long experience better prepared for Temeraire's radical notions, and said, "Women are generally smaller and weaker than men, Temeraire, less able to endure the privations of service."

"I have never noticed that Captain Harcourt is much smaller than any of the rest of you," Temeraire said; well he might not, speaking from a height of some thirty feet and a weight topping eighteen tons. "Besides, I am smaller than Maximus, and Messoria is smaller than me; but that does not mean we cannot still fight."

"It is different for dragons than for people," Laurence said. "Among other things, women must bear children, and care for them through childhood, where your kind lay eggs and hatch ready to look to your own needs."

Temeraire blinked at this intelligence. "You do not

hatch out of eggs?" he asked, in deep fascination. "How then—"

"I beg your pardon, I think I see Purbeck looking for me," Riley said, very hastily, and escaped at a speed remarkable, Laurence thought somewhat resentfully, in a man who had lately consumed nearly a quarter of his own weight again in food.

"I cannot really undertake to explain the process to you; I have no children of my own," Laurence said. "In any case, it is late; and if you wish to make a long flight tomorrow, you had better rest well tonight."

"That is true, and I am sleepy," Temeraire said, yawning and letting his long forked tongue unroll, tasting the air. "I think it will keep clear; we will have good weather for the flight." He settled himself. "Good night, Laurence; you will come early?"

"Directly after breakfast, I am entirely at your disposal," Laurence promised. He stayed stroking Temeraire gently until the dragon drifted into sleep; his hide was still very warm to the touch, likely from the last lingering heat of the galley, its ovens finally given some rest after the long preparations. At last, Temeraire's eyes closing to the thinnest of slits, Laurence got himself back onto his feet and climbed down to the quarterdeck.

The men had mostly cleared away or were napping on deck, save those surly few set as lookouts and muttering of their unhappy lot in the rigging, and the night air was pleasantly cool. Laurence walked a ways aft to stretch his legs before going below; the midshipman standing watch, young Tripp, was yawning almost as wide as Temeraire; he closed his mouth with a snap and jerked to embarrassed attention when Laurence passed.

"A pleasant evening, Mr. Tripp," Laurence said, concealing his amusement; the boy was coming along well, from what Riley had said, and bore little resemblance anymore to the idle, spoiled creature who had been foisted upon them by his family. His wrists showed bare for several inches past the ends of his sleeves, and the back of his coat had split so many times that in the end it had been necessary to expand it by the insertion of a panel of blue-dyed sailcloth, not quite the same shade as the rest, so he had an odd stripe running down the middle. Also his hair had grown curly, and bleached to almost yellow by the sun; his own mother would likely not recognize him.

"Oh, yes, sir," Tripp said, enthusiastically. "Such wonderful food, and they gave me a whole dozen of those sweet dumplings at the end, too. It is a pity we cannot always be eating so."

Laurence sighed over this example of youthful resilience; his own stomach was not at all comfortable yet. "Mind you do not fall asleep on watch," he said; after such a dinner it would be astonishing if the boy was not sorely tempted, and Laurence had no desire to see him suffer the ignominious punishment.

"Never, sir," Tripp said, swallowing a fresh yawn and finishing the sentence out in a squeak. "Sir," he asked, nervously, in a low voice, when Laurence would have gone, "May I ask you—you do not suppose that Chinese spirits would show themselves to a fellow who was not a member of their family, do you?"

"I am tolerably certain you will not see any spirits on watch, Mr. Tripp, unless you have concealed some in your coat pocket," Laurence said, dryly. This took a moment to puzzle out, then Tripp laughed, but still nervously, and Laurence frowned. "Has someone been telling you stories?" he asked, well aware of what such rumors could do to the state of a ship's crew.

"No, it is only that—well, I thought I saw someone, forward, when I went to turn the glass. But I spoke, and he quite vanished away; I am sure he was a Chinaman, and oh, his face was so white!"

"That is quite plain: you saw one of the servants who cannot speak our tongue, coming from the head, and startled him into ducking away from what he thought would be a scolding of some sort. I hope you are not inclined to superstition, Mr. Tripp; it is something which must be tolerated in the men, but a sad flaw in an officer." He spoke sternly, hoping by firmness to keep the boy from spreading the tale, at least; and if the fear kept him wakeful for the rest of the night, it would be so much the better.

"Yes, sir," Tripp said, rather dismally. "Good night, sir."

Laurence continued his circuit of the deck, at a leisurely pace that was all he could muster. The exercise was settling his stomach; he was almost inclined to take another turn, but the glass was running low, and he did not wish to disappoint Temeraire by rising late. As he made to step down into the fore hatch, however, a sudden heavy blow landed on his back and he lurched, tripped, and pitched headfirst down the ladder-way.

His hand grasped automatically for the guideline, and after a jangling twist he found the steps with his feet, catching himself against the ladder with a thump. Angry, he looked up and nearly fell again, recoiling from the pallid white face, incomprehensibly deformed, that was peering closely into his own out of the dark.

"Good God in Heaven," he said, with great sincerity; then he recognized Feng Li, Yongxing's servant, and breathed again: the man only looked so strange because he was dangling upside-down through the hatch, barely inches from falling himself. "What the devil do you mean, lunging about the deck like this?" he demanded, catching the man's flailing hand and setting it onto the guideline, so he could right himself. "You ought to have better sea-legs by now."

Feng Li only stared in mute incomprehension, then

hauled himself back onto his feet and scrambled down the ladder past Laurence pell-mell, disappearing below-decks to where the Chinese servants were quartered with speed enough to call it vanishing. With his dark blue clothing and black hair, as soon as his face was out of sight he was almost invisible in the dark. "I cannot blame Tripp in the least," Laurence said aloud, now more generously inclined towards the boy's silliness; his heart was still pounding disgracefully as he continued on to his quarters.

Laurence roused the next morning to yells of dismay and feet running overhead; he dashed at once for the deck to find the foremainsail yard tumbled to the deck in two pieces, the enormous sail draped half over the fore-castle, and Temeraire looking at once miserable and embarrassed. "I did not mean to," he said, sounding gravelly and quite unlike himself, and sneezed again, this time managing to turn his head away from the ship: the force of the eruption cast up a few waves that slopped against the larboard side.

Keynes was already climbing up to the deck with his bag, and laid his ear against Temeraire's chest. "Hm." He said nothing more, listening in many places, until Laurence grew impatient and prompted him.

"Oh, it is certainly a cold; there is nothing to be done but wait it out, and dose him for coughing when that should begin. I am only seeing if I might hear the fluid moving in the channels which relate to the divine wind," Keynes said absently. "We have no notion of the anatomy of the particular trait; a pity we have never had a specimen to dissect."

Temeraire drew back at this, putting his ruff down, and snorted; or rather tried to: instead he blew mucus out all over Keynes's head. Laurence himself sprang back only just in time, and could not feel particularly sorry for the surgeon: the remark had been thoroughly tactless.

Temeraire croaked out, "I am quite well, we can still go flying," and looked at Laurence in appeal.

"Perhaps a shorter flight now, and then again in the afternoon, if you are still not tired," Laurence offered, looking at Keynes, who was ineffectually trying to get the slime from his face.

"No, in warm weather like this he can fly just as usual if he likes to; no need to baby him," Keynes said, rather shortly, managing to clear his eyes at least. "So long as you are sure to be strapped on tight, or he will sneeze you clean off. Will you excuse me?"

So in the end Temeraire had his long flight after all: the *Allegiance* left dwindling behind in the blue-water depths, and the ocean shading to jeweled glass as they drew nearer the coast: old cliffs, softened by the years and sloping gently to the water under a cloak of unbroken green, with a fringe of jagged grey boulders at their base to break the water. There were a few small stretches of pale sand, none large enough for Temeraire to land even if they had not grown wary; but otherwise the trees were impenetrable, even after they had flown straight inland for nearly an hour.

It was lonely, and as monotonous as flying over empty ocean; the wind among the leaves instead of the lapping of the waves, only a different variety of silence. Temeraire looked eagerly at every occasional animal cry that broke the stillness, but saw nothing past the ground cover, so thickly overgrown were the trees. "Does no one live here?" he asked, eventually.

He might have been keeping his voice low because of the cold, but Laurence felt the same inclination to preserve the quiet, and answered softly, "No; we have flown too deep. Even the most powerful tribes live only along the coasts, and never venture so far inland; there are too many feral dragons and other beasts, too savage to confront."

They continued on without speaking for some time; the sun was very strong, and Laurence drifted neither awake nor asleep, his head nodding against his chest. Unchecked, Temeraire kept on his course, the slow pace no challenge to his endurance; when at last Laurence roused, on Temeraire's sneezing again, the sun was past its zenith: they would miss dinner.

Temeraire did not express a wish to stay longer when Laurence said they ought to turn around; if anything he quickened his pace. They had gone so far that the coastline was out of sight, and they flew back only by Laurence's compass, with no landmarks to guide them through the unchanging jungle. The smooth curve of the ocean was very welcome, and Temeraire's spirits rose as they struck out again over the waves. "At least I am not tiring anymore, even if I am sick," he said, and then sneezed himself thirty feet directly upwards, with a sound not unlike cannon-fire.

They did not reach the *Allegiance* again until nearly dark, and Laurence discovered he had missed more than his dinner-hour. Another sailor besides Tripp had also spied Feng Li on deck the night before, with similar results, and during Laurence's absence the story of the ghost had already gone round the ship, magnified a dozen times over and thoroughly entrenched. All his attempted explanations were useless, the ship's company wholly convinced: three men now swore they had seen the ghost dancing a jig upon the foresail yard the night before, foretelling its doom; others from the middle watch claimed the ghost had been wafting about the rigging all night long.

Liu Bao himself flung fuel onto the fire; having inquired and heard the tale during his visit to the deck the next day, he shook his head and opined that the ghost was a sign that someone aboard had acted immorally with a woman. This qualified nearly every man aboard; they muttered a great deal about foreign ghosts with unreasonably prudish sensibilities, and discussed the subject anxiously at meals, each one trying to persuade himself and his messmates that *he* could not possibly be the guilty culprit; *his* infraction had been small and innocent, and in any case he had always meant to marry her, the instant he returned.

As yet general suspicion had not fallen onto a single individual, but it was only a matter of time; and then the wretch's life would hardly be worth living. In the meantime, the men went about their duties at night only reluctantly, going so far as to refuse orders which would have required them to be alone on any part of the deck. Riley attempted to set an example to the men by walking out of sight during his watches, but this had less effect than might have been desired by his having to visibly steel himself first. Laurence roundly scolded Allen, the first of his own crew to mention the ghost in his hearing, so no more was said in front of him; but the aviators showed themselves inclined to stay close to Temeraire on duty, and to come to and from their quarters in groups.

Temeraire was himself too uncomfortable to pay a great deal of attention. He found the degree of fear baffling, and expressed some disappointment at never seeing the specter when so many others had evidently had a glimpse; but for the most part he was occupied in sleeping, and directing his frequent sneezes away from the ship. He tried to conceal his coughing at first when it developed, reluctant to be dosed: Keynes had been brewing the medicine in a great pot in the galley since the first evidence of Temeraire's illness, and the foul stench rose through the boards ominously. But late on the third day he was seized with a fit he could not suppress, and Keynes and his assistants trundled the pot of medicine up onto the dragondeck: a thick, almost gelatinous brownish mixture, swimming in a glaze of liquid orange fat.

Temeraire stared down into the pot unhappily. "Must I?" he asked.

"It will do its best work drunk hot," Keynes said, implacable, and Temeraire squeezed his eyes shut and bent his head to gulp.

"Oh; oh, *no*," he said, after the first swallow; he seized the barrel of water which had been prepared for him and upended it into his mouth, spilling much over his chops and neck and onto the deck as he guzzled. "I cannot possibly drink any more of it," he said, putting the barrel down. But with much coaxing and exhortation, he at length got down the whole, miserable and retching all the while.

Laurence stood by, stroking him anxiously: he did not dare speak again. Keynes had been so very cutting at his first suggestion of a brief respite. Temeraire at last finished and slumped to the deck, saying passionately, "I will *never* be ill again, *ever*," but despite his unhappiness, his coughing was indeed silenced, and that night he slept more easily, his breathing a good deal less labored.

Laurence stayed on deck by his side as he had every night of the illness; with Temeraire sleeping quiet he had ample opportunity to witness the absurd lengths the men practiced to avoid the ghost: going two at a time to the head, and huddling around the two lanterns left on deck instead of sleeping. Even the officer of the watch stayed uneasily close, and looked pale every time he took the walk along the deck to turn the glass and strike the bell.

Nothing would cure it but distraction, and of that there was little prospect: the weather was holding fair, and there was little chance of meeting any enemy who would offer battle; any ship which did not wish to fight could easily outrun them. Laurence could not really wish for either, in any case; the situation could only be tolerated until they reached port, where the break in the journey would hopefully dispel the myth.

Temeraire snuffled in his sleep and half-woke, coughing wetly, and sighed in misery. Laurence laid a hand on him and opened the book on his lap again; the lantern swaying beside him gave a light, if an unreliable one, and he read slowly aloud until Temeraire's eyelids sank heavily down again.

Chapter 9

"I DO NOT mean to tell you your business," General Baird said, showing very little reluctance to do so. "But the winds to India are damned unpredictable this time of year, with the winter monsoon barely over. You are as likely to find yourselves blown straight back here. You had much better wait for Lord Caledon to arrive, especially after this news about Pitt."

He was a younger man, but long-faced and serious, with a very decided mouth; the high upstanding collar of his uniform pushed up his chin and gave his neck a stiff, elongated look. The new British governor not yet arrived, Baird was temporarily in command of the Capetown settlement, and ensconced in the great fortified castle in the midst of the town at the foot of the great flat-topped Table Mount. The courtyard was brilliant with sun, hazy glints cast off the bayonets of the troops drilling smartly on the grounds, and the encircling walls blocked the best part of the breeze which had cooled them on the walk up from the beach.

"We cannot be sitting in port until June," Hammond said. "It would be much better if we were to sail and be delayed at sea, with an obvious attempt to make haste, than to be idle in front of Prince Yongxing. He has already been asking me how much longer we expect the journey to take, and where else we may be stopping."

"I am perfectly happy to get under way as soon as we are resupplied, for my part," Riley said, putting down his empty teacup and nodding to the servant to fill it again. "She is not a fast ship by any means, but I would lay a thousand pounds on her against any weather we might meet."

"Not, of course," he said to Laurence later, somewhat anxiously, as they walked back to the *Allegiance,* "that I would really like to try her against a typhoon. I never meant anything of the sort; I was thinking only of ordinary bad weather, perhaps a little rain."

Their preparations for the long remaining stretch of ocean went ahead: not merely buying livestock, but also packing and preserving more salt meat, as there were no official naval provisions yet to be had from the port. Fortunately there was no shortage of supply; the settlers did not greatly resent the mild occupation, and they were happy enough to sell from their herds. Laurence was more occupied with the question of demand, for Temeraire's appetite was greatly diminished since he had been afflicted by the cold, and he had begun to pick querulously at his food, complaining of a lack of flavor.

There was no proper covert, but, alerted by Volly, Baird had anticipated their arrival and arranged the clearing of a large green space near the landing ground so the dragon could rest comfortably. Temeraire having flown to this stable location, Keynes could perform a proper inspection: the dragon was directed to lay his head flat and open his jaws wide, and the surgeon climbed inside with a lantern, picking his way carefully among the hand-sized teeth to peer down into Temeraire's throat.

Watching anxiously from outside with Granby, Laurence could see that Temeraire's narrow forked tongue, ordinarily pale pink, was presently coated thickly with white, mottled with virulent red spots.

"I expect that is why he cannot taste anything; there is

nothing out of the ordinary in the condition of his passages," Keynes said, shrugging as he climbed out of Temeraire's jaws, to applause: a crowd of children, both settlers and natives, had gathered around the clearing's fence to watch, fascinated as if at a circus. "And they use their tongues for scent also, which must be contributing to the difficulties."

"Surely this is not a usual symptom?" Laurence asked.

"I don't recall ever seeing a dragon lose his appetite over a cold," Granby put in, worriedly. "In the ordinary line of things, they get hungrier."

"He is only pickier than most about his food," Keynes said. "You will just have to force yourself to eat until the illness has run its course," he added, to Temeraire, sternly. "Come, here is some fresh beef; let us see you finish the whole."

"I will try," Temeraire said, heaving a sigh that came rather like a whine through his stuffed nose. "But it is very tiresome chewing on and on when it does not taste like anything." He obediently if unenthusiastically downed several large hunks, but only mauled a few more pieces about without swallowing much of them, and then went back to blowing his nose into the small pit which had been dug for this purpose, wiping it against a heap of broad palm leaves.

Laurence watched silently, then took the narrow pathway winding from the landing grounds back to the castle: he found Yongxing resting in the formal guest quarters with Sun Kai and Liu Bao. Thin curtains had been pinned up to dim the sunlight instead of the heavy velvet drapes, and two servants were making a breeze by standing at the full-open windows and waving great fans of folded paper; another stood by unobtrusively, refilling the envoys' cups with tea. Laurence felt untidy and hot in contrast, his collar wet and limp against his neck after the day's exertions, and dust thick on his boots, spattered also with blood from Temeraire's unfinished dinner.

After the translator was summoned and some pleasantries exchanged, he explained the situation and said, as gracefully as he could manage, "I would be grateful if you would lend me your cooks to make some dish for Temeraire, in your style, which might have some stronger flavor than fresh meat alone."

He had scarcely finished asking before Yongxing was giving orders in their language; the cooks were dispatched to the kitchens at once. "Sit and wait with us," Yongxing said, unexpectedly, and had a chair brought for him, draped over with a long narrow silk cloth.

"No, thank you, sir; I am all over dirt," Laurence said, eyeing the beautiful drapery, pale orange and patterned with flowers. "I do very well."

But Yongxing only repeated the invitation; yielding, Laurence gingerly sat down upon the very edge of the chair, and accepted the cup of tea which he was offered. Sun Kai nodded at him, in an odd approving fashion. "Have you heard anything from your family, Captain?" he inquired through the translator. "I hope all is well with them."

"I have had no fresh news, sir, though I thank you for the concern," Laurence said, and passed another quarter of an hour in further small talk of the weather and the prospects for their departure, wondering a little at this sudden change in his reception.

Shortly a couple of lamb carcasses, on a bed of pastry and dressed with a gelatinous red-orange sauce, emerged from the kitchens and were trundled along the path to the clearing on great wooden trays. Temeraire brightened at once, the intensity of the spice penetrating even his dulled senses, and made a proper meal. "I was hungry after all," he said, licking sauce from his chops and putting his head down to be cleaned off more thoroughly.

Laurence hoped he was not doing Temeraire some harm by the measure: some traces of the sauce got on his hand as he wiped Temeraire clean, and it literally burnt upon the skin, leaving marks. But Temeraire seemed comfortable enough, not even asking more water than usual, and Keynes opined that keeping him eating was of the greater importance.

Laurence scarcely needed to ask for the extended loan of the cooks; Yongxing not only agreed but made it a point to supervise and press them to do more elaborate work, and his own physician was called for and recommended the introduction of various herbs into the dishes. The poor servants were sent out into the markets—silver the only language they shared with the local merchants—to collect whatever ingredients they could find, the more exotic and expensive the better.

Keynes was skeptical but unworried, and Laurence, being more conscious of owing gratitude than truly grateful, and guilty over his lack of sincerity, did not try to interfere with the menus, even as the servants daily trooped back from the markets with a succession of increasingly bizarre ingredients: penguins, served stuffed with grain and berries and their own eggs; smoked elephant meat brought in by hunters willing to risk the dangerous journey inland; shaggy, fat-tailed sheep with hair instead of wool; and the still-stranger spices and vegetables. The Chinese insisted on these last, swearing they were healthy for dragons, though the English custom had always been to feed them a steady diet of meat alone. Temeraire, for his part, ate the complicated dishes one after another with no ill-effects other than a tendency to belch foully afterwards.

The local children had become regular visitors, emboldened by seeing Dyer and Roland so frequently climbing on and about Temeraire; they began to view the search for ingredients as a game, cheering every new dish, or occasionally hissing those they felt insufficiently imaginative. The native children were members of the various tribes which lived about the region. Most lived by herding, but others by foraging in the mountains and the forests beyond, and these in particular joined in the fun, daily bringing items which their older relations had found too bizarre for their own consumption.

The crowning triumph was a misshapen and overgrown fungus brought back to the clearing by a group of five children with an air of triumph, its roots still covered with wet black dirt: mushroom-like, but with three brown-spotted caps instead of one, arranged one atop the other along the stem, the largest nearly two feet across, and so fetid they carried it with faces averted, passing it among one another with much shrieking laughter.

The Chinese servants took it back to the castle kitchens with great enthusiasm, paying the children with handfuls of colored ribbons and shells. Only shortly thereafter, General Baird appeared in the clearing, to complain: Laurence followed him back to the castle and understood the objections before he had fairly entered the complex. There was no visible smoke, but the air was suffused with the cooking smell, something like a mixture of stewed cabbage and the wet green mold which grew on the deck beams in humid weather; sour, cloying, and lingering upon the tongue. The street on the other side of the wall from the kitchens, ordinarily thronged with local merchants, was deserted; and the halls of the castle were nearly uninhabitable from the miasma. The envoys were quartered in a different building, well away from the kitchens, and so had not been personally affected, but the soldiers were quartered directly by and could not possibly be asked to eat in the repulsive atmosphere.

The laboring cooks, whose sense of smell, Laurence could only think, had been dulled by the week of producing successively more pungent dishes, protested through the interpreter that the sauce was not done, and all the persuasion Laurence and Baird together could muster was required to make them surrender the great stew-pot. Baird shamelessly ordered a couple of unlucky privates to carry it over to the clearing, the pot suspended between them on a broad tree branch. Laurence followed after them, trying to breathe shallowly.

However, Temeraire received it with enthusiasm, far more pleased that he could actually perceive the smell than put off by its quality. "It seems perfectly nice to me," he said, and nodded impatiently for it to be poured over his meat. He devoured an entire one of the local humpbacked oxen slathered in the stuff, and licked the insides of the pot clean, while Laurence watched dubiously from as far a distance as was polite.

Temeraire sprawled into a blissful somnolence after his meal, murmuring approval and hiccoughing a little between words, almost drunkenly. Laurence came closer, a little alarmed to see him so quickly asleep, but Temeraire roused at the prodding, beaming and enthusiastic, and insisted on nuzzling at Laurence closely. His breath had grown as unbearable as the original stench; Laurence averted his face and tried not to retch, very glad to escape when Temeraire fell asleep again and he could climb out of the affectionate embrace of the dragon's forelegs.

Laurence had to wash and shift his clothes before he could consider himself presentable. Even afterwards, he could still catch the lingering odor in his hair; too much to bear, he thought, and felt himself justified in carrying the protest back to the Chinese. It gave no offense, but it was not received with quite the gravity he had hoped for: indeed Liu Bao laughed uproariously when Laurence had described the effects of the mushroom; and when Laurence suggested that perhaps they might organize a more regular and limited set of dishes, Yongxing dismissed the notion, saying, "We cannot insult a *tien-lung* by offering him the same day in and day out; the cooks will just have to be more careful."

Laurence left without managing to carry his point, and with the suspicion that his control over Temeraire's diet had been usurped. His fears were soon confirmed. Temeraire woke the next day after an unusually long sleep, much improved and no longer so congested. The cold vanished entirely after a few days more, but though Laurence hinted repeatedly that there was no further need for assistance, the prepared dishes continued to come. Temeraire certainly made no objections, even as his sense of smell began to be restored. "I think I am beginning to be able to tell the spices from one another," he said, licking his claws daintily clean: he had taken to picking up the food in his forelegs to eat, rather than simply feeding from the tubs. "Those red things are called hua jiao, I like them very much."

"So long as you are enjoying your meals," Laurence said. "I can hardly say anything more without being churlish," he confided to Granby later that evening, over their own supper in his cabin. "If nothing else at least their efforts made him more comfortable, and kept him eating healthily; I cannot now say thank you, no, especially when he likes it."

"If you ask me, it is still nothing less than interference," Granby said, rather disgruntled on his behalf. "And however are we to keep him fed in this style, when we have taken him back home?"

Laurence shook his head, both at the question and at the use of *when;* he would gladly have accepted uncertainty on the former point, if he might have had any assurance of the latter.

* * *

The *Allegiance* left Africa behind sailing almost due east with the current, which Riley thought better than trying to beat up along the coast into the capricious winds that still blew more south than north for the moment, and not liking to strike out across the main body of the Indian Ocean. Laurence watched the narrow hook of the land darken and fade into the ocean behind them; four months into the journey, and they were now more than halfway to China.

A similarly disconsolate mood prevailed among the rest of the ship's company as they left behind the comfortable port and all its attractions. There had been no letters waiting in Capetown, as Volly had brought their mail with him, and little prospect of receiving any word from home ahead, unless some faster-sailing frigate or merchantman passed them by; but few of those would be sailing to China so early in the season. They thus had nothing to anticipate with pleasure, and the ghost still loomed ominously in all their hearts.

Preoccupied by their superstitious fears, the sailors were not as attentive as they ought to have been. Three days out of port, Laurence woke before dawn out of an uneasy sleep to the sound, penetrating easily through the bulkhead that separated his quarters from the next cabin, of Riley savaging poor Lieutenant Beckett, who had been on the middle watch. The wind had shifted and risen during the night, and in confusion Beckett had put them on the wrong heading and neglected to reef the main and mizzen: ordinarily his mistakes were corrected by the more experienced sailors, who would cough meaningfully until he hit upon the right order to give, but more anxious to avoid the ghost and stay out of the rigging, no one had on this occasion given him warning, and now the *Allegiance* had been blown far north out of her course.

The swell was rising some fifteen feet in height under a

lightening sky, the waves pale, green-tinted, and translucent as glass under their soapy white lather, leaping up into sharp peaks and spilling down again over themselves in great clouds of spray. Climbing to the dragondeck, Laurence pulled the hood of his sou'wester further forward, lips already dry and stiff with salt. Temeraire was curled tightly in upon himself, as far from the edge of the deck as he could manage, his hide wet and glossy in the lantern-light.

"I do not suppose they could build up the fires a little in the galley?" Temeraire asked, a little plaintively, poking his head out from under his wing, eyes squinted down to slits to avoid the spray; he coughed a little for emphasis. This was quite possibly a piece of dramatics, for Temeraire had otherwise thoroughly recovered from his cold before their leaving port, but Laurence had no desire to risk its recurrence. Though the water was bathwater-warm, the wind still gusting erratically from the south had a chill. He marshaled the crew to collect oilskins to cover Temeraire and had the harness-men stitch them together so they would stay.

Temeraire looked very odd under the makeshift quilt, only his nose visible, and shuffling awkwardly like an animated heap of laundry whenever he wished to change position. Laurence was perfectly content so long as he was warm and dry, and ignored the muffled sniggering from the forecastle; also Keynes, who made noises about coddling patients and encouraging malingering. The weather precluded reading on deck, so he climbed a little way under the covers himself to sit with Temeraire and keep him company. The insulation kept in not only the heat from the galley below but the steady warmth of Temeraire's own body as well; Laurence soon needed to shed his coat, and grew drowsy against Temeraire's side, responding only vaguely and without much attention to the conversation.

"Are you asleep, Laurence?" Temeraire asked; Laurence roused with the question, and wondered if he had indeed been asleep a long time, or whether perhaps a fold of the oilskin quilt had fallen down to obscure the opening: it was grown very dark.

He pushed his way out from under the heavy oilskins; the ocean had smoothed out almost to a polished surface, and directly ahead a solid bank of purple-black clouds stretched across the whole expanse of the eastern horizon, its puffy, windswept fringe lit from behind by the sunrise into thick red color; deeper in the interior, flashes of sudden lightning briefly limned the edges of towering cloud masses. Far to the north, a ragged line of clouds was marching to join the greater multitude ahead of them, curving across the sky to a point just past the ship. The sky directly above was still clear.

"Pray have the storm-chains fetched, Mr. Fellowes," Laurence said, putting down his glass. The rigging was already full of activity.

"Perhaps you should ride the storm out aloft," Granby suggested, coming to join him at the rail. It was a natural suggestion to make: though Granby had been on transports before, he had served at Gibraltar and the Channel almost exclusively and did not have much experience of the open sea. Most dragons could stay aloft a full day, if only coasting on the wind, and well-fed and watered beforehand. It was a common way to keep them out of the way when a transport came into a thunderstorm or a squall: this was neither.

In answer, Laurence only shook his head briefly. "It is just as well we have put together the oilskins; he will be much easier with them beneath the chains," he said, and saw Granby take his meaning.

The storm-chains were brought up piecemeal from below, each iron link as thick around as a boy's wrist, and laid over Temeraire's back in crosswise bands. Heavy cables, wormed and parceled to strengthen them, were laced through all the chain links and secured to the four double-post bitts in the corners of the dragondeck. Laurence inspected all the knots anxiously, and had several redone before he pronounced himself satisfied.

"Do the bonds catch you anywhere?" he asked Temeraire. "They are not too tight?"

"I cannot move with all of these chains upon me," Temeraire said, trying the narrow limits of his movement, the end of his tail twitching back and forth uneasily as he pushed against the restraints. "It is not at all like the harness; what are these for? Why must I wear them?"

"Pray do not strain the ropes," Laurence said, worried, and went to look: fortunately none had frayed. "I am sorry for the need," he added, returning, "but if the seas grow heavy, you must be fast to the deck: else you could slide into the ocean, or by your movement throw the ship off her course. Are you very uncomfortable?"

"No, not very," Temeraire said, but unhappily. "Will it be for long?"

"While the storm lasts," Laurence said, and looked out past the bow: the cloudbank was fading into the dim and leaden mass of the sky, the newly risen sun swallowed up already. "I must go and look at the glass."

The mercury was very low in Riley's cabin: empty, and no smell of breakfast beyond the brewing coffee. Laurence took a cup from the steward and drank it standing, hot, and went back on deck; in his brief absence the sea had risen perhaps another ten feet, and now the *Allegiance* was showing her true mettle, her iron-bound prow slicing the waves cleanly, and her enormous weight pressing them away to either side.

Storm-covers were being laid down over the hatches; Laurence made a final inspection of Temeraire's restraints, then said to Granby, "Send the men below; I will take the first watch." He ducked under the oilskins by Temeraire's head again and stood by him, stroking the soft muzzle. "We are in for a long blow, I am afraid," he said. "Could you eat something more?"

"I ate yesterday late, I am not hungry," Temeraire said; in the dark recesses of the hood his pupils had widened, liquid and black, with only the thinnest crescent rims of blue. The iron chains moaned softly as he shifted his weight again, a higher note against the steady deep creaking of the timber, the ship's beams working. "We have been in a storm before, on the *Reliant*," he said. "I did not have to wear such chains then."

"You were much smaller, and so was the storm," Laurence said, and Temeraire subsided, but not without a wordless grumbling murmur of discontent; he did not pursue conversation, but lay silently, occasionally scraping his talons against the edges of the chains. He was lying with his head pointed away from the bow, to avoid the spray; Laurence could look out past his muzzle and watch the sailors, busy getting on the storm-lashings and taking in the topsails, all noise but the low metallic grating muffled by the thick layer of fabric.

By two bells in the forenoon watch, the ocean was coming over the bulwarks in thick overlapping sheets, an almost continuous waterfall pouring over the edge of the dragondeck onto the forecastle. The galleys had gone cold; there would be no fires aboard until the storm had blown over. Temeraire huddled low to the deck and complained no more but drew the oilskin more closely around them, his muscles twitching beneath the hide to shake off the rivulets that burrowed deep between the layers. "All hands, all hands," Riley was saying, distantly, through the wind; the bosun took up the call with his bellowing voice cupped in his hand, and the men came scrambling up onto the deck, *thump-thump* of many hurrying feet through the planking, to begin the work of shortening sail and getting her before the wind.

The bell was rung without fail at every turn of the half-hourglass, their only measure of time; the light had failed early on, and sunset was only an incremental increase of darkness. A cold blue phosphorescence washed the deck, carried on the surface of the water, and illuminated the cables and edges of the planks; by its weak glimmering the crests of the waves could be seen, growing steadily higher.

Even the *Allegiance* could not break the present waves, but must go climbing slowly up their faces, rising so steeply that Laurence could look straight down along the deck and see the bottom of the wave trenches below. Then at last her bow would get over the crest: almost with a leap she would tilt over onto the far side of the collapsing wave, gather herself, and plunge deep and with shattering force into the surging froth at the bottom of the trench. The broad fan of the dragondeck then rose streaming, scooping a hollow out of the next wave's face; and she began the slow climb again from the beginning, only the drifting sand in the glass to mark the difference between one wave and the next.

Morning: the wind as savage, but the swell a little lighter, and Laurence woke from a restless, broken sleep. Temeraire refused food. "I cannot eat anything, even if they could bring it me," he said, when Laurence asked, and closed his eyes again: exhausted more than sleeping, and his nostrils caked white with salt.

Granby had relieved him on watch; he and a couple of the crew were on deck, huddled against Temeraire's other side. Laurence called Martin over and sent him to fetch some rags. The present rain was too mixed with spray to be fresh, but fortunately they were not short of water, and the fore scuttlebutt had been full before the storm. Clinging with both hands to the life-lines stretched fore and aft the length of the deck, Martin crept slowly along to the barrel, and brought the rags dripping back.

Temeraire barely stirred as Laurence gently wiped the salt rims away from his nose.

A strange, dingy uniformity above with neither clouds nor sun visible; the rain came only in short drenching bursts flung at them by the wind, and at the summit of the waves the whole curving horizon was full of the heaving, billowing sea. Laurence sent Granby below when Ferris came up, and took some biscuit and hard cheese himself; he did not care to leave the deck. The rain increased as the day wore on, colder now than before; a heavy cross-sea pounded the *Allegiance* from either side, and one towering monster broke its crest nearly at the height of the foremast, the mass of water coming down like a blow upon Temeraire's body and jarring him from his fitful sleep with a start.

The flood knocked the handful of aviators off their feet, sent them swinging wildly from whatever hold they could get upon the ship. Laurence caught Portis before the midwingman could be washed off the edge of the dragondeck and tumbled down the stairs; but then he had to hold on until Portis could grip the life-line and steady himself. Temeraire was jerking against the chains, only half-awake and panicked, calling for Laurence; the deck around the base of the bitts was beginning to warp under his strength.

Scrambling over the wet deck to lay hands back on Temeraire's side, Laurence called reassurance. "It was only a wave; I am here," he said urgently. Temeraire stopped fighting the bonds and lowered himself panting to the deck: but the ropes had been stretched. The chains were looser now just when they were needed most, and the sea was too violent for landsmen, even aviators, to be trying to resecure the knots.

The *Allegiance* took another wave on her quarter and leaned alarmingly; Temeraire's full weight slid against the chains, further straining them, and instinctively he dug his claws into the deck to try and hold on; the oak planking splintered where he grasped at it. "Ferris, here; stay with him," Laurence bellowed, and himself struck out across the deck. Waves flooding the deck in succession now; he moved from one line to the next blindly, his hands finding purchase for him without conscious direction.

The knots were soaked through and stubborn, drawn tight by Temeraire's pulling against them. Laurence could only work upon them when the ropes came slack, in the narrow spaces between waves; every inch gained by hard labor. Temeraire was lying as flat as he could manage, the only help he could provide; all his other attention was given to keeping his place.

Laurence could see no one else across the deck, obscured by flying spray, nothing solid but the ropes burning his hands and the squat iron posts, and Temeraire's body a slightly darker region of the air. Two bells in the first dog watch: somewhere behind the clouds, the sun was setting. Out of the corner of his eye he saw a couple of shadows moving nearby; in a moment Leddowes was kneeling beside him, helping with the ropes. Leddowes hauled while Laurence tightened the knots, both of them clinging to each other and the iron bitts as the waves came, until at last the metal of the chains was beneath their hands: they had taken up the slack.

Nearly impossible to speak over the howl; Laurence simply pointed at the second larboard bitt, Leddowes nodded, and they set off. Laurence led, staying by the rail; easier to climb over the great guns than keep their footing out in the middle of the deck. A wave passed by and gave them a moment of calm; he was just letting go the rail to clamber over the first carronade when Leddowes shouted.

Turning, Laurence saw a dark shape coming at his head and flung up a protective hand only from instinct: a

terrific blow like being struck with a poker landed on his
arm. He managed to get a hand on the breeching of the
carronade as he fell; he had only a confused impression
of another shadow moving above him, and Leddowes,
terrified and staring, was scrambling back away with
both hands raised. A wave crashed over the side and Leddowes was abruptly gone.

Laurence clung to the gun and choked on salt water,
kicking for some purchase: his boots were full of water
and heavy as stone. His hair had come loose; he threw
his head back to get it out of his eyes, and managed to
catch the descending pry-bar with his free hand. Behind
it he saw with a shock of recognition Feng Li's face looming white, terrified and desperate. Feng Li tried to pull
the bar away for another attempt, and they wrestled it
back and forth, Laurence half-sprawling on the deck
with his boot-heels skidding over the the wet planks.

The wind was a third party to the battle, trying to
drive them apart, and ultimately victorious: the bar slipped
from Laurence's rope-numb fingers. Feng Li, still standing, went staggering back with arms flung wide as if to
embrace the blast of the wind: full willing, it carried him
backwards over the railing and into the churning water;
he vanished without trace.

Laurence clawed back to his feet and looked over the
rail: no sign of Feng Li or Leddowes, either; he could not
even see the surface of the water for the great clouds of
mist and fog rising from the waves. No one else had even
seen the brief struggle. Behind him, the bell was clanging
again for the turn of the glass.

Too confused with fatigue to make any sense of the
murderous attack, Laurence said nothing, other than to
briefly tell Riley the men had been lost overboard; he
could not think what else to do, and the storm occupied
all the attention he could muster. The wind began to fall

the next morning; by the start of the afternoon watch, Riley was confident enough to send the men to dinner, though by shifts. The heavy mass of cloud cover broke into patches by six bells, the sunlight streaming down in broad, dramatic swaths from behind the still-dark clouds, and all the hands privately and deeply satisfied despite their fatigue.

They were sorry over Leddowes, who had been well-liked and a favorite with all, but as for a long-expected loss rather than a dreadful accident: he was now proven to have been the prey of the ghost all along, and his mess-mates had already begun magnifying his erotic misdeeds in hushed voices to the rest of the crew. Feng Li's loss passed without much comment, nothing more than coincidence to their minds: if a foreigner with no sea-legs liked to go frolicking about on deck in a typhoon, there was nothing more to be expected, and they had not known him well.

The aftersea was still very choppy, but Temeraire was too unhappy to keep bound; Laurence gave the word to set him loose as soon as the crew had returned from their own dinner. The knots had swelled in the warm air, and the ropes had to be hacked through with axes. Set free, Temeraire shrugged the chains to the deck with a heavy thump, turned his head around, and dragged the oilskin blanket off with his teeth; then he shook himself all over, water running down in streams off his hide, and announced militantly, "I am going flying."

He leapt aloft without harness or companion, leaving them all behind and gaping. Laurence made an involuntary startled gesture after him, useless and absurd, and then dropped his arm, sorry to have so betrayed himself. Temeraire was only stretching his wings after the long confinement, nothing more; or so he told himself. He was deeply shocked, alarmed; but he could only feel the sensation dully, the exhaustion like a smothering weight lying over all his emotions.

"You have been on deck for three days," Granby said, and led him down below carefully. Laurence's fingers felt thick and clumsy, and did not quite want to grip the ladder rails. Granby gripped his arm once, when he nearly slipped, and Laurence could not quite stifle an exclamation of pain: there was a tender, throbbing line where the first blow from the pry-bar had struck across his upper arm.

Granby would have taken him to the surgeon at once, but Laurence refused. "It is only a bruise, John; and I had rather not make any noise about it yet." But then he had perforce to explain why: disjointedly, but the story came out as Granby pressed him.

"Laurence, this is outrageous. The fellow tried to murder you; we must do something," Granby said.

"Yes," Laurence answered, meaninglessly, climbing into his cot; his eyes were already closing. He had the dim awareness of a blanket being laid over him, and the light dimming; nothing more.

He woke clearer in his head, if not much less sore in body, and hurried from his bed at once: the *Allegiance* was low enough in the water he could at least tell that Temeraire had returned, but with the blanketing fatigue gone, Laurence had full consciousness to devote to worry. Coming out of his cabin thus preoccupied, he nearly fell over Willoughby, one of the harness-men, who was sleeping stretched across the doorway. "What are you doing?" Laurence demanded.

"Mr. Granby set us on watches, sir," the young man said, yawning and rubbing his face. "Will you be going up on deck then now?"

Laurence protested in vain; Willoughby trailed after him like an overzealous sheepdog all the way up to the dragondeck. Temeraire sat up alertly as soon as he caught sight of them, and nudged Laurence along into the shelter of his body, while the rest of the aviators drew closed their ranks behind him: plainly Granby had not kept the secret.

"How badly are you hurt?" Temeraire nosed him all over, tongue flickering out for reassurance.

"I am perfectly well, I assure you, nothing more than a bump on the arm," Laurence said, trying to fend him off; though he could not help being privately glad to see that Temeraire's fit of temper had at least for the moment subsided.

Granby ducked into the curve of Temeraire's body, and unrepentantly ignored Laurence's cold looks. "There; we have worked out watches amongst ourselves. Laurence, you do not suppose it was some sort of accident, or that he mistook you for someone else, do you?"

"No." Laurence hesitated, then reluctantly admitted, "This was not the first attempt. I did not think anything of it at the time, but now I am almost certain he tried to knock me down the fore hatch, after the New Year's dinner."

Temeraire growled deeply, and only with difficulty restrained himself from clawing at the deck, which already bore deep grooves from his thrashing about during the storm. "I am glad he fell overboard," he said venomously. "I hope he was eaten by sharks."

"Well, I am not," Granby said. "It will make it a sight more difficult to prove whyever he was at it."

"It cannot have been anything of a personal nature," Laurence said. "I had not spoken ten words to him, and he would not have understood them if I had. I suppose he could have run mad," he said, but with no real conviction.

"Twice, and once in the middle of a typhoon," Granby said, contemptuously, dismissing the suggestion. "No; I am not going to stretch that far: for my part, he must have done it under orders, and that means their prince is most likely behind it all, or I suppose one of those other Chinamen; we had better find out double-quick who, before they try it again."

This notion Temeraire seconded with great energy, and Laurence blew out a heavy sigh. "We had better call Hammond to my cabin in private and tell him about it," he said. "He may have some idea what their motives might be, and we will need his help to question the lot of them, anyway."

Summoned below, Hammond listened to the news with visible and increasing alarm, but his ideas were of quite another sort. "You seriously propose we should interrogate the Emperor's brother and his retinue like a gang of common criminals; accuse them of conspiracy to murder; demand alibis and evidence— You may as well put a torch to the magazine and scuttle the ship; our mission will have as much chance of success that way as the other. Or, no: more chance, because at least if we are all dead and at the bottom of the ocean there can be no cause for quarrel."

"Well, what do you propose, then, that we ought to just sit and smile at them until they do manage to kill Laurence?" Granby demanded, growing angry in his turn. "I suppose that would suit you just as well; one less person to object to your handing Temeraire over to them, and the Corps can go hang for all you care."

Hammond wheeled round on him. "My first care is for our country, and not for any one man or dragon, as yours ought to be if you had any proper sense of duty—"

"That is quite enough, gentlemen," Laurence cut in. "Our first duty is to establish a secure peace with China, and our first hope must be to achieve it without the loss of Temeraire's strength; on either score there can be no dispute."

"Then neither duty nor hope will be advanced by this

course of action," Hammond snapped. "If you did manage to find any evidence, what do you imagine could be done? Do you think we are going to put Prince Yongxing in chains?"

He stopped and collected himself for a moment. "I see no reason, no evidence whatsoever, to suggest Feng Li was not acting alone. You say the first attack came after the New Year; you might well have offended him at the feast unknowingly. He might have been a fanatic angered by your possession of Temeraire, or simply mad; or you might be mistaken entirely. Indeed, that seems to me the most likely—both incidents in such dim, confused conditions; the first under the influence of strong drink, the second in the midst of the storm—"

"For the love of Christ," Granby said rudely, making Hammond stare. "And Feng Li was shoving Laurence down hatchways and trying to knock his head in for some perfectly good reason, of course."

Laurence himself had been momentarily bereft of speech at this offensive suggestion. "If, sir, any of your suppositions are true, then any investigation would certainly reveal as much. Feng Li could not have concealed lunacy or such zealotry from all his country-men, as he could from us; if I had offended him, surely he would have spoken of it."

"And in ascertaining as much, this investigation would only require offering a profound insult to the Emperor's brother, who may determine our success or failure in Peking," Hammond said. "Not only will I not abet it, sir, I absolutely forbid it; and if you make any such ill-advised, reckless attempt, I will do my very best to convince the captain of the ship that it is his duty to the King to confine you."

This naturally ended the discussion, so far as Hammond was concerned in it; but Granby came back after closing the door behind him, with more force than strictly necessary. "I don't know that I have ever been more tempted to push a fellow's nose in for him. Laurence, Temeraire could translate for us, surely, if we brought the fellows up to him."

Laurence shook his head and went for the decanter; he was roused and knew it, and he did not immediately rely upon his own judgment. He gave Granby a glass, took his own to the stern lockers, and sat there drinking and looking out at the ocean: a steady dark swell of five feet, no more, rolling against her larboard quarter.

He set the glass aside at last. "No: I am afraid we must think better of it, John. Little as I like Hammond's mode of address, I cannot say that he is wrong. Only think, if we did offend him and the Emperor with such an investigation, and yet found no evidence, or worse yet some rational explanation—"

"—we could say hail and farewell to any chance of keeping Temeraire," Granby finished for him, with resignation. "Well, I suppose you are right and we will have to lump it for now; but I am damned if I like it."

Temeraire took a still-dimmer view of this resolution. "I do not care if we do not have any proof," he said angrily. "I am not going to sit and wait for him to kill you. The next time he comes out on deck I will kill *him*, instead, and that will put an end to it."

"No, Temeraire, you cannot!" Laurence said, appalled.

"I am perfectly sure I can," Temeraire disagreed. "I suppose he might not come out on deck again," he added, thoughtfully, "but then I could always knock a hole through the stern windows and come at him that way. Or perhaps we could throw in a bomb after him."

"You *must* not," Laurence amended hastily. "Even had we proof, we could hardly move against him; it would be grounds for an immediate declaration of war."

"If it would be so terrible to kill him, why is it not so

terrible for him to kill *you*?" Temeraire demanded. "Why is he not afraid of our declaring war on him?"

"Without proper evidence, I am sure Government would hardly take such a measure," Laurence said; he was fairly certain Government would not declare war *with* evidence, but that, he felt, was not the best argument for the moment.

"But we are not allowed to *get* evidence," Temeraire said. "And also I am not allowed to kill him, and we are supposed to be polite to him, and all of it for the sake of Government. I am very tired of this Government, which I have never seen, and which is always insisting that I must do disagreeable things, and does no good to anybody."

"All politics aside, we cannot be sure Prince Yongxing had anything to do with the matter," Laurence said. "There are a thousand unanswered questions: why he should even wish me dead, and why he would set a man-servant on to do it, rather than one of his guards; and after all, Feng Li could have had some reason of his own of which we know nothing. We cannot be killing people only on suspicion, without evidence; that would be to commit murder ourselves. You could not be comfortable afterwards, I assure you."

"But I could, too," Temeraire muttered, and subsided into glowering.

To Laurence's great relief, Yongxing did not come back up on deck for several days after the incident, which served to let the first heat of Temeraire's temper cool; and when at last he did make another appearance, it was with no alteration of manner at all: he greeted Laurence with the same cool and distant civility, and proceeded to give Temeraire another recitation of poetry, which after a little while caught Temeraire's interest, despite himself, and made him forget to keep glaring: he did not have a resentful nature. If Yongxing were conscious of any guilt whatsoever, it did not show in the slightest, and Laurence began to question his own judgment.

"I could easily have been mistaken," he said unhappily, to Granby and Temeraire, after Yongxing had quitted the deck again. "I cannot find I remember the details anymore; and after all I was half-stunned with fatigue. Maybe the poor fellow only came up to try and help, and I am inventing things out of whole cloth; it seems more fantastic to me with every moment. That the Emperor of China's brother should be trying to have me assassinated, as though I were any threat to him, is absurd. I will end by agreeing with Hammond, and calling myself a drunkard and a fool."

"Well, I'll call you neither," Granby said. "I can't make any sense of it myself, but the notion Feng Li just took a fancy to knock you on the head is all stuff. We will just have to keep a guard on you, and hope this prince doesn't prove Hammond wrong."

Chapter 10

᠅

*I*T WAS NEARLY three weeks more, passing wholly without incident, before they sighted the island of New Amsterdam: Temeraire delighted by the glistening heaps of seals, most sunbathing lazily upon the beaches and the more energetic coming to the ship to frolic in her wake. They were not shy of the sailors, nor even of the Marines who were inclined to use them for target practice, but when Temeraire descended into the water, they vanished away at once, and even those on the beach humped themselves sluggishly further away from the waterline.

Deserted, Temeraire swam about the ship in a disgruntled circle, then climbed back aboard: he had grown more adept at this maneuver with practice, and now barely set the *Allegiance* to bobbing. The seals gradually returned, and did not seem to object to him peering down at them more closely, though they dived deep again if he put his head too far into the water.

They had been carried southward by the storm nearly into the forties and had lost almost all their easting as well: a cost of more than a week's sailing. "The one benefit is that I think the monsoon has set in, finally," Riley said, consulting Laurence over his charts. "From here, we can strike out for the Dutch East Indies directly; it will be a good month and a half without landfall, but I have sent the boats to the island, and with a few days of sealing to add to what we already have, we should do nicely."

The barrels of seal meat, salted down, stank profoundly; and two dozen more fresh carcasses were hung in meat-lockers from the catheads to keep them cool. The next day, out at sea again, the Chinese cooks butchered almost half of these on deck, throwing the heads, tails, and entrails overboard with shocking waste, and served Temeraire a heap of steaks, lightly seared. "It is not bad, with a great deal of pepper, and perhaps more of those roasted onions," he said after tasting, now grown particular.

Still as anxious to please as ever, they at once altered the dish to his liking. He then devoured the whole with pleasure and laid himself down for a long nap, wholly oblivious to the great disapproval of the ship's cook and quartermasters, and the crew in general. The cooks had not cleaned after themselves, and the upper deck was left nearly awash in blood; this having taken place in the afternoon, Riley did not see how he could ask the men to wash the decks a second time for the day. The smell was overpowering as Laurence sat down to dinner with him and the other senior officers, especially as the small windows were obliged to be kept shut to avoid the still-more-pungent smell of the remaining carcasses hanging outside.

Unhappily, Riley's cook had thought along the same lines as the Chinese cooks: the main dish upon the table was a beautifully golden pie, a week's worth of butter gone into the pastry along with the last of the fresh peas from Capetown, accompanied by a bowl of bubbling-hot gravy; but when cut into, the smell of the seal meat was too distinctly recognizable, and the entire table picked at their plates.

"It is no use," Riley said, with a sigh, and scraped his serving back into the platter. "Take it down to the midshipmen's mess, Jethson, and let them have it; it would be a pity to waste." They all followed suit and made do with the remaining dishes, but it created a sad vacancy on the table, and as the steward carried away the platter, he could be heard through the door, talking loudly of "foreigners what don't know how to behave civilized, and spoil people's appetite."

They were passing around the bottle for consolation when the ship gave a queer jerk, a small hop in the water unlike anything Laurence had ever felt. Riley was already going to the door when Purbeck said suddenly, "Look there," and pointed out the window: the chain of the meat-locker was dangling loose, and the cage was gone.

They all stared; then a confusion of yells and screams erupted on deck, and the ship yawed abruptly to starboard, with the gunshot sound of cracking wood. Riley rushed out, the rest of them hard on his heels. As Laurence went up the ladder-way another crash shook her; he slipped down four rungs, and nearly knocked Granby off the ladder.

They popped out onto the deck jack-in-the-box fashion, all of them together; a bloody leg with buckled shoe and silk stocking was lying across the larboard gangway, all that was left of Reynolds, who had been the midshipman on duty, and two more bodies had fetched up against a splintered half-moon gap in the railing, apparently bludgeoned to death. On the dragondeck, Temeraire was sitting up on his haunches, looking around wildly; the other men on deck were leaping up into the rigging or scrambling for the forward ladder-way, struggling against the midshipmen who were trying to come up.

"Run up the colors," Riley said, shouting over the noise, even as he leapt to try and grapple with the double-wheel, calling several other sailors to come and help him; Basson, the coxswain, was nowhere to be seen, and the ship was still drifting off her course. She was moving steadily, so they had not grounded on a reef, and there was no sign of any other ship, the horizon clear all around. "Beat to quarters."

The drumroll started and drowned out any hope of learning what was going on, but it was the best means of getting the panicking men back into order, the most urgent matter of business. "Mr. Garnett, get the boats over the side, if you please," Purbeck called loudly, striding out to the middle of the rail, fixing on his hat; he had as usual worn his best coat to dinner, and made a tall, official figure. "Griggs, Masterson, what do you mean by this?" he said, addressing a couple of the hands peering down fearfully from the tops. "Your grog is stopped for a week; get down and go along to your guns."

Laurence pushed forward along the gangway, forcing a lane against the men now running to their proper places: one of the Marines hopping past, trying to pull on a freshly blacked boot, his hands greasy and slipping on the leather; the gun-crews for the aft carronades scrambling over one another. "Laurence, Laurence, what is it?" Temeraire called, seeing him. "I was asleep; what has happened?"

The *Allegiance* rocked abruptly over to one side, and Laurence was thrown against the railing; on the far side of the ship, a great jet of water fountained up and came splashing down upon the deck, and a monstrous draconic head lifted up above the railing: enormous, luridly orange eyes set behind a rounded snout, with ridges of webbing tangled with long trailers of black seaweed. An arm was still dangling from the creature's mouth, limply; it opened its maw and threw its head back with a jerk, swallowing the rest: its teeth were washed bright red with blood.

Riley called for the starboard broadside, and on deck Purbeck was drawing three of the gun-crews together around one of the carronades: he meant them to point it at the creature directly. They were casting loose its tackles, the strongest men blocking the wheels; all sweating and utterly silent but for low grunting, working as fast as they could, greenish-pale; the forty-two-pounder could not be easily handled.

"Fire, fire, you fucking yellow-arsed millers!" Macready yelling hoarsely in the tops, already reloading his own gun. The other Marines belatedly set off a ragged volley, but the bullets did not penetrate; the serpentine neck was clad in thickly overlapping scales, blue and silver-gilt. The sea-serpent made a low croaking noise and lunged at the deck, striking two men flat and seizing another in its mouth; Doyle's shrieks could be heard even from within, his legs kicking frantically.

"No!" Temeraire said. "Stop; *arrêtez*!" and followed this with a string of words in Chinese also; the serpent looked at him incuriously, with no sign of understanding, and bit down: Doyle's legs fell abruptly back to the deck, severed, blood spurting briefly in mid-air before they struck.

Temeraire held quite motionless with staring horror, his eyes fixed on the serpent's crunching jaws and his ruff completely flattened against his neck; Laurence shouted his name, and he came alive again. The fore- and main-masts lay between him and the sea-serpent; he could not come at the creature directly, so he leapt off the bow and winged around the ship in a tight circle to come up behind it.

The sea-serpent's head turned to follow his movement, rising higher out of the water; it laid spindly forelegs on the *Allegiance*'s railing as it lifted itself out, webbing stretched between unnaturally long taloned fingers. Its body was much narrower than Temeraire's, thickening only slightly along its length, but in size its head was larger, with eyes larger than dinner platters, terrible in their unblinking, dull savagery.

Temeraire dived; his talons skidded along the silver hide, but he managed to find purchase by putting his forearms nearly around the body: despite the serpent's length, it was narrow enough for him to grasp. The serpent croaked again, gurgling deep in its throat, and clung to the *Allegiance,* the sagging jowly folds of flesh along its throat working with its cries. Temeraire set himself and hauled back, wings beating the air furiously: the ship leaned dangerously under their combined force, and yells could be heard from the hatchways, where water was coming in through the lowest gunports.

"Temeraire, cut loose," Laurence shouted. "She will overset."

Temeraire was forced to let go; the serpent seemed to only have a mind to get away from him now: it crawled forward onto the ship, knocking askew the mainsail yards and tearing the rigging as it came, head weaving from side to side. Laurence saw his own reflection, weirdly elongated, in the black pupil; then the serpent blinked sideways, a thick translucent sheath of skin sliding over the orb, and moved on past; Granby was pulling him back towards the ladder-way.

The creature's body was immensely long; its head and forelegs vanished beneath the waves on the other side of the ship, and its hindquarters had not yet emerged, the scales shading to deeper blue and purple iridescence as the length of it kept coming, undulating onwards. Laurence had never seen one even a tenth the size; the Atlantic serpents reached no more than twelve feet even in the warm waters off the coast of Brazil, and those in the Pacific dived when ships drew near, rarely seen as anything more than fins breaking the water.

The master's-mate Sackler was coming up the ladder-way, panting, with a big sliver spade, seven inches wide, hastily tied onto a spar: he had been first mate on a South Seas whaler before being pressed. "Sir, sir; tell them to 'ware; oh Christ, it'll loop us," he yelled up, seeing Laurence through the opening, even as he threw the spade onto the deck and hauled himself out after.

With the reminder, Laurence remembered on occasion seeing a swordfish or tunny hauled up with a sea-serpent wrapped about it, strangling: it was their favorite means of seizing prey. Riley had heard the warning also; he was calling for axes, swords. Laurence seized one from the first basket handed up the ladder-way, and began chopping next to a dozen other men. But the body moved on without stopping; they made some cuts into pale, grey-white blubber, but did not even reach flesh, nowhere near cutting through.

"The head, watch for the head," Sackler said, standing at the rail with the cutting-spade ready, hands clenched and shifting anxiously around the pole; Laurence handed off his axe and went to try and give Temeraire some direction: he was still hovering above in frustration, unable to grapple with the sea-serpent while it was so entangled with the ship's masts and rigging.

The sea-serpent's head broke the water again, on the same side, just as Sackler had warned, and the coils of the body began to draw tight; the *Allegiance* groaned, and the railing cracked and began to give way under the pressure.

Purbeck had the gun positioned and ready. "Steady, men; wait for the downroll."

"Wait, wait!" Temeraire called: Laurence could not see why.

Purbeck ignored him and called out, "Fire!" The carronade roared, and the shot went flying across the water, struck the sea-serpent on the neck, and flew onwards before sinking. The creature's head was knocked sideways by the impact, and a burning smell of cooked meat rose; but the blow was not mortal: it only gargled in pain and began to tighten still further.

Purbeck never flinched, steady though the serpent's body was scarcely half a foot away from him now. "Spunge your gun," he said as soon as the smoke had died away, setting the men on another round. But it would be another three minutes at least before they could fire again, hampered by the awkward position of the gun and the confusion of three gun-crews flung together.

Abruptly a section of the starboard railing just by the gun burst under the pressure into great jagged splinters, as deadly as those scattered by cannon-fire. One stabbed Purbeck deep in the flesh of the arm, purple staining his coat sleeve instantly. Chervins threw up his arms, gargling around the shard in his throat, and slumped over the gun; Dyfydd hauled his body off onto the floor, never flagging despite the splinter stuck right through his jaw, the other end poking out the underside of his chin and dripping blood.

Temeraire was still hovering back and forth near the serpent's head, growling at it. He had not roared, perhaps afraid of doing so close to the *Allegiance*: a wave like that which had destroyed the *Valérie* would sink them just as easily as the serpent itself. Laurence was on the verge of ordering him to take the risk regardless: the men were hacking frantically, but the tough hide was resisting them, and in any moment the *Allegiance* might be broken beyond repair: if her futtocks cracked, or worse the keel bent, they might never be able to bring her into port again.

But before he could call, Temeraire suddenly gave a low frustrated cry, beat up into the air, and folded his wings shut: he fell like a stone, claws outstretched, and struck the sea-serpent's head directly, driving it below the water's surface. His momentum drove him beneath the waves also, and a deep purpling cloud of blood filled the water. "Temeraire!" Laurence cried, scrambling heedless over the shuddering, jerking body of the serpent, half-crawling and half-running along the length of the blood-slippery deck; he climbed out over the rail and onto the mainmast chains, while Granby grabbed at him and missed.

He kicked his boots off into the water, no very coherent plan in mind; he could swim only a little, and he had no knife or gun. Granby was trying to climb out to join him, but could not keep his feet with the ship sawing to and fro like a nursery rocking-horse. Abruptly a great shiver traveled in reverse along the silver-grey length of the serpent's body which was all that was visible; its hindquarters and tail surfaced in a convulsive leap, then fell back into the water with a tremendous splash; and it lay still at last.

Temeraire popped back out through the surface like a cork, bouncing partway out of the water and splashing down again: he coughed and spluttered, and spat: there was blood all over his jaws. "I think she is dead," he said, between his wheezing gasps for air, and slowly paddled himself to the ship's side: he did not climb aboard, but leaned against the *Allegiance*, breathing deeply and relying on his native buoyancy to keep him afloat. Laurence clambered over to him on the fretwork like a boy, and perched there stroking him, as much for his own comfort as Temeraire's.

Temeraire being too weary to climb back aboard at once, Laurence took one of the small boats and pulled Keynes around to inspect him for any signs of injury. There were some scratches—in one wound an ugly, sawedged tooth lodged—but none severe; Keynes, however, listened to Temeraire's chest again and looked grave, and opined that some water had entered the lungs.

With much encouragement from Laurence, Temeraire pulled himself back aboard; the *Allegiance* sagged more than usual, both from his fatigue and her own state of disarray, but he eventually managed to climb back aboard, though causing some fresh damage to the railing. Not even Lord Purbeck, devoted as he was to the ship's appearance, begrudged Temeraire the cracked banisters; indeed a tired but wholehearted cheer went up as he thumped down at last.

"Put your head down over the side," Keynes said, once Temeraire was fairly established on the deck; he groaned a little, wanting only to sleep, but obeyed. After leaning precariously far, and complaining in a stifled voice that he was growing dizzy, he did manage to cough up some quantity of salt water. Having satisfied Keynes, he shuffled himself slowly backwards until his position on the deck was more secure, and curled into a heap.

"Will you have something to eat?" Laurence said. "Something fresh; a sheep? I will have them prepare it for you however you like."

"No, Laurence, I cannot eat anything, not at all," Temeraire said, muffled, his head hidden under his wing and a shudder visible between his shoulder-blades. "Pray let them take her away."

The body of the sea-serpent still lay sprawled across the *Allegiance:* the head had bobbed to the surface on the larboard side, and now the whole impressive extent of it could be seen. Riley sent men in boats to measure it from nose to tail: more than 250 feet, at least twice the length of the largest Regal Copper Laurence had ever heard of, which had rendered it thus capable of encircling the whole vessel, though its body was less than twenty feet in diameter.

"Kiao, a sea-dragon," Sun Kai called it, having come up on deck to see what had happened; he informed them that there were similar creatures in the China Sea, though ordinarily smaller.

No one suggested eating it. After the measurements had been done, and the Chinese poet, also something of an artist, permitted to render an illustration, the axes were applied to it once more. Sackler led the effort with practiced strokes of the cutting-spade, and Pratt severed the thick armored column of the spine with three heavy blows. After this its own weight and the slow forward motion of the *Allegiance* did the rest of the work almost at once: the remaining flesh and hide parted with a sound like tearing fabric, and its separate halves slid away off the opposite sides.

There was already a great deal of activity in the water around the body: sharks tearing at the head, and other fishes also; now an increasingly furious struggle arose around the hacked and bloody ends of the two halves. "Let us get under way as best we can," Riley said to Purbeck; though the main- and mizzen sails and rigging had been badly mauled, the foremast and its rigging were untouched but for a few tangled ropes, and they managed to get a small spread of sail before the wind.

They left the corpse drifting on the surface behind them and got under way; in an hour or so it was little more than a silvery line on the water. Already the deck had been washed down, freshly scrubbed and sanded with holystone, and sluiced clean again, water pumped up with great enthusiasm, and the carpenter and his mates were engaged in cutting a couple of spars to replace the mainsail and mizzen topsail yards.

The sails had suffered greatly: spare sailcloth had to be brought up from stores, and this was found to have been rat-chewed, to Riley's fury. Some hurried patchwork was done, but the sun was setting, and the fresh cordage could not be rigged until morning. The men were let go by watches to supper, and then to sleep without the usual inspection.

Still barefoot, Laurence took some coffee and ship's biscuit when Roland brought it him, but stayed by Temeraire, who remained subdued and without appetite. Laurence tried to coax him out of the low spirits, worried that perhaps he had taken some deeper injury, not immediately apparent, but Temeraire said dully, "No, I am not hurt at all, nor sick; I am perfectly well."

"Then what has distressed you so?" Laurence at length asked, tentatively. "You did so very well today, and saved the ship."

"All I did was kill her; I do not see it is anything to be so proud of," Temeraire said. "She was not an enemy, fighting us for some cause; I think she only came because she was hungry, and then I suppose we frightened her, with the shooting, and that is why she attacked us; I wish I could have made her understand and leave."

Laurence stared: it had not occurred to him that Temeraire might not have viewed the sea-serpent as the monstrous creature it seemed to him. "Temeraire, you cannot think that beast anything like a dragon," he said. "It had no speech, nor intelligence; I dare say you are right that it came looking for food, but any animal can hunt."

"Why should you say such things?" Temeraire said. "You mean that she did not speak English, or French, or Chinese, but she was an ocean creature; how ought she have learned any human languages, if she was not tended by people in the shell? I would not understand them myself otherwise, but that would not mean I did not have intelligence."

"But surely you must have seen she was quite without reason," Laurence said. "She ate four of the crew, and killed six others: men, not seals, and plainly not dumb beasts; if she were intelligent, it would have been inhuman—uncivilized," he amended, stumbling over his choice of words. "No one has ever been able to tame a sea-serpent; even the Chinese do not say differently."

"You may as well say, that if a creature will not serve people, and learn their habits, it is not intelligent, and had just as well be killed," Temeraire said, his ruff quivering; he had lifted his head, stirred-up.

"Not at all," Laurence said, trying to think of how he could give comfort; to him the lack of sentience in the creature's eyes had been wholly obvious. "I am saying only that if they were intelligent, they would be able to learn to communicate, and we would have heard of it. After all, many dragons do not choose to take on a handler, and refuse to speak with men at all; it does not happen so very often, but it does, and no one thinks dragons unintelligent for it," he added, thinking he had chanced on a happy example.

"But what happens to them, if they do?" Temeraire said. "What should happen to me, if I were to refuse to obey? I do not mean a single order; what if I did not wish to fight in the Corps at all."

So far this had all been general; the suddenly narrower question startled Laurence, giving the conversation a more ominous cast. Fortunately, there was little work to be done with so light a spread of sail: the sailors were gathered on the forecastle, gambling with their grog rations and intent on their game of dice; the handful of aviators remaining on duty were talking together softly at the rail. There was no one likely to overhear, for which Laurence was grateful: others might misunderstand, and think Temeraire unwilling, even disloyal in some way. For his own part he could not believe there was any real risk of Temeraire's choosing to leave the Corps and all his friends; he tried to answer calmly. "Feral dragons are housed in the breeding grounds, very comfortably. If you chose, you might live there also; there is a large one in the north of Wales, on Cardigan Bay, which I understand is very beautiful."

"And if I did not care to live there, but wished to go somewhere else?"

"But how would you eat?" Laurence said. "Herds

which could feed a dragon would be raised by men, and their property."

"If men have penned up all the animals and left none wild, I cannot think it reasonable of them to complain if I take one now and again," Temeraire said. "But even making such allowance, I could hunt for fish. What if I chose to live near Dover, and fly as I liked, and eat fish, and did not bother anyone's herds; should I be allowed?"

Too late Laurence saw he had wandered onto dangerous ground, and bitterly regretted having led the conversation in this direction. He knew perfectly well Temeraire would be allowed nothing of the sort. People would be terrified at the notion of a dragon living loose among them, no matter how peaceable the dragon might be. The objections to such a scheme would be many and reasonable, and yet from Temeraire's perspective the denial would represent an unjust curtailment of his liberties. Laurence could not think how to reply without aggravating his sense of injury.

Temeraire took his silence for the answer it was, and nodded. "If I would not go, I should be put in chains again, and dragged off," he said. "I would be forced to go to the breeding grounds, and if I tried to leave, I would not be allowed; and the same for any other dragon. So it seems to me," he added, grimly, a suggestion of a low growling anger beneath his voice, "that we are just like slaves; only there are fewer of us, and we are much bigger and dangerous, so we are treated generously where they are treated cruelly; but we are still not free."

"Good God, that is not so," Laurence said, standing up: appalled, dismayed, at his own blindness as much as the remark. Small wonder if Temeraire had flinched from the storm-chains, if such a train of thought had been working through his imagination before now, and Laurence did not believe that it could be the result solely of the recent battle.

"No, it is not so; wholly unreasonable," Laurence repeated; he knew himself inadequate to debate with Temeraire on most philosophical grounds, but the notion was inherently absurd, and he felt he must be able to convince Temeraire of the fact, if only he could find the words. "It is as much to say that I am a slave, because I am expected to obey the orders of the Admiralty: if I refused, I would be dismissed the service and very likely hanged; that does not mean I am a slave."

"But you have chosen to be in the Navy and the Corps," Temeraire said. "You might resign, if you wished, and go elsewhere."

"Yes, but then I should have to find some other profession to support myself, if I did not have enough capital to live off the interest. And indeed, if you did not wish to be in the Corps, I have enough to purchase an estate, somewhere in the north, or perhaps Ireland, and stock the grounds. You might live there exactly as you liked, and no one could object." Laurence breathed again as Temeraire mulled this over; the militant light had faded a little from his eyes, and gradually his tail ceased its restless mid-air twitching and coiled again into a neatly spiraled heap upon the deck, the curving horns of his ruff lying more easily against his neck.

Eight bells rang softly, and the sailors left their dice game, the new watch coming on deck to put out the last handful of lights. Ferris came up the dragondeck stairs, yawning, with a handful of fresh crewmen still rubbing the sleep from their eyes; Baylesworth led the earlier watch below, the men saying, "Good night, sir; good night, Temeraire," as they went by, many of them patting Temeraire's flank.

"Good night, gentlemen," Laurence answered, and Temeraire gave a low warm rumble.

"The men may sleep on deck if they like, Mr. Tripp," Purbeck was saying, his voice carrying along from the stern. The ship's night settled upon her, the men gladly dropping along the forecastle, heads pillowed on coiled hawsers and rolled-up shirts; all darkness but for the solitary stern lantern, winking far at the other end of the ship, and the starlight; there was no moon, but the Magellanic Clouds were particularly bright, and the long cloudy mass of the Milky Way. Presently silence fell; the aviators also had disposed of themselves along the larboard railing, and they were again as nearly alone as they might be on board. Laurence had sat down once more, leaning against Temeraire's side; there was a waiting quality to Temeraire's silence.

And at length Temeraire said, "But if you did," as if there had been no break in the conversation; although not with the same heat of anger as before. "If you purchased an estate for me, that would still be your doing, and not mine. You love me, and would do anything you could to ensure my happiness; but what of a dragon like poor Levitas, with a captain of Rankin's sort, who did not care for his comfort? I do not understand what precisely capital is, but I am sure I have none of my own, nor any way of getting it."

He was at least not so violently distressed as before, but rather now sounded weary, and a little sad. Laurence said, "You do have your jewels, you know; the pendant alone is worth some ten thousand pounds, and it was a clear gift; no one could dispute that it is your own property in law."

Temeraire bent his head to inspect the piece of jewelry, the breastplate which Laurence had purchased for him with much of the prize-money for the *Amitié*, the frigate which had carried his egg. The platinum had suffered some small dents and scratches in the course of the journey, which remained because Temeraire would not suffer to be parted from it long enough for them to be sanded out, but the pearl and sapphires were as brilliant as ever.

"So is that what capital is, then? Jewels? No wonder it is so nice. But Laurence, that makes no difference; it was still your present, after all, not something which I won myself."

"I suppose no one has ever thought of offering dragons a salary, or prize-money. It is no lack of respect, I promise you; only that money does not seem to be of much use to dragons."

"It is of no use, because we are not permitted to go anywhere, or do as we like, and so have nothing to spend it upon," Temeraire said. "If I had money, I am sure I still could not go to a shop and buy more jewels, or books; we are even chided for taking our food out of the pen when it suits us."

"But it is not because you are a slave that you cannot go where you like, but because people would naturally be disturbed by it, and the public good must be consulted," Laurence said. "It would do you no good to go into town and to a shop if the keeper had fled before you came."

"It is not fair that we should be thus restricted by others' fears, when we have not done anything wrong; you must see it is so, Laurence."

"No, it is not just," Laurence said, reluctantly. "But people will be afraid of dragons no matter how they are told it is safe; it is plain human nature, foolish as it may be, and there is no managing around it. I am very sorry, my dear." He laid his hand on Temeraire's side. "I wish I had better answers for your objections; I can only add to these, that whatever inconveniences society may impose upon you, I would no more consider you a slave than myself, and I will always be glad to serve you in overcoming these as I may."

Temeraire huffed out a low sigh, but nudged Laurence affectionately and drew a wing down more closely about him; he said no more on the subject, but instead asked for the latest book, a French translation of the Arabian Nights, which they had found in Capetown. Laurence was glad enough to be allowed to thus escape, but uneasy: he did not think he had been very successful in the task of reconciling Temeraire to a situation with which Laurence had always thought him well-satisfied.

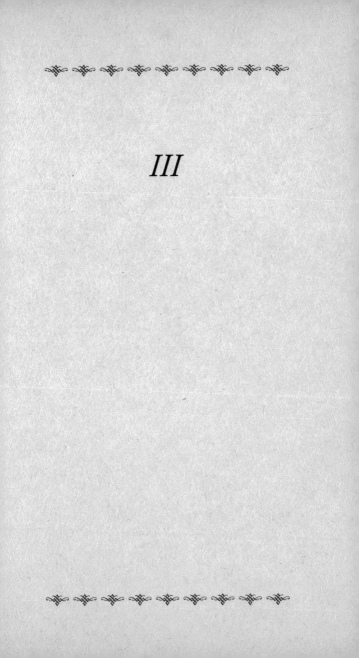

III

Chapter 11

Jane, I must ask you to forgive the long gap in this Letter, and the few hasty Words that are all by which I can amend the same now. I have not had Leisure to take up my pen these three weeks—since we passed out of Banka Strait we have been much afflicted by malarial Fevers. I have escaped sickness myself, and most of my men, for which Keynes opines we must be grateful to Temeraire, believing that the heat of his body in some wise dispels the Miasmas which cause the ague, and our close association thus affords some protection.

But we have been spared only to increase of Labor: Captain Riley has been confined to his bed since almost the very first, and Lord Purbeck falling ill, I have stood watch in turn with the ship's third and fourth lieutenants, Franks and Beckett. Both are willing young men, and Franks does his best, but is by no means yet prepared for the Duty of overseeing so vast a Ship as the *Allegiance,* nor to maintain discipline among her Crew—stammers, I am sorry to say, which explains his seeming Rudeness at table, which I had earlier remarked upon.

This being summer, and Canton proper barred to Westerners, we will put in at Macao tomorrow morning, where the ship's surgeon hopes to find Jesuit's bark to replenish our supply, and I some British merchantman, here out of season, to bear this home to you and to England. This will be my last Opportunity, as by special dispensation from Prince Yongxing we have Permission to continue on northward to the Gulf of Zhi-Li, so we may reach Peking through Tien-sing. The savings of time will be enormous, but as no Western ships are permitted north of Canton ordinarily, we cannot hope to find any British vessels once we have left port.

We have passed three French merchantmen already in our Approach, more than I had been used to see in this part of the World, though it has been some seven years since the occasion of my last visit to Canton, and foreign Vessels of all kinds are more numerous than formerly. At the present hour, a sometimes obscuring Fog lies over the harbor, and impedes the view of my glass, so I cannot be certain, but I fear there may also be a Man-of-War, though perhaps Dutch rather than French; certainly it is not one of our own. The *Allegiance* is of course in no direct danger, being on a wholly different Scale and under the Protection of the Imperial Crown, which the French cannot dare to slight in these Waters, but we fear that the French may have some Embassy of their own in train, which must naturally have or shortly form the Design of disrupting our own Mission.

On the subject of my earlier Suspicions, I can say nothing more. No further Attempts have been made, at least, though our sadly reduced Numbers would have made easier any such stroke, and I begin to hope that Feng Li acted from some inscrutable motive of his own, and not at the Behest of another.

The Bell has rung—I must go on Deck. Allow me to

send with this all my Affection and Respect, and believe me always,

> Yr. obdt. srvt,
> Wm. Laurence
> June 16, 1806

*T*HE FOG PERSISTED through the night, lingering as the *Allegiance* made her final approach to Macao harbor. The long curving stretch of sand, circled by tidy, square buildings in the Portuguese style and a neatly planted row of saplings, had all the comfort of familiarity, and most of the junks having their sails still furled might almost have been small dinghies at anchor in Funchal or Portsmouth roads. Even the softly eroded, green-clad mountains revealed as the grey fog trailed away would not have been out of place in any Mediterranean port.

Temeraire had been perched up on his hindquarters with eager anticipation; now he gave up looking and lowered himself to the deck in dissatisfaction. "Why, it does not look at all different," he said, cast down. "I do not see any other dragons, either."

The *Allegiance* herself, coming in off the ocean, was under heavier cover, and her shape was not initially clear to those on shore, revealed only as the sluggishly creeping sun burnt off the mists and she came farther into the harbor, a breath of wind pushing the fog off her bows. Then a nearly violent notice was taken: Laurence had put in at the colony before, and expected some bustle, perhaps exaggerated by the immense size of the ship, quite unknown in these waters, but was taken aback by the noise which arose almost explosively from the shore.

"*Tien-lung, tien-lung!*" The cry carried across the water, and many of the smaller junks, more nimble, came bounding across the water to meet them, crowding each other so closely they often bumped each other's hulls and the *Allegiance* herself, with all the hooting and shouting the crew could do to try and fend them off.

More boats were being launched from the shore even as they let go the anchor, with much caution necessitated by their unwelcome close company. Laurence was startled to see Chinese women coming down to the shore in their queer, mincing gait, some in elaborate and elegant dress, with small children and even infants in tow; and cramming themselves aboard any junk that had room to spare with no care for their garments. Fortunately the wind was mild and the current gentle, or the wallowing, overloaded vessels would certainly have been overset with a terrible loss of life. As it was they somehow made their way near the *Allegiance,* and when they drew near, the women seized their children and held them up over their heads, almost waving them in their direction.

"What on earth do they mean by it?" Laurence had never seen such an exhibition: by all his prior experience the Chinese women were exceedingly careful to seclude themselves from Western gaze, and he had not even known so many lived in Macao at all. Their antics were drawing the curious attention of the Westerners of the port also now, both along the shore and upon the decks of the other ships with which they shared the harbor. Laurence saw with sinking feelings that his previous night's assessment had not been incorrect: indeed rather short of the mark, for there were two French warships in the harbor, both handsome and trim, one a two-decker of some sixty-four guns and the smaller a heavy frigate of forty-eight.

Temeraire had been observing with a great deal of interest, snorting in amusement at some of the infants, who looked very ridiculous in their heavily embroidered gowns, like sausages in silk and gold thread, and mostly wailing unhappily at being dangled in mid-air. "I will ask them," he said, and bent over the railing to address one of the more energetic women, who had actually knocked over a rival to secure a place at the boat's edge for herself and her offspring, a fat boy of maybe two who somehow managed to bear a resigned, phlegmatic expression on his round-cheeked face despite being thrust nearly into Temeraire's teeth.

He blinked at her reply, and settled back on his haunches. "I am not certain, because she does not sound quite the same," he said, "but I think she says they are here to see me." Affecting unconcern, he turned his head and with what he evidently thought were covert motions rubbed at his hide with his nose, polishing away imaginary stains, and further indulged his vanity by arranging himself to best advantage, his head poised high and his wings shaken out and folded more loosely against his body. His ruff was standing broadly out in excitement.

"It is good luck to see a Celestial." Yongxing seemed to think this perfectly obvious, when applied to for some additional explanation. "They would never have a chance to see one otherwise—they are only merchants."

He turned from the spectacle dismissively. "We with Liu Bao and Sun Kai will be going on to Guangzhou to speak with the superintendant and the viceroy, and to send word of our arrival to the Emperor," he said, using the Chinese name for Canton, and waited expectantly; so that Laurence had perforce to offer him the use of the ship's barge for the purpose.

"I beg you will allow me to remind you, Your Highness, we may confidently expect to reach Tien-sing in three weeks' time, so you may consider whether to hold any communications for the capital." Laurence meant only to save him some effort; the distance was certainly better than a thousand miles.

But Yongxing very energetically made clear that he viewed this suggestion as nearly scandalous in its neglect of due respect to the throne, and Laurence was forced to apologize for having made it, excusing himself by a lack of knowledge of local custom. Yongxing was not mollified; in the end Laurence was glad to pack him and the other two envoys off at the cost of the services of the barge, though it left him and Hammond only the jolly-boat to convey them to their own rendezvous ashore: the ship's launch was already engaged in ferrying over fresh supplies of water and livestock.

"Is there anything I can bring you for your relief, Tom?" Laurence asked, putting his head into Riley's cabin.

Riley lifted his head from the pillows where he lay before the windows and waved a weak, yellow-tinged hand. "I am a good deal better. But I would not say no to a good port, if you can find a decent bottle in the place; I think my mouth has been turned down forever from the godawful quinine."

Reassured, Laurence went to take his leave of Temeraire, who had managed to coax the ensigns and runners into scrubbing him down, quite unnecessarily. The Chinese visitors were grown more ambitious, and had begun to throw gifts of flowers aboard, and other things also, less innocuous. Running up to Laurence very pale, Lieutenant Franks forgot to stutter in his alarm. "Sir, they are throwing burning incense onto the ship, pray, pray make them stop."

Laurence climbed up to the dragondeck. "Temeraire, will you please tell them nothing lit can be thrown at the ship. Roland, Dyer, mind what they throw, and if you see anything else that may carry a risk of fire, throw it back over at once. I hope they have better sense than to try setting off crackers," he added, without much confidence.

"I will stop them if they do," Temeraire promised. "You will see if there is somewhere I can come ashore?"

"I will, but I cannot hold out much hope; the entire territory is scarcely four miles square, and thoroughly built-up," Laurence said. "But at least we can fly over it, and perhaps even over Canton, if the mandarins do not object."

The English Factory was built facing directly onto the main beach, so there was no difficulty in finding it; indeed, their attention drawn by the gathered crowd, the Company commissioners had sent a small welcoming party to await them on shore, led by a tall young man in the uniform of the East India Company's private service, with aggressive sideburns and a prominent aquiline nose, giving him a predatory look rather increased than diminished by the alert light in his eyes. "Major Heretford, at your service," he said, bowing. "And may I say, sir, we are damned glad to see you," he added, with a soldier's frankness, once they were indoors. "Sixteen months; we had begun to think no notice would be taken of it at all."

With an unpleasant shock Laurence was recalled to the memory of the seizure of the East India merchant ships by the Chinese, all the long months ago: preoccupied by his own concerns over Temeraire's status and distracted by the voyage, he had nearly forgotten the incident entirely; but of course it could hardly have been concealed from the men stationed here. They would have spent the intervening months on fire to answer the profound insult.

"No action has been taken, surely?" Hammond asked, with an anxiety that gave Laurence a fresh distaste for him; there was a quality of fear to it. "It would of all things be most prejudicial."

Heretford eyed him sidelong. "No, the commissioners thought best under the circumstances to conciliate the Chinese, and await some more official word," in a tone that left very little doubt of where his own inclinations would have led him.

Laurence could not but find him sympathetic, though in the ordinary course he did not think very highly of the

Company's private forces. But Heretford looked intelligent and competent, and the handful of men under his command showed signs of good discipline: their weapons well-kept, and their uniforms crisp despite the nearly sopping heat.

The boardroom was shuttered against the heat of the climbing sun, with fans laid ready at their places to stir the moist, stifling air. Glasses of claret punch, cooled with ice from the cellars, were brought once the introductions had been completed. The commissioners were happy enough to take the post which Laurence had brought, and promised to see it conveyed back to England; this concluding the exchange of pleasantries, they launched a delicate but pointed inquiry after the aims of the mission.

"Naturally we are pleased to hear that Government has compensated Captains Mestis and Holt and Greggson, and the Company, but I cannot possibly overstate the damage which the incident has done to our entire operations." Sir George Staunton spoke quietly, but forcefully for all that; he was the chief of the commissioners despite his relative youth by virtue of his long experience of the nation. As a boy of twelve, he had accompanied the Macartney embassy itself in his father's train, and was one of the few British men perfectly fluent in the language.

Staunton described for them several more instances of bad treatment, and went on to say, "These are entirely characteristic, I am sorry to say. The insolence and rapacity of the administration has markedly increased, and towards us only; the Dutch and the French meet with no such treatment. Our complaints, which previously they treated with some degree of respect, are now summarily dismissed, and in fact only draw worse down upon us."

"We have been almost daily fearing to be ordered out entirely," Mr. Grothing-Pyle added to this; he was a portly man, his white hair somewhat disordered by the

vigorous action of his fan. "With no insult to Major
Heretford or his men," he nodded to the officer, "we
would be hard-pressed to withstand such a demand, and
you can be sure the French would be happy to help the
Chinese enforce it."

"And to take our establishments for their own once
we were expelled," Staunton added, to a circle of nodding heads. "The arrival of the *Allegiance* certainly puts
us in a different position, vis-à-vis the possibility of
resistance—"

Here Hammond stopped him. "Sir, I must beg leave to
interrupt you. There is no contemplation of taking the
Allegiance into action against the Chinese Empire: none;
you must put such a thought out of your minds entirely."
He spoke very decidedly, though he was certainly the
youngest man at the table, except for Heretford; a palpable coolness resulted. Hammond paid no attention. "Our
first and foremost goal is to restore our nation to enough
favor with the court to keep the Chinese from entering
into an alliance with France. All other designs are in-
significant by comparison."

"Mr. Hammond," Staunton said, "I cannot believe
there is any possibility of such an alliance; nor that it can
be so great a threat as you seem to imagine. The Chinese
Empire is no Western military power, impressive as their
size and their ranks of dragons may be to the inexperienced eye," Hammond flushed at this small jab, perhaps
not unintentional, "and they are militantly uninterested
in European affairs. It is a matter of policy with them to
affect even if not feel a lack of concern with what passes
beyond their borders, ingrained over centuries."

"Their having gone to the lengths of dispatching Prince
Yongxing to Britain must surely weigh with you, sir, as
showing that a change in policy may be achieved, if the
impetus be sufficient," Hammond said coolly.

They argued the point and many others with increasing politeness, over the course of several hours. Laurence had a struggle to keep his attention on the conversation, liberally laced as it was with references to names and incidents and concerns of which he knew nothing: some local unrest among the peasants and the state of affairs in Thibet, where apparently some sort of outright rebellion was in progress; the trade deficit and the necessity of opening more Chinese markets; difficulties with the Inca over the South American route.

But little though Laurence felt able to form his own conclusions, the conversation served another purpose for him. He grew convinced that while Hammond was thoroughly informed, his view of the situation was in direct contradiction on virtually all points with the established opinions of the commissioners. In one instance, the question of the kowtow ceremony was raised and treated by Hammond as inconsequential: naturally they would perform the full ritual of genuflection, and by so doing hopefully amend the insult given by Lord Macartney's refusal to do so in the previous embassy.

Staunton objected forcefully. "Yielding on this point with no concessions in return can only further degrade our standing in their eyes. The refusal was not made without reason. The ceremony is meant for envoys of tributary states, vassals of the Chinese throne, and having objected to it on these grounds before, we cannot now perform it without appearing to give way to the outrageous treatment they have meted out to us. It would of all things be most prejudicial to our cause, as giving them encouragement to continue."

"I can scarcely admit that anything could be more prejudicial to our cause, than to willfully resist the customs of a powerful and ancient nation in their own territory, because they do not meet our own notions of etiquette," Hammond said. "Victory on such a point can only be won by the loss of every other, as proved by the complete failure of Lord Macartney's embassy."

"I find I must remind you that the Portuguese prostrated themselves not only to the Emperor but to his portrait and letters, at every demand the mandarins made, and their embassy failed quite as thoroughly," Staunton said.

Laurence did not like the notion of groveling before any man, Emperor of China or no; but he thought it was not merely his own preferences which inclined him to Staunton's opinion on the matter. Abasement to such a degree could not help but provoke disgust even in a recipient who demanded the gesture, it seemed to him, and only lead to even more contemptuous treatment. He was seated on Staunton's left for dinner, and through their more casual conversation grew increasingly convinced of the man's good judgment; and all the more doubtful of Hammond's.

At length they took their leave and returned to the beach to await the boat. "This news about the French envoy worries me more than all the rest together," Hammond said, more to himself than to Laurence. "De Guignes is dangerous; how I wish Bonaparte had sent anyone else!"

Laurence made no response; he was unhappily conscious that his own sentiments were much the same towards Hammond himself, and he would gladly have exchanged the man if he could.

Prince Yongxing and his companions returned from their errand late the following day, but when applied to for permission to continue the journey, or even to withdraw from the harbor, he refused point-blank, insisting that the *Allegiance* should have to wait for further instructions. Whence these were to come, and when, he did not say; and in the meantime the local ships continued their pilgrimages even into the night, carrying great hanging paper lanterns in the bows to light their way.

Laurence struggled out of sleep very early the next morning to the sound of an altercation outside his door: Roland, sounding very fierce despite her clear, high treble, saying something in a mixture of English and Chinese, which she had begun to acquire from Temeraire. "What is that damned noise there?" he called strongly.

She peered in through the door, which she held only a little ajar, wide enough for her eye and mouth; over her shoulder he could see one of the Chinese servants making impatient gestures, and trying to get at the doorknob. "It is Huang, sir, he is making a fuss and says the prince wants you to come up to the deck at once, though I told him you had only gone to sleep after the middle watch."

He sighed and rubbed his face. "Very good, Roland; tell him I will come." He was in no humor to be up; late in his evening's watch, another visiting boat piloted by a young man more entreprenurial than skilled had been caught broadside by a wave. Her anchor, improperly set, had come flying up and struck the *Allegiance* from beneath, jabbing a substantial hole in her hold and soaking much of the newly purchased grain. At the same time the little boat had overturned herself, and though the harbor was not distant, the passengers in their heavy silk garments could not make their own way to safety, but had to be fished out by lantern-light. It had been a long and tiresome night, and he had been up watch and watch dealing with the mess before finally gaining his bed only in the small hours of the morning. He splashed his face with the tepid water in the basin and put on his coat with reluctance before going up to the deck.

Temeraire was talking with someone; Laurence had to look twice before he even realized that the other was in fact a dragon, like none he had ever seen before. "Laurence, this is Lung Yu Ping," Temeraire said, when Laurence had climbed up to the dragondeck. "She has brought us the post."

Facing her, Laurence found their heads were nearly on a level: she was smaller even than a horse, with a broad curving forehead and a long arrow-shaped muzzle, and an enormously deep chest rather along greyhound proportions. She could not have carried anyone on her back except a child, and wore no harness but a delicate collar of yellow silk and gold, from which hung a fine mesh like thin chainmail which covered her chest snugly, fixed to her forearms and talons by golden rings.

The mesh was washed with gold, striking against her pale green hide; her wings were a darker shade of green, and striped with narrow bands of gold. They were also unusual in appearance: narrow and tapered, and longer than she was; even folded upon her back, their long tips dragged along the ground behind her like a train.

When Temeraire had repeated the introductions in Chinese, the little dragon sat up on her haunches and bowed. Laurence bowed in return, amused to greet a dragon thus on an equal plane. The forms satisfied, she poked her head forward to inspect him more closely, leaning over to look him up and down on both sides with great interest; her eyes were very large and liquid, amber in color, and thickly lidded.

Hammond was standing and talking with Sun Kai and Liu Bao, who were inspecting a curious letter, thick and with many seals, the black ink liberally interspersed with vermilion markings. Yongxing stood a little way apart, reading a second missive written in oddly large characters upon a long rolled sheet of paper; he did not share this letter, but rolled it shut again, put it away privately, and rejoined the other three.

Hammond bowed to them and came to translate the news for Laurence. "We are directed to let the ship continue on to Tien-sing, while we come on ahead by air," he said, "and they insist we must leave at once."

"Directed?" Laurence asked, in confusion. "But I do not understand; where have these orders come from? We cannot have had word from Peking already; Prince Yongxing sent word only three days ago."

Temeraire addressed a question to Ping, who tilted her head and replied in deep, unfeminine tones which came echoing from her barrel chest. "She says she brought it from a relay station at Heyuan, which is four hundred of something called *li* from here, and the flight is a little more than two hours," he said. "But I do not know what that means in terms of distance."

"One mile is three *li*," Hammond said, frowning as he tried to work it out; Laurence, quicker at figuring in his head, stared at her: if there was no exaggeration, that meant Yu Ping had covered better than 120 miles in her flight. At such a rate, with couriers flying in relays, the message could indeed have come from Peking, nearly two thousand miles distant; the idea was incredible.

Yongxing, overhearing, said impatiently, "Our message is of highest priority, and traveled by Jade Dragons the entire route; of course we have received word back. We cannot delay in this fashion when the Emperor has spoken. How quickly can you be ready to leave?"

Still staggered, Laurence collected himself and protested that he could not leave the *Allegiance* at present, but would have to wait until Riley was well enough to rise from his bed. In vain: Yongxing did not even have a chance to protest before Hammond was vociferously arguing his point. "We cannot possibly begin by offending the Emperor," he said. "The *Allegiance* can certainly remain here in port until Captain Riley is recovered."

"For God's sake, that will only worsen the situation," Laurence said impatiently. "Half the crew is already gone to fever; she cannot lose the other half to desertion." But the argument was a compelling one, particularly once it had been seconded by Staunton, who had come across to the ship by prior arrangement to take breakfast with Laurence and Hammond.

"Whatever assistance Major Heretford and his men can give Captain Riley, I am happy to promise," Staunton said. "But I do agree; they stand very much on ceremony here, and neglect of the outward forms is as good as a deliberate insult: I beg you not to delay."

With this encouragement, and after some consultation with Franks and Beckett, who with more courage than truth pronounced themselves prepared to handle the duty alone, and a visit to Riley belowdecks, Laurence at last yielded. "After all, we are not at the docks anyway because of her draft, and we have enough fresh supplies by now that Franks can haul in the boats and keep all the men aboard," Riley pointed out. "We will be sadly held up behind you no matter what, but I am much better, and Purbeck also; we will press on as soon as we can, and rendezvous with you at Peking."

But this only set off a fresh series of problems: the packing was already under way when Hammond's cautious inquiries determined that the Chinese invitation was by no means a general one. Laurence himself was from necessity accepted as an adjunct to Temeraire, Hammond as the King's representative only grudgingly permitted to come along, but the suggestion that Temeraire's crew should come along, riding in harness, was rejected with horror.

"I am not going anywhere without the crew along to guard Laurence," Temeraire put in, hearing of the difficulty, and conveyed this to Yongxing directly in suspicious tones; for emphasis he settled himself on the deck with finality, his tail drawn about him, looking quite immovable. A compromise was shortly offered that Laurence should choose ten of his crew, to be conveyed by some other Chinese dragons whose dignity would be less outraged by performing the service.

"What use ten men will be in the middle of Peking, I should like to know," Granby observed tartly, when Hammond brought this offer back to the cabin; he had not forgiven the diplomat for his refusal to investigate the attempt on Laurence's life.

"What use you imagine a hundred men would be, in the case of any real threat from the Imperial armies, I should like to know," Hammond answered with equal sharpness. "In any case, it is the best we can do; I had a great deal of work to gain their permission for so many."

"Then we will have to manage." Laurence scarcely even looked up; he was at the same time sorting through his clothing, and discarding those garments which had been too badly worn by the journey to be respectable. "The more important point, so far as safety is concerned, is to make certain the *Allegiance* is brought to anchor within a distance which Temeraire can reach in a single flight, without difficulty. Sir," he said, turning to Staunton, who had come down to sit with them, at Laurence's invitation, "may I prevail upon you to accompany Captain Riley, if your duties will allow it? Our departure will at one stroke rob him of all interpreters, and the authority of the envoys; I am concerned for any difficulties which he may encounter on the journey north."

"I am entirely at his service and yours," Staunton said, inclining his head; Hammond did not look entirely satisfied, but he could not object under the circumstances, and Laurence was privately glad to have found this politic way of having Staunton's advice on hand, even if his arrival would be delayed.

Granby would naturally accompany him, and so Ferris had to remain to oversee those men of the crew who could not come; the rest of the selection was a more painful one. Laurence did not like to seem to be showing any kind of favoritism, and indeed he did not want to leave Ferris without all of the best men. He settled finally for Keynes and Willoughby, of the ground crew: he had come to rely on the surgeon's opinion, and despite having to leave the harness behind, he felt it necessary to have at least one of the harness-men along, to direct the others in getting Temeraire rigged-out in some makeshift way if some emergency required.

Lieutenant Riggs interrupted his and Granby's deliberations with a passionate claim to come along, and bring his four best shots also. "They don't need us here; they have the Marines aboard, and if anything should go wrong the rifles will do you best, you must see," he said. As a point of tactics this was quite true; but equally true, the riflemen were the rowdiest of his young officers as a group, and Laurence was dubious about taking so many of them to court after they had been nearly seven months at sea. Any insult to a Chinese lady would certainly be resented harshly, and his own attention would be too distracted to keep close watch over them.

"Let us have Mr. Dunne and Mr. Hackley," Laurence said finally. "No; I understand your arguments, Mr. Riggs, but I want steady men for this work, men who will not go astray; I gather you take my meaning. Very good. John, we will have Blythe along also, and Martin from the top-men."

"That leaves two," Granby said, adding the names to the tally.

"I cannot take Baylesworth also; Ferris will need a reliable second," Laurence said, after briefly considering the last of his lieutenants. "Let us have Therrows from the bellmen instead. And Digby for the last: he is a trifle young, but he has handled himself well, and the experience will do him good."

"I will have them on deck in fifteen minutes, sir," Granby said, rising.

"Yes; and send Ferris down," Laurence said, already writing his orders. "Mr. Ferris, I rely on your good judgment," he continued, when the acting second lieutenant had come. "There is no way to guess one-tenth part of what may arise under the circumstances. I have written you a formal set of orders, in case Mr. Granby and myself should be lost. If that be the case your first concern must be Temeraire's safety, and following that the crew's, and their safe return to England."

"Yes, sir," Ferris said, downcast, and accepted the sealed packet; he did not try to argue for his inclusion, but left the cabin with unhappily bowed shoulders.

Laurence finished repacking his sea-chest: thankfully he had at the beginning of the voyage set aside his very best coat and hat, wrapped in paper and oilskin at the bottom of his chest, with a view towards preserving them for the embassy. He shifted now into the leather coat and trousers of heavy broadcloth which he wore for flying; these had not been too badly worn, being both more resilient and less called-on during the course of the journey. Only two of his shirts were worth including, and a handful of neckcloths; the rest he laid aside in a small bundle, and left in the cabin locker.

"Boyne," he called, putting his head out the door and spying a seaman idly splicing some rope. "Light this along to the deck, will you?" The sea-chest dispatched, he penned a few words to his mother and to Jane and took them to Riley, the small ritual only heightening the sensation which had crept upon him, as of being on the eve of battle.

The men were assembled on deck when he came up, their various chests and bags being loaded upon the launch. The envoys' baggage would mostly be remaining aboard, after Laurence had pointed out nearly a day would be required to unload it; even so, their bare necessities outweighed all the baggage of the crewmen.

Yongxing was on the dragondeck handing over a sealed letter to Lung Yu Ping; he seemed to find nothing at all unusual in entrusting it directly to the dragon, riderless as she was, and she herself took it with practiced skill, holding it so delicately between her long taloned claws she might almost have been gripping it. She tucked it carefully into the gold mesh she wore, to rest against her belly.

After this, she bowed to him and then to Temeraire and waddled forward, her wings ungainly for walking. But at the edge of the deck, she snapped them out wide, fluttered them a little, then sprang with a tremendous leap nearly her full length into the air, already beating furiously, and in an instant had diminished into a tiny speck above.

"Oh," Temeraire said, impressed, watching her go. "She flies very high; I have never gone so far aloft."

Laurence was not unimpressed, either, and stood watching through his glass for a few minutes more himself; by then she was wholly out of sight, though the day was clear.

Staunton drew Laurence aside. "May I make a suggestion? Take the children along. If I may speak from my own experience as a boy, they may well be useful. There is nothing like having children present to convey peaceful intentions, and the Chinese have an especial respect for filial relations, both by adoption as well as by blood. You can quite naturally be said to be their guardian, and I am certain I can persuade the Chinese they ought not be counted against your tally."

Roland overheard: instantly she and Dyer stood shining-eyed and hopeful before Laurence, full of silent pleading, and with some hesitation he said, "Well—if the Chinese have no objection to their addition to the party—" This was enough encouragement; they vanished belowdecks for their own bags, and came scrambling back up even before Staunton had finished negotiating for their inclusion.

"It still seems very silly to me," Temeraire said, in what was meant to be an undertone. "I could easily carry all of you, and everything in that boat besides. If I must fly alongside, it will surely take much longer."

"I do not disagree with you, but let us not reopen the discussion," Laurence said tiredly, leaning against Temeraire and stroking his nose. "*That* will take more time than could possibly be saved by any other means of transport."

Temeraire nudged him comfortingly, and Laurence closed his eyes a moment; the moment of quiet after the three hours of frantic hurry brought all his fatigue from the missed night of sleep surging back to the fore. "Yes, I am ready," he said, straightening up; Granby was there. Laurence settled his hat upon his head and nodded to the crew as he went by, the men touching their foreheads; a few even murmured, "Good luck, sir," and "Godspeed, sir."

He shook Franks's hand, and stepped over the side to the yowling accompaniment of pipes and drums, the rest of the crew already aboard the launch. Yongxing and the other envoys had already been lowered down by means of the bosun's chair, and were ensconced in the stern under a canopy for shelter from the sun. "Very well, Mr. Tripp; let us get under way," Laurence said to the midshipman, and they were off, the high sloping sides of the *Allegiance* receding as they raised the gaff mainsail and took the southerly wind past Macao and into the great sprawling delta of the Pearl River.

Chapter 12

❧

$\mathcal{T}$HEY DID NOT follow the usual curve of the river to Whampoa and Canton, but instead took an earlier eastern branch towards the city of Dongguan: now drifting with the wind, now rowing against the slow current, past the broad square-bordered rice fields on either side of the river, verdant green with the tops of the shoots beginning to protrude beyond the water's surface. The stench of manure hung over the river like a cloud.

Laurence drowsed nearly the entire journey, only vaguely conscious of the futile attempts made by the crew to be quiet, their hissing whispers causing instructions to be repeated three times, gradually increasing to the usual volume. Any occasional slip, such as dropping a coil of rope too heavily, or stumbling over one of the thwarts, brought forth a stream of invective and injunctions to be quiet that were considerably louder than the ordinary noise would have been. Nevertheless he slept, or something close to it; every so often he would open his eyes and look up, to be sure of Temeraire's form still pacing them overhead.

He woke from a deeper sleep only after dark: the sail was being furled, and a few moments later the launch bumped gently against a dock, followed by the quiet ordinary cursing of the sailors tying-up. There was very little light immediately at hand but the boat's lanterns, only enough to show a broad stairway leading down into the water, the lowest steps disappearing beneath the river's surface; to either side of these only the dim shadows of native junks drawn up onto the beach.

A parade of lanterns came towards them from further in on the shore, the locals evidently warned to expect their arrival: great glowing spheres of deep orange-red silk, stretched taut over thin bamboo frames, reflecting like flames in the water. The lamp-bearers spread out along the edges of the walls in careful procession, and suddenly a great many Chinese were climbing aboard the ship, seizing on the various parts of the baggage, and transferring these off without so much as a request for permission, calling out to one another cheerfully as they worked.

Laurence was at first disposed to complain, but there was no cause: the entire operation was being carried out with admirable efficiency. A clerk had seated himself at the base of the steps with something like a drawing-table upon his lap, making a tally of the different parcels on a paper scroll as they passed by him, and at the same time marking each one plainly. Instead Laurence stood up and tried to unstiffen his neck surreptitiously by small movements to either side, without any undignified stretching. Yongxing had already stepped off the boat and gone into the small pavilion on the shore; from inside, Liu Bao's booming voice could be heard calling for what even Laurence had come to recognize as the word for "wine," and Sun Kai was on the bank speaking with the local mandarin.

"Sir," Laurence said to Hammond, "will you be so good as to ask the local officials where Temeraire has come to ground?"

Hammond made some inquiries of the men on the bank, frowned, and said to Laurence in an undertone, "They say he has been taken to the Pavilion of Quiet Waters, and that we are to go elsewhere for the night; pray make some objection at once, loudly, so I may have an excuse to argue with them; we ought not set a precedent of allowing ourselves to be separated from him."

Laurence, who if not prompted would have at once made a great noise, found himself cast into confusion by the request to play-act; he stammered a little, and said in a raised but awkwardly tentative voice, "I must see Temeraire at once, and be sure he is well."

Hammond turned back at once to the attendants, spreading his hands in apology, and spoke urgently; under their scowls, Laurence did his best to look stern and unyielding, feeling thoroughly ridiculous and angry all at once, and eventually Hammond turned back with satisfaction and said, "Excellent; they have agreed to take us to him."

Relieved, Laurence nodded and turned back to the ship's crew. "Mr. Tripp, let these gentlemen show you and the men where to sleep; I will speak with you in the morning before you return to the *Allegiance*," he told the midshipman, who touched his hat, and then he climbed up onto the stairs.

Without discussion, Granby arranged the men in a loose formation around him as they walked along the broad, paved roads, following the guide's bobbing lantern; Laurence had the impression of many small houses on either side, and deep wheel-ruts were cut into the paving-stones, all sharp edges worn soft and curving with the impression of long years. He felt wide-awake after the long day drowsing, and yet there was something curiously dream-like about walking through the foreign dark, the soft black boots of the guide making hushing noises over the stones, the smoke of cooking fires drifting from the nearby houses, muted light filtering from behind screens and out of windows, and once a snatch of unfamiliar song in a woman's voice.

They came at last to the end of the wide straight road,

and the guide led them up the broad stairway of a pavilion and between massive round columns of painted wood, the roof so far overhead that its shape was lost in the darkness. The low rumbled breathing of dragons echoed loudly in the half-enclosed space, close all around them, and the tawny lantern-light gleamed on scales in every direction, like heaped mounds of treasure around the narrow aisle through the center. Hammond drew unconsciously closer to the center of their party, and caught his breath once, as the lantern reflected from a dragon's half-open eye, turning into a disk of flat, shining gold.

They passed through another set of columns and into an open garden, with water trickling somewhere in the darkness, and the whisper of broad leaves rubbing against one another overhead. A few more dragons lay sleeping here, one sprawled across the path; the guide poked him with the stick of the lantern until he grudgingly moved away, never even opening his eyes. They climbed more stairs up to another pavilion, smaller than the first, and here at last found Temeraire, curled up alone in the echoing vastness.

"Laurence?" Temeraire said, lifting his head as they came in, and nuzzled at him gladly. "Will you stay? It is very strange to be sleeping on land again. I almost feel as though the ground is moving."

"Of course," Laurence said, and the crew laid themselves down without complaint: the night was pleasantly warm, and the floor made of inlaid squares of wood, smoothed down by years, and not uncomfortably hard. Laurence took his usual place upon Temeraire's forearm; after sleeping through the journey, he was wakeful, and told Granby he would take the first watch. "Have you been given something to eat?" he asked Temeraire, once they were settled.

"Oh, yes," Temeraire said drowsily. "A roast pig, very large, and some stewed mushrooms. I am not at all hungry. It was not a very difficult flight, after all, and nothing very interesting either to see before the sun went down; except those fields were strange, that we came past, full of water."

"The rice fields," Laurence said, but Temeraire was already asleep, and shortly began to snore: the noise was decidedly louder in the confines of the pavilion even though it had no walls. The night was very quiet, and the mosquitoes were not too much of a torment, thankfully; they evidently did not care for the dry heat given off by a dragon's body. There was very little to mark the time, with the sky concealed by the roof, and Laurence lost track of the hours. No interruption in the stillness of the night, except that once a noise in the courtyard drew his attention: a dragon landing, turning a milky pearlescent gaze towards them, reflecting the moonlight very much like a cat's eyes; but it did not come near the pavilion, and only padded away deeper into the darkness.

Granby woke for his turn at watch; Laurence composed himself to sleep: he, too, felt the old familiar illusion of the earth shifting, his body remembering the movement of the ocean even now that they had left it behind.

He woke startled: the riot of color overhead was strange until he understood he was looking at the decoration upon the ceiling, every scrap of wood painted and enameled in brilliant peacocky colors and shining gilt. He sat up and looked about himself with fresh interest: the round columns were painted a solid red, set upon square bases of white marble, and the roof was at least thirty feet overhead: Temeraire would have had no difficulty coming in underneath it.

The front of the pavilion opened onto a prospect of the courtyard which he found interesting rather than beautiful: paved with grey stones around a winding path of reddish ones, full of queerly shaped rocks and trees, and of course dragons: there were five sprawled over the grounds in various attitudes of repose, except for one already awake and grooming itself fastidiously by the enormous pool which covered the northeast corner of the grounds. The dragon was a shade of greyish blue not very different from the present color of the sky, and curiously the tips of its four claws were painted a bright red; as Laurence watched it finished its morning ablutions and took to the air.

Most of the dragons in the yard seemed of a similar breed, though there was a great deal of variety among them in size, in the precise shade of their color, and in the number and placement of their horns; some were smooth-backed and others had spiked ridges. Shortly a very different kind of dragon came out of the large pavilion to the south: larger and crimson-red, with gold-tinted talons and a bright yellow crest running from its many-horned head and along its spine. It drank from the pool and yawned enormously, displaying a double row of small but wicked teeth, and a set of four larger curving fangs among them. Narrower halls, with walls interspersed with small archways, ran to east and west of the courtyard, joining the two pavilions; the red dragon went over to one of the archways now and yelled something inside.

A few moments later a woman came stumbling out through the archway, rubbing her face and making wordless groaning noises. Laurence stared, then looked away, embarrassed, she was naked to the waist. The dragon nudged her hard and knocked her back entirely into the pond. It certainly had a reviving effect: she rose up sputtering and wide-eyed, and then yammered back at the grinning dragon in a passion before going back inside the hall. She came out again a few minutes later, now fully dressed in what seemed to be a sort of padded jerkin, dark blue cotton edged with broad bands of red, with wide sleeves, and carrying a rig made also of fabric: silk, Laurence thought. This she threw upon the dragon all by herself, still talking loudly and obviously disgruntled all the while; Laurence was irresistibly reminded of Berkley and Maximus, even though Berkley had never spoken so many words together in his life: something in the irreverent quality of their relations.

The rig secured, the Chinese aviator scrambled aboard and the two went aloft with no further ceremony, disappearing from the pavilion to whatever their day's duties might be. All the dragons were now beginning to stir, another three of the big scarlet ones coming out of the pavilion, and more people to come from the halls: men from the east, and a few more women from the west.

Temeraire himself twitched under Laurence, and then opened his eyes. "Good morning," he said, yawning, then, "Oh!" his eyes wide as he looked around, taking in the opulent decoration and the bustle going on in the courtyard. "I did not realize there were so many other dragons here, or that it was so grand," he said, a little nervously. "I hope they are friendly."

"I am sure they cannot but be gracious, when they realize you have come from so far," Laurence said, climbing down so Temeraire could stand. The air was close and heavy with moisture, the sky remaining uncertain and grey; it would be hot again, he thought. "You ought to drink as much as you can," he said. "I have no notion how often they will want to stop and rest along the way today."

"I suppose," Temeraire said, reluctantly, and stepped out of the pavilion and into the court. The increasing hubbub came to an abrupt and complete halt; the dragons and their companions alike stared openly, and then there was a general movement back and away from him. Laurence was for a moment shocked and offended; then he saw that they were all, men and dragons, bowing themselves very low to the ground. They had only been opening a clear path to the pond.

There was perfect silence. Temeraire uncertainly walked through the parted ranks of the other dragons to the pond, rather hastily drank his fill, and retreated to the raised pavilion; only when he had gone again did the general activity resume, with much less noise than earlier, and a good deal of peering into the pavilion, while pretending to do nothing of the sort. "They were very nice to let me drink," Temeraire said, almost whispering, "but I wish they would not stare so."

The dragons seemed disposed to linger, but one after another they all set off, except for a few plainly older ones, their scales faded at the edges, who returned to basking upon the courtyard stones. Granby and the rest of the crew had woken over the intervening time, sitting up to watch the spectacle with as much interest as the other dragons had taken in Temeraire; now they roused fully, and began to straighten their clothing. "I suppose they will send someone for us," Hammond was saying, brushing futilely at his wrinkled breeches; he had been dressed formally, rather than in the riding gear which all the aviators had put on. At that very moment, Ye Bing, one of the young Chinese attendants from the ship, came through the courtyard, waving to draw their attention.

Breakfast was not what Laurence was used to, being a sort of thin rice porridge mixed with dried fish and slices of horrifically discolored eggs, served with greasy sticks of crisp, very light bread. The eggs he pushed to the side, and forced himself to eat the rest, on the same advice which he had given to Temeraire; but he would have given a great deal for some properly cooked eggs and bacon. Liu Bao poked Laurence in the arm with his chopsticks and pointed at the eggs with some remark: he was eating his own with very evident relish.

"What do you suppose is the matter with them?" Granby asked in an undertone, prodding his own eggs doubtfully.

Hammond, inquiring of Liu Bao, said just as doubtfully, "He says they are thousand-year eggs." Braver than the rest of them, he picked one of the slices up and ate it; chewed, swallowed, and looked thoughtful while they waited his verdict. "It tastes almost pickled," he said. "Not rotten, at any rate." He tried another piece, and ended by eating the whole serving; for his own part, Laurence left the lurid yellow-and-green things alone.

They had been brought to a sort of guest hall not far from the dragon pavilion for the meal; the sailors were there waiting and joined them for the breakfast, grinning rather maliciously. They were no more pleased at being left out of the adventure than the rest of the aviators had been, and not above making remarks about the quality of food which the party could expect for the rest of their journey. Afterwards, Laurence took his final parting from Tripp. "And be sure you tell Captain Riley that all is ship-shape, in those exact words," he said; it had been arranged between them that any other message, regardless how reassuring, would mean something had gone badly wrong.

A couple of mule-led carts were waiting for them outside, rather rough-hewn and clearly without springs; their baggage had gone on ahead. Laurence climbed in and held on grimly to the side as they rattled along down the road. The streets at least were not more impressive by daylight: very broad, but paved with old rounded cobblestones, whose mortar had largely worn away. The wheels of the cart ran along in deep sloping ruts between stones, bumping and leaping over the uneven surface.

There was a bustle of people all around, who stared with great curiosity at them, often putting down their work to follow after them for some short distance. "And this is not even a city?" Granby looked around with interest, making some attempt to tally the numbers. "There seem to be a great many people, for only a town."

"There are some two hundred millions of people in the country, by our latest intelligence," Hammond said absently, himself busy taking down notes in a journal; Laurence shook his head at the appalling number, more than ten times the size of England's population.

Laurence was more startled for his part to see a dragon come walking down the road in the opposite direction. Another of the blue-grey ones; it was wearing a queer sort of silk harness with a prominent breast-pad, and when they had passed it by, he saw that three little dragonets, two of the same variety and one of the red color, were tramping along behind, each attached to the harness also as if on leading-strings.

Nor was this dragon the only one in the streets: they shortly passed by a military station, with a small troop of blue-clad infantrymen drilling in its courtyard, and a couple of the big red dragons were sitting outside the gate talking and exclaiming over a dice game which their captains were playing. No one seemed to take any particular notice of them; the hurrying peasants carrying their loads went by without a second glance, occasionally climbing over one of the splayed-out limbs when other routes were blocked.

Temeraire was waiting for them in an open field, with two of the blue-grey dragons also on hand, wearing mesh harnesses which were being loaded up with baggage by attendants. The other dragons were whispering amongst themselves and eyeing Temeraire sidelong. He looked uncomfortable, and greatly relieved to see Laurence.

Having been loaded, the dragons now crouched down onto all fours so the attendants could climb aloft and raise small pavilions on their backs: very much like the tents which were used for long flights among British aviators. One of the attendants spoke to Hammond, and gestured to one of the blue dragons. "We are to ride on that one," Hammond said to Laurence aside, then asked something else of the attendant, who shook his head, and answered forcefully, pointing again to the second dragon.

Before the reply could even be translated, Temeraire sat up indignantly. "Laurence is not riding any other dragon," he said, putting out a possessive claw and nearly knocking Laurence off his feet, herding him closer; Hammond scarcely had to repeat the sentiments in Chinese.

Laurence had not quite realized the Chinese did not mean for even him to ride with Temeraire. He did not like the idea of Temeraire having to fly with no company on the long trip, and yet he could not help but think the point a small one; they would be flying in company, in sight of one another, and Temeraire could be in no real danger. "It is only for the one journey," he said to Temeraire, and was surprised to find himself overruled at once not by Temeraire, but by Hammond.

"No; the suggestion is unacceptable, cannot be entertained," Hammond said.

"Not at all," Temeraire said, in perfect agreement, and actually growled when the attendant tried to continue the argument.

"Mr. Hammond," Laurence said, with happy inspiration, "pray tell them, if it is the notion of harness which is at issue, I can just as easily lock on to the chain of Temeraire's pendant; as long as I do not need to go climbing about it will be secure enough."

"They cannot possibly argue with that," Temeraire said, pleased, and interrupted the argument immediately to make the suggestion, which was grudgingly accepted.

"Captain, may I have a word?" Hammond drew him

aside. "This attempt is of a piece with last night's arrangements. I must urge you, sir, by no means agree to continue on should we somehow come to be parted; and be on your guard if they should make further attempts to separate you from Temeraire."

"I take your point, sir; and thank you for the advice," Laurence said, grimly, and looked narrowly at Yongxing; though the prince had never stooped to involve himself directly in any of the discussions, Laurence suspected his hand behind them, and he had hoped that the failure of the shipboard attempts to part them would at least have precluded these efforts.

After these tensions at the journey's outset, the long day's flight itself was uneventful, except for the occasional leap in Laurence's stomach when Temeraire would swoop down for a closer look at the ground: the breastplate did not keep entirely still throughout the flight, and shifted far more than harness. Temeraire was considerably quicker than the other two dragons, with more endurance, and could easily catch them up even if he lingered half-an-hour in sight-seeing at a time. The most striking feature, to Laurence, was the exuberance of the population: they scarcely passed any long stretch of land that was not under cultivation of some form, and every substantial body of water was crammed full of boats going either direction. And of course the real immensity of the country: they traveled from morning to night, with only an hour's pause for dinner each day at noon, and the days were long.

An almost endless expanse of broad, flat plains, checkered with rice fields and interspersed with many streams, yielded after some two days' travel to hills, and then to the slow puckering rise of mountains. Towns and villages of varying size punctuated the countryside below, and occasionally people working in the fields would stop and watch them flying overhead, if Temeraire came low enough to be recognized as a Celestial. Laurence at first thought the Yangtze another lake; one of respectable size but not extraordinary, being something less than a mile wide, with its east and west banks shrouded in a fine, grey drizzle; only when they had come properly over-head could he see the mighty river sprawling endlessly away, and the slow procession of junks appearing and vanishing through the mists.

After having passed two nights in smaller towns, Lau-rence had begun to think their first establishment an un-usual case, but their residence that night in the city of Wuchang dwarfed it into insignificance: eight great pavil-ions arranged in a symmetric octagonal shape, joined by narrower enclosed halls, around a space deserving to be called a park more than a garden. Roland and Dyer made at first a game of trying to count the dragons inhabiting it, but gave up the attempt somewhere after thirty; they lost track of their tally when a group of small purple dragons landed and darted in a flurry of wings and limbs across the pavilion, too many and too quick to count.

Temeraire drowsed; Laurence put aside his bowl: an-other plain dinner of rice and vegetables. Most of the men were already asleep, huddled in their cloaks, the rest silent; rain still coming down in a steady, steaming cur-tain beyond the walls of the pavilion, the overrun clatter-ing off the upturned corners of the tiled roof. Along the slopes of the river valley, faintly visible, small yellow bea-cons burnt beneath open-walled huts to mark the way for dragons flying through the night. Soft grumbling breath echoing from the neighboring pavilions, and far away a more piercing cry, ringing clear despite the muf-fling weight of the rain.

Yongxing had been spending his nights apart from the rest of the company, in more private quarters, but now he came out of seclusion and stood at the edge of the

pavilion looking out into the valley: in another moment
the call came again, nearer. Temeraire lifted up his head
to listen, the ruff around his neck rising up alertly; then
Laurence heard the familiar leathery snapping of wings,
mist and steam rolling away from the stones for the
descending dragon, a white ghostly shadow coalescing
from the silver rain. She folded great white wings and
came pacing towards them, her talons clicking on the
stones; the attendants going between pavilions shrank
away from her, averting their faces, hurrying by, but
Yongxing walked down the steps into the rain, and she
lowered her great, wide-ruffed head towards him, calling
his name in a clear, sweet voice.

"Is that another Celestial?" Temeraire asked him,
hushed and uncertain; Laurence only shook his head and
could not answer: she was a shockingly pure white, a
color he had never before seen in a dragon even in spots
or streaks. Her scales had the translucent gleam of fine,
much-scraped vellum, perfectly colorless, and the rims of
her eyes were a glassy pink mazed with blood vessels so
engorged as to be visible even at a distance. Yet she had
the same great ruff, and the long narrow tendrils fringing
her jaws, just as Temeraire did: the color alone was un-
natural. She wore a heavy golden torque set with rubies
around the base of her neck, and gold talon-sheaths
tipped with rubies upon all of her foreleg claws, the deep
color echoing the hue of her eyes.

She nudged Yongxing caressingly back into the shelter
of the temple and came in after him, first shivering her
wings quickly to let cascades of rain roll away in streams;
she alloted them barely a glance, her eyes flickering rapidly
over them and away, before she jealously coiled herself
around Yongxing, to murmur quietly with him in the far
corner of the pavilion. Servants came bringing her some
dinner, but dragging their heels, uneasily, though they
had shown no such similar reluctance around any of the

other dragons, and indeed visible satisfaction in Temeraire's presence. She did not seem to merit their fear; she ate quickly and daintily, not letting so much as a drop spill out of the dish, and otherwise paid them no mind.

The next morning Yongxing briefly presented her to them as Lung Tien Lien, and then led her away to breakfast in private; Hammond had made quiet inquiries enough to tell them a little more over their own meal: "She is certainly a Celestial," he said. "I suppose it is a kind of albinism; I have no idea why it should make them all so uneasy."

"She was born in mourning colors, of course she is unlucky," Liu Bao said, when he was cautiously applied to for information, as if this were self-evident, and he added, "The Qianlong Emperor was going to give her to a prince out in Mongolia, so her bad luck wouldn't hurt any of his sons, but Yongxing insisted on having her himself instead of letting a Celestial go outside the Imperial family. He could have been Emperor himself, but of course you couldn't have an Emperor with a cursed dragon, it would be a disaster for the State. So now his brother is the Jiaqing Emperor. Such is the will of Heaven!" With this philosophical remark, he shrugged and ate another piece of fried bread. Hammond took this news bleakly, and Laurence shared his dismay: pride was one thing; principle implacable enough to sacrifice a throne for, something else entirely.

The two bearer dragons accompanying them had been changed for another one of the blue-grey breed and one of a slightly larger kind, deep green with blue streaks and a sleek hornless head; they still regarded Temeraire with the same staring awe, however, and Lien with nervous respect, and kept well to themselves. Temeraire had by now reconciled himself to the state of majestic solitude; and in any case he was thoroughly occupied in glancing sidelong at Lien with fascinated curiosity, until she turned to stare pointedly at him in return and he ducked his head, abashed.

She wore this morning an odd sort of headdress, made of thin silk draped between gold bars, which stood out over her eyes rather like a canopy and shaded them; Laurence wondered that she should find it necessary, with the sky still unrelieved and grey. But the hot, sullen weather broke almost abruptly during their first few hours of flight, through gorges winding among old mountains: their sloping southern faces lush and green, and the northern almost barren. A cool wind met their faces as they came out into the foothills, and the sun breaking from the clouds was almost painfully bright. The rice fields did not reappear, but long expanses of ripening wheat took their place, and once they saw a great herd of brown oxen creeping slowly across a grassy plain, heads to the ground as they munched away.

A little shed was planted on a hill, overlooking the herd, and beside it several massive spits turned, entire cows roasting upon them, a fragrant smoky smell rising upwards. "Those look tasty," Temeraire observed, a little wistfully. He was not alone in the sentiment: as they approached, one of their companion dragons put on a sudden burst of speed and swooped down. A man came out of the shed and held a discussion with the dragon, then went inside again; he came out carrying a large plank of wood and laid it down before the dragon, which carved a few Chinese symbols into the plank with its talon.

The man took away the plank, and the dragon took away a cow: plainly it had been making a purchase. It lifted back up into the air at once to rejoin them, crunching its cow happily as it flew: it evidently did not think it necessary to let its passengers off for any of the proceedings. Laurence thought he could see poor Hammond looking faintly green as it slurped the intestines up with obvious pleasure.

"We could try to purchase one, if they will take guineas," Laurence offered to Temeraire, a little dubiously; he had brought gold rather than paper money with him, but had no idea if the herdsman would accept it.

"Oh, I am not really hungry," Temeraire said, preoccupied by a wholly different thought. "Laurence, that was writing, was it not? What he did on the plank?"

"I believe so, though I do not set myself up as an expert on Chinese writing," Laurence said. "You are more likely to recognize it than I."

"I wonder if all Chinese dragons know how to write," Temeraire said, dismal at the notion. "They will think me very stupid if I am the only one who cannot. I must learn somehow; I always thought letters had to be made with a pen, but I am sure I could do that sort of carving."

Perhaps in courtesy to Lien, who seemed to dislike bright sunlight, they now paused during the heat of the day at another wayside pavilion for some dinner and for the dragons to rest, and flew on into the evening instead; beacons upon the ground lit their way at irregular intervals, and in any case Laurence could chart their course by the stars: turning now more sharply to the northeast, with the miles slipping quickly past. The days continued hot, but no longer so extraordinarily humid, and the nights were wonderfully cool and pleasant; signs of the force of the northern winters were apparent, however: the pavilions were walled on three sides, and set up from the ground on stone platforms which held stoves so the floors could be heated.

Peking sprawled out a great distance from beyond the city walls, which were numerous and grand, with many square towers and battlements not unlike the style of European castles. Broad streets of grey stone ran in straight lines to the gates and within, so full of people, of horses, of carts, all of them moving, that from above they seemed like rivers. They saw many dragons also, both on the streets and in the sky, leaping into the air for short flights from one quarter of the city to another, sometimes with a crowd of people hanging off them and evidently traveling in this manner. The city was divided with extraordinary regularity into square sections, except for the curving sprawl of four small lakes actually within the walls. To the east of these lay the great Imperial palace itself, not a single building but formed of many smaller pavilions, walled in and surrounded by a moat of murky water: in the setting sun, all the roofs within the complex shone as if gilded, nestled among trees with their spring growth still fresh and yellow-green, throwing long shadows into the plazas of grey stone.

A smaller dragon met them in mid-air as they drew near: black with canary-yellow stripes and wearing a collar of dark green silk, he had a rider upon his back, but spoke to the other dragons directly. Temeraire followed the other dragons down, to a small round island in the southernmost lake, less than half-a-mile from the palace walls. They landed upon a broad pier of white marble which jutted out into the lake, for the convenience of dragons only, as there were no boats in evidence.

This pier ended in an enormous gateway: a red structure more than a wall and yet too narrow to be considered a building, with three square archways as openings, the two smallest many times higher than Temeraire's head and wide enough for four of him to walk abreast; the central was even larger. A pair of enormous Imperial dragons stood at attention on either side, very like Temeraire in conformity but without his distinctive ruff, one black and the other a deep blue, and beside them a long file of soldiers: infantrymen in shining steel caps and blue robes, with long spears.

The two companion dragons walked directly through

the smaller archways, and Lien paced straightaway through the middle, but the yellow-striped dragon barred Temeraire from following, bowed low, and said something in apologetic tones while gesturing to the center archway. Temeraire answered back shortly, and sat down on his haunches with an air of finality, his ruff stiff and laid back against his neck in obvious displeasure. "Is something wrong?" Laurence asked quietly; through the archway he could see a great many people and dragons assembled in the courtyard beyond, and obviously some ceremony was intended.

"They want you to climb down, and go through one of the small archways, and for me to go through the large one," Temeraire said. "But I am not putting you down alone. It sounds very silly to me, anyway, to have three doors all going to the same place."

Laurence wished rather desperately for Hammond's advice, or anyone's for that matter; the striped dragon and his rider were equally nonplussed at Temeraire's recalcitrance, and Laurence found himself looking at the other man and meeting with an almost identical expression of confusion. The dragons and soldiers in the archway remained as motionless and precise as statues, but as the minutes passed those assembled on the other side must have come to realize something was wrong. A man in richly embroidered blue robes came hurrying through the side corridor, and spoke to the striped dragon and his rider; then looked askance at Laurence and Temeraire and hurried back to the other side.

A low murmur of conversation began, echoing down the archway, then was abruptly cut off; the people on the far side parted, and a dragon came through the archway towards them, a deep glossy black very much like Temeraire's own coloring, with the same deep blue eyes and wing-markings, and a great standing ruff of translucent black stretched among ribbed horns of vermilion, another Celestial. She stopped before them and spoke in deep resonant tones; Laurence felt Temeraire first stiffen and then tremble, his own ruff rising slowly up, and Temeraire said, low and uncertainly, "Laurence, this is my mother."

Chapter 13

LAURENCE LATER LEARNED from Hammond that passage through the central gate was reserved for the use of the Imperial family, and dragons of that breed and the Celestials only, hence their refusal to let Laurence himself pass through. At the moment, however, Qian simply led Temeraire in a short flight over the gateway and into the central courtyard beyond, thus neatly severing the Gordian knot.

The problem of etiquette resolved, they were all ushered into an enormous banquet, held within the largest of the dragon pavilions, with two tables waiting. Qian was herself seated at the head of the first table, with Temeraire upon her left and Yongxing and Lien upon her right. Laurence was directed to sit some distance down the table, with Hammond across and several more seats down; the rest of the British party was placed at the second table. Laurence did not think it politic to object: the separation was not even the length of the room, and in any case Temeraire's attention was entirely engaged at present. He was speaking to his mother with an almost timid air, very unlike himself and clearly overawed: she was larger than he, and the faint translucence of her scales indicated a great age, as did her very grand manners. She wore no harness, but her ruff was adorned with enormous yellow topazes affixed to the spines, and a deceptively fragile neckpiece of filigree gold, studded with more topazes and great pearls.

Truly gigantic platters of brass were set before the dragons, each bearing an entire roasted deer, antlers intact: oranges stuck with cloves were impaled upon them, creating a fragrance not at all unpleasant to human senses, and their bellies were stuffed with a mixture of nuts and very bright red berries. The humans were served with a sequence of eight dishes, smaller though equally elaborate. After the dismal food along the course of the journey, even the highly exotic repast was very welcome, however.

Laurence had assumed there should be no one for him to talk to, as he sat down, unless he tried to shout across to Hammond, there being no translator present so far as he could tell. On his left side sat a very old mandarin, wearing a hat with a pearlescent white jewel perched on top and a peacock feather dangling down from the back over a truly impressive queue, still mostly black despite the profusion of wrinkles engraved upon his face. He ate and drank with single-minded intensity, never even trying to address Laurence at all: when the neighbor on his other side leaned over and shouted in the man's ear, Laurence realized that he was very deaf, as well as being unable to speak English.

But shortly after he had seated himself, he was taken aback to be addressed from his other side in English, heavy with French accents: "I hope you have had a comfortable journey," said the smiling, cheerful voice. It was the French ambassador, dressed in long robes in the Chinese style rather than in European dress; that and his dark hair accounted for Laurence not having distinguished him at once from the rest of the company.

"You will permit that I make myself known to you, I hope, despite the unhappy state of affairs between our countries," De Guignes continued. "I can claim an informal acquaintance, you see; my nephew tells me he owes his life to your magnanimity."

"I beg your pardon, sir, I have not the least notion to what you refer," Laurence said, puzzled by this address. "Your nephew?"

"Jean-Claude De Guignes; he is a lieutenant in our Armée de l'Air," the ambassador said, bowing, still smiling. "You encountered him this last November over your Channel, when he made an attempt to board you."

"Good God," Laurence said, exclaiming, distantly recalling the young lieutenant who had fought so vigorously in the convoy action, and he willingly shook De Guignes's hand. "I remember; most extraordinary courage. I am so very happy to hear that he has quite recovered, I hope?"

"Oh yes, in his letter he expected to rise from his hospital any day; to go to prison of course, but that is better than going to a grave," De Guignes said, with a prosaic shrug. "He wrote me of your interesting journey, knowing I had been dispatched here to your destination; I have been with great pleasure expecting you this last month since his letter arrived, with hopes of expressing my admiration for your generosity."

From this happy beginning, they exchanged some more conversation on neutral topics: the Chinese climate, the food, and the startling number of dragons. Laurence could not help but feel a certain kinship with him, as a fellow Westerner in the depths of the Oriental enclave, and though De Guignes was himself not a military man, his familiarity with the French aerial corps made him sympathetic company. They walked out together at the close of the meal, following the other guests into the courtyard, where most of these were being carried away by dragon in the same manner they had seen earlier in the city.

"It is a clever mode of transport, is it not?" De Guignes said, and Laurence, watching with interest, agreed wholeheartedly: the dragons, mostly of what he now considered the common blue variety, wore light harnesses of many silk straps draped over their backs, to which were hung numerous loops of broad silk ribbons. The passengers climbed up the loops to the topmost empty one, which they slid down over their arms and underneath the buttocks: they could then sit in comparative stability, clinging to the main strap, so long as the dragon flew level.

Hammond emerged from the pavilion and caught sight of them, eyes widening, and hastened to join them; he and De Guignes smiled and spoke with great friendliness, and as soon as the Frenchman had excused himself and departed in company with a pair of Chinese mandarins, Hammond instantly turned to Laurence and demanded, in a perfectly shameless manner, to have the whole of their conversation recounted.

"Expecting us for a month!" Hammond was appalled by the intelligence, and managed to imply without actually saying anything openly offensive that he thought Laurence had been a simpleton to take De Guignes at face value. "God only knows what mischief he may have worked against us in that time; pray have no more private conversation with him."

Laurence did not respond to these remarks as he rather wanted to, and instead went away to Temeraire's side. Qian had been the last to depart, taking a caressing leave of Temeraire, nudging him with her nose before leaping aloft; her sleek black form disappeared into the night quickly, and Temeraire stood watching after her very wistfully.

The island had been prepared for their residence as a compromise measure; the property of the Emperor, it possessed several large and elegant dragon pavilions, with establishments intended for human use conjoined to these. Laurence and his party were allowed to establish themselves in a residence attached to the largest of the pavilions, facing across a broad courtyard. The building was a handsome one, and large, but the upper floor was wholly taken up by a host of servants greatly exceeding their needs; although seeing how these ranged themselves almost underfoot throughout the house, Laurence began to suspect they were intended equally as spies and guards.

His sleep was heavy, but broken before dawn by servants poking their heads in to see if he were awake; after the fourth such attempt in ten minutes, Laurence yielded with no good grace and rose with a head still aching from the previous day's free flow of wine. He had little success in conveying his desire for a washbasin, and at length resorted to stepping outside into the courtyard to wash in the pond there. This posed no difficulty, as there was an enormous circular window little less than his height set in the wall, the lower sill barely off the ground.

Temeraire was sprawled luxuriously across the far end, lying flattened upon his belly with even his tail stretched out to its full extent, still fast asleep and making occasional small pleased grunts as he dreamed. A system of bamboo pipes emerged from beneath the pavement, evidently used to heat the stones, and these spilled a cloud of hot water into the pond, so Laurence could make more comfortable ablutions than he had expected. The servants hovered in visible impatience all the time, and looked rather scandalized at his stripping to the waist to wash. When at last he came back in, they pressed Chinese dress upon him: soft trousers and the stiff-collared gown which seemed nearly universal among them. He resisted a moment, but a glance over at his own clothes showed them sadly wrinkled from the travel; the native dress was at least neat, if not what he was used to, and not physically uncomfortable, though he felt very nearly indecent without a proper coat or neckcloth.

A functionary of some sort had come to breakfast with them and was already waiting at table, which was evidently the source of the servants' urgency. Laurence bowed rather shortly to the stranger, named Zhao Wei, and let Hammond carry the conversation while he drank a great deal of the tea: fragrant and strong, but not a dish of milk to be seen, and the servants only looked blank when the request was translated for them.

"His Imperial Majesty has in his benevolence decreed you are to reside here for the length of your visit," Zhao Wei was saying; his English was by no means polished, but understandable; he had a rather prim and pinched look, and eyed Laurence's still-unskilled use of the chopsticks with an expression of disdain hovering about his mouth. "You may walk in the courtyard as you desire, but you are not to leave the residence without making a formal request and receiving permission."

"Sir, we are most grateful, but you must be aware that if we are not to be allowed free movement during the day, the size of this house is by no means adequate to our needs," Hammond said. "Why, only Captain Laurence and myself had private rooms last night, and those small and ill-befitting our standing, while the rest of our compatriots were housed in shared quarters and very cramped."

Laurence had noticed no such inadequacy, and found both the attempted restrictions on their movement and Hammond's negotiations for more space mildly absurd, the more so as it transpired, from their conversation, that the whole of the island had been vacated in deference to Temeraire. The complex could have accommodated a dozen dragons in extreme comfort, and there were sufficient human residences that every man of Laurence's crew might have had a building to himself. Still, their residence was in perfectly good repair, comfortable, and far more spacious than their shipboard quarters for the last seven months; he could not see the least reason for desiring additional space any more than for denying them the liberty of the island. But Hammond and Zhao Wei continued to negotiate the matter with a measured gravity and politeness.

Zhao Wei at length consented to their being allowed to take walks around the island in the company of the servants, "so long as you do not go to the shores or the docks, and do not interfere in the patrols of the guardsmen." With this Hammond pronounced himself satisfied. Zhao Wei sipped at his tea, and then added, "Of course, His Majesty wishes Lung Tien Xiang to see something of the city. I will conduct him upon a tour after he has eaten."

"I am certain Temeraire and Captain Laurence will find it most edifying," Hammond said immediately, before Laurence could even draw breath. "Indeed, sir, it was very kind of you to arrange for native clothing for Captain Laurence, so he will not suffer from excessive curiosity."

Zhao Wei only now took notice of Laurence's clothing, with an expression that made it perfectly plain he was nothing whatsoever involved; but he bore his defeat in reasonably good part. He said only, "I hope you will be ready to leave shortly, Captain," with a small inclination of the head.

"And we may walk through the city itself?" Temeraire asked, with much excitement, as he was scrubbed and sluiced clean after his breakfast, holding out his forehands one at a time with the talons outspread to be brushed vigorously with soapy water. His teeth even received the same treatment, a young serving-maid ducking inside his mouth to scrub the back ones.

"Of course?" Zhao Wei said, showing some sincere puzzlement at the question.

"Perhaps you may see something of the training grounds of the dragons here, if there are any within the city bounds," Hammond suggested: he had accompanied them outside. "I am sure you would find it of interest, Temeraire."

"Oh, yes," Temeraire said; his ruff was already up and half-quivering.

Hammond gave Laurence a significant glance, but Laurence chose to ignore it entirely: he had little desire to play the spy, or to prolong the tour, however interesting the sights might be. "Are you quite ready, Temeraire?" he asked instead.

They were transported to the shore by an elaborate but awkward barge, which wallowed uncertainly under Temeraire's weight even in the placidity of the tiny lake; Laurence kept close to the tiller and watched the lubberly pilot with a grim and censorious eye: he would dearly have loved to take her away from the fellow. The scant distance to shore took twice as long to cover as it ought to have. A substantial escort of armed guards had been detached from their patrols on the island to accompany them on the tour. Most of these fanned out ahead to force a clear path through the streets, but some ten kept close on Laurence's heels, jostling one another out of any kind of formation in what seemed to be an attempt to keep him blocked almost by a human wall from wandering away.

Zhao Wei took them through another of the elaborate red-and-gold gateways, this one set in a fortified wall and yielding onto a very broad avenue. It was manned by several guards in the Imperial livery, as well as by two dragons also under gear: one of the by-now-familiar red ones, and the other a brilliant green with red markings. Their captains were sitting together sipping tea under an awning, their padded jerkins removed against the day's heat, and both were women.

"I see you have women captains also," Laurence said to Zhao Wei. "Do they serve with particular breeds, then?"

"Women are companions to those dragons who go into the army," Zhao Wei said. "Naturally only the lower breeds would choose to do that sort of work. Over there, that green one is one of the Emerald Glass. They are too lazy and slow to do well on the examinations, and the Scarlet Flower breed all like fighting too much, so they are not good for anything else."

"Do you mean to say that only women serve in your aerial corps?" Laurence asked, sure he had misunderstood; yet Zhao Wei only nodded a confirmation. "But what reason can there be for such a policy; surely you do not ask women to serve in your infantry, or navy?" Laurence protested.

His dismay was evident, and Zhao Wei, perhaps feeling a need to defend his nation's unusual practice, proceeded to narrate the legend which was its foundation. The details were of course romanticized: a girl had supposedly disguised herself as a man to fight in her father's stead, had become companion to a military dragon and saved the empire by winning a great battle; as a consequence, the Emperor of the time had pronounced girls acceptable for service with dragons.

But these colorful exaggerations aside, it seemed that the nation's policy itself was accurately described: in times of conscription, the head of each family had at one time been required to serve or send a child in his stead. Girls being considerably less valued than boys, they had become the preferred choice to fill out the quota when possible. As they could only serve in the aerial corps, they had come to dominate this branch of the service until eventually the force became exclusive.

The telling of the legend, complete with recitation of its traditional poetic version, which Laurence suspected lost a great deal of color in the translation, carried them past the gate and some distance along the avenue towards a broad grey-flagged plaza set back from the road itself, and full of children and hatchlings. The boys sat cross-legged on the floor in front, the hatchlings coiled up neatly behind, and all together in a queer mixture of childish voices and the more resonant draconic tones were parroting a human teacher who stood on a podium in front, reading loudly from a great book and beckoning the students to repeat after every line.

Zhao Wei waved his hand towards them. "You wanted to see our schools. This is a new class, of course; they are only just beginning to study the Analects."

Laurence was privately baffled at the notion of subjecting dragons to study and written examinations. "They do not seem paired off," he said, studying the group.

Zhao Wei looked blankly at him, and Laurence clarified, "I mean, the boys are not sitting with their own hatchlings, and the children seem rather young for them, indeed."

"Oh, those dragonets are much too young to have chosen any companions yet," Zhao Wei said. "They are only a few weeks old. When they have lived fifteen months, then they will be ready to choose, and the boys will be older."

Laurence halted in surprise, and turned to stare at the little hatchlings again; he had always heard that dragons had to be tamed directly at hatching, to keep them from becoming feral and escaping into the wild, but this seemed plainly contradicted by the Chinese example. Temeraire said, "It must be very lonely. I would not have liked to be without Laurence when I hatched, at all." He lowered his head and nudged Laurence with his nose. "And it would also be very tiresome to have to hunt all the time for yourself when you are first hatched; I was always hungry," he added, more prosaically.

"Of course the hatchlings do not have to hunt for themselves," Zhao Wei said. "They must study. There are dragons who tend the eggs and feed the young. That is much better than having a person do it. Otherwise a dragonet could not help but become attached, before he was wise enough to properly judge the character and virtues of his proposed companion."

This was a pointed remark indeed, and Laurence answered it coolly, "I suppose that may be a concern, if you have less regulation of how men are to be chosen for such an opportunity. Among us, of course, a man must ordinarily serve for many years in the Corps before he can be considered worthy even to be presented to a hatchling. In such circumstances, it seems to me that an early attachment such as you decry may be instead the foundation of a lasting deeper affection, more rewarding to both parties."

They continued on into the city proper, and now with a view of his surroundings from a more ordinary perspective than from the air, Laurence was struck afresh by the great breadth of the streets, which seemed to almost have been designed with dragons in mind. They gave the city a feeling of spaciousness altogether different from London; though the absolute number of people was, he guessed, nearly equal. Temeraire was here more staring than stared-at; the populace of the capital were evidently used to the presence of the more exalted breeds, while he had never been out into a city before, and his head craned nearly in a loop around his own neck as he tried to look in three directions at once.

Guards roughly pushed ordinary travelers out of the way of green sedan-chairs, carrying mandarins on official duties. Along one broad way a wedding procession brilliant with scarlet and gold were winding their shouting, clapping way through the streets, with musicians and spitting fireworks in their train and the bride well-concealed in a draped chair: a wealthy match to judge by the elaborate proceedings. Occasional mules plodded along under cartloads, inured to the presence of the dragons, their hooves clopping along the stones; but Laurence did not see any horses on the main avenues, nor carriages: likely they could not be tamed to bear the presence of so many dragons. The air smelled quite differently: none of the sour grassy stench of manure and horse piss inescapable in London, but instead the faintly sulfurous smell of dragon waste, more pronounced when the wind blew from the northeast; Laurence suspected some larger cesspools lay in that quarter of the city.

And everywhere, everywhere dragons: the blue ones, most common, were engaged in the widest variety of tasks. In addition to those Laurence saw ferrying people about with their carrying harnesses, others bore loads of freight; but a sizable number also seemed to be traveling alone on more important business, wearing collars of varying colors, much like the different colors of the mandarins' jewels. Zhao Wei confirmed that these were signifiers of rank, and the dragons so adorned members of the civil service. "The *Shen-lung* are like people, some are clever and some are lazy," he said, and added, to Laurence's great interest, "Many superior breeds have risen from the best of them, and the wisest may even be honored with an Imperial mating." Dozens of other breeds also were to be seen, some with and others without human companions, engaged on many errands. Once two Imperial dragons came by going in the opposite direction, and inclined their heads to Temeraire politely as they passed; they were adorned with scarves of red silk knotted and wrapped in chains of gold and sewn all over with small pearls, very elegant, to which Temeraire gave a sidelong covetous eye.

They came shortly into a market district, the stores lavishly decorated with carving and gilt, and full of goods. Silks of glorious color and texture, some of much finer quality than anything Laurence had ever seen in London; great skeins and wrapped yards of the plain blue cotton as yarn and cloth, in different grades of quality both by thickness and by the intensity of the dye. And porcelain, which in particular caught Laurence's attention; unlike his father, he was no connoisseur of the art, but the precision in the blue-and-white designs seemed also superior to those dishes which he had seen imported, and the colored dishes particularly lovely.

"Temeraire, will you ask if he would take gold?" he asked; Temeraire was peering into the shop with much interest, while the merchant eyed his looming head in the doorway anxiously; this at least seemed one place even in China where dragons were not quite welcome. The merchant looked doubtful, and addressed some questions to Zhao Wei; after this, he consented at least to take a half-guinea and inspect it. He rapped it on the side of the table and then called in his son from a back room: having few teeth left himself, he gave it to the younger man to bite upon. A woman seated in the back peeped around the corner, interested by the noise, and was admonished loudly and without effect until she stared her fill at Laurence and withdrew again; but her voice came from the back room stridently, so she seemed also to be participating in the debate.

At last the merchant seemed satisfied, but when Laurence picked up the vase which he had been examining, he immediately jumped forward and took it away, with a torrent of words; motioning Laurence to stay, he went into the back room. "He says that is not worth so much," Temeraire explained.

"But I have only given him half a pound," Laurence protested; the man came back carrying a much larger vase, in a deep, nearly glowing red, shading delicately to a pure white at the top, and with an almost mirrored gloss. He put it down on the table and they all looked at it with admiration; even Zhao Wei did not withhold a murmur of approval, and Temeraire said, "Oh, that is very pretty."

Laurence pressed another few guineas on the shopkeeper with some difficulty, and still felt guilty at carrying it away, swathed in many protective layers of cotton rags; he had never seen a piece so lovely before, and he was already anxious for its survival through the long journey. Emboldened by this first success, he embarked on other purchases, of silk and other porcelain, and after that a small pendant of jade, which Zhao Wei, his façade of disdain gradually yielding to enthusiasm for the shopping expedition, pointed out to him, explaining that the symbols upon it were the start of the poem about the legendary woman dragon-soldier. It was apparently a good-luck symbol often bought for a girl about to embark upon such a career. Laurence rather thought Jane Roland would like it, and added it to the growing pile; very soon Zhao Wei had to detail several of his soldiers to carry the various packages: they no longer seemed so concerned about Laurence's potential escape as about his loading them down like cart-horses.

Prices for many of the goods seemed considerably lower than Laurence was used to, in general; more than could be accounted for by the cost of freight. This alone was not a surprise, after hearing the Company commissioners in Macao talk about the rapacity of the local mandarins and the bribes they demanded, on top of the state duties. But the difference was so high that Laurence had to revise significantly upwards his guesses of the degree of extortion. "It is a great pity," Laurence said to Temeraire, as they came to the end of the avenue. "If only the trade were allowed to proceed openly, I suppose these merchants could make a much better living, and the craftsmen, too; having to send all their wares through Canton is what allows the mandarins there to be so unreasonable. Probably they do not even want to bother, if they can sell the goods here, so we receive only the dregs of their market."

"Perhaps they do not want to sell the nicest pieces so far away. That is a very pleasant smell," Temeraire said, approvingly, as they crossed a small bridge into another district, surrounded by a narrow moat of water and a low stone wall. Open shallow trenches full of smoldering coals lined the street to either side, with animals cooking over them, spitted on metal spears and being basted with great swabs by sweating, half-naked men: oxen, pigs, sheep, deer, horses, and smaller, less-identifiable creatures; Laurence did not look very closely. The sauces dripped and scorched upon the stones, raising thick wafting clouds of aromatic smoke. Only a handful of people were buying here, nimbly dodging among the dragons who made up the better part of the clientele.

Temeraire had eaten heartily that morning: a couple of young venison, with some stuffed ducks as a relish; he did not ask to eat, but looked a little wistfully at a smaller purple dragon eating roast suckling pigs off a skewer. But down a smaller alley Laurence also saw a tired-looking blue dragon, his hide marked with old sores from the silk carrying-harness he wore, turning sadly away from a beautifully roasted cow and pointing instead at a small, rather burnt sheep left off to the side: he took it away to a corner and began eating it very slowly, stretching it out, and he did not disdain the offal or the bones.

It was natural that if dragons were expected to earn their bread, there should be some less fortunate than others; but Laurence felt it somehow criminal to see one going hungry, particularly when there was so much extravagant waste at their residence and elsewhere. Temeraire did not notice, his gaze fixed on the displays. They came out of the district over another small bridge which led them back onto the broad avenue where they had begun. Temeraire sighed deeply with pleasure, releasing the aroma only slowly from his nostrils.

Laurence, for his part, was fallen quiet; the sight had dispelled his natural fascination with all the novelty of their surroundings and the natural interest inherent in a foreign capital of such extents, and without such distraction he was inescapably forced to recognize the stark contrast in the treatment of dragons. The city streets were not wider than in London by some odd coincidence, or a question of taste, or even for the greater grandeur which they offered; but plainly designed that dragons might live in full harmony with men, and that this design was accomplished, to the benefit of all parties, he could not dispute: the case of misery which he had seen served rather to illustrate the general good.

The dinner-hour was hard upon them, and Zhao Wei turned their route back towards the island; Temeraire also grown quieter as they left the market precincts behind, and they walked along in silence until they reached the gateway; there pausing he looked back over his shoulder at the city, its activity undiminished. Zhao Wei caught the look and said something to him in Chinese. "It is very nice," Temeraire answered him, and added, "but I cannot compare it: I have never walked in London, or even in Dover."

They took their leave from Zhao Wei briefly, outside the pavilion, and went in again together. Laurence sat heavily down upon a wooden bench, while Temeraire began to pace restlessly back and forth, his tail-tip switching back and forth with agitation. "It is not true, at all," he burst out at last. "Laurence, we have gone everywhere we liked; I have been in the streets and to shops, and no one has run away or been frightened: not in the south and not here. People are not afraid of dragons, not in the least."

"I must beg your pardon," Laurence said quietly. "I confess I was mistaken: plainly men can be accustomed. I expect with so many dragons about, all men here are raised with close experience of them, and lose their fear. But I assure you I have not lied to you deliberately; the same is not true in Britain. It must be a question of use."

"If use can make men stop being afraid, I do not see why we should be kept penned up so they may continue to be frightened," Temeraire said.

To this Laurence could make no answer, and did not try; instead he retreated to his own room to take a little dinner; Temeraire lay down for his customary afternoon nap in a brooding, restless coil, while Laurence sat alone, picking unenthusiastically over his plate. Hammond came to inquire after what they had seen; Laurence answered him as briefly as he could, his irritation of spirit ill-concealed, and in short order Hammond went away rather flushed and thin-lipped.

"Has that fellow been pestering you?" Granby said, looking in.

"No," Laurence said tiredly, getting up to rinse his hands in the basin he had filled from the pond. "Indeed, I am afraid I was plainly rude to him just now, and he did not deserve it in the least: he was only curious how they raise the dragons here, so he could argue with them that Temeraire's treatment in England has not been so ill."

"Well, as far as I am concerned he deserved a trimming," Granby said. "I could have pulled out my hair when I woke up and he told me smug as a deacon that he had packed you off alone with some Chinaman; not that Temeraire would let any harm come to you, but anything could happen in a crowd, after all."

"No, nothing of the kind was attempted at all; our guide was a little rude to begin, but perfectly civil by the end." Laurence glanced over at the bundles stacked in the corner, where Zhao Wei's men had left them. "I begin to think Hammond was right, John; and it was all old-maid flutters and imagination," he said, unhappily; it seemed to him, after the long day's tour, that the prince hardly needed to stoop to murder, with the many advantages of his country to serve as gentler and no less persuasive arguments.

"More likely Yongxing gave up trying aboard ship, and has just been waiting to get you settled in under his eyes," Granby said pessimistically. "This is a nice enough cottage, I suppose, but there are a damned lot of guards skulking about."

"All the more reason not to fear," Laurence said. "If they meant to kill me, they could have done so by now, a dozen times over."

"Temeraire would hardly stay here if the Emperor's own guards killed you, and him already suspicious," Granby said. "Most like he would do his best to kill the lot of them, and then I hope find the ship again and go back home; though it takes them very hard, losing a captain, and he might just as easily go and run into the wild."

"We can argue ourselves in circles this way forever." Laurence lifted his hands impatiently and let them drop again. "At least today, the only wish which I saw put in action was to make a desirable impression upon Temeraire." He did not say that this goal had been thoroughly accomplished and with little effort; he did not know how to draw a contrast against the treatment of dragons in the West without sounding at best a complainer and at worst nearly disloyal: he was conscious afresh that he had not been raised an aviator, and he was unwilling to say anything that might wound Granby's feelings.

"You are a damned sight too quiet," Granby said, unexpectedly, and Laurence gave a guilty start: he had been sitting and brooding in silence. "I am not surprised he took a liking to the city, he is always on fire for anything new; but is it that bad?"

"It is not only the city," Laurence said finally. "It is the respect which is given to dragons; and not only to himself: they all of them have a great deal of liberty, as a matter of course. I think I saw a hundred dragons at least today, wandering through the streets, and no one took any notice of them."

"And God forbid we should take a flight over Regent's Park but we have shrieks of murder and fire and flood all at once, and ten memoranda sent us from the Admiralty," Granby agreed, with a quick flash of resentment. "Not that we *could* set down in London if we wanted to: the streets are too narrow for anything bigger than a Winchester. From what we have seen even just from the air, this place is laid out with a good deal more sense. It is no wonder they have ten beasts to our one, if not more."

Laurence was deeply relieved to find Granby taking no offense against him, and so willing to discuss the subject. "John, do you know, here they do not assign handlers until the dragon is fifteen months of age; until then they are raised by other dragons."

"Well, that seems a rotten waste to me, letting dragons sit around nursemaiding," Granby said. "But I suppose they can afford it. Laurence, when I think what we could do with a round dozen of those big scarlet fellows that they have sitting around getting fat everywhere; it makes you weep."

"Yes; but what I meant to say was, they seem not to have any ferals at all," Laurence said. "Is it not one in ten that we lose?"

"Oh, not nearly so many, not in modern times," Granby said. "We used to lose Longwings by the dozen, until Queen Elizabeth had the bright idea of setting her serving-maid to one and we found they would take to girls like lambs, and then it turned out the Xenicas would, too. And Winchesters often used to nip off like lightning before you could get a stitch of harness on them, but nowadays we hatch them inside and let them flap about for a bit before bringing out the food. Not more than one in thirty, at the most, if you do not count the eggs we lose in the breeding grounds: the ferals already there hide them from us sometimes."

Their conversation was interrupted by a servant; Laurence tried to wave the man away, but with apologetic bows and a tug on Laurence's sleeve, he made clear he wished to lead them out to the main dining chamber: Sun Kai, unexpectedly, had come to take tea with them.

Laurence was in no mood for company, and Hammond, who joined them to serve as translator, as yet remained stiff and unfriendly; they made an awkward and mostly silent company. Sun Kai inquired politely about their accommodations, and then about their enjoyment of the country, which Laurence answered very shortly; he could not help some suspicion that this might be some attempt at probing Temeraire's state of mind, and still more so when Sun Kai at last came however to the purpose for his visit.

"Lung Tien Qian sends you an invitation," Sun Kai said. "She hopes you and Temeraire will take tea with her tomorrow in the Ten Thousand Lotus palace, in the morning before the flowers open."

"Thank you, sir, for bearing the message," Laurence said, polite but flat. "Temeraire is anxious to know her better." The invitation could hardly be refused, though he was by no means happy to see further lures thrown out to Temeraire.

Sun Kai nodded equably. "She, too, is anxious to know more of her offspring's condition. Her judgment carries much weight with the Son of Heaven." He sipped his tea and added, "Perhaps you will wish to tell her of your nation, and the respect which Lung Tien Xiang has won there."

Hammond translated this, and then added, quickly enough that Sun Kai might think it part of the translation of his own words, "Sir, I trust you see this is a tolerably clear hint. You must make every effort to win her favor."

"I cannot see why Sun Kai would give me any advice at all in the first place," Laurence said, after the envoy had left them again. "He has always been polite enough, but not what anyone would call friendly."

"Well, it's not much advice, is it?" Granby said. "He only said to tell her that Temeraire is happy: that's hardly something you couldn't have thought of alone, and it makes a polite noise."

"Yes; but we would not have known to value her good opinion quite so highly, or think this meeting of any particular importance," Hammond said. "No; for a diplomat, he has said a great deal indeed, as much as he could, I imagine, without committing himself quite openly to us. This is most heartening," he added, with what Laurence felt was excessive optimism, likely born of frustration: Hammond had so far written five times to the Emperor's ministers, to ask for a meeting where he might present his credentials: every note had been returned unopened, and a flat refusal had met his request to go out from the island to meet the handful of other Westerners in the town.

"She cannot be so very maternal, if she agreed to send him so far away in the first place," Laurence said to Granby, shortly after dawn the next morning; he was inspecting his best coat and trousers, which he had set out to air overnight, in the early light: his cravat needed pressing, and he thought he had noticed some frayed threads on his best shirt.

"They usually aren't, you know," Granby said. "Or at least, not after the hatching, though they get broody over the eggs when they are first laid. Not that they don't care at all, but after all, a dragonet can take the head off a goat five minutes after it breaks the shell; they don't need mothering. Here, let me have that; I can't press without scorching, but I can do up a seam." He took the shirt and needle from Laurence and set to repairing the tear in the cuff.

"Still, she would not care to see him neglected, I am sure," Laurence said. "Though I wonder that she is so deeply in the Emperor's counsel; I would have imagined that if they sent any Celestial egg away, it would only have been of a lesser line. Thank you, Dyer; set it there," he said, as the young runner came in bearing the hot iron from the stove.

His appearance polished so far as he could manage, Laurence joined Temeraire in the courtyard; the striped dragon had returned to escort them. The flight was only a short one, but curious: they flew so low they could see small clumps of ivy and rootlings that had managed to establish themselves upon the yellow-tiled roofs of the palace buildings, and see the colors of the jewels upon the mandarins' hats as the ministers went hurrying through the enormous courtyards and walkways below, despite the early hour of the morning.

The particular palace lay within the walls of the immense Forbidden City, easily identifiable from aloft: two huge dragon pavilions on either side of a long pond almost choked with water-lilies, the flowers still closed within their buds. Wide sturdy bridges spanned the pond, arched high for decoration, and a courtyard flagged with black marble lay to the south, just now being touched with first light.

The yellow-striped dragon landed here and bowed them along; as Temeraire padded by, Laurence could see other dragons stirring in the early light under the eaves of the great pavilions. An ancient Celestial was creeping stiffly out from the bay farthest to the southeast, the tendrils about his jaw long and drooping as mustaches. His enormous ruff was leached of color, and his hide gone so translucent the black was now redly tinted with the color of the flesh and blood beneath. Another of the yellow-striped dragons paced him carefully, nudging him occasionally with his nose towards the sun-drenched courtyard; the Celestial's eyes were a milky blue, the pupils barely visible beneath the cataracts.

A few other dragons emerged also: Imperials rather than Celestials, lacking the ruff and tendrils, and with more variety in their hue: some were as black as Temeraire, but others a deep indigo-washed blue; all very dark, however, except for Lien, who emerged at the same time out of a separate and private pavilion, set back and alone among the trees, and came to the pond to drink. With her white hide, she looked almost unearthly among the rest; Laurence felt it would be difficult to fault anyone for indulging in superstition towards her, and indeed the other dragons consciously gave her a wide berth. She ignored them entirely in return and yawned wide and red, shaking her head vigorously to scatter away the clinging drops of water, and then paced away into the gardens in solitary dignity.

Qian herself was waiting for them at one of the central pavilions, flanked by two Imperial dragons of particularly graceful appearance, all of them adorned with elaborate jewels. She inclined her head courteously and flicked a talon against a standing bell nearby to summon servants; the attending dragons shifted their places to make room for Laurence and Temeraire on her right, and the human servants brought Laurence a comfortable chair.

Qian made no immediate conversation, but gestured towards the lake; the line of the morning sun was now traveling swiftly northward over the water as the sun crept higher, and the lotus buds were unfolding in almost balletic progression; they numbered literally in the thousands, and made a spectacle of glowing pink color against the deep green of their leaves.

As the last unfurled flowers came to rest, the dragons all tapped their claws against the flagstones in a clicking noise, a kind of applause. Now a small table was brought for Laurence and great porcelain bowls painted in blue and white for the dragons, and a black, pungent tea poured for them all. To Laurence's surprise the dragons drank with enjoyment, even going so far as to lick up the leaves in the bottom of their cups. He himself found the tea curious and over-strong in flavor: almost the aroma of smoked meat, though he drained his cup politely as well. Temeraire drank his own enthusiastically and very fast, and then sat back with a peculiar uncertain expression, as though trying to decide whether he had liked it or not.

"You have come a very long way," Qian said, addressing Laurence; an unobtrusive servant had stepped forward to her side to translate. "I hope you are enjoying your visit with us, but surely you must miss your home?"

"An officer in the King's service must be used to go where he is required, madam," Laurence said, wondering if this was meant as a suggestion. "I have not spent more than a sixmonth at my own family's home since I took ship the first time, and that was as a boy of twelve."

"That is very young, to go so far away," Qian said. "Your mother must have had great anxiety for you."

"She had the acquaintance of Captain Mountjoy, with whom I served, and we knew his family well," Laurence said, and seized the opening to add, "You yourself had no such advantage, I regret, on being parted from Temeraire; I would be glad to satisfy you on whatever points I might, if only in retrospect."

She turned her head to the attending dragons. "Perhaps Mei and Shu will take Xiang to see the flowers more closely," she said, using Temeraire's Chinese name. The two Imperials inclined their heads and stood up expectantly waiting for Temeraire.

Temeraire looked a little worriedly at Laurence, and said, "They are very nice from here?"

Laurence felt rather anxious himself at the prospect of a solitary interview, with so little sense of what might please Qian, but he mustered a smile for Temeraire and said, "I will wait here with your mother; I am sure you will enjoy them."

"Be sure not to bother Grandfather or Lien," Qian added to the Imperial dragons, who nodded as they led Temeraire away.

The servants refilled his cup and Qian's bowl from a fresh kettle, and she lapped at it in a more leisurely way. Presently she said, "I understand Temeraire has been serving in your army."

There was unmistakably a note of censure in her voice, which did not need translation. "Among us, all those dragons who can, serve in defense of their home: that is no dishonor, but the fulfillment of our duty," Laurence said. "I assure you we could not value him more highly. There are very few dragons among us: even the least are greatly prized, and Temeraire is of the highest order."

She rumbled low and thoughtfully. "Why are there so few dragons, that you must ask your most valued to fight?"

"We are a small nation, nothing like your own," Laurence said. "Only a handful of smaller wild breeds were native to the British Isles, when the Romans came and began to tame them. Since then, by cross-breeding our lines have multiplied, and thanks to careful tending of our cattle herds, we have been able to increase our numbers, but still we cannot support nearly so many as you here possess."

She lowered her head and regarded him keenly. "And among the French, how are dragons treated?"

Instinctively Laurence was certain British treatment of dragons was superior and more generous than that of any other Western nation; but he was unhappily aware he would have considered it also superior to China's, if he had not come and already seen plainly otherwise. A month before, he could easily have spoken with pride of how British dragons were cared for. Like all of them, Temeraire had been fed and housed on raw meat and in bare clearings, with constant training and little entertainment. Laurence thought he might as well brag of raising children in a pigsty to the Queen, as speak of such conditions to this elegant dragon in her flower-decked palace. If the French were no better, they were hardly worse; and he would have thought very little of anyone who covered the faults in his own service by blackening another's.

"In ordinary course, the practices in France are much the same as ours, I believe," he said at last. "I do not know what promises were made you, in Temeraire's particular case, but I can tell you that Emperor Napoleon himself is a military man: even as we left England he was in the field, and any dragon who was his companion would hardly remain behind while he went to war."

"You are yourself descended from kings, I understand," Qian said unexpectedly, and turning her head spoke to one of the servants, who hurried forward with a long rice-paper scroll and unrolled it upon the table: with amazement, Laurence saw it was a copy, in a much finer hand and larger, of the familial chart which he had drawn so long ago at the New Year banquet. "This is correct?" she inquired, seeing him so startled.

It had never occurred to him that the information would come to her ears, nor that she would find it of interest. But he at once swallowed any reluctance: he would puff off his consequence to her day and night if it would win her approval. "My family is indeed an old one, and proud; you see I myself have gone into service in the Corps, and count it an honor," he said, though guilt pricked at him; certainly no one in the circles of his birth would have called it as much.

Qian nodded, apparently satisfied, and sipped again at her tea while the servant carried the chart away again. Laurence cast about for something else to say. "If I may be so bold, I think I may with confidence say on behalf of my Government that we would gladly agree to whatever conditions the French accepted, on your first sending Temeraire's egg to them."

"Many considerations besides remain" was all she said in response to this overture, however.

Temeraire and the two Imperials were already coming back from their walk, Temeraire having evidently set a rather hurried pace; at the same time, the white dragon came walking past as she returned to her own quarters with Yongxing now by her side, speaking with her in a low voice, one hand affectionately resting upon her side. She walked slowly, so he could keep pace, and also the several attendants trailing reluctantly after burdened with large scrolls and several books: still the Imperials held well back and waited to let them pass before coming back into the pavilion.

"Qian, why is she that color?" Temeraire asked, peeking back out at Lien after she had gone by. "She looks so very strange."

"Who can understand the workings of Heaven?" Qian said repressively. "Do not be disrespectful. Lien is a great scholar; she was *chuang-yuan*, many years ago, though she did not need to submit to the examinations at all, being a Celestial, and also she is your elder cousin. She was sired by Chu, who was hatched of Xian, as was I."

"Oh," Temeraire said, abashed. More timidly he asked, "Who was my sire?"

"Lung Qin Gao," Qian said, and twitched her tail; she looked rather pleased by the recollection. "He is an Imperial dragon, and is at present in the south in Hangzhou: his companion is a prince of the third rank, and they are visiting the West Lake."

Laurence was startled to learn Celestials could so breed true with Imperials: but on his tentative inquiry Qian confirmed as much. "That is how our line continues. We cannot breed among ourselves," she said, and added, quite unconscious of how she was staggering him, "There are only myself and Lien now, who are female, and besides Grandfather and Chu, there are only Chuan and Ming and Zhi, and we are all cousins at most."

"Only eight of them, altogether?" Hammond stared and sat down blankly: as well he might.

"I don't see how they can possibly continue on like that forever," Granby said. "Are they so mad to keep them only for the Emperors, that they'll risk losing the whole line?"

"Evidently from time to time a pair of Imperials will give birth to a Celestial," Laurence said, between bites; he was sitting down at last to his painfully late dinner, in his bedroom: seven o'clock and full darkness outside, and he had swelled himself near to bursting with tea in an effort to stave off hunger over the visit which had stretched to many hours. "That is how the oldest fellow there now was born; and he is sire to the lot of them, going back four or five generations."

"I cannot make it out in the least," Hammond said, paying no attention to the rest of the conversation. "Eight Celestials; why on earth would they ever have given him away? Surely, at least for breeding—I cannot, I *cannot* credit it; Bonaparte cannot have impressed them so, not secondhand and from a continent away. There must be something else, something which I have not grasped. Gentlemen, you will excuse me," he added, distractedly, and rose and left them alone. Laurence finished his meal without much appetite and set down his chopsticks.

"She did not say no to our keeping him, at any rate," Granby said into the silence, but dismally.

Laurence said, after a moment, more to quell his own inner voices, "I could not be so selfish to even try and deny him the pleasure of making the better acquaintance of his own kindred, or learning about his native land."

"It is all stuff and nonsense in the end, Laurence," Granby said, trying to comfort him. "A dragon won't be parted from his captain for all the gems in Araby, and all the calves in Christendom, too, for that matter."

Laurence rose and went to the window. Temeraire had curled up for the night upon the heated courtyard stones once again. The moon had risen, and he was very beautiful to look at in the silver light, with the blossom-heavy trees on either side hanging low above him and a dappled reflection in the pond, all his scales gleaming.

"That is true; a dragon will endure a great deal sooner than be parted from his captain. It does not follow that a decent man would ask it of him," Laurence said, very low, and let the curtain fall.

Chapter 14

❖

 $\mathcal{T}$ EMERAIRE HIMSELF WAS quiet the day after their visit. Laurence went out to sit with him, and gazed at him with anxiety; but he did not know how to broach the subject of what distressed him, nor what to say. If Temeraire was grown discontented with his lot in England, and wished to stay, there was nothing to be done. Hammond would hardly argue, so long as he was able to complete his negotiations; he cared a good deal more for establishing a permanent embassy and winning some sort of treaty than for getting Temeraire home. Laurence was by no means inclined to force the issue early.

Qian had told Temeraire, on their departure, to make himself free of the palace, but the same invitation had not been extended to Laurence. Temeraire did not ask permission to go, but he looked wistfully into the distance, and paced the courtyard in circles, and refused Laurence's offer to read together. At last growing sick of himself, Laurence said, "Would you wish to go and see Qian again? I am sure she would welcome your visit."

"She did not ask you," Temeraire said, but his wings fanned halfway out, irresolute.

"There can be no offense intended in a mother liking to see her offspring privately," Laurence said, and this excuse was sufficient; Temeraire very nearly glowed with pleasure and set off at once. He returned only late that evening, jubilant and full of plans to return.

"They have started teaching me to write," he said. "I have already learned twenty-five characters today; shall I show you?"

"By all means," Laurence answered, and not only to humor him; grimly he set himself to studying the symbols Temeraire laid down, and copying them down as best he could with a quill instead of a brush while Temeraire pronounced them for his benefit, though he looked rather doubtful at Laurence's attempts to reproduce the sounds. He did not make much progress, but the effort alone made Temeraire so very happy that he could not begrudge it, and concealed the intense strain which he had suffered under the entire seeming endless day.

Infuriatingly, however, Laurence had to contend not only with his own feelings, but with Hammond on the subject as well. "*One* visit, in your company, could serve as reassurance and give her the opportunity of making your acquaintance," the diplomat said. "But this continued solitary visiting cannot be allowed. If he comes to prefer China and agrees of his own volition to stay, we will lose any hope of success: they will pack us off at once."

"That is enough, sir," Laurence said angrily. "I have no intention of insulting Temeraire by suggesting that his natural wish to become acquainted with his kind in any way represents a lack of fidelity."

Hammond pressed the point, and the conversation grew heated; at last Laurence concluded by saying, "If I must make this plain, so be it: I do not consider myself as under your command. I have been given no instructions to that effect, and your attempt to assert an authority without official foundation is entirely improper."

Their relations had already been tolerably cool; now they became frigid, and Hammond did not come to have dinner with Laurence and his officers that night. The next day, however, he came early into the pavilion, before Temeraire had left on his visit, accompanied by Prince Yongxing. "His Highness has been kind enough to come and see how we do; I am sure you will join me in welcoming him," he said, with rather hard emphasis on the last words, and Laurence rather reluctantly rose to make his most formal leg.

"You are very kind, sir; as you see you find us very comfortable," he said, with stiff politeness, and wary; he still did not trust Yongxing's intentions in the least.

Yongxing inclined his head a very little, equally stiff and unsmiling, and then turned and beckoned to a young boy following him: no more than thirteen years of age, wearing wholly nondescript garments of the usual indigo-dyed cotton. Glancing up at him, the boy nodded and walked past Laurence, directly up to Temeraire, and made a formal greeting: he raised his hands up in front of himself, fingers wrapped over one another, and inclined his head, saying something in Chinese at the same time. Temeraire looked a little puzzled, and Hammond interjected hastily, "Tell him yes, for Heaven's sake."

"Oh," said Temeraire, uncertainly, but said something to the boy, evidently affirmative. Laurence was startled to see the boy climb up onto Temeraire's foreleg, and arrange himself there. Yongxing's face was as always difficult to read, but there was a suggestion of satisfaction to his mouth; then he said, "We will go inside and take tea," and turned away.

"Be sure not to let him fall," Hammond added hastily to Temeraire, with an anxious look at the boy, who was sitting cross-legged, with great poise, and seemed as likely to fall off as a Buddha statue to climb off its pediment.

"Roland," Laurence called; she and Dyer had been working their trigonometry in the back corner. "Pray see if he would like some refreshment."

She nodded and went to talk to the boy in her broken Chinese while Laurence followed the other men across the courtyard and into the residence. Already the servants had hastily rearranged the furniture: a single draped chair for Yongxing, with a footstool, and armless chairs placed at right angles to it for Laurence and Hammond. They brought the tea with great ceremony and attention, and throughout the process Yongxing remained perfectly silent. Nor did he speak once the servants had at last withdrawn, but sipped at his tea, very slowly.

Hammond at length broke the silence with polite thanks for the comfort of their residence, and the attentions which they had received. "The tour of the city, in particular, was a great kindness; may I ask, sir, if it was your doing?"

Yongxing said, "It was the Emperor's wish. Perhaps, Captain," he added, "you were favorably impressed?"

It was very little a question, and Laurence said, shortly, "I was, sir; your city is remarkable." Yongxing smiled, a small dry twist of the lips, and did not say anything more, but then he scarcely needed to; Laurence looked away, all the memory of the coverts in England and the bitter contrast fresh in his mind.

They sat in dumb-show a while longer; Hammond ventured again, "May I inquire as to the Emperor's health? We are most eager, sir, as you can imagine, to pay the King's respects to His Imperial Majesty, and to convey the letters which I bear."

"The Emperor is in Chengde," Yongxing said dismissively. "He will not return to Peking soon; you will have to be patient."

Laurence was increasingly angry. Yongxing's attempt to insinuate the boy into Temeraire's company was as blatant as any of the previous attempts to separate the two of them, and yet now Hammond was making not the least objection, and still trying to make polite conversation in the face of insulting rudeness. Pointedly, Laurence said, "Your Highness's companion seems a very likely young man; may I inquire if he is your son?"

Yongxing frowned at the question and said only, "No," coldly.

Hammond, sensing Laurence's impatience, hastily intervened before Laurence could say anything more. "We are of course only too happy to attend the Emperor's convenience; but I hope we may be granted some additional liberty, if the wait is likely to be long; at least as much as has been given the French ambassador. I am sure, sir, you have not forgotten their murderous attack upon us, at the outset of our journey, and I hope you will allow me to say, once again, that the interests of our nations march far more closely together than yours with theirs."

Unchecked by any reply, Hammond went on; he spoke passionately and at length about the dangers of Napoleon's domination of Europe, the stifling of the trade which should otherwise bring great wealth to China, and the threat of an insatiable conqueror spreading his empire ever wider—perhaps, he added, ending on their very doorstep, "For Napoleon has already made one attempt, sir, to come at us in India, and he makes no secret that his ambition is to exceed Alexander. If he should ever be successful, you must realize his rapacity will not be satisfied there."

The idea that Napoleon should subdue Europe, conquer the Russian and the Ottoman Empires both, cross the Himalayas, establish himself in India, and still have energy left to wage war on China, was to Laurence a piece of exaggeration that would hardly convince anyone; and as for trade, he knew that argument carried no weight at all with Yongxing, who had so fervently spoken of China's self-sufficiency. Nevertheless the prince did not interrupt Hammond at all from beginning to end, listened to the entire long speech frowning, and then at the end of it, when Hammond concluded with a renewed plea to be granted the same freedoms as De Guignes, Yongxing received it in silence, sat a long time, and then said only, "You have as much liberty as he does; anything more would be unsuitable."

"Sir," Hammond said, "perhaps you are unaware that we have not been permitted to leave the island, nor to communicate with any official even by letter."

"Neither is he permitted," Yongxing said. "It is not proper for foreigners to wander through Peking, disrupting the affairs of the magistrates and the ministers: they have much to occupy them."

Hammond was left baffled by this reply, confusion writ plain on his face, and Laurence, for his part, had sat through enough; plainly Yongxing meant nothing but to waste their time, while the boy flattered and fawned over Temeraire. As the child was not his own son, Yongxing had surely chosen him from his relations especially for great charm of personality and instructed him to be as insinuating as ever he might. Laurence did not truly fear that Temeraire would take a preference to the boy, but he had no intention of sitting here playing the fool for the benefit of Yongxing's scheming.

"We cannot be leaving the children unattended this way," he said abruptly. "You will excuse me, sir," and rose from the table already bowing.

As Laurence had suspected, Yongxing had no desire to sit and make conversation with Hammond except to provide the boy an open field, and he rose also to take his leave of them. They returned all together to the courtyard, where Laurence found, to his private satisfaction, that the boy had climbed down from Temeraire's arm and was engaged in a game of jacks with Roland and Dyer, all of them munching on ship's biscuit, and Temeraire had wandered out to the pier, to enjoy the breeze coming off the lake.

Yongxing spoke sharply, and the boy sprang up with a guilty expression; Roland and Dyer looked equally abashed, with glances towards their abandoned books. "We thought it was only polite to be hospitable," Roland said hurriedly, looking to see how Laurence would take this.

"I hope he has enjoyed the visit," Laurence said, mildly, to their relief. "Back to your work, now." They hurried back to their books, and, the boy called to heel, Yongxing swept away with a dissatisfied mien, exchanging a few words with Hammond in Chinese; Laurence gladly watched him go.

"At least we may be grateful that De Guignes is as restricted in his movements as we are," Hammond said after a moment. "I cannot think Yongxing would bother to lie on the subject, though I cannot understand how—" He stopped in puzzlement and shook his head. "Well, perhaps I may learn a little more tomorrow."

"I beg your pardon?" Laurence said, and Hammond absently said, "He said he would come again, at the same time; he means to make a regular visit of it."

"He may mean whatever he likes," Laurence said, angrily, at finding Hammond had thus meekly accepted further intrusions on his behalf, "but *I* will not be playing attendance on him; and why you should choose to waste your time cultivating a man you know very well has not the least sympathy for us is beyond me."

Hammond, answered with some heat, "Of course Yongxing has no natural sympathy for us; why should he or any other man here? Our work is to win them over, and if he is willing to give us the chance to persuade him, it is our duty to try, sir; I am surprised that the effort of remaining civil and drinking a little tea should so try your patience."

Laurence snapped, "And I am surprised to find you so unconcerned over this attempt at supplanting me, after all your earlier protests."

"What, with a twelve-year-old boy?" Hammond said, so very incredulous it was nearly offensive. "I, sir, in my turn, am astonished at your taking alarm *now;* and perhaps if you had not been so quick to dismiss my advice before, you should not have so much need to fear."

"I do not fear in the least," Laurence said, "but neither am I disposed to tolerate so blatant an attempt, or to have us submit tamely to a daily invasion whose only purpose is to give offense."

"I will remind you, Captain, as you did me not so very long ago, that just as you are not under my authority, *I* am not under *yours,*" Hammond said. "The conduct of our diplomacy has very clearly been placed in my hands, and thank Heaven: if we were relying upon you, by now I dare say you would be blithely flying back to England, with half our trade in the Pacific sinking to the bottom of the ocean behind you."

"Very well; you may do as you like, sir," Laurence said, "but you had best make plain to him that I do not mean to leave this protégé of his alone with Temeraire anymore, and I think you will find him less eager to be *persuaded* afterwards; and do not imagine," he added, "that I will tolerate having the boy let in when my back is turned, either."

"As you are disposed to think me a liar and an unscrupulous schemer, I see very little purpose in denying I should do any such thing," Hammond said angrily, coloring up.

He departed instantly, leaving Laurence still angry but ashamed and conscious of having been unfair; he would himself have called it grounds for a challenge. By the next morning, when from the pavilion he saw Yongxing going away with the boy, having evidently cut short the visit on being denied access to Temeraire, his guilt was sharp enough that he made some attempt to apologize, with little success: Hammond would have none of it.

"Whether he took offense at your refusing to join us, or whether you were correct about his aims, can make no difference now," he said, very coldly. "If you will excuse me, I have letters to write," and so quitted the room.

Laurence gave it up and instead went to say farewell to Temeraire, only to have his guilt and unhappiness both renewed at seeing in Temeraire's manner an almost furtive excitement, a very great eagerness to be gone. Hammond was hardly wrong: the idle flattery of a child was nothing to the danger of the company of Qian and the Imperial dragons, no matter how devious Yongxing's motives or how sincere Qian's; there was only less honest excuse for complaining of her.

Temeraire would be gone for hours, but the house being small and the chambers separated mainly by screens of rice paper, Hammond's angry presence was nearly palpable inside, so Laurence stayed in the pavilion after he had gone, attending to his correspondence: unnecessarily, as it was now five months since he had received any letters, and little of any interest had occurred since the welcoming dinner party, now two weeks old; he was not disposed to write of the quarrel with Hammond.

He dozed off over the writing, and woke rather abruptly, nearly knocking heads with Sun Kai, who was bending over him and shaking him. "Captain Laurence, you must wake up," Sun Kai was saying.

Laurence said automatically, "I beg your pardon; what is the matter?" and then stared: Sun Kai had spoken in quite excellent English, with an accent more reminiscent of Italian than Chinese. "Good Lord, have you been able to speak English all this time?" he demanded, his mind leaping to every occasion on which Sun Kai had stood on the dragondeck, privy to all their conversations, and now revealed as having understood every word.

"There is no time at present for explanations," Sun Kai said. "You must come with me at once: men are coming here to kill you, and all your companions also."

It was near on five o'clock in the afternoon, and the lake and trees, framed in the pavilion doors, were golden in the setting light; birds were speaking occasionally from up in the rafters where they nested. The remark, delivered in perfectly calm tones, was so ludicrous Laurence did not at first understand it, and then stood up in outrage. "I am not going anywhere in response to such a threat, with so little explanation," he said, and raised his voice. "Granby!"

"Everything all right, sir?" Blythe had been occupying himself in the neighboring courtyard on some busy-work, and now poked his head in, even as Granby came running.

"Mr. Granby, we are evidently to expect an attack," Laurence said. "As this house does not admit of much security, we will take the small pavilion to the south, with the interior pond. Establish a lookout, and let us have fresh locks in all the pistols."

"Very good," Granby said, and dashed away again; Blythe, in his customary silence, picked up the cutlasses he had been sharpening and offered Laurence one before wrapping up the others and carrying them with his whetstone to the pavilion.

Sun Kai shook his head. "This is great foolishness," he said, following after Laurence. "The very largest gang of *hunhun* are coming from the city. I have a boat waiting just here, and there is time yet for you and all your men to get your things and come away."

Laurence inspected the pavilion entryway; as he had remembered, the pillars were made of stone rather than wood, and nearly two feet in diameter, very sturdy, and the walls of a smooth grey brick under their layer of red paint. The roof was of wood, which was a pity, but he thought the glazed tile would not catch fire easily. "Blythe, will you see if you can arrange some elevation for Lieutenant Riggs and his riflemen out of those stones in the garden? Pray assist him, Willoughby; thank you."

Turning around, he said to Sun Kai, "Sir, you have not said where you would take me, nor who these assassins are, nor whence they have been sent; still less have you given us any reason to trust you. You have certainly deceived us so far as your knowledge of our language. Why you should so abruptly reverse yourself, I have no idea, and after the treatment which we have received, I am in no humor to put myself into your hands."

Hammond came with the other men, looking confused, and came to join Laurence, greeting Sun Kai in Chinese. "May I inquire what is happening?" he asked stiffly.

"Sun Kai has told me to expect another attempt at assassination," Laurence said. "See if you can get anything more clear from him; in the meantime, I must assume we are shortly to come under attack, and make arrangements. He can speak perfect English," he added. "You need not resort to Chinese." He left Sun Kai with a visibly startled Hammond, and joined Riggs and Granby at the entryway.

"If we could knock a couple of holes in this front wall, we could shoot down at any of them coming," Riggs said, tapping the brick. "Otherwise, sir, we're best off laying down a barricade mid-room, and shooting as they come in; but then we can't have fellows with swords at the entryway."

"Lay and man the barricade," Laurence said. "Mr. Granby, block as much of this entryway as you can, so they cannot come in more than three or four abreast if you can manage it. We will form up the rest of the men to either side of the opening, well clear of the field of fire, and hold the door with pistols and cutlasses between volleys while Mr. Riggs and his fellows reload."

Granby and Riggs both nodded. "Right you are," Riggs said. "We have a couple of spare rifles along, sir; we could use you at the barricade."

This was rather transparent, and Laurence treated it with the contempt which it deserved. "Use them for second shots as you can; we cannot waste the guns in the hands of any man who is not a trained rifleman."

Keynes came in almost staggering under a basket of sheets, with three of the elaborate porcelain vases from their residence laid on top. "You are not my usual kind of patients," he said, "but I can bandage and splint you, at any rate. I will be in the back by the pond. And I have brought these to carry water in," he added, sardonic, jerking his chin at the vases. "I suppose they would bring fifty pounds each in auction, so let that be an encouragement not to drop them."

"Roland, Dyer; which of you is the better hand at reloading?" Laurence asked. "Very well; you will both help Mr. Riggs for the first three volleys, then Dyer, you are to help Mr. Keynes, and run back and forth with the water jugs as that duty permits."

"Laurence," Granby said in an undertone, when the others had gone, "I don't see any sign of all those guards anywhere, and they have always been used to patrol at this hour; they must have been called away by someone."

Laurence nodded silently and waved him back to work. "Mr. Hammond, you will pray go behind the barricade," he said, as the diplomat came to his side, Sun Kai with him.

"Captain Laurence, I beg you to listen to me," Hammond said urgently. "We had much better go with Sun Kai at once. These attackers he expects are young bannermen, members of the Tartar tribes, who from poverty and lack of occupation have gone into a sort of local brigandage, and there may be a great many of them."

"Will they have any artillery?" Laurence asked, paying no attention to the attempt at persuasion.

"Cannon? No, of course not; they do not even have muskets," Sun Kai said, "but what does that matter? There may be one hundred of them or more, and I have heard rumors that some among them have even studied Shaolin Quan, in secret, though it is against the law."

"And some of them may be, however distantly, kin to the Emperor," Hammond added. "If we were to kill one, it could easily be used as a pretext for taking offense, and casting us out of the country; you must see we ought to leave at once."

"Sir, you will give us some privacy," Laurence said to Sun Kai, flatly, and the envoy did not argue, but silently bowed his head and moved some distance away.

"Mr. Hammond," Laurence said, turning to him, "you yourself warned me to beware of attempts to separate me from Temeraire, now only consider: if he should return here, to find us gone, with no explanation and all our baggage gone also, how should he ever find us again? Perhaps he might even be convinced that we had been given a treaty and left him deliberately behind, as Yongxing once desired me to do."

"And how will the case be improved if he returns and finds you dead, and all of us with you?" Hammond said impatiently. "Sun Kai has before now given us cause to trust him."

"I give less weight to a small piece of inconsequential advice than you do, sir, and more to a long and deliberate lie of omission; he has unquestionably spied on us from the very beginning of our acquaintance," Laurence said. "No; we are not going with him. It will not be more than a few hours before Temeraire returns, and I am confident in our holding out that long."

"Unless they have found some means of distracting him, and keeping him longer at his visit," Hammond said. "If the Chinese government meant to separate us from him, they could have done so by force at any time during his absence. I am sure Sun Kai can arrange to have a message sent to him at his mother's residence once we have gone to safety."

"Then let him go and send the message now, if he likes," Laurence said. "You are welcome to go with him."

"No, sir," Hammond said, flushing, and turned on his heel to speak with Sun Kai. The former envoy shook his head and left, and Hammond went to take a cutlass from the ready heap.

They worked for another quarter of an hour, hauling in three of the queer-shaped boulders from outside to make the barricade for the riflemen, and dragging over the enormous dragon-couch to block off most of the entryway. The sun had gone by now, but the usual lanterns did not make their appearance around the island, nor any signs of human life at all.

"Sir!" Digby hissed suddenly, pointing out into the grounds. "Two points to starboard, outside the doors of the house."

"Away from the entry," Laurence said; he could not see anything in the twilight, but Digby's young eyes were better than his. "Willoughby, douse that light."

The soft *click-click* of the guns being cocked, the echo of his own breath in his ears, the constant untroubled hum of the flies and mosquitoes outside; these were at first the only noise, until use filtered them out and he could hear the light running footsteps outside: a great many men, he thought. Abruptly there was a crash of wood, several yells. "They've broken into the house, sir," Hackley whispered hoarsely from the barricades.

"Quiet, there," Laurence said, and they kept a silent vigil while the sound of breaking furniture and shattering glass came from the house. The flare of torches outside cast shadows into the pavilion, weaving and leaping in strange angles as a search commenced. Laurence heard men calling to each other outside, the sound coming down from the eaves of the roof. He glanced back; Riggs nodded, and the three riflemen raised their guns.

The first man appeared in the entrance and saw the wooden slab of the dragon-couch blocking it. "My shot," Riggs said clearly, and fired: the Chinaman fell dead with his mouth open to shout.

But the report of the gun brought more cries from outside, and men came bursting in with swords and torches in their hands; a full volley fired off, killing another three, then one more shot from the last rifle, and Riggs called, "Prime and reload!"

The quick slaughter of their fellows had checked the advance of the larger body of men, and clustered them in the opening left in the doorway. Yelling "Temeraire!" and "England!" the aviators launched themselves from the shadows, and engaged the attackers close at hand.

The torchlight was painful to Laurence's eyes after the long wait in the dark, and the smoke of the burning wood mingled with that from the musketry. There was no room for any real swordplay; they were engaged hilt-to-hilt, except when one of the Chinese swords broke—they smelled of rust—and a few men fell over. Otherwise they were all simply heaving back against the pressure of dozens of bodies, trying to come through the narrow opening.

Digby, being too slim to be of much use in the human wall, was stabbing at the attackers between their legs, their arms, through any space left open. "My pistols,"

Laurence shouted at him; no chance to pull them free himself: he was holding his cutlass with two hands, one upon the hilt and another laid upon the flat of the blade, keeping off three men. They were packed so close together they could not move either way to strike at him, but could only raise and lower their swords in a straight line, trying to break his blade through sheer weight.

Digby pulled one of the pistols out of its holster, and fired, taking the man directly before Laurence between the eyes. The other two involuntarily pulled back, and Laurence managed to stab one in the belly, then seized the other by the sword-arm and threw him to the ground; Digby put a sword into his back, and he lay still.

"Present arms!" Riggs yelled, from behind, and Laurence bellowed, "Clear the door!" He swung a cut at the head of the man engaged with Granby, making him flinch back, and they scrambled back together, the polished stone floor already slick under their bootheels. Someone pushed the dripping jug into his hand; he swallowed a couple of times and passed it on, wiping his mouth and his forehead against his sleeve. The rifles all fired at once, and another couple of shots after; then they were back into the fray.

The attackers had already learned to fear the rifles, and they had left a little clear space before the door, many milling about a few paces off under the torches; they nearly filled the courtyard before the pavilion: Sun Kai's estimate had not been exaggerated. Laurence shot a man six paces away, then flipped the pistol in his hand; as they came rushing back on, he clubbed another in the side of the head, and then he was again pushing back against the weight of the swords, until Riggs shouted again.

"Well done, gentlemen," Laurence said, breathing deeply. The Chinese had retreated at the shout and were not immediately at the door; Riggs had experience enough to hold the volley until they advanced again. "For the moment, the advantage is ours. Mr. Granby, we will divide into two parties. Stay back this next wave, and we shall alternate. Therrows, Willoughby, Digby, with me; Martin, Blythe, and Hammond, with Granby."

"I can go with both, sir," Digby said. "I'm not tired at all, truly; it's less work for me, since I can't help to hold them."

"Very well, but be sure to take water between, and stay back on occasion," Laurence said. "There are a damned lot of them, as I dare say you have all seen," he said candidly. "But our position is a good one, and I have no doubt we can hold them as long as ever need be, so long as we pace ourselves properly."

"And see Keynes at once to be tied up if you take a cut or a blow—we cannot afford to lose anyone to slow bleeding," Granby added to this, while Laurence nodded. "Only sing out, and someone will come to take your place in line."

A sudden feverish many-voiced yell rose from outside, the men working themselves up to facing the volley, then a pounding of running feet, and Riggs shouted, "Fire!" as the attackers stormed the entryway again.

The fighting at the door was a greater strain now with fewer of them to hand, but the opening was sufficiently narrow that they could hold it even so. The bodies of the dead were forming a grisly addition to their barrier, piled now two and even three deep, and some of the attackers were forced to stretch over them to fight. The reloading time seemed queerly long, an illusion; Laurence was very glad of the rest when at last the next volley was ready. He leaned against the wall, drinking again from the vase; his arms and shoulders were aching from the constant pressure, and his knees.

"Is it empty, sir?" Dyer was there, anxious, and Laurence handed him the vase: he trotted away back towards the pond, through the haze of smoke shrouding the middle of the room; it was drifting slowly upwards, into the cavernous emptiness above.

Again the Chinese did not immediately storm the door, with the volley waiting. Laurence stepped a little way back into the pavilion and tried to look out, to see if he could make anything out beyond the front line of the struggle. But the torches dazzled his eyes too much: nothing but an impenetrable darkness beyond the first row of shining faces staring intently towards the entryway, feverish with the strain of battle. The time seemed long; he missed the ship's glass, and the steady telling of the bell. Surely it had been an hour or two, by now; Temeraire would come soon.

A sudden clamor from outside, and a new rhythm of clapping hands. His hand went without thought to the cutlass hilt; the volley went off with a roar. "For England and the King!" Granby shouted, and led his group into the fray.

But the men at the entry were drawing back to either side, Granby and his fellows left standing uneasily in the opening. Laurence wondered if maybe they had some artillery after all. But instead abruptly a man came running at them down the open aisle, alone, as if intent on throwing himself onto their swords: they stood set, waiting. Not three paces distant he leapt into the air, landed somehow sideways against the column, and sprang off it literally over their heads, diving, and tucked himself neatly into a rolling somersault along the stone floor.

The maneuver defied gravity more thoroughly than any skylarking Laurence had ever seen done; ten feet into the air and down again with no propulsion but his own legs. The man leapt up at once, unbruised, now at Granby's back with the main wave of attackers charging the entryway again. "Therrows, Willoughby," Laurence bellowed to the men in his group, unnecessarily: they were already running to hold him back.

The man had no weapon, but his agility was beyond anything; he jumped away from their swinging swords in a manner that made them seem accomplices in a stage play rather than in deadly earnest, trying to kill him; and from his greater distance, Laurence could see he was drawing them steadily back, towards Granby and the others, where their swords could only become dangers to their comrades.

Laurence clapped on to his pistol and drew it out, his hands following the practiced sequence despite the dark and the furor; in his head he listened to the chant of the great-gun exercise, so nearly parallel. Ramrod down the muzzle with a rag, twice, and then he pulled back the hammer to half-cocked, groping after the paper cartridge in his hip pouch.

Therrows suddenly screamed and fell, clutching his knee. Willoughby's head turned to look; his sword was held defensively, at the level of his chest, but in that one moment of incaution the Chinese man leapt again impossibly high and struck him full on the jaw with both feet. The sound of his neck snapping was grisly; he was lifted an inch straight up off the ground, arms splaying out wide, and then collapsed into a heap, his head lolling side-to-side upon the ground. The Chinese man tumbled to the ground from his leap, landed on his shoulder, rolling lightly back up, and turned to look at Laurence.

Riggs was yelling from behind him, "Make ready! Faster, damn you, make ready!"

Laurence's hands were still working. Tearing open the cartridge of black powder with his teeth, a few grains like sand bitter on his tongue. Powder straight down the muzzle, then the round lead ball after, the paper in for wadding, rammed down hard; no time to check the primer, and he raised the gun and blew out the man's brains, barely more than arm's reach away.

Laurence and Granby dragged Therrows back over to Keynes while the Chinese backed away from the waiting volley. He was sobbing quietly, his leg dangling useless; "I'm sorry, sir," he kept saying, choked.

"For Heaven's sake, enough moan," Keynes said sharply, when they put him down, and slapped Therrows across the face with a distinct lack of sympathy. The young man gulped, but stopped, and hastily scrubbed an arm across his face. "The kneecap is broken," Keynes said, after a moment. "A clean enough break, but he won't be standing again for a month."

"Get over to Riggs when you have been splinted, and reload for them," Laurence told Therrows, then he and Granby dashed back to the entryway.

"We'll take rest by turns," Laurence said, kneeling down by the others. "Hammond, you first; go and tell Riggs to keep one rifle back, loaded, at all times, if they should try and send another fellow over that way."

Hammond was visibly heaving for breath, his cheeks marked with spots of bright red; he nodded and said hoarsely, "Leave your pistols, I will reload."

Blythe, gulping water from the vase, abruptly choked, spat out a fountain, and yelled, "Sweet Christ in Heaven!" and made them all jump. Laurence looked around wildly: a bright orange goldfish two fingers long was wriggling on the stones in the puddled water. "Sorry," Blythe said, panting. "I felt the bugger squirming in my mouth."

Laurence stared, then Martin started laughing, and for a moment they were all grinning at one another; then the rifles cracked off, and they were back to the door.

The attackers made no attempt at setting the pavilion on fire, which surprised Laurence; they had torches enough, and wood was plentiful around the island. They did try smoke, building small bonfires to either side of the building under the eaves, but through either some trick of the pavilion's design, or simply the prevailing wind, a drifting air current carried the smoke up and out through the yellow-tiled roof. It was unpleasant enough, but not deadly, and near the pond the air was fresh. Each round the one man resting would go back there, to drink and clear his lungs, and have the handful of scratches they had all by now accumulated smeared with salve and bound up if still bleeding.

The gang tried a battering ram, a fresh-cut tree with the branches and leaves still attached, but Laurence called, "Stand aside as they come, and cut at their legs." The bearers ran themselves directly onto the blades with great courage, trying to break through, but even the three steps that led up to the pavilion door were enough to break their momentum. Several at the head fell with gashes showing bone, to be clubbed to death with pistol-butts, and then the tree itself toppled forward and halted their progress. The British had a few frantic minutes of hacking off the branches, to clear the view for the rifle-men; by then the next volley was more than ready, and the attackers gave up the attempt.

After this the battle settled into a sort of grisly rhythm; each round of fire won them even more time to rest now, the Chinese evidently disheartened by their failure to break in through the small British line, and by the very great slaughter. Every bullet found its mark; Riggs and his men had been trained to make shots from the back of a dragon, flying sometimes at thirty knots in the heat of battle, and with less than thirty yards to the entryway, they could scarcely miss. It was a slow, grinding way to fight, every minute seeming to consume five times its proper length; Laurence began to count the time by volleys.

"We had better go to three shots only a volley, sir,"

Riggs said, coughing, when Laurence knelt to speak with him, his next rest spell. "It'll hold them all the same, now they've had a taste, and though I brought all the cartridges we had, we're not bloody infantry. I have Therrows making us more, but we have enough powder for another thirty rounds at most, I think."

"That will have to do," Laurence said. "We will try and hold them longer between volleys. Start resting one man every other round, also." He emptied his own cartridge box and Granby's into the general pile: only another seven, but that meant two rounds more at least, and the rifles were of more value than the pistols.

He splashed his face with water at the pond, smiling a little at the darting fish which he could see more clearly now, his eyes perhaps adjusting to the dark. His neckcloth was soaked quite through with sweat; he took it off and wrung it out over the stones, then could not bring himself to put it back on once he had exposed his grateful skin to the air. He rinsed it clean and left it spread out to dry, then hurried back.

Another measureless stretch of time, the faces of the attackers growing blurry and dim in the doorway. Laurence was struggling to hold off a couple of men, shoulder-to-shoulder with Granby, when he heard Dyer's high treble cry out, "Captain! Captain!" from behind. He could not turn and look; there was no opportunity for pause.

"I have them," Granby panted, and kicked the man in front in the balls with his heavy Hessian boot; he engaged the other hilt-to-hilt, and Laurence pulled away and turned hurriedly around.

A couple of men were standing dripping on the edge of the pond, and another pulling himself out: they had somehow found whatever reservoir fed the pond, and swum through it underneath the wall. Keynes was sprawled unmoving on the floor, and Riggs and the other riflemen were running over, still reloading frantically as they went. Hammond had been resting: he was swinging furiously at the two other men, pushing them back towards the water, but he did not have much science: they had short knives, and would get under his guard in a moment.

Little Dyer seized one of the great vases and flung it, still full of water, into the man bending over Keynes's body with his knife; it shattered against his head and knocked him down to the floor, dazed and slipping in the water. Roland, running over, snatched up Keynes's tenaculum, and dragged the sharp hooked end across the man's throat before he could arise, blood spurting in a furious jet from the severed vein, through his grasping fingers.

More men were coming out of the pond. "Fire at will," Riggs shouted, and three went down, one of them shot with only his head protruding from the water, sinking back down below the surface in a spreading cloud of blood. Laurence was up beside Hammond, and together they forced the two he was struggling against back into the water: while Hammond kept swinging, Laurence stabbed one with the point of his cutlass, and clubbed the other with the hilt; he fell unconscious into the water, open-mouthed, and bubbles rose in a profusion from his lips.

"Push them all into the water," Laurence said. "We must block up the passage." He climbed into the pond, pushing the bodies against the current; he could feel a greater pressure coming from the other side, more men trying to come through. "Riggs, get your men back to the front and relieve Granby," he said. "Hammond and I can hold them here."

"I can help also," Therrows said, limping over: he was a tall fellow, and could sit down on the edge of the pond and put his good leg against the mass of bodies.

"Roland, Dyer, see if there is anything to be done for

Keynes," Laurence said over his shoulder, and then looked
when he did not hear a response immediately: they were
both being sick in the corner, quietly.

Roland wiped her mouth and got up, looking rather
like an unsteady-legged foal. "Yes, sir," she said, and she
and Dyer tottered over to Keynes. He groaned as they
turned him over: there was a great clot of blood on his
head, above the eyebrow, but he opened his eyes dazedly
as they bound it up.

The pressure on the other side of the mass of bodies
weakened, and slowly ceased; behind them the guns spoke
again and again with suddenly quickened pace, Riggs
and his men firing almost at the rate of redcoats. Laurence, trying to look over his shoulder, could not see anything through the haze of smoke.

"Therrows and I can manage, go!" Hammond gasped
out. Laurence nodded and slogged out of the water, his
full boots dragging like stones; he had to stop and pour
them out before he could run to the front.

Even as he came, the shooting stopped: the smoke so
thick and queerly bright they could not see anyone through
it, only the broken heap of bodies around the floor at
their feet. They stood waiting, Riggs and his men reloading more slowly, their fingers shaking. Then Laurence
stepped forward, using a hand on the column for balance: there was nowhere to stand but on the corpses.

They came out blinking through the haze, into the
early-morning sunlight, startling up a flock of crows that
lifted from the bodies in the courtyard and fled shrieking
hoarsely over the water of the lake. There was no one left
moving in sight: the rest of the attackers had fled. Martin
abruptly fell over onto his knees, his cutlass clanging un-
musically on the stones; Granby went to help him up and
ended by falling down also. Laurence groped to a small
wooden bench before his own legs gave out; not caring

very much that he was sharing it with one of the dead, a smooth-faced young man with a trail of red blood drying on his lips and a purpled stain around the ragged bullet wound in his chest.

There was no sign of Temeraire. He had not come.

Chapter 15

※

$\mathcal{S}$UN KAI FOUND THEM scarcely more than dead themselves, an hour later; he had come warily into the courtyard from the pier with a small group of armed men: perhaps ten or so and formally dressed in guard uniforms, unlike the scruffy and unkempt members of the gang. The smoldering bonfires had gone out of their own accord, for lack of fuel; the British were dragging the corpses into the deepest shade, so they would putrefy less horribly.

They were all of them half-blind and numb with exhaustion, and could offer no resistance; helpless to account for Temeraire's absence and with no other idea of what to do, Laurence submitted to being led to the boat, and thence to a stuffy, enclosed palanquin, whose curtains were drawn tight around him. He slept instantly upon the embroidered pillows, despite the jostling and shouts of their progress, and knew nothing more until at last the palanquin was set down, and he was shaken back to wakefulness.

"Come inside," Sun Kai said, and pulled on him until he rose; Hammond and Granby and the other crewmen were emerging in similarly dazed and battered condition from other sedan-chairs behind him. Laurence followed unthinking up the stairs into the blessedly cool interior of a house, fragrant with traces of incense; along a narrow hallway and to a room which faced onto the garden courtyard. There he at once surged forward and leapt over the low balcony railing: Temeraire was lying curled asleep upon the stones.

"Temeraire," Laurence called, and went towards him; Sun Kai exclaimed in Chinese and ran after him, catching his arm before he could touch Temeraire's side; then the dragon raised up his head and looked at them, curiously, and Laurence stared: it was not Temeraire at all.

Sun Kai tried to drag Laurence down to the ground, kneeling down himself; Laurence shook him off, managing with difficulty to keep his balance. He noticed only then a young man of perhaps twenty, dressed in elegant silk robes of dark yellow embroidered with dragons, sitting on a bench.

Hammond had followed Laurence and now caught at his sleeve. "For God's sake, kneel," he whispered. "This must be Prince Mianning, the crown prince." He himself went down to both knees, and pressed his forehead to the ground just as Sun Kai was doing.

Laurence stared a little stupidly down at them both, looked at the young man, and hesitated; then he bowed deeply instead, from the waist: he was mortally certain he could not bend a single knee without falling down to both, or more ignominiously upon his face, and he was not yet willing to perform the kowtow to the Emperor, much less the prince.

The prince did not seem offended, but spoke in Chinese to Sun Kai; he rose, and Hammond also, very slowly. "He says we can rest here safely," Hammond said to Laurence. "I beg you to believe him, sir; he can have no need to deceive us."

Laurence said, "Will you ask him about Temeraire?" Hammond looked at the other dragon blankly. "That is not him," Laurence added. "It is some other Celestial, it is not Temeraire."

Sun Kai said, "Lung Tien Xiang is in seclusion in the Pavilion of Endless Spring. A messenger is waiting to bring him word, as soon as he emerges."

"He is well?" Laurence asked, not bothering to try and make sense of this; the most urgent concern was to understand what might have kept Temeraire away.

"There is no reason to think otherwise," Sun Kai said, which seemed evasive. Laurence did not know how to press him further; he was too thick with fatigue. But Sun Kai took pity on his confusion and added more gently, "He is well. We cannot interrupt his seclusion, but he will come out sometime today, and we will bring him to you then."

Laurence still did not understand, but he could not think of anything else to do at the moment. "Thank you," he managed. "Pray thank His Highness for his hospitality, for us; pray convey our very deep thanks. I beg he will excuse any inadequacy in our address."

The prince nodded and dismissed them with a wave. Sun Kai herded them back over the balcony into their rooms, and stood watching over them until they had collapsed upon the hard wooden bed platforms; perhaps he did not trust them not to leap up and go wandering again. Laurence almost laughed at the improbability of it, and fell asleep mid-thought.

"Laurence, Laurence," Temeraire said, very anxiously; Laurence opened his eyes and found Temeraire's head poked in through the balcony doors, and a darkening sky beyond. "Laurence, you are not hurt?"

"Oh!" Hammond had woken, and fallen off his bed in startlement at finding himself cheek-to-jowl with Temeraire's muzzle. "Good God," he said, painfully climbing to his feet and sitting back down upon the bed. "I feel like a man of eighty with gout in both legs."

Laurence sat up with only a little less effort; every

muscle had stiffened up during his rest. "No, I am quite well," he said, reaching out gratefully to put a hand on Temeraire's muzzle and feel the reassurance of his solid presence. "You have not been ill?"

He did not mean it to sound accusing, but he could hardly imagine any other excuse for Temeraire's apparent desertion, and perhaps some of his feeling was clear in his tone. Temeraire's ruff drooped. "No," he said, miserably. "No, I am not sick at all."

He volunteered nothing more, and Laurence did not press him, conscious of Hammond's presence: Temeraire's shy behavior did not bode a very good explanation for his absence, and as little as Laurence might relish the prospect of confronting him, he liked the notion of doing so in front of Hammond even less. Temeraire withdrew his head to let them come out into the garden. No acrobatic leaping this time: Laurence levered himself out of bed and stepped slowly and carefully over the balcony rail. Hammond, following, was almost unable to lift his foot high enough to clear the rail, though it was scarcely two feet off the ground.

The prince had left, but the dragon, whom Temeraire introduced to them as Lung Tien Chuan, was still there. He nodded to them politely, without much interest, then went straight back to working upon a large tray of wet sand in which he was scratching symbols with a talon: writing poetry, Temeraire explained.

Having made his bow to Chuan, Hammond groaned again as he lowered himself onto a stool, muttering under his breath with a degree of profanity more appropriate to the seamen from whom he had likely first heard the oaths. It was not a very graceful performance, but Laurence was perfectly willing to forgive him that and more after the previous day's work. He had never expected Hammond to do as much, untrained, untried, and in disagreement with the whole enterprise.

"If I may be so bold, sir, allow me to recommend you take a turn around the garden instead of sitting," Laurence said. "I have often found it answer well."

"I suppose I had better," Hammond said, and after a few deep breaths heaved himself back up to his feet, not disdaining the offer of Laurence's hand, and walking very slowly at first. But Hammond was a young man: he was already walking more easily after they had gone halfway round. With the worst of his pain relieved, Hammond's curiosity revived: as they continued walking around the garden he studied the two dragons closely, his steps slowing as he turned first from one to the other and back. The courtyard was longer than it was wide. Stands of tall bamboo and a few smaller pine trees clustered at the ends, leaving the middle mostly open, so the two dragons lay opposite each other, head-to-head, making the comparison easier.

They were indeed as like as mirror images, except for the difference in their jewels: Chuan wore a net of gold draped from his ruff down the length of his neck, studded with pearls: very splendid, but it looked likely to be inconvenient in any sort of violent activity. Temeraire had also battle-scars, of which Chuan had none: the round knot of scales on his breast from the spiked ball, now several months old, and the smaller scratches from other battles. But these were difficult to see, and aside from these the only difference was a certain undefinable quality in their posture and expression, which Laurence could not have adequately described for another's interpretation.

"Can it be chance?" Hammond said. "All Celestials may be related, but such a degree of similarity? I cannot tell them apart."

"We are hatched from twin eggs," Temeraire said, lifting up his head as he overheard this. "Chuan's egg was first, and then mine."

"Oh, I have been unutterably slow," Hammond said, and sat down limply on the bench. "Laurence—Laurence—" His face was almost shining from within, and he reached out groping towards Laurence, and seized his hand and shook it. "Of course, of *course:* they did not want to set up another prince as a rival for the throne, that is why they sent away the egg. My God, how relieved I am!"

"Sir, I hardly dispute your conclusions, but I cannot see what difference it makes to our present situation," Laurence said, rather taken aback by this enthusiasm.

"Do you not see?" Hammond said. "Napoleon was only an excuse, because he is an emperor on the other side of the world, as far away as they could manage from their own court. And all this time I have been wondering how the devil De Guignes ever managed to approach them, when they would scarcely let me put my nose out of doors. Ha! The French have no alliance, no real understanding with them at all."

"That is certainly cause for relief," Laurence said, "but their lack of success does not seem to me to directly improve our position; plainly the Chinese have now changed their minds, and desire Temeraire's return."

"No, do you not see? Prince Mianning still has every reason to want Temeraire gone, if he could render another claimant eligible for the throne," Hammond said. "Oh, this makes all the difference in the world. I have been groping in the dark; now I have some sense of their motives, a great deal more comes clear. How much longer will it be until the *Allegiance* arrives?" he asked suddenly, looking up at Laurence.

"I know too little about the likely currents and the prevailing winds in the Bay of Zhitao to make any accurate estimate," Laurence said, taken aback. "A week at least, I should think."

"I wish to God Staunton were here already. I have a

thousand questions and not enough answers," Hammond said. "But I can at least try and coax a little more information from Sun Kai: I hope he will be a little more forthright now. I will go and seek him; I beg your pardon."

At this, he turned and ducked back into the house. Laurence called after him belatedly, "Hammond, your clothes—!" for his breeches were unbuckled at the knee, they and his shirt hideously bloodstained besides, and his stockings thoroughly laddered: he looked a proper spectacle. But it was too late: he had gone.

Laurence supposed no one could blame them for their appearance, as they had been brought over without baggage. "Well, at least he is gone to some purpose; and we cannot but be relieved by this news that there is no alliance with France," he said to Temeraire.

"Yes," Temeraire said, but unenthusiastically. He had been quite silent all this time, brooding and coiled about the garden. The tip of his tail continued flicking back and forth restlessly at the edge of the nearer pond and spattering thick black spots onto the sun-heated flagstones, which dried almost as quickly as they appeared.

Laurence did not immediately press him for explanation, even now Hammond had gone, but came and sat by his head. He hoped deeply that Temeraire would speak of his own volition, and not require questioning.

"Are all the rest of my crew all right also?" Temeraire asked after a moment.

Laurence said, "Willoughby has been killed, I am very sorry to tell you. A few injuries besides, but nothing else mortal, thankfully."

Temeraire trembled and made a low keening sound deep in his throat. "I ought to have come. If I had been there, they could never have done it."

Laurence was silent, thinking of poor Willoughby: a damned ugly waste. "You did very wrong not to send word," he said finally. "I cannot hold you culpable in Willoughby's death. He was killed early, before you would ordinarily have come back, and I do not think I would have done anything differently, had I known you were not returning. But certainly you have violated your leave."

Temeraire made another small unhappy noise and said, low, "I have failed in my duty; have I not? So it was my fault, then, and there is nothing else to be said about it."

Laurence said, "No, if you had sent word, I would have thought nothing of agreeing to your extended absence: we had every reason to think our position perfectly secure. And in all justice, you have never been formally instructed in the rules of leave in the Corps, as they have never been necessary for a dragon, and it was my responsibility to be sure you understood.

"I am not trying to comfort you," he added, seeing that Temeraire shook his head. "But I wish you to feel what you have in fact done wrong, and not to distract yourself improperly with false guilt over what you could not have controlled."

"Laurence, you do not understand," Temeraire said. "I have always understood the rules quite well; that is not why I did not send word. I did not mean to stay so long, only I did not notice the time passing."

Laurence did not know what to say. The idea that Temeraire had not noticed the passage of a full night and day, when he had always been used to come back before dark, was difficult to swallow, if not impossible. If such an excuse had been given him by one of his men, Laurence would have outright called it a lie; as it was, his silence betrayed what he thought of it.

Temeraire hunched his shoulders and scratched a little at the ground, his claws scraping the stones with a noise that made Chuan look up and put his ruff back, with a quick rumble of complaint. Temeraire stopped; then all at once he said abruptly, "I was with Mei."

"With who?" Laurence said, blankly.

"Lung Qin Mei," Temeraire said, "—she is an Imperial."

The shock of understanding was near a physical blow. There was a mixture of embarrassment, guilt, and confused pride in Temeraire's confession which made everything plain.

"I see," Laurence said with an effort, as controlled as ever he had been in his life. "Well—" He stopped, and mastered himself. "You are young, and—and have never courted before; you cannot have known how it would take you," he said. "I am glad to know the reason; that is some excuse." He tried to believe his own words; he did believe them; only he did not particularly want to forgive Temeraire's absence on such grounds. Despite his quarrel with Hammond over Yongxing's attempts to supplant him with the boy, Laurence had never really feared losing Temeraire's affections; it was bitter, indeed, to find himself so unexpectedly with real cause for jealousy after all.

They buried Willoughby in the grey hours of the morning, in a vast cemetery outside the city walls, to which Sun Kai brought them. It was crowded for a burial place, even considering the extent, with many small groups of people paying respects at the tombs. These visitors' interest was caught by both Temeraire's presence and the Western party, and shortly something of a procession had formed behind them, despite the guards who pushed off any too-curious onlookers.

But though the crowd shortly numbered several hundreds of people, they maintained an attitude of respect, and fell to perfect silence while Laurence somberly spoke a few words for the dead and led his men in the Lord's Prayer. The tomb was above-ground, and built of white stone, with an upturned roof very like the local houses; it looked elaborate even in comparison with the neighboring mausoleums. "Laurence, if it wouldn't be disrespectful, I think his mother would be glad of a sketch," Granby said quietly.

"Yes, I ought to have thought of it myself," Laurence said. "Digby, do you think you could knock something together?"

"Please allow me to have an artist prepare one," Sun Kai interjected. "I am ashamed not to have offered before. And assure his mother that all the proper sacrifices will be made; a young man of good family has already been selected by Prince Mianning to carry out all the rites." Laurence assented to these arrangements without investigating further; Mrs. Willoughby was, as he recalled, a rather strict Methodist, and he was sure would be happier not to know more than that her son's tomb was so elegant and would be well-maintained.

Afterwards Laurence returned to the island with Temeraire and a few of the men to collect their possessions, which had been left behind in the hurry and confusion. All the bodies had been cleared away already, but the smoke-blackened patches remained upon the outer walls of the pavilion where they had sheltered, and dried bloodstains upon the stones; Temeraire looked at them a long time, silently, and then turned his head away. Inside the residence, furniture had been wildly overturned, the rice-paper screens torn through, and most of their chests smashed open, clothing flung onto the floor and trampled upon.

Laurence walked through the rooms as Blythe and Martin began collecting whatever they could find in good enough condition to bother with. His own chamber had been thoroughly pillaged, the bed itself flung up on its side against the wall, as if they had thought him maybe cowering underneath, and his many bundles from the shopping expedition thrown rudely about the room. Powder and bits of shattered porcelain trickled out across the floor behind some of them like a trail, strips of torn and frayed silk hanging almost decoratively about the room. Laurence bent down and lifted up the large shapeless package of the red vase, fallen over in a corner of the room, and slowly took off the wrappings; and then he found himself looking upon it through an unaccountable blurring of his vision: the shining surface wholly undamaged, not even chipped, and in the afternoon sun it poured out over his hands a living richness of deep and scarlet light.

The true heart of the summer had struck the city now: the stones grew hot as worked anvils during the day, and the wind blew an endless stream of fine yellow dust from the enormous deserts of the Gobi to the west. Hammond was engaged in a slow elaborate dance of negotiations, which so far as Laurence could see proceeded only in circles: a sequence of wax-sealed letters coming back and forth from the house, some small trinkety gifts received and sent in return, vague promises and less action. In the meantime, they were all growing short-tempered and impatient, except for Temeraire, who was occupied still with his education and his courting. Mei now came to the residence to teach him daily, elegant in an elaborate collar of silver and pearls; her hide was a deep shade of blue, with dapplings of violet and yellow upon her wings, and she wore many golden rings upon her talons.

"Mei is a very charming dragon," Laurence said to Temeraire after her first visit, feeling he might as well be properly martyred; it had not escaped his attention that Mei was very lovely, at least as far as he was a judge of draconic beauty.

"I am glad you think so also," Temeraire said, brightening; the points of his ruff raised and quivered. "She was hatched only three years ago, and has just passed the first examinations with honor. She has been teaching me how to read and write, and has been very kind; she has not at all made fun of me, for not knowing."

She could not have complained of her pupil's progress, Laurence was sure. Already Temeraire had mastered the technique of writing in the sand tray-tables with his talons, and Mei praised his calligraphy done in clay; soon she promised to begin teaching him the more rigid strokes used for carving in soft wood. Laurence watched him scribbling industriously late into the afternoon, while the light lasted, and often played audience for him in Mei's absence: the rich sonorous tones of Temeraire's voice pleasant though the words of the Chinese poetry were meaningless, except when he stopped in a particularly nice passage to translate.

The rest of them had little to occupy their time: Mianning occasionally gave them a dinner, and once an entertainment consisting of a highly unmusical concert and the tumbling of some remarkable acrobats, nearly all young children and limber as mountain goats. Occasionally they drilled with their small-arms in the courtyard behind the residence, but it was not very pleasant in the heat, and they were glad to return to the cool walks and gardens of the palace after.

Some two weeks following their remove to the palace, Laurence sat reading in the balcony overlooking the courtyard, where Temeraire slept, while Hammond worked on papers at the writing-desk within the room. A servant came bearing them a letter: Hammond broke the seal and scanned the lines, telling Laurence, "It is from Liu Bao, he has invited us to dine at his home."

"Hammond, do you suppose there is any chance he might be involved?" Laurence asked reluctantly, after a moment. "I do not like to suggest such a thing, but after all, we know he is not in Mianning's service, like Sun Kai is; could he be in league with Yongxing?"

"It is true we cannot rule out his possible involvement," Hammond said. "As a Tartar himself, Liu Bao would likely have been able to organize the attack upon us. Still, I have learned he is a relation of the Emperor's mother, and an official in the Manchu White Banner; his support would be invaluable, and I find it hard to believe he would openly invite us if he meant anything underhanded."

They went warily, but their plans for caution were thoroughly undermined as they arrived, met unexpectedly at the gates by the rich savory smell of roasted beef. Liu Bao had ordered his now well-traveled cooks to prepare a traditional British dinner for them, and if there was rather more curry than one would expect in the fried potatoes, and the currant-studded pudding inclined to be somewhat liquid, none of them found anything to complain of in the enormous crown roast, the upstanding ribs jeweled with whole onions, and the Yorkshire pudding was improbably successful.

Despite their very best efforts, the last plates were again carried away almost full, and there was some doubt whether a number of the guests would not have to be carted off in the same manner, including Temeraire. He had been served with plain, freshly butchered prey, in the British manner, but the cooks could not restrain themselves entirely and had served him not merely a cow or sheep, but two of each, as well as a pig, a goat, a chicken, and a lobster. Having done his duty by each course, he now crawled out into the garden uninvited with a little moan and collapsed into a stupor.

"That is all right, let him sleep!" Liu Bao said, waving

away Laurence's apology. "We can sit in the moon-viewing terrace and drink wine."

Laurence girded himself, but for once Liu Bao did not press the wine on them them too enthusiastically. It was quite pleasant to sit, suffused with the steady genial warmth of inebriation, the sun going down behind the smoke-blue mountains and Temeraire drowsing in an aureate glow before them. Laurence had entirely if irrationally given up the idea of Liu Bao's involvement: it was impossible to be suspicious of a man while sitting in his garden, full of his generous dinner; and even Hammond was half-unwillingly at his ease, blinking with the effort of keeping awake.

Liu Bao expressed some curiosity as to how they had come to take up residence with Prince Mianning. For further proofs of his innocence, he received the news of the gang attack with real surprise, and shook his head sympathetically. "Something has to be done about these *hunhun*, they are really getting out of hand. One of my nephews got involved with them a few years ago, and his poor mother worried herself almost to death. But then she made a big sacrifice to Guanyin and built her a special altar in the nicest place in their south garden, and now he has married and taken up studying." He poked Laurence in the side. "You ought to try studying yourself! It will be embarrassing for you if your dragon passes the examinations and you don't."

"Good God, could that possibly make a difference in their minds, Hammond?" Laurence asked, sitting up appalled. For all his efforts, Chinese remained to him as impenetrable as if it were enciphered ten times over, and as for sitting examinations next to men who had been studying for them since the age of seven—

But, "I am only teasing you," Liu Bao said good-humoredly, much to Laurence's relief. "Don't be afraid. I suppose if Lung Tien Xiang really wants to stay companion to an unlettered barbarian, no one can argue with him."

"He is joking about calling you that, of course," Hammond added to the translation, but a little doubtfully.

"I *am* an unlettered barbarian, by their standards of learning, and not stupid enough to make pretensions to be anything else," Laurence said. "I only wish that the negotiators took your view of it, sir," he added to Liu Bao. "But they are quite fixed that a Celestial may only be companion to the Emperor and his kin."

"Well, if the dragon will not have anyone else, they will have to live with it," Liu Bao said, unconcerned. "Why doesn't the Emperor adopt you? That would save face for everyone."

Laurence was disposed to think this a joke, but Hammond stared at Liu Bao with quite a different expression. "Sir, would such a suggestion be seriously entertained?"

Liu Bao shrugged and filled their cups again with wine. "Why not? The Emperor has three sons to perform the rites for him, he doesn't need to adopt anyone; but another doesn't hurt."

"Do you mean to pursue the notion?" Laurence asked Hammond, rather incredulous, as they made their staggering way out to the sedan-chairs waiting to bear them back to the palace.

"With your permission, certainly," Hammond said. "It is an extraordinary idea to be sure, but after all it would be understood on all sides as only a formality. Indeed," he continued, growing more enthusiastic, "I think it would answer in every possible respect. Surely they would not lightly declare war upon a nation related by such intimate ties, and only consider the advantages to our trade of such a connection."

Laurence could more easily consider his father's likely reaction. "If you think it a worthwhile course to pursue, I will not forestall you," he said reluctantly, but he did not think the red vase, which he had been hoping to use as something of a peace-offering, would be in any way adequate to mend matters if Lord Allendale should learn that Laurence had given himself up for adoption like a foundling, even to the Emperor of China.

Chapter 16

❦

"Iᴛ ᴡᴀs ᴀ close-run affair before we arrived, that much I can tell you," Riley said, accepting a cup of tea across the breakfast table with more eagerness than he had taken the bowl of rice porridge. "I have never seen the like: a fleet of twenty ships, with two dragons for support. Of course they were only junks, and not half the size of a frigate, but the Chinese navy ships were hardly any bigger. I cannot imagine what they were about, to let a lot of pirates get so out of hand."

"I was impressed by their admiral, however; he seemed a rational sort of man," Staunton put in. "A lesser man would not have liked being rescued."

"He would have been a great gaby to prefer being sunk," Riley said, less generous.

The two of them had arrived only that morning, with a small party from the *Allegiance:* having been shocked by the story of the murderous gang attack, they were now describing the adventure of their own passage through the China Sea. A week out of Macao, they had encountered a Chinese fleet attempting to subdue an enormous band of pirates, who had established themselves in the Zhoushan Islands to prey upon both domestic shipping and the smaller ships of the Western trade.

"There was not much trouble once we were there, of course," Riley went on. "The pirate dragons had no armaments—the crews tried to fire arrows at us, if you can credit it—and no sense of range at all; dived so low we could hardly miss them at musket-shot, much less with the pepper-guns. They sheered off pretty quick after a taste of that, and we sank three of the pirates with a single broadside."

"Did the Admiral say anything about how he would report the incident?" Hammond asked Staunton.

"I can only tell you that he was punctilious in expressing his gratitude. He came aboard our ship, which was I believe a concession on his part."

"And let him have a good look at our guns," Riley said. "I fancy he was more interested in those than in being polite. But at any rate, we saw him to port, and then came on; she's anchored in Tien-sing harbor now. No chance of our leaving soon?"

"I do not like to tempt fate, but I hardly think so," Hammond said. "The Emperor is still away on his summer hunting trip up to the north, and he will not return to the Summer Palace for several weeks more. At that time I expect we will be given a formal audience.

"I have been putting forward this notion of adoption, which I described to you, sir," he added to Staunton. "We have already received some small amount of support, not only from Prince Mianning, and I have high hopes that the service which you have just performed for them will sway opinion decisively in our favor."

"Is there any difficulty in the ship's remaining where she is?" Laurence asked with concern.

"For the moment, no, but I must say, supplies are dearer than I had looked for," Riley said. "They have nothing like salt meat for sale, and the prices they ask for cattle are outrageous; we have been feeding the men on fish and chickens."

"Have we outrun our funds?" Laurence too late began to regret his purchases. "I have been a little extravagant, but I do have some gold left, and they make no bones about taking it once they see it is real."

"Thank you, Laurence, but I don't need to rob you; we are not in dun territory yet," Riley said. "I am mostly thinking about the journey home—with a dragon to feed, I hope?"

Laurence did not know how to answer the question; he made some evasion, and fell silent to let Hammond carry on the conversation.

After their breakfast, Sun Kai came by to inform them that a feast and an entertainment would be held that evening, to welcome the new arrivals: a great theatrical performance. "Laurence, I am going to go and see Qian," Temeraire said, poking his head into the room while Laurence contemplated his clothing. "You will not go out, will you?"

He had grown singularly more protective since the assault, refusing to leave Laurence unattended; the servants had all suffered his narrow and suspicious inspection for weeks, and he had put forward several thoughtful suggestions for Laurence's protection, such as devising a schedule which should arrange for Laurence's being kept under a five-man guard at all hours, or drawing in his sand-table a proposed suit of armor which would not have been unsuited to the battlefields of the Crusades.

"No, you may rest easy; I am afraid I will have enough to do to make myself presentable," Laurence said. "Pray give her my regards; will you be there long? We cannot be late tonight, this engagement is in our honor."

"No, I will come back very soon," Temeraire said, and true to his word returned less than an hour later, ruff quivering with suppressed excitement and clutching a long narrow bundle carefully in his forehand.

Laurence came out into the courtyard at his request, and Temeraire nudged the package over to him rather abashedly. Laurence was so taken aback he only stared at first, then he slowly removed the silk wrappings and opened the lacquered box: an elaborate smooth-hilted saber lay next to its scabbard on a yellow silk cushion. He lifted it from its bed: well-balanced, broad at the base, with the curved tip sharpened along both edges; the surface watered like good Damascus steel, with two blood grooves cut along the back edge to lighten the blade.

The hilt was wrapped in black ray-skin, the fittings of gilded iron adorned with gold beads and small pearls, and a gold dragon-head collar at the base of the blade with two small sapphires for eyes. The scabbard itself of black lacquered wood was also decorated with broad gold bands of gilded iron, and strung with strong silk cords: Laurence took his rather shabby if serviceable cutlass off his belt and buckled the new one on.

"Does it suit you?" Temeraire asked anxiously.

"Very well indeed," Laurence said, drawing out the blade for practice: the length admirably fitted to his height. "My dear, this is beyond anything; however did you get it?"

"Well, it is not all my doing," Temeraire said. "Last week, Qian admired my breastplate, and I told her you had given it to me; then I thought I would like to give you a present also. She said it was usual for the sire and dame to give a gift when a dragon takes a companion, so I might choose one for you from her things, and I thought this was the nicest." He turned his head to one side and another, inspecting Laurence with deep satisfaction.

"You must be quite right; I could not imagine a better," Laurence said, attempting to master himself; he felt quite absurdly happy and absurdly reassured, and on going back inside to complete his dress could not help but stand and admire the sword in the mirror.

Hammond and Staunton had both adopted the Chinese scholar-robes; the rest of his officers wore their

bottle-green coats, trousers, and Hessians polished to
a gleam; neckcloths had been washed and pressed, and
even Roland and Dyer were perfectly smart, having been
set on chairs and admonished not to move the moment
they were bathed and dressed. Riley was similarly elegant in Navy blue, knee-breeches and slippers, and the
four Marines whom he had brought from the ship in
their lobster-red coats brought up the end of their company in style as they left the residence.

A curious stage had been erected in the middle of the
plaza where the performance was to be held: small, but
marvelously painted and gilded, with three different levels. Qian presided at the center of the northern end of the
court, Prince Mianning and Chuan on her left, and a
place for Temeraire and the British party reserved upon
her right. Besides the Celestials, there were also several
Imperials present, including Mei, seated farther down
the side and looking very graceful in a rig of gold set with
polished jade: she nodded to Laurence and Temeraire
from her place as they took their seats. The white dragon,
Lien, was there also, seated with Yongxing to one side, a
little apart from the rest of the guests; her albino col-
oration again startling by contrast with the dark-hued
Imperials and Celestials on every side, and her proudly
raised ruff today adorned with a netting of fine gold mesh,
with a great pendant ruby lying upon her forehead.

"Oh, there is Miankai," Roland said in undertones to
Dyer, and waved quickly across the square to a boy sitting by Mianning's side. The boy wore robes similar to
the crown prince's, of the same dark shade of yellow, and
an elaborate hat; he sat very stiff and proper. Seeing
Roland's wave, he lifted his hand partway to respond,
then dropped it again hastily, glanced down the table
towards Yongxing, as if to see if he had been noticed in
the gesture, and sat back relieved when he realized he
had not drawn the older man's attention.

"How on earth do you know Prince Miankai? Has he ever come by the crown prince's residence?" Hammond asked. Laurence also would have liked to know, as on his orders the runners had not been allowed out of their quarters alone at all, and ought not have had any opportunity of getting to know anyone else, even another child.

Roland looking up at him said, surprised, "Why, you presented him to us, on the island," and Laurence looked hard again. It might have been the boy who had visited them before, in Yongxing's company, but it was almost impossible to tell; swathed in the formal clothing, the boy looked entirely different.

"Prince Miankai?" Hammond said. "The boy Yongxing brought was Prince Miankai?" He might have said something more; certainly his lips moved. But nothing at all could be heard over the sudden roll of drums: the instruments evidently hidden somewhere within the stage, but the sound quite unmuffled and about the volume of a moderate broadside, perhaps twenty-four guns, at close range.

The performance was baffling, of course, being entirely transacted in Chinese, but the movement of the scenery and the participants was clever: figures rose and dropped between the three different levels, flowers bloomed, clouds floated by, the sun and moon rose and set; all amid elaborate dances and mock swordplay. Laurence was fascinated by the spectacle, though the noise was scarcely to be imagined, and after some time his head began to ache sadly. He wondered if even the Chinese could understand the words being spoken, what with the din of drums and jangling instruments and the occasional explosion of firecrackers.

He could not apply to Hammond or Staunton for explanation: through the entire proceeding the two of them were attempting to carry on a conversation in pantomime, and paying no attention whatsoever to the stage. Hammond had brought an opera-glass, which they used only to peer across the courtyard at Yongxing, and the gouts of smoke and flame which formed part of the first act's extraordinary finale only drew their exclamations of annoyance at disrupting the view.

There was a brief gap in the proceedings while the stage was reset for the second act, and the two of them seized the few moments to converse. "Laurence," Hammond said, "I must beg your pardon; you were perfectly right. Plainly Yongxing did mean to make the boy Temeraire's companion in your place, and now at last I understand *why*: he must mean to put the boy on the throne, somehow, and establish himself as regent."

"Is the Emperor ill, or an old man?" Laurence said, puzzled.

"No," Staunton said meaningfully. "Not in the least."

Laurence stared. "Gentlemen, you sound as though you are accusing him of regicide and fratricide both; you cannot be serious."

"I only wish I were not," Staunton said. "If he does make such an attempt, we might end in the middle of a civil war, with nothing more likely for us than disaster regardless of the outcome."

"It will not come to that now," Hammond said, confidently. "Prince Mianning is no fool, and I expect the Emperor is not, either. Yongxing brought the boy to us incognito for no good reason, and they will not fail to see that, nor that it is of a piece with the rest of his actions, once I lay them all before Prince Mianning. First his attempts to bribe you, with terms that I now wonder if he had the authority to offer, and then his servant attacking you on board the ship; and recall, the *hunhun* gang came at us directly after you refused to allow him to throw Temeraire and the boy into each other's company; all of it forms a very neat and damning picture."

He spoke almost exultantly, not very cautious, and started when Temeraire, who had overheard all, said with dawning anger, "Are you saying that we have evidence, now, then? That Yongxing has been behind all of this—that he is the one who tried to hurt Laurence, and had Willoughby killed?" His great head rose and swiveled at once towards Yongxing, his slit pupils narrowing to thin black lines.

"Not here, Temeraire," Laurence said hurriedly, laying a hand on his side. "Pray do nothing for the moment."

"No, no," Hammond said also, alarmed. "I am not yet certain, of course; it is only hypothetical, and we cannot take any action against him ourselves—we must leave it in their hands—"

The actors moved to take their places upon the stage, putting an end to the immediate conversation; yet beneath his hand Laurence could feel the angry resonance deep within Temeraire's breast, a slow rolling growl that found no voice but lingered just short of sound. His talons gripped at the edges of the flagstones, his spiked ruff at half-mast and his nostrils red and flaring; he paid no more mind to the spectacle, all his attention given over to watching Yongxing.

Laurence stroked his side again, trying to distract him: the square was crowded full of guests and scenery, and he did not like to imagine the results if Temeraire were to leap to some sort of action, for all he would gladly have liked to indulge his own anger and indignation towards the man. Worse, Laurence could not think how Yongxing was to be dealt with. The man was still the Emperor's brother, and the plot which Hammond and Staunton imagined too outrageous to be easily believed.

A crash of cymbals and deep-voiced bells came from behind the stage, and two elaborate rice-paper dragons descended, crackling sparks flying from their nostrils; beneath them nearly the entire company of actors came running out around the base of the stage, swords and paste-jeweled knives waving, to enact a great battle. The drums again rolled out their thunder, the noise so vast it was almost like the shock of a blow, driving air out of his lungs. Laurence gasped for breath, then slowly put a groping hand up to his shoulder and found a short dagger's hilt jutting from below his collarbone.

"Laurence!" Hammond said, reaching for him, and Granby was shouting at the men and thrusting aside the chairs: he and Blythe put themselves in front of Laurence. Temeraire was turning his head to look down at him.

"I am not hurt," Laurence said, confusedly: there was queerly no pain at first, and he tried to stand up, to lift his arm, and then felt the wound; blood was spreading in a warm stain around the base of the knife.

Temeraire gave a shrill, terrible cry, cutting through all the noise and music; every dragon reared back on its hindquarters to stare, and the drums stopped abruptly: in the sudden silence Roland was crying out, "He threw it, over there, I saw him!" and pointing at one of the actors.

The man was empty-handed, in the midst of all the others still carrying their counterfeit weapons, and dressed in plainer clothing. He saw that his attempt to hide among them had failed and turned to flee too late; the troupe ran screaming in all directions as Temeraire flung himself almost clumsily into the square.

The man shrieked, once, as Temeraire's claws caught and dragged mortally deep furrows through his body. Temeraire threw the bloody corpse savaged and broken to the ground; for a moment he hung over it low and brooding, to be sure the man was dead, and then raised his head and turned on Yongxing; he bared his teeth and hissed, a murderous sound, and stalked towards him. At once Lien sprang forward, placing herself protectively in front of Yongxing; she struck down Temeraire's reaching talons with a swipe of her own foreleg and growled.

In answer, Temeraire's chest swelled out, and his ruff, queerly, stretched: something Laurence had never seen before, the narrow horns which made it up expanding outwards, the webbing drawn along with it. Lien did not flinch at all, but snarled almost contemptuously at him, her own parchment-pale ruff unfolding wide; the blood vessels in her eyes swelled horribly, and she stepped farther into the square to face him.

At once there was a general hasty movement to flee the courtyard. Drums and bells and twanging strings made a terrific noise as the rest of the actors decamped from the stage, dragging their instruments and costumes with them; the audience members picked up the skirts of their robes and hurried away with a little more dignity but no less speed.

"Temeraire, no!" Laurence called, understanding too late. Every legend of dragons dueling in the wild invariably ended in the destruction of one or both: and the white dragon was clearly the elder and larger. "John, get this damned thing out," he said to Granby, struggling to unwind his neckcloth with his good hand.

"Blythe, Martin, hold his shoulders," Granby directed them, then laid hold of the knife and pulled it loose, grating against bone; the blood spurted for a single dizzy moment, and then they clapped a pad made of their neckcloths over the wound, and tied it firmly down.

Temeraire and Lien were still facing each other, feinting back and forth in small movements, barely more than a twitch of the head in either direction. They did not have much room to maneuver, the stage occupying so much of the courtyard, and the rows of empty seats still lining the edges. Their eyes never left each other.

"There's no use," Granby said quietly, gripping Laurence by the arm, helping him to his feet. "Once they've set themselves on to duel like that, you can only get killed, trying to get between them, or distract him from the battle."

"Yes, very well," Laurence said harshly, putting off their hands. His legs had steadied, though his stomach was knotted and uncertain; the pain was not worse than he could manage. "Get well clear," he ordered, turning around to the crew. "Granby, take a party back to the residence and bring back our arms, in case that fellow should try to set any of the guards on him."

Granby dashed away with Martin and Riggs, while the other men climbed hastily over the seats and got back from the fighting. The square was now nearly deserted, except for a few curiosity-seekers with more bravery than sense, and those most intimately concerned: Qian observing with a look at once anxious and disapproving, and Mei some distance behind her, having retreated in the general rush and then crept partway back.

Prince Mianning also remained, though withdrawn a prudent distance: even so, Chuan was fidgeting and plainly concerned. Mianning laid a quieting hand on Chuan's side and spoke to his guards: they snatched up young Prince Miankai and carried him off to safety, despite his loud protests. Yongxing watched the boy taken away and nodded to Mianning coolly in approval, himself disdaining to move from his place.

The white dragon abruptly hissed and struck out: Laurence flinched, but Temeraire had reared back in the bare nick of time, the red-tipped talons passing scant inches from his throat. Now up on his powerful back legs, he crouched and sprang, claws outstretched, and Lien was forced to retreat, hopping back awkwardly and off-balance. She spread her wings partway to catch her footing, and sprang aloft when Temeraire pressed her again; he followed her up at once.

Laurence snatched Hammond's opera-glass away unceremoniously and tried to follow their path. The white dragon was the larger, and her wingspan greater; she quickly outstripped Temeraire and looped about gracefully, her deadly intentions plain: she meant to plummet down on him from above. But the first flush of battle-fury past, Temeraire had recognized her advantage, and put his experience to use; instead of pursuing her, he angled away and flew out of the radiance of the lanterns, melting into the darkness.

"Oh, well done," Laurence said. Lien was hovering uncertainly mid-air, head darting this way and that, peering into the night with her queer red eyes; abruptly Temeraire came flashing straight down towards her, roaring. But she flung herself aside with unbelievable quickness: unlike most dragons attacked from above, she did not hesitate more than a moment, and as she rolled away she managed to score Temeraire flying past: three bloody gashes opened red against his black hide. Drops of thick blood splashed onto the courtyard, shining black in the lantern-light. Mei crept closer with a small whimpering cry; Qian turned on her, hissing, but Mei only ducked down submissively and offered no target, coiling anxiously against a stand of trees to watch more closely.

Lien was making good use of her greater speed, darting back and away from Temeraire, encouraging him to spend his strength in useless attempts to hit her; but Temeraire grew wily: the speed of his slashes was just a little less than he could manage, a fraction slow. At least so Laurence hoped; rather than the wound giving him so much pain. Lien was successfully tempted closer: Temeraire suddenly flashed out with both foreclaws at once, and caught her in belly and breast; she shrieked out in pain and beat away frantically.

Yongxing's chair fell over clattering as the prince surged to his feet, all pretense of calm gone; now he stood watching with fists clenched by his sides. The wounds did not look very deep, but the white dragon seemed quite stunned by them, keening in pain and hovering to lick the gashes. Certainly none of the palace dragons had any scars; it occurred to Laurence that very likely they had never been in real battle.

Temeraire hung in the air a moment, talons flexing, but when she did not turn back to close with him again, he seized the opening and dived straight down towards Yongxing, his real target. Lien's head snapped up; she shrieked again and threw herself after him, beating with all her might, injury forgotten. She caught even with him just shy of the ground and flung herself upon him, wings and bodies tangling, and wrenched him aside from his course.

They struck the ground rolling together, a single hissing, savage, many-limbed beast clawing at itself, neither dragon paying any attention now to scratches or gouges, neither able to draw in the deep breaths that could let them use the divine wind against one another. Their thrashing tails struck everywhere, knocking over potted trees and scalping a mature stand of bamboo with a single stroke; Laurence seized Hammond's arm and dragged him ahead of the crashing hollow trunks as they collapsed down upon the chairs with an echoing drum-like clatter.

Shaking leaves from his hair and the collar of his coat, Laurence awkwardly raised himself on his one good arm from beneath the branches. In their frenzy, Temeraire and Lien had just knocked askew a column of the stage. The entire grandiose structure began to lean over, sliding by degrees towards the ground, almost stately. Its progress towards destruction was quite plain to see, but Mianning did not take shelter: the prince had stepped over to offer Laurence a hand to rise, and perhaps had not understood his very real danger; his dragon Chuan, too, was distracted, trying to keep himself between Mianning and the duel.

Thrusting himself up with an effort from the ground, Laurence managed to knock Mianning down even as the whole gilt-and-painted structure smashed into the court-yard stones, bursting into foot-long shards of wood. He bent low over the prince to shield them both, covering the back of his neck with his good arm. Splinters jabbed him painfully even through the padded broadcloth of his heavy coat, one sticking him badly in the thigh where he had only his trousers, and another, razor-sharp, sliced his scalp above the temple as it flew.

Then the deadly hail was past, and Laurence straight-ened wiping blood from the side of his face to see Yong-xing, with a deeply astonished expression, fall over: a great jagged splinter protruding from his eye.

Temeraire and Lien managed to disentangle them-selves and sprang apart into facing crouches, still growl-ing, their tails waving angrily. Temeraire glanced back over his shoulder towards Yongxing first, meaning to make another try, and halted in surprise: one foreleg poised in the air. Lien snarled and leapt at him, but he dodged instead of meeting her attack, and then she saw.

For a moment she was perfectly still, only the tendrils of her ruff lifting a little in the breeze, and the thin run-nels of red-black blood trickling down her legs. She walked very slowly over to Yongxing's body and bent her head low, nudging him just a little, as if to confirm for herself what she must already have known.

There was no movement, not even a last nerveless twitching of the body, as Laurence had sometimes seen in the suddenly killed. Yongxing lay stretched out his full height; the surprise had faded with the final slackening of the muscles, and his face was now composed and unsmil-ing, his hands lying one outflung and slightly open, the other fallen across his breast, and his jeweled robes still glittering in the sputtering torchlight. No one else came near; the handful of servants and guards who had not abandoned the clearing huddled back at the edges, staring, and the other dragons all kept silent.

Lien did not scream out, as Laurence had dreaded, or even make any sound at all; she did not turn again on Temeraire, either, but very carefully with her talons brushed away the smaller splinters that had fallen onto Yongxing's robes, the broken pieces of wood, a few shredded leaves of bamboo; then she gathered the body up in both her foreclaws, and carrying it flew silently away into the dark.

Chapter 17

※

LAURENCE TWITCHED AWAY from the restless, pinching hands, first in one direction then the other: but there was no escape, either from them or from the dragging weight of the yellow robes, stiff with gold and green thread, and pulled down by the gemstone eyes of the dragons embroidered all over them. His shoulder ached abominably under the burden, even a week after the injury, and they would keep trying to move his arm to adjust the sleeves.

"Are you not ready yet?" Hammond said anxiously, putting his head into the room. He admonished the tailors in rapid-fire Chinese; and Laurence closed his mouth on an exclamation as one managed to poke him with a too-hasty needle.

"Surely we are not late; are we not expected at two o'clock?" Laurence asked, making the mistake of turning around to see a clock, and being shouted at from three directions for his pains.

"One is expected to be many hours early for any meeting with the Emperor, and in this case we must be more punctilious than less," Hammond said, sweeping his own blue robes out of the way as he pulled over a stool. "You are quite sure you remember the phrases, and their order?"

Laurence submitted to being drilled once more; it was

at least good for distraction from his uncomfortable position. At last he was let go, one of the tailors following them halfway down the hall, making a last adjustment to the shoulders while Hammond tried to hurry him.

Young Prince Miankai's innocent testimony had quite damned Yongxing: the boy had been promised his own Celestial, and had been asked how he would like to be Emperor himself, though with no great details on how this was to be accomplished. Yongxing's whole party of supporters, men who like him believed all contact with the West ought to be severed, had been cast quite into disgrace, leaving Prince Mianning once more ascendant in the court: and as a result, further opposition to Hammond's proposal of adoption had collapsed. The Emperor had sent his edict approving the arrangements, and as this was to the Chinese the equivalent of commanding them done instantly, their progress now became as rapid as it had been creeping heretofore. Scarcely had the terms been settled than servants were swarming through their quarters in Mianning's palace, sweeping away all their possessions into boxes and bundles.

The Emperor had taken up residence now at his Summer Palace in the Yuanmingyuan Garden: half a day's journey from Peking by dragon, and thence they had been conveyed almost pell-mell. The vast granite courtyards of the Forbidden City had turned anvils under the punishing summer sun, which was muted in the Yuanmingyuan by the lush greenery and the expanses of carefully tended lakes; Laurence had found it little wonder the Emperor preferred this more comfortable estate.

Only Staunton had been granted permission to accompany Laurence and Hammond into the actual ceremony of adoption, but Riley and Granby led the other men as an escort: their numbers fleshed out substantially by guards and mandarins loaned by Prince Mianning to give Laurence what they considered a respectable num-

ber. As a party they left the elaborate complex where
they had been housed, and began the journey to the audience hall where the Emperor would meet them. After an
hour's walk, crossing some six streams and ponds, their
guides pausing at regular intervals to point out to them
particularly elegant features of the landscaped grounds,
Laurence began to fear they had indeed not left in good
time: but at last they came to the hall, and were led to the
walled court to await the Emperor's pleasure.

The wait itself was interminable: slowly soaking the
robes through with sweat as they sat in the hot, breath-
less courtyard. Cups of ices were brought to them, also
many dishes of hot food, which Laurence had to force
himself to sample; bowls of milk and tea; and presents: a
large pearl on a golden chain, quite perfect, and some
scrolls of Chinese literature, and for Temeraire a set of
gold-and-silver talon-sheaths, such as his mother occasionally wore. Temeraire was alone among them unfazed
by the heat; delighted, he put the talon-sheaths on at
once and entertained himself by flashing them in the
sunlight, while the rest of the party lay in an increasing
stupor.

At last the mandarins came out again and with deep
bows led Laurence within, followed by Hammond and
Staunton, and Temeraire behind them. The audience
chamber itself was open to the air, hung with graceful
light draperies, the fragrance of peaches rising from a
heaped bowl of golden fruit. There were no chairs but
the dragon-couch at the back of the room, where a great
male Celestial presently sprawled, and the simple but
beautifully polished rosewood chair which held the Emperor.

He was a stocky, broad-jawed man, unlike the thin-
faced and rather sallow Mianning, and with a small
mustache squared off at the corners of his mouth, not yet
touched with grey though he was nearing fifty. His clothes

were very magnificent, in the brilliant yellow hue which they had seen nowhere else but on the private guard outside the palace, and he wore them entirely unconsciously; Laurence thought not even the King had looked so casually in state robes, on those few occasions when he had attended at court.

The Emperor was frowning, but thoughtful rather than displeased, and nodded expectantly as they came in; Mianning stood among many other dignitaries to either side of the throne, and inclined his head very slightly. Laurence took a deep breath and lowered himself carefully to both knees, listening to the mandarin hissing off the count to time each full genuflection. The floor was of polished wood covered with gorgeously woven rugs, and the act itself was not uncomfortable; he could just glimpse Hammond and Staunton following along behind him as he bowed each time to the floor.

Still it went against the grain, and Laurence was glad to rise at last with the formality met; thankfully the Emperor made no unwelcome gesture of condescension, but only ceased to frown: there was a general air of release from tension in the room. The Emperor now rose from his chair and led Laurence to the small altar on the eastern side of the hall. Laurence lit the stands of incense upon the altar and parroted the phrases which Hammond had so laboriously taught him, relieved to see Hammond's small nod: he had made no mistakes, then, or at least none unforgivable.

He had to genuflect once more, but this time before the altar, which Laurence was ashamed to acknowledge even to himself was easier by far to bear, though closer to real blasphemy; hurriedly, under his breath, he said a Lord's Prayer, and hoped that should make quite clear that he did not really mean to be breaking the commandment. Then the worst of the business was over: now Temeraire was called forward for the ceremony which would formally bind them as companions, and Laurence could make the required oaths with a light heart.

The Emperor had seated himself again to oversee the proceedings; now he nodded approvingly, and made a brief gesture to one of his attendants. At once a table was brought into the room, though without any chairs, and more of the cool ices served while the Emperor made inquiries to Laurence about his family, through Hammond's mediation. The Emperor was taken aback to learn that Laurence was himself unmarried and without children, and Laurence was forced to submit to being lectured on the subject at great length, quite seriously, and to agree that he had been neglecting his family duties. He did not mind very much: he was too happy not to have misspoken, and for the ordeal to be so nearly over.

Hammond himself was nearly pale with relief as they left, and had actually to stop and sit down upon a bench on their way to their quarters. A couple of servants brought him some water and fanned him until the color came back into his face and he could stagger on. "I congratulate you, sir," Staunton said, shaking Hammond's hand as they at last left him to lie down in his chamber. "I am not ashamed to say I would not have believed it possible."

"Thank you; thank you," Hammond could only repeat, deeply affected; he was nearly toppling over.

Hammond had won for them not only Laurence's formal entrée into the Imperial family, but the grant of an estate in the Tartar city itself. It was not quite an official embassy, but as a practical matter it was much the same, as Hammond could now reside there indefinitely at Laurence's invitation. Even the kowtow had been dealt with to everyone's satisfaction: from the British point of view, Laurence had made the gesture not as a representative of the Crown, but as an adopted son, while the Chinese were content to have their proper forms met.

"We have already had several very friendly messages

from the mandarins at Canton through the Imperial post, did Hammond tell you?" Staunton said to Laurence, as they stood together outside their own rooms. "The Emperor's gesture to remit all duties on British ships for the year will of course be a tremendous benefit to the Company, but in the long run this new mind-set amongst them will by far prove the more valuable. I suppose—" Staunton hesitated; his hand was already on the screen-frame, ready to go inside. "I suppose you could not find it consistent with your duty to stay? I need scarcely say that it would be of tremendous value to have you here, though of course I know how great our need for dragons is, back home."

Retiring at last, Laurence gladly exchanged his clothes for plain cotton robes, and went outside to join Temeraire in the fragrant shade of a bank of orange trees. Temeraire had a scroll laid out in his frame, but was gazing out across the nearby pond rather than reading. In view, a graceful nine-arched bridge crossed the pond, mirrored in black shadows against the water now dyed yellow-orange with the reflections of the late sunlight, the lotus flowers closing up for the night.

He turned his head and nudged Laurence in greeting. "I have been watching: there is Lien," he said, pointing with his nose across the water. The white dragon was crossing over the bridge, all alone except for a tall, dark-haired man in blue scholar-robes walking by her side, who looked somehow unusual; after a moment squinting, Laurence realized the man did not have a shaved forehead nor a queue. Midway Lien paused and turned to look at them: Laurence put a hand on Temeraire's neck, instinctively, in the face of that unblinking red gaze.

Temeraire snorted, and his ruff came up a little way, but she did not stay: her neck proudly straight and haughty, she turned away again and continued past, vanishing shortly among the trees. "I wonder what she will do now," Temeraire said.

Laurence wondered also; certainly she would not find another willing companion, when she had been held unlucky even before her late misfortunes. He had even heard several courtiers make remarks to the effect that she was responsible for Yongxing's fate; deeply cruel, if she had heard them, and still-less-forgiving opinion held that she ought to be banished entirely. "Perhaps she will go into some secluded breeding grounds."

"I do not think they have particular grounds set aside for breeding here," Temeraire said. "Mei and I did not have to—" Here he stopped, and if it were possible for a dragon to blush, he certainly would have undertaken it. "But perhaps I am wrong," he said hastily.

Laurence swallowed. "You have a great deal of affection for Mei."

"Oh, yes," Temeraire said, wistfully.

Laurence was silent; he picked up one of the hard little yellow fruits that had fallen unripe, and rolled it in his hands. "The *Allegiance* will sail with the next favorable tide, if the wind permits," he said finally, very low. "Would you prefer us to stay?" Seeing that he had surprised Temeraire, he added, "Hammond and Staunton tell me we could do a great deal of good for Britain's interests here. If you wish to remain, I will write to Lenton, and let him know we had better be stationed here."

"Oh," Temeraire said, and bent his head over the reading frame: he was not paying attention to the scroll, but only thinking. "You would rather go home, though, would you not?"

"I would be lying if I said otherwise," Laurence said heavily. "But I would rather see you happy; and I cannot think how I could make you so in England, now you have seen how dragons are treated here." The disloyalty nearly choked him; he could go no further.

"The dragons here are not all smarter than British dragons," Temeraire said. "There is no reason Maximus or Lily could not learn to read and write, or carry on some other kind of profession. It is not right that we are kept penned up like animals, and never taught anything but how to fight."

"No," Laurence said. "No, it is not." There was no possible answer to make, all his defense of British custom undone by the examples which he had seen before him in every corner of China. If some dragons went hungry, that was hardly a counter. He himself would gladly have starved sooner than give up his own liberty, and he would not insult Temeraire by mentioning it even as a sop.

They were silent together for a long space of time, while the servants came around to light the lamps; the quarter-moon rising hung mirrored in the pond, luminous silver, and Laurence idly threw pebbles into the water to break the reflection into gilt ripples. It was hard to imagine what he would do in China, himself, other than serve as a figurehead. He would have to learn the language somehow after all, at least spoken if not the script.

"No, Laurence, it will not do. I cannot stay here and enjoy myself, while back home they are still at war, and need me," Temeraire said finally. "And more than that, the dragons in England do not even know that there is any other way of doing things. I will miss Mei and Qian, but I could not be happy while I knew Maximus and Lily were still being treated so badly. It seems to me my duty to go back and arrange things better there."

Laurence did not know what to say. He had often chided Temeraire for revolutionary thoughts, a tendency to sedition, but only jokingly; it had never occurred to him Temeraire would ever make any such attempt deliberately, outright. Laurence had no idea what the official reaction would be, but he was certain it would not be taken calmly. "Temeraire, you cannot possibly—" he said, and stopped, the great blue eyes expectantly upon him.

"My dear," he said quietly, after a moment, "you put me to shame. Certainly we ought not be content to leave things as they are, now we know there is a better way."

"I thought you would agree," Temeraire said, in satisfaction. "Besides," he added, more prosaically, "my mother tells me that Celestials are not supposed to fight, at all, and only studying all the time does not sound very exciting. We had much better go home." He nodded, and looked back at his poetry. "Laurence," he said, "the ship's carpenter could make some more of these reading frames, could he not?"

"My dear, if it will make you happy he shall make you a dozen," Laurence said, and leaned against him, full of gratitude despite his concerns, to calculate by the moon when the tide should turn again for England and for home.

Selected extracts from
"A Brief Discourse upon the Oriental Breeds, with
Reflections upon the Art of Draconic Husbandry"

Presented before the Royal Society, June 1801

by Sir Edward Howe, F.R.S.

THE "VAST UNTRAMMELED serpentine hordes" of the
Orient are become a byword in the West, feared and admired at
once, thanks in no small part to the well-known accounts of
pilgrims from an earlier and more credulous era, which, while
of inestimable value at the time of their publication in shedding
light upon the perfect darkness which preceded them, to the
modern scholar can hardly be of any use, suffering as they do
from the regrettable exaggeration which was in earlier days the
mode, either from sincere belief on the part of the author or the
less innocent yet understandable desire to satisfy a broader audience, anticipatory of monsters and delights incalculable in
any tales of the Orient.

A sadly inconsistent collection of reports has thus come forward to the present day, some no better than pure fiction and
nearly all others distortions of the truth, which the reader
would do better to discount wholesale than to trust in any particular. I will mention one illustrative example, the Sui-Riu of
Japan, familiar to the student of draconic lore from the 1613
account of Captain John Saris, whose letters confidently described as fact its ability to summon up a thunderstorm out of a
clear blue sky. This remarkable claim, which should thus arro-
gate the powers of Jove to a mortal creature, I will discredit
from my own knowledge: I have seen one of the Sui-Riu and
observed its very real capacity to swallow massive quantities of
water and expel them in violent gusts, a gift which renders it inexpressibly valuable not only in battle, but in the protection of
the wooden buildings of Japan from the dangers of fire. An un-
wary traveler caught in such a torrent might well imagine the
skies to have opened up over his head with a thunderclap, but
these deluges proceed quite unaccompanied by lightning or

rain-cloud, are of some few moments' duration, and, needless to say, not supernatural in the least.

Such errors I will endeavor to avoid in my own turn, rather trusting to the plain facts, presented without excessive ornamentation, to suffice for my more knowledgeable audience . . .

We can without hesitation dismiss as ridiculous the estimate, commonly put forth, that in China one may find a dragon for every ten men: a count which, if it were remotely near the truth and our understanding of the *human* population not entirely mistaken, should certainly result in that great nation's being so wholly overrun by the beasts that the hapless traveler bringing us this intelligence should have had great difficulty in finding even a place to stand. The vivid picture drawn for us by Brother Mateo Ricci, of the temple gardens full of serpentine bodies one overlapping the other, which has so long dominated the Western imagination, is not a wholly false one; however, one must understand that among the Chinese, dragons live rather within the cities than without, their presence thus all the more palpable, and they furthermore move hither and yon with far greater freedom, so that the dragon seen in the market square in the afternoon will often be the same individual observed earlier in morning ablutions at the temple, and then again, some hours later, dining at the cattle-yards upon the city border.

For the size of the population as a whole, we have I am sorry to say no sources upon which I am prepared to rely. However, the letters of the late Father Michel Benoît, a Jesuit astronomer who served in the court of the Qianlong Emperor, report that, upon the occasion of the Emperor's birthday, two companies of their aerial corps were engaged to overfly the Summer Palace in performance of acrobatics; which he himself, in company with two other Jesuit clerks, then personally witnessed.

These companies, consisting of some dozen dragons apiece, are roughly equivalent to the largest of Western formations, and each assigned to one company of three hundred men. Twenty-five such companies form each of the eight banner divisions of the aerial armies of the Tartars, which would yield twenty-four hundred dragons acting in concert with sixty thousand men: already a more than respectable number, yet the number of companies has grown substantially since the founding of the dynasty, and the army is at present a good deal closer to twice the size. We may thus reliably conclude that there are some five thousand dragons in military service in China; a number at once plausible and extraordinary, which gives some small notion of the overall population.

The very grave difficulties inherent in the management of even so many as a hundred dragons together in any singular and protracted military operation are well known in the West, and greatly constrain for practical purposes the size of our own aerial corps. One cannot move herds of cattle so quickly as dragons, nor can dragons carry their food with them live. How the supply of so vast a number of dragons may be orchestrated plainly poses a problem of no small order; indeed, for this purpose the Chinese have established an entire Ministry of Draconic Affairs . . .

. . . it may be that the ancient Chinese practice of keeping their coins strung upon cords is due to the former necessity of providing a means of handling money to dragons; however, this is a relic of earlier times, and since at least the Tang Dynasty, the present system has been in place. The dragon is furnished, upon reaching maturity, with an individual hereditary mark, showing sire and dame as well as the dragon's own rank; this having being placed on record with the Ministry, all funds due to the dragon are then paid into the general treasury and disbursed again on reception of markers which the dragon gives to those merchants, primarily herdsmen, whom it chooses to patronize.

This would seem upon the face of it a system wholly unworkable; one may well imagine the results were a government to so administer the wages of its citizenry. However, it most curiously appears that it does not occur to the dragons to forge a false mark when making their purchases; they receive such a suggestion with surprise and profound disdain, even if hungry and short of funds. Perhaps one may consider this as evidence of a sort of innate honor existing among dragons, or in any event family pride; yet at the same time, they will without hesitation or any consciousness of shame seize any opportunity which offers of taking a beast from an unattended herd or stall and never consider leaving payment behind; this is not viewed by them as any form of theft, and indeed in such a case the guilty dragon may be found devouring his ill-gotten prey while sitting directly beside the pen from which it was seized, and ignoring with perfect ease the complaints of the unhappy herdsman who has returned too late to save his flock.

Themselves scrupulous in the use of their own marks, the

dragons are also rarely made victims of any unscrupulous person who might think to rob them by submitting falsified markers to the Ministry. Being as a rule violently jealous of their wealth, dragons will at once on arriving in any settled place go to inquire as to the state of their accounts and scrutinize all expenses, and so quickly notice any unwarranted charge upon their funds or missing payment; and by all reports the well-known reactions of dragons to being robbed has no less force when that theft occurs in this manner indirectly and out of their view. Chinese law expressly waives any penalty for a dragon who kills a man proven guilty of such a theft; the ordinary sentence is indeed the exposure of the perpetrator to the dragon. Such a sentence of sure and violent death may seem to us a barbaric punishment, and yet I have been assured several times over by both master and dragon that this is the only means of consoling a dragon so abused and restoring it to calm.

This same necessity of placating the dragons has also ensured the steady continuance of the system over the course of better than a thousand years; any conquering dynasty made it nearly their first concern to stabilize the flow of funds, as one can well imagine the effects of a riot of angry dragons . . .

The soil of China is not naturally more arable than that of Europe; the vast necessary herds are rather supported through an ancient and neatly contrived scheme of husbandry whereby the herdsmen, having driven some portion of their flocks into the towns and cities to sate the hungry dragons, returning carry away with them great loads of the richly fermented night-soil collected in the dragon-middens of the town, to exchange with the farmers in their rural home districts. This practice of using dragon night-soil as fertilizer in addition to the manure of cattle, almost unknown here in the West due to the relative scarcity of dragons and the remoteness of their habitations, seems especially efficacious in renewing the fertility of the soil; why this should be so is a question as yet unanswered by modern science, and yet well-evidenced by the productivity of the Chinese husbandmen, whose farms, I am reliably informed, regularly produce a yield nearly an order of magnitude greater than our own . . .

Acknowledgments

A SECOND NOVEL POSES a fresh set of challenges and alarms, and I am especially grateful to my editors, Betsy Mitchell of Del Rey, and Jane Johnson and Emma Coode of HarperCollins UK, for their insights and excellent advice. I also owe many thanks to my team of beta readers on this one for all their help and encouragement: Holly Benton, Francesca Coppa, Dana Dupont, Doris Egan, Diana Fox, Vanessa Len, Shelley Mitchell, Georgina Paterson, Sara Rosenbaum, L. Salom, Micole Sudberg, Rebecca Tushnet, and Cho We Zen.

Many thanks to my sterling agent, Cynthia Manson, for all her help and guidance; and to my family for all their continuing advice and support and enthusiasm. And I'm lucky beyond measure in my very best and in-house reader, my husband, Charles.

And I want to say a special thanks to Dominic Harman, who has been doing one brilliant cover after another for both the American and British editions; it's a thrill beyond measure to see my dragons given life in his art.

Here is an excerpt from *Black Powder War*
by Naomi Novik, the third adventure
in the thrilling Temeraire series!

Available in mass market
paperback from Del Rey

*T*HE HOT WIND blowing into Macao was sluggish and unrefreshing, only stirring up the rotting salt
smell of the harbor, the fish-corpses and great knots of
black-red seaweed, the effluvia of human and dragon
wastes. Even so the sailors were sitting crowded along
the rails of the *Allegiance* for a breath of the moving air,
leaning against one another to get a little room. A little
scuffling broke out amongst them from time to time, a
dull exchange of shoving back and forth, but these
quarrels died almost at once in the punishing heat.

Temeraire lay disconsolately upon the dragondeck,
gazing towards the white haze of the open ocean, the
aviators on duty lying half-asleep in his great shadow.
Laurence himself had sacrificed dignity so far as to take
off his coat, as he was sitting in the crook of Temeraire's
foreleg and so concealed from view.

"I am sure I could pull the ship out of the harbor," Temeraire said, not for the first time in the past week; and
sighed when this amiable plan was again refused. In a
calm he might indeed have been able to tow even the
enormous dragon transport, but against a direct head-
wind he could only exhaust himself to no purpose.

"Even in a calm you could scarcely pull her any great
distance," Laurence added consolingly. "A few miles
may be of some use out in the open ocean, but at present

we may as well stay in harbor, and be a little more comfortable; we would make very little speed even if we could get her out."

"It seems a great pity to me that we must always be waiting on the wind, when everything else is ready and we are also," Temeraire said. "I would so like to be home *soon:* there is so very much to be done." His tail thumped hollowly upon the boards, for emphasis.

"I beg you will not raise your hopes too high," Laurence said, himself a little hopelessly: urging Temeraire to restraint had so far not produced any effect, and he did not expect a different event now. "You must be prepared to endure some delays; at home as much as here."

"Oh! I promise I will be patient," Temeraire said, and immediately dispelled any small notion Laurence might have had of relying upon this promise by adding, unconscious of any contradiction, "but I am quite sure the Admiralty will see the justice of our case very quickly. Certainly it is only fair that dragons should be paid, if our crews are."

Having been at sea from the age of twelve onwards, before the accident of chance which had made him the captain of a dragon rather than a ship, Laurence enjoyed an extensive familiarity with the gentlemen of the Admiralty Board who oversaw the Navy and the Aerial Corps both, and a keen sense of justice was hardly their salient feature. The offices seemed rather to strip their occupants of all ordinary human decency and real qualities: creeping, nip-farthing political creatures, very nearly to a man. The vastly superior conditions for dragons here in China had forced open Laurence's unwilling eyes to the evils of their treatment in the West, but as for the Admiralty's sharing that view, at least so far as it would cost the country tuppence, he was not sanguine.

In any case, he could not help privately entertaining the hope that once at home, back at their post on the

Channel and engaged in the honest business of defending their country, Temeraire might, if not give over his goals, then at least moderate them. Laurence could make no real quarrel with the aims, which were natural and just; but England was at war, after all, and he was conscious, as Temeraire was not, of the impudence in demanding concessions from their own Government under such circumstances: very like mutiny. Yet he had promised his support and would not withdraw it. Temeraire might have stayed here in China, enjoying all the luxuries and freedoms which were his birthright, as a Celestial. He was coming back to England largely for Laurence's sake, and in hopes of improving the lot of his comrades-in-arms; despite all Laurence's misgivings, he could hardly raise a direct objection, though it at times felt almost dishonest not to speak.

"It is very clever of you to suggest we should begin with pay," Temeraire continued, heaping more coals of fire onto Laurence's conscience; he had proposed it mainly for its being less radical a suggestion than many of the others which Temeraire had advanced, such as the wholesale demolition of quarters of London to make room for thoroughfares wide enough to accommodate dragons, and the sending of draconic representatives to address Parliament, which aside from the difficulty of their getting into the building would certainly have resulted in the immediate flight of all the human members. "Once we have pay, I am sure everything else will be easier. Then we can always offer people money, which they like so much, for all the rest; like those cooks which you have hired for me. That is a very pleasant smell," he added, not a non sequitur: the rich smoky smell of well-charred meat was growing so strong as to rise over the stench of the harbor.

Laurence frowned and looked down: the galley was situated directly below the dragondeck, and wispy ribbons of smoke, flat and wide, were seeping up from between the boards of the deck. "Dyer," he said, beckoning to one of his runners, "go and see what they are about, down there."

Temeraire had acquired a taste for the Chinese style of dragon cookery which the British quartermaster, expected only to provide freshly butchered cattle, was quite unable to satisfy, so Laurence had found two Chinese cooks willing to leave their country for the promise of substantial wages. The new cooks spoke no English, but they lacked nothing in self-assertion; already professional jealousy had nearly brought the ship's cook and his assistants to pitched battle with them over the galley stoves, and produced a certain atmosphere of competition.

Dyer trotted down the stairs to the quarterdeck and opened the door to the galley: a great rolling cloud of smoke came billowing out, and at once there was a shout and halloâ of "Fire!" from the look-outs up in the rigging. The watch-officer rang the bell frantically, the clapper scraping and clanging; Laurence was already shouting, "To stations!" and sending his men to their fire crews.

All lethargy vanished at once, the sailors running for buckets, pails; a couple of daring fellows darted into the galley and came out dragging limp bodies: the cook's mates, the two Chinese, and one of the ship's boys, but no sign of the ship's cook himself. Already the dripping buckets were coming in a steady flow, the bosun roaring and thumping his stick against the foremast to give the men the rhythm, and one after another the buckets were emptied through the galley doors. But still the smoke came billowing out, thicker now, through every crack and seam of the deck, and the bitts of the dragondeck were scorching hot to the touch: the rope coiled over two of the iron posts was beginning to smoke.

Young Digby, quick-thinking, had organized the other

ensigns: the boys were hurrying together to unwind the cable, swallowing hisses of pain when their fingers brushed against the hot iron. The rest of the aviators were ranged along the rail, hauling up water in buckets flung over the side and dousing the dragondeck: steam rose in white clouds and left a grey crust of salt upon the already warping planks, the deck creaking and moaning like a crowd of old men. The tar between the seams was liquefying, running in long black streaks along the deck with a sweet, acrid smell as it scorched and smoked. Temeraire was standing on all four legs now, mincing from one place to another for relief from the heat, though Laurence had seen him lie with pleasure on stones baked by the full strength of the midday sun.

Captain Riley was in and among the sweating, laboring men, shouting encouragement as the buckets swung back and forth, but there was an edge of despair in his voice. The fire was too hot, the wood seasoned by the long stay in harbor under the baking heat; and the vast holds were filled with goods for the journey home: delicate china wrapped in dry straw and packed in wooden crates, bales of silks, new-laid sailcloth for repairs. The fire had only to make its way four decks down, and the stores would go up in quick hot flames running all the way back to the powder magazine, and carry her all away.

The morning watch, who had been sleeping below, were now fighting to come up from the lower decks, open-mouthed and gasping with the smoke chasing them out, breaking the lines of water-carriers in their panic: though the *Allegiance* was a behemoth, her forecastle and quarterdeck could not hold her entire crew, not with the dragondeck nearly in flames. Laurence seized one of the stays and pulled himself up on the railing of the deck, looking for his crew in and amongst the milling crowd: most had already been out upon the dragondeck, but a handful remained unaccounted for: Therrows, his leg still in splints after the battle in Peking; Keynes, the surgeon, likely at his books in the privacy of his cabin; and he could see no sign of Emily Roland, his other runner: she was scarcely turned eleven, and could not easily have pushed her way out past the heaving, struggling men.

A thin, shrill kettle-whistle erupted from the galley chimneys, the metal cowls beginning to droop towards the deck, slowly, like flowers gone to seed. Temeraire hissed back in instinctive displeasure, drawing his head back up to all the full length of his neck, his ruff flattening against his neck. His great haunches had already tensed to spring, one foreleg resting on the railing. "Laurence, is it quite safe for you there?" he called anxiously.

"Yes, we will be perfectly well, go aloft at once," Laurence said, even as he waved the rest of his men down to the forecastle, concerned for Temeraire's safety with the planking beginning to give way. "We may better be able to come at the fire once it has come up through the deck," he added, principally for the encouragement of those hearing him; in truth, once the dragondeck fell in, he could hardly imagine they would be able to put out the blaze.

"Very well, then I will go and help," Temeraire said, and took to the air.

A handful of men less concerned with preserving the ship than their own lives had already lowered the jolly-boat into the water off the stern, hoping to make their escape unheeded by the officers engaged in the desperate struggle against the fire; they dived off in panic as Temeraire unexpectedly darted around the ship and descended upon them. He paid no attention to the men, but seized the boat in his talons, ducked it underwater like a ladle, and heaved it up into the air, dripping water and oars. Carefully keeping it balanced, he flew back and poured it out over the dragondeck: the sudden deluge went hissing and spitting over the planks, and tumbled in a brief waterfall over the stairs and down.

"Fetch axes!" Laurence called urgently. It was desperately hot, sweating work, hacking at the planks with steam rising and their axe blades skidding on the wet and tar-soaked wood, smoke pouring out through every cut they made. All struggled to keep their footing each time Temeraire deluged them once again; but the constant flow of water was the only thing that let them keep at their task, the smoke otherwise too thick. As they labored, a few of the men staggered and fell unmoving upon the deck: no time even to heave them down to the quarterdeck, the minutes too precious to sacrifice. Laurence worked side by side with his armorer, Pratt, long thin trails of black-stained sweat marking their shirts as they swung the axes in uneven turns, until abruptly the planking cracked with gunshot sounds, a great section of the dragondeck all giving way at once and collapsing into the eager hungry roar of the flames below.

For a moment Laurence wavered on the verge; then his first lieutenant, Granby, was pulling him away. They staggered back together, Laurence half-blind and nearly falling into Granby's arms; his breath would not quite come, rapid and shallow, and his eyes were burning. Granby dragged him partway down the steps, and then another torrent of water carried them in a rush the rest of the way, to fetch up against one of the forty-two-pounder carronades on the forecastle. Laurence managed to pull himself up the railing in time to vomit over the side, the bitter taste in his mouth still less strong than the acrid stink of his hair and clothes.

The rest of the men were abandoning the dragondeck, and now the enormous torrents of water could go straight down at the flames. Temeraire had found a steady rhythm, and the clouds of smoke were already less: black sooty water was running out of the galley doors onto the quarterdeck. Laurence felt queerly shaken and ill, heaving deep breaths that did not seem to fill his lungs. Riley was rasping out hoarse orders through the speaking-trumpet, barely loud enough to be heard over the hiss of smoke; the bosun's voice was gone entirely: he was pushing the men into rows with his bare hands, pointing them at the hatchways; soon there was a line organized, handing up the men who had been overcome or trampled below: Laurence was glad to see Therrows being lifted out. Temeraire poured another torrent upon the last smoldering embers; then Riley's coxswain Basson poked his head out of the main hatch, panting, and shouted, "No more smoke coming through, sir, and the planks above the berth-deck ain't worse than warm: I think she's out."

A heartfelt ragged cheer went up. Laurence was beginning to feel he could get his wind back again, though he still spat black with every coughing breath; with Granby's hand he was able to climb to his feet. A haze of smoke like the aftermath of cannon-fire lay thickly upon the deck, and when he climbed up the stairs he found a gaping charcoal fire-pit in place of the dragondeck, the edges of the remaining planking crisped like burnt paper. The body of the poor ship's cook lay like a twisted cinder amongst the wreckage, skull charred black and his wooden legs burnt to ash, leaving only the sad stumps to the knee.

Having let down the jolly-boat, Temeraire hovered above uncertainly a little longer and then let himself drop into the water beside the ship: there was nowhere left for him to land upon her. Swimming over and grasping at the rail with his claws, he craned up his great head to peer anxiously over the side. "You are well, Laurence? Are all my crew all right?"

"Yes; I have made everyone," Granby said, nodding to Laurence. Emily, her cap of sandy hair speckled grey with soot, came to them dragging a jug of water from the scuttlebutt: stale and tainted with the smell of the harbor, and more delicious than wine.

Riley climbed up to join them. "What a ruin," he said, looking over the wreckage. "Well, at least we have saved her, and thank Heaven for that; but how long it will take before we can sail now, I do not like to think." He gladly accepted the jug from Laurence and drank deep before handing it on to Granby. "And I am damned sorry; I suppose all your things must be spoilt," he added, wiping his mouth: senior aviators had their quarters towards the bow, one level below the galley.

"Good God," Laurence said, blankly, "and I have not the least notion what has happened to my coat."

"Four; four days," the tailor said in his limited English, holding up fingers to be sure he had not been misunderstood; Laurence sighed and said, "Yes, very well." It was small consolation to think that there was no shortage of time: two months or more would be required to repair the ship, and until then he and all his men would be cooling his heels on shore. "Can you repair the other?"

They looked together down at the coat which Laurence had brought him as a pattern: more black than bottle-green now, with a peculiar white residue upon the buttons and smelling strongly of smoke and salt water both. The tailor did not say *no* outright, but his expression spoke volumes. "You take this," he said instead, and going into the back of his workshop brought out another garment: not a coat, precisely, but one of the quilted jackets such as the Chinese soldiers wore, like a tunic opening down the front, with a short upturned collar.

"Oh, well—" Laurence eyed it uneasily; it was made of silk, in a considerably brighter shade of green, and handsomely embroidered along the seams with scarlet and gold: the most he could say was that it was not as ornate as the formal robes to which he had been subjected on prior occasions.

But he and Granby were to dine with the commissioners of the East India Company that evening; he could not present himself half-dressed, or keep himself swathed in the heavy cloak which he had put on to come to the shop. He was glad enough to have the Chinese garment when, returning to his new quarters on shore, Dyer and Roland told him there was no proper coat to be had in town for any money whatsoever: not very surprising, as respectable gentlemen did not choose to look like aviators, and the dark green of their broadcloth was not a popular color in the Western enclave.

"Perhaps you will set a new fashion," Granby said, somewhere between mirth and consolation; a lanky fellow, he was himself wearing a coat seized from one of the hapless midwingmen, who, having been quartered on the lower decks, had not suffered the ruin of their own clothes. With an inch of wrist showing past his coat sleeves and his pale cheeks as usual flushed with sunburn, he looked at the moment rather younger than his twenty years and six, but at least no one would look askance. Laurence, being a good deal more broad-shouldered, could not rob any of the younger officers in the same manner, and though Riley had handsomely offered, Laurence did not mean to present himself in a blue coat, as if he were ashamed of being an aviator and wished to pass himself off as still a naval captain.

He and his crew were now quartered in a spacious house set directly upon the waterfront, the property of a local Dutch merchant more than happy to let it to them and remove his household to apartments farther into the town, where he would not have a dragon on his doorstep. Temeraire had been forced by the destruction of his dragondeck to sleep on the beach, much to the dismay of the Western inhabitants; to his own disgust as well, the shore being inhabited by small and irritating crabs which persisted in treating him like the rocks in which they made their homes and attempting to conceal themselves upon him while he slept.

Laurence and Granby paused to bid him farewell on their way to the dinner. Temeraire, at least, approved Laurence's new costume; he thought the shade a pretty one, and admired the gold buttons and thread particularly. "And it looks handsome with the sword," he added, having nosed Laurence around in a circle the better to inspect him: the sword in question was his very own gift, and therefore in his estimation the most important part of the ensemble. It was also the one piece for which Laurence felt he need not blush: his shirt, thankfully hidden beneath the coat, not all the scrubbing in the world could save from disgrace; his breeches did not bear close examination; and as for his stockings, he had resorted to his tall Hessian boots.

They left Temeraire settling down to his own dinner under the protective eyes of a couple of midwingmen and a troop of soldiers under the arms of the East India Company, part of their private forces; Sir George Staunton had loaned them to help guard Temeraire not from danger but over-enthusiastic well-wishers. Unlike the Westerners who had fled their homes near the shore, the Chinese were not alarmed by dragons, living from childhood in their midst, and the tiny handful of Celestials so rarely left the Imperial precincts that to see one, and better yet to touch, was counted an honor and an assurance of good fortune.

Staunton had also arranged this dinner by way of offering the officers some entertainment and relief from their anxieties over the disaster, unaware that he would be putting the aviators to such desperate shifts in the article of clothing. Laurence had not liked to refuse the generous invitation for so trivial a reason, and had hoped to the last that he might find something more respectable to wear; now he came ruefully prepared to share his travails over the dinner-table, and bear the amusement of the company.

His entrance was met with a polite if astonished silence, at first; but he had scarcely paid his respects to Sir George and accepted a glass of wine before murmurs began. One of the older commissioners, a gentleman who liked to be deaf when he chose, said quite clearly, "Aviators and their starts; who knows what they will take into their heads next," which made Granby's eyes glitter with suppressed anger; and a trick of the room made some less consciously indiscreet remarks audible also.

"What do you suppose he means by it?" inquired Mr. Chatham, a gentleman newly arrived from India, while eyeing Laurence with interest from the next window over; he was speaking in low voices with Mr. Grothing-Pyle, a portly man whose own interest was centered upon the clock, and in judging how soon they should go in to dinner.

"Hm? Oh; he has a right to style himself an Oriental prince now if he likes," Grothing-Pyle said, shrugging, after an incurious glance over his shoulder. "And just as well for us, too. Do you smell venison? I have not tasted venison in a year."

Laurence turned his own face to the open window, appalled and offended in equal measure. Such an interpretation had never even occurred to him; his adoption by the Emperor had been purely and strictly *pro forma*, a matter of saving face for the Chinese, who had insisted that a Celestial might not be companion to any but a direct connection of the Imperial family; while on the British side it had been eagerly accepted as a painless means of resolving the dispute over the capture of Temeraire's egg. Painless, at least, to everyone but Laurence, already in possession of one proud and imperious father, whose wrathful reaction to the adoption he anticipated with no small dismay. True, that consideration had not stopped him: he would have willingly accepted anything short of treason to avoid being parted from Temeraire. But he had certainly never sought or desired so signal and queer an honor, and to have men think him a ludicrous kind of social climber, who should value Oriental titles above his own birth, was deeply mortifying.

The embarrassment closed his mouth. He would have gladly shared the story behind his unusual clothing as an anecdote; as an excuse, never. He spoke shortly in reply to the few remarks offered him; anger made him pale and, if he had only known it, gave his face a cold, forbidding look, almost dangerous, which made conversation near him die down. He was ordinarily good-humored in his expression, and though he was not darkly tanned, the many years laboring in the sun had given his looks a warm bronzed cast; the lines upon his face were mostly smiling: all the more contrast now. These men owed, if not their lives, at least their fortunes to the success of the diplomatic mission to Peking, whose failure would have meant open warfare and an end to the China trade, and whose success had cost Laurence a blood-letting and the life of one of his men; he had not expected any sort of effusive thanks and would have spurned them if offered, but to meet with derision and incivility was something entirely different.

"Shall we go in?" Sir George said, sooner than usual, and at the table he made every effort to break the uneasy atmosphere which had settled over the company: the butler was sent back to the cellar half-a-dozen times, the wines growing more extravagant with each visit, and the food was excellent despite the limited resources accessible to Staunton's cook: among the dishes was a very handsome fried carp, laid upon a ragout of the small crabs, now victims in their turn, and for centerpiece a pair of fat haunches of venison roasted, accompanied by a dish full of glowing jewel-red currant jelly.

The conversation flowed again; Laurence could not be insensible to Staunton's real and sincere desire to see him and all the company comfortable, and he was not of an implacable temper to begin with; still less when encouraged with the best part of a glorious burgundy just come into its prime. No one had made any further remarks about coats or imperial relations, and after several courses Laurence had thawed enough to apply himself with a will to a charming trifle assembled out of Naples biscuits and sponge-cake, with a rich brandied custard flavored with orange, when a commotion outside the dining room began to intrude, and finally a single piercing shriek, like a woman's cry, interrupted the increasingly loud and slurred conversation.

Silence fell, glasses stopped in mid-air, some chairs were pushed back; Staunton rose, a little wavering, and begged their pardon. Before he could go to investigate, the door was thrust abruptly open, Staunton's anxious servant stumbling back into the room still protesting volubly in Chinese. He was gently but with complete firmness being pressed aside by another Oriental man, dressed in a padded jacket and a round, domed hat rising above a thick roll of dark wool; the stranger's clothing was dusty and stained yellow in places, and not much like the usual native dress, and on his gauntleted hand perched an angry-looking eagle, brown and golden feathers ruffled up and a yellow eye glaring; it clacked its beak and shifted its perch uneasily, great talons puncturing the heavy block of padding.

When they had stared at him and he at them in turn, the stranger further astonished the room by saying, in pure drawing-room accents, "I beg your pardon, gentlemen, for interrupting your dinner; my errand cannot wait. Is Captain William Laurence here?"

Laurence was at first too bemused with wine and surprise to react; then he rose and stepped away from the table, to accept a sealed oilskin packet under the eagle's unfriendly stare. "I thank you, sir," he said. At a second glance, the lean and angular face was not entirely Chinese: the eyes, though dark and faintly slanting, were rather more Western in shape, and the color of his skin, much like polished teak wood, owed less to nature than to the sun.

The stranger inclined his head politely. "I am glad to have been of service." He did not smile, but there was a glint in his eye suggestive of amusement at the reaction of the room, which he was surely accustomed to provoking; he threw the company all a final glance, gave Staunton a small bow, and left as abruptly as he had come, going directly past a couple more of the servants who had come hurrying to the room in response to the noise.

"Pray go and give Mr. Tharkay some refreshment," Staunton said to the servants in an undertone, and sent them after him; meanwhile Laurence turned to his packet. The wax had been softened by the summer heat, the impression mostly lost, and the seal would not easily come away or break, pulling like soft candy and trailing sticky threads over his fingers. A single sheet within only, written from Dover in Admiral Lenton's own hand, and in the abrupt style of formal orders: a single look was enough to take it in.

. . . and you are hereby required without the loss of a Moment to proceed to Istanbul, there to receive by the Offices of Avraam Maden, in the service of H.M. Selim III, three Eggs now through agreement the Property of His Majesty's Corps, to be secured against the Elements with all due care for their brooding and thence delivered straightaway to the charge of those

Officers appointed to them, who shall await you at the covert at Dunbar . . .

The usual grim epilogues followed, *herein neither you nor any of you shall fail, or answer the contrary at your peril;* Laurence handed the letter to Granby, then nodded to him to pass the letter to Riley and to Staunton, who had joined them in the privacy of the library.

"Laurence," Granby said, after handing it on, "we cannot sit here waiting for repairs with a months-long sea-journey after that; we must get going at once."

"Well, how else do you mean to go?" Riley said, looking up from the letter, which he was reading over Staunton's shoulder. "There's not another ship in port that could hold Temeraire's weight for even a few hours; you can't fly straight across the ocean without a place to rest."

"It's not as though we were going to Nova Scotia, and could only go by sea," Granby said. "We must take the overland route instead."

"Oh, come now," Riley said impatiently.

"Well, and why not?" Granby demanded. "Even aside from the repairs, it's going by sea that is out of the way, we lose ages having to circle around India. Instead we can make a straight shot across Tartary—"

"Yes, and you can jump in the water and try to swim all the way to England, too," Riley said. "Sooner is better than late, but late is better than never; the *Allegiance* will get you home quicker than that."

Laurence listened to their conversation with half an ear, reading the letter again with fresh attention. It was difficult to separate the true degree of urgency from the general tenor of a set of orders; but though dragon eggs might take a long time indeed to hatch, they were unpredictable and could not be left sitting indefinitely. "And we must consider, Tom," he said to Riley, "that it might easily be as much as five months' sailing to Basra if we are unlucky in the way of weather, and from there we should have a flight overland to Istanbul in any case."

"And as likely to find three dragonets as three eggs at the end of it, no use at all," Granby said; when Laurence asked him, he gave as his firm opinion that the eggs could not be far from hatching; or at least not so far as to set their minds at ease. "There aren't many breeds who go for longer than a couple of years in the shell," he explained, "and the Admiralty won't have bought eggs less than halfway through their brooding: any younger than that, and you cannot be sure they will come off. We cannot lose the time; why they are sending us to get them instead of a crew from Gibraltar I don't in the least understand."

Laurence, less familiar with the various duty stations of the Corps, had not yet considered this possibility, and now it struck him also as odd that the task had been delegated to them, being so much farther distant. "How long ought it take them to get to Istanbul from there?" he asked, disquieted; even if much of the coast along the way were under French control, patrols could not be everywhere, and a single dragon flying should have been able to find places to rest.

"Two weeks, perhaps a little less flying hard all the way," Granby said. "While I don't suppose we can make it in less than a couple of months, ourselves, even going overland."

Staunton, who had been listening anxiously to their deliberations, now interjected, "Then must not these orders by their very presence imply a certain lack of urgency? I dare say it has taken three months for the letter to come this far. A few months more, then, can hardly make a difference; otherwise the Corps would have sent someone nearer."

"If anyone nearer could be sent," Laurence said, grimly. England was hard-up enough for dragons that even one or two could not easily be spared in any sort of a crisis, certainly not for a month going and coming back, and certainly not a heavy-weight in Temeraire's class. Bonaparte might once again be threatening invasion across the Channel, or launching attacks against the Mediterranean Fleet, leaving only Temeraire, and the handful of dragons stationed in Bombay and Madras, at any sort of liberty.

"No," Laurence concluded, having contemplated these unpleasant possibilities, "I do not think we can make any such assumption, and in any case there are not two ways to read *without the loss of a Moment*, not when Temeraire is certainly able to go. I know what I would think of a captain with such orders who lingered in port when tide and wind were with him."

Seeing him thus beginning to lean towards a decision, Staunton at once began, "Captain, I beg you will not seriously consider taking so great a risk," while Riley, more blunt with nine years' acquaintance behind him, said, "For God's sake, Laurence, you cannot mean to do any such crazy thing."

He added, "And I do not call it *lingering in port,* to wait for the *Allegiance* to be ready; if you like, taking the overland route should rather be like setting off headlong into a gale, when a week's patience will bring clear skies."

"You make it sound as though we might as well slit our own throats as go," Granby exclaimed. "I don't deny it would be awkward and dangerous with a caravan, lugging goods all across Creation, but with Temeraire, no one will give us any trouble, and we only need a place to drop for the night."

"And enough food for a dragon the size of a first-rate," Riley fired back.

Staunton, nodding, seized on this avenue at once. "I think you cannot understand the extreme desolation of the regions you would cross, nor their vastness." He hunted through his books and papers to find Laurence several maps of the region: an inhospitable place even on parchment, with only a few lonely small towns breaking up the stretches of nameless wasteland, great expanses of desert entrenched behind mountains; on one dusty and crumbling chart a spidery old-fashioned hand had written *heere ys no water 3 wekes* in the empty yellow bowl of the desert. "Forgive me for speaking so strongly, but it is a reckless course, and I am convinced not one which the Admiralty can have meant you to follow."

"And I am convinced Lenton should never have conceived of our whistling six months down the wind," Granby said. "People do come and go overland; what about that fellow Marco Polo, and wasn't that nearly two centuries ago?"

"Yes, and what about the Fitch and Newbery expedition, after him," Riley said. "Three dragons all lost in the mountains, in a five-day blizzard, through just such reckless behavior—"

"This man Tharkay, who brought the letter," Laurence said to Staunton, interrupting an exchange which bade fair to end in hot words, Riley's tone growing rather sharp and Granby's pale skin flushing up with tell-tale color. "He came overland, did he not?"

"I hope you do not mean to take him for your model," Staunton said. "One man can go where a group cannot, and manage on very little, particularly a rough adventurer such as he. More to the point, he risks only himself when he goes: you must consider that in your charge is an inexpressibly valuable dragon, whose loss must be of greater importance than even this mission."

* * *

"Oh, pray let us be gone at once," said the inexpressibly valuable dragon, when Laurence had carried the question, still unresolved, back to him. "It sounds very exciting to me." Temeraire was wide-awake now in the relative cool of the evening, and his tail was twitching back and forth with enthusiasm, producing moderate walls of sand to either side upon the beach, not much above the height of a man. "What kind of dragons will the eggs be? Will they breathe fire?"

"Lord, if they would only give us a Kazilik," Granby said. "But I expect it will be ordinary middle-weights: these kinds of bargains are made to bring a little fresh blood into the lines."

"How much more quickly would we be at home?" Temeraire asked, cocking his head sideways so he could focus one eye upon the maps, which Laurence had laid out over the sand. "Why, only see how far out of our way the sailing takes us, Laurence, and it is not as though I must have wind always, as the ship does: we will be home again before the end of summer," an estimate as optimistic as it was unlikely, Temeraire not being able to judge the scale of the map so very well; but at least they would likely be in England again by late September, and that was an incentive almost powerful enough to overrule all caution.

"And yet I cannot get past it," Laurence said. "We were assigned to the *Allegiance,* and Lenton must have assumed we would come home by her. To go haring-off along the old silk roads has an impetuous flavor; and you need not try and tell me," he added repressively to Temeraire, "that there is nothing to worry about."

"But it *cannot* be so very dangerous," Temeraire said, undaunted. "It is not as though I were going to let you go off all alone, and get hurt."

"That you should face down an army to protect us I

have no doubt," Laurence said, "but a gale in the mountains even you cannot defeat." Riley's reminder of the ill-fated expedition lost in the Karakorum Pass had resonated unpleasantly. Laurence could envision all too clearly the consequences should they run into a deadly storm: Temeraire borne down by the frozen wind, wet snow and ice forming crusts upon the edges of his wings, beyond where any man of the crew could reach to break them loose; the whirling snow blinding them to the hazards of the cliff walls around them and turning them in circles; the dropping chill rendering him by insensible degrees heavier and more sluggish—and worse prey to the ice, with no shelter to be found. In such circumstances, Laurence would be forced to choose between ordering him to land, condemning him to a quicker death in hopes of sparing the lives of his men, or letting them all continue on the slow grinding road to destruction together: a horror beside which Laurence could contemplate death in battle with perfect equanimity.

"So then the sooner we go, the better, for having an easy crossing of it," Granby argued. "August will be better than October for avoiding blizzards."

"And for being roasted alive in the desert instead," Riley said.

Granby rounded on him. "I don't mean to say," he said, with a smoldering look in his eye that belied his words, "that there is anything old-womanish in all these objections—"

"For there is not, indeed," Laurence broke in sharply. "You are quite right, Tom; the danger is not a question of blizzards in particular, but that we have not the first understanding of the difficulties particular to the journey. And that we must remedy, first, before we engage either to go or to wait."

*　*　*

"If you offer the fellow money to guide you, of course he will say the road is safe," Riley said. "And then just as likely leave you halfway to nowhere, with no recourse."

Staunton also tried again to dissuade Laurence, when he came seeking Tharkay's direction the next morning. "He occasionally brings us letters, and sometimes will do errands for the Company in India," Staunton said. "His father was a gentleman, I believe a senior officer, and took some pains with his education; but still the man cannot be called reliable, for all the polish of his manners. His mother was a native woman, Thibetan or Nepalese, or something like; and he has spent the better part of his life in the wild places of the earth."

"For my part, I should rather have a guide half-British than one who can scarcely make himself understood," Granby said afterwards, as he and Laurence together picked their way along the back streets of Macao; the late rains were still puddled in the gutters, a thin slick of green overlaid on the stagnating waste. "And if Tharkay were not so much a gypsy he wouldn't be of any use to us; it is no good complaining about that."

At length they found Tharkay's temporary quarters: a wretched little two-story house in the Chinese quarter with a drooping roof, held up mostly by its neighbors to either side, all of them leaning against one another like drunken old men, with a landlord who scowled before leading them within, muttering.

Tharkay was sitting in the central court of the house, feeding the eagle gobbets of raw flesh from a dish; the fingers of his left hand were marked with white scars where the savage beak had cut him on previous feedings, and a few small scratches bled freely now, unheeded. "Yes, I came overland," he said, to Laurence's inquiry, "but I would not recommend you the same road, Captain; it is not a comfortable journey, when compared against sea travel." He did not interrupt his task, but held up another strip of meat for the eagle, which snatched it out of his fingers, glaring at them furiously with the dangling bloody ends hanging from its beak as it swallowed.

It was difficult to know how to address him: neither a superior servant, nor a gentleman, nor a native, all his refinements of speech curiously placed against the scruff and tumble of his clothing and his disreputable surroundings; though perhaps he could have gotten no better accommodations, curious as his appearance was, and with the hostile eagle as his companion. He made no concessions, either, to his odd, in-between station; a certain degree of presumption almost in his manner he was less formal than Laurence would himself have used to so new an acquaintance, almost in active defiance against being held at a servant's distance.

But Tharkay answered their many questions readily enough, and having fed his eagle and set it aside, hooded, to sleep, he even opened up the kit which had carried him there so that they might inspect the vital equipment: a special sort of desert tent, fur-lined and with leather-reinforced holes spaced evenly along the edges, which he explained could be lashed quickly together with similar tents to form a single larger sheet to shield a camel, or in larger numbers a dragon, against sandstorm or hail or snow. There was also a snug leather-wrapped canteen, well-waxed to keep the water in, and a small tin cup tied on with string, marks engraved into it halfway and near the rim; a neat small compass, in a wooden case, and a thick journal full of little hand-sketched maps, and directions taken down in a small, neat hand.

All of it showed signs of use and good upkeep; plainly he knew what he was about, and he did not show himself over-eager, as Riley had feared, for their custom. "I had not thought of returning to Istanbul," Tharkay said instead, when Laurence at last came around to inquiring if he would be their guide. "I have no real business there."

"But have you any elsewhere?" Granby said. "We will have the devil of a time getting there without you, and you should be doing your country a service."

"And you will be handsomely paid for your trouble," Laurence added.

"Ah, well, in that case," Tharkay said, a wry twist to his smile.

"Just when you think you've seen every variation possible on the dragon story, along comes Naomi Novik to prove you wrong. Her wonderful Temeraire is a dragon for the ages."
—TERRY BROOKS

RIDE ALONG WITH
THE TEMERAIRE SERIES
by NAOMI NOVIK!

HIS MAJESTY'S DRAGON

Fate sweeps British naval captain Will Laurence into an uncertain future—and an unexpected kinship with a most extraordinary creature—after a dragon egg captured from a French ship falls into his hands. Thrust into the rarefied world of the Aerial Corps as master of the dragon Temeraire, Laurence faces a crash course in the daring tactics of airborne battle.

THRONE OF JADE

China has discovered that its rare dragon egg, intended for Napoleon, has fallen into British hands—and an angry Chinese delegation vows to reclaim the remarkable beast. Captain Laurence has no choice but to accompany Temeraire back to the Far East—a long voyage fraught with peril, intrigue, and the untold terrors of the deep.

BLACK POWDER WAR

Three valuable dragon eggs have been purchased from the Ottoman Empire, and Captain Laurence and Temeraire must detour to Istanbul to escort the precious cargo back to England. But what chance do they have against the massed forces of Bonaparte's implacable army?

www.delreybooks.com